CRUEL AND beautiful

A.M. HARGROVE & TERRI E. LAINE

Acknowledgements

There is a group of people who deserve our thanks, namely our beta readers. Their patience with us during our first project together is deeply appreciated. When we started this, we didn't dream it would end up here and without their input, it never would've happened. So here's our biggest bestest thank you to the following people: Jill Patten, Adriane Leigh, Michelle Leighton, Liz Crowe, Andrea Stafford, and Kat Grimes.

We'd also like to thank Sara Eirew for putting up with us in all the changes we asked her to make in the cover. We can't begin to name them. (Runs and hides in shame!) Thank you, Sara!

A hearty thanks goes out to Anne Chaconas at Bad Ass Marketing for, well, her Bad Ass Marketing!

And a big thanks to Julie, Kris, Rick, and Amy at Red Coat PR for all their help, too!

PROLOGUE

A RASPY VOICE WAKES ME up. That's not quite true because I don't really sleep anymore. My body hovers in that place that's not exactly sleep and not exactly awareness. After the last year, I'm not sure if I'll ever get a solid night's sleep again.

"Cate?"

"Yeah? What is it?" I'm instantly on high alert.

"I think it's time. I want to go to the hospital."

The words I've dreaded for weeks punch me in the gut. But I refuse to let him see it. "Yeah, okay. Let me get dressed."

"Cate? I think you need to call 911. I'm pretty sure I can't get up to walk." He inhales and it's then I hear the faint rattle deep in his chest. Oh, god, how will I ever get through this?

"Drew?" I lean over him and press my cheek against his. What used to be firm flesh is now nothing but skin wrapped around bone. My hands latch onto his shoulders and it's much the same. All the mass has vanished, stolen by the disease that ravages his beautiful body and soul.

"It's going to be fine, Cate, I promise. Things will be good. Just call 911." He struggles to clear his throat.

Always the positive one. I want to yell and scream, stomp my feet and smash things. But I do none of that. I look into his cloudy blue eyes that were once so clear and stunning and only nod. I pick up the bedside phone and make the call, asking the voice on the other end to tell the paramedics not to use the sirens or flashers and explain why. When they arrive at our house, I lead them to Drew, and then follow the ambulance to the hospital. On the way, I make the dreaded family calls.

Hollow. That's what I am as I watch them wheel Drew in on the gurney. Everything has been ripped out of me—my guts, my heart, my soul. I bite my knuckle as I stand there. He knows what's happening. He's a doctor. He's charted everything out and explained it all to me, though I've refused to believe half of it. Why did he have to be right? My mind only wants to accept certain things. And this isn't one of them.

When we finally get to a room, he sleeps. The deep purple smudges beneath his eyes are a stark contrast to his pale skin. It reminds me of a time when he used to be so tanned. And his hair, which is downy fuzz grown back from the last and final round of failed chemo, is so different now from the thick mass of messy waves that were always sun streaked, even in winter. In this state, little more than a skeleton, he's still my perfect Drew. And I ask myself again, for the thousandth time, how am I going to deal with this?

Later in the day, when Drew wakes up, he beckons me to his bedside.

"Cate, you know when I first saw you at that party, I knew you were my one. My it girl. And then you put up such damn resistance to me, I didn't think I'd ever get you out on a date. But I did."

I suck on my lower lip, trying not to outright sob as I remember.

The left corner of his upper lip curls, his little trademark that I love so much. It plows into me like a damn tank and I want to crawl into the bed next to him and cling to him forever.

"I knew if I could get you out on a date, I could win you over. Thank god I did. You've been my life, Cate, my reason for being. I'm only sorry it all turned out like this. This," and he motions with his hand up and down his body, "wasn't part of my plan for you. I wanted the whole deal—marriage, and we got that, but I wanted kids, an SUV, a big house, and grandkids, too. I'm so sorry I fucked it all up, babe. But listen, I love you more than my life. And hear me out now. I want you to go home."

I nod and suck back my tears. "Okay. I'm going to go home

and shower, because I'm kind of rank. I love you too, Drew. More than I can say."

"Cate, stop. That's not what I meant. I want you to promise me something, okay? Swear to me right now." His voice is firm, much stronger than it has been in days.

"Okay. What is it?"

"I want you to leave this room now and go home, but I don't want you to come back after you shower. I want you to say your goodbyes to me right here, right now."

"What!? What are you saying?" My heart stutters in my throat.

"I'm saying what you think I'm saying. I love you so much more than having you sit here by my side for the next few days. I don't want that. You swore to me, Cate."

"Drew, I can't."

"Yes, you can. Now, go. Turn around, walk through that door, and don't ever look back. All my stuff is boxed exactly like I asked you to, and you know what to do with it. My parents and yours will be here, along with Ben. But you, you don't need to be here. I don't want you to be here. I want you to remember me as I was, when I was healthy, during our best times. Now, look at that door and take your first steps into your new life, Cate. And promise me you'll live. Just live, Cate. Do it for me."

ONE
Present

---◆---

Two years and four months later

THE BITTER COLD SLIPS THROUGH my wool coat as if it's mesh, causing me to hug myself tighter. As I make my way across the street, the countdown on the crosswalk sign nearly ends, and I quicken my steps. The way my luck goes these days, I won't make it across in time. Instead, I'm likely to get run over by a tiny Smart car, of all things, because DC cabbies are just as crazy as the ones in New York. And somehow I'll survive, only without the use of any of my limbs.

Just as my feet land on the curb, a cab roars by, sending a slushy wave of ice and snow against the back of my legs and the bottom half of my coat. I shiver as the cold seeps into my very bones.

"Great," I mutter, dusting myself off while sidestepping the ice patches that litter the sidewalks after yesterday's winter storm. Of all the luck. Washington, DC is supposed to be the exception to northern winters, or so I've been told. It's just far enough south to squeak past the worst of the northern winter weather. Much like Charleston, historically, old man winter doesn't dump buckets of snow in the area—or at least until I decided to make this place my home.

Yesterday's snow nearly beat the record of earliest recorded snowfall on October 5, 1892. We've missed that by a grand seven

4

days. Great for me—*not*. I'm not a fan of the white stuff, which is why I chose DC over the Big Apple. My needs were simple and my requirements few when I made the decision to leave South Carolina about a year ago, two of which were to be in a big city and preferably north. What I didn't bank on is living in a place where cold is the norm more months out of the year than not. Guess the joke's on me.

Jarred from my inner thoughts, I take the wrong step and end up slipping and sliding with wide arching, wind-milling arms. The comical movements do nothing to stop the momentum and I lose my footing. A hand snakes out from nowhere and takes hold of my arm while another steadies my hip. I have to glance way up to see my savior, who is somewhere in the stratosphere above me.

Immediately, the dull gray of the day disappears and I find myself swimming in an ocean of tropical blue. Disbelief clouds my gaze because instantly I recognize the person who saved me. It's as if fate decided to play Russian roulette with my life and I've finally pulled the trigger with a voracious bang.

"Hi," I stammer.

The man with the aqua eyes and a face I can study forever stares at me a second longer than awkward. A wide-eyed gaze confirms he is just as surprised to see me.

When he speaks, his voice is as deep as the shit I stand in. There is too much history between us. Yet, for a second, the sexy glint in his eyes glamours away all my reticent thoughts of the past.

"Hi. I...ah... never expected to see you here." That's the understatement of the century. "On the streets of DC of all places, and me playing rescuer." His southern drawl glides off his tongue like warm honey.

Jostled some more by passersby, he doesn't let go. Instead, he silently steers me out of the line of foot traffic over to the side of a building next to an ATM machine.

Although we are both almost covered head to foot in winter gear, we are close enough that I feel the heat rolling off of him. Thoughts of the past flitter across my brain like the odd saying that someone walked over my grave, and I shiver.

His gloved hand rubs down my arm as if he notices.

"Are you living here now?"

I nod stupidly because he has to be the last person I'd ever thought I would see again, especially since I've been mostly running away from him.

"Yes. You?" I ask, truly curious if he's visiting or not.

A cloud of frost escapes his mouth when he sighs and runs a gloved hand through hair that appears highlighted by the sun despite the season. "I'm not sure."

My brows rise as I give him a conspicuous look before responding with a half laugh. "That's odd. Either you are or you're not." My tone, although playful, doesn't stop my gut from twisting into complicated knots.

He shrugs. "I'm testing the waters. Now that I've finished my fellowship—"

"You've finished?" I blurt, surprised by his admission.

His smile is warm but doesn't quite meet his eyes. And I feel foolish for even asking. Of course he finished. He was close to completion when I ran.

"Don't," he whispers, moving in closer.

Even on the crowded street his quiet word rings in my ears. The way he looks at me, it's as if he's reading my soul. All of a sudden, I feel the anguish he must see on my face. He holds my gaze a second longer. Then he straightens and continues as if no time apart has passed between us.

"I'm temporarily working with one of the top guys in oncology. A doctor in his practice is out on maternity leave. I'm filling in, but it has the potential to lead to a full-time position. It could be an opportunity of a lifetime. However, I need to figure out if I like the area enough to make a permanent move. You know my heart's in Charleston. The rest is up to fate."

That word again. Has fate placed him in my path? What are the odds that I'd slip and he'd be the one to catch me, miles and miles away from our hometown?

There are many reasons why I shouldn't be curious. The biggest of which is that I'd left Charleston after he gave me many reasons to stay.

"I should head back to work. I'm already late," I mutter with averted eyes.

His hand halts my escape, making it impossible to move around him. Earnest eyes search mine before he decides what he wants to say.

"We should have lunch or dinner? Something to do with a meal. I know your favorite is Italian. Word has it there is a good restaurant not too far from here."

"I don't know," I admit honestly. My captured eyes break from his in favor of the ground, searching for an escape hatch. As beautiful as the man is, so much pain surrounds any possible relationship between us. I hurt him when I left and I hurt myself as well.

A finger lifts my chin as he forces me to stare into his gorgeous eyes.

"We don't have to talk about the past—Charleston, the hospital, any of it. It can be as if we're meeting for the first time. We can make a brand new start."

My heart gallops like a thoroughbred on a wild boar hunt.

"Drew—"

He shakes his head again. "No, let's try something new."

He takes a small step back before proffering his hand.

"Hi, I'm Andy."

"Andy?" I'm sure my eyebrows shoot into my hairline.

He leans in and whispers, "Calling me anything else would remind you of the past."

I bite my bottom lip because the name does stir ugly emotions in my stomach. They are the kind that turns my face red with fat tears spilling down my cheeks. I've run from those emotions and the man before me.

Unable to do anything else with the hand offered to me as if in truce, I take it with a faint smile. "Hi, Andy."

He keeps my hand for many seconds, much longer than any stranger would. When we finally let go, a crooked smile that should be properly named a sexy smirk appears on his face. "Nice to meet you, Cate." He playfully waggles his eyebrows. "Can I have your number?"

The cliché line should be cheesy, but the way he says it would make any woman's panties melt.

I glance away, not wanting him to see how affected I am. More than that, he subtly lets me know that he realizes I've changed my number. That means he's tried to call me despite it all. The fact that he doesn't give me crap about it adds value to his declaration of a fresh start.

He uses his black leather-gloved hand to touch my cheek and draw me from my inner turmoil. I'm forced to face him and the truth of my actions.

"I see your pretty little head working. We're here in DC away from everything. No one has to know," he says before letting me go.

The idea that our family or friends might catch the slightest clue we're considering dating freaks me out. After everything, I still haven't forgiven myself. I shake that thought away. In a moment of free will, I pull my phone from my pocket. God only knows if I'm making the right decision, but I'm tired of running. Let me rephrase that. I'm tired of running from *him*.

"What's yours?"

His smile thaws me from my face all the way to my toes. He doesn't answer. The pads of his gloved thumb glide over my cheeks.

"You're still as beautiful as the first day I saw you."

His eyes laser onto mine in a way that sends a shockwave to my core. Just like then, I'm embarrassed by my reaction to him. The idea of his touch makes my center clench with expectation.

I watch his lips move as he recites his number. It's a wonder how I manage to hear him, as I'm transfixed thinking about all the things he can do with his capable mouth. The text I send is simple. Three words, the order of which come from my inner vixen.

Lunch Dinner or Breakfast.

Wanting to be sexy for the first time in ages, I begin to stroll away after a quick farewell with an extra bounce in my step only to slip again.

When he catches me for a second time, he whispers, "If you keep falling, I'll think you want my hands on you. And that will mean our first meal together will be breakfast."

His steamy words blow across my cheek and the heat causes a shudder to run through me. Since he's at my back, I can't see his expression. But I know well enough that his face sports a cocky grin. Only when I turn to say something, he's already walking away in the opposite direction. I roll my lower lip in and gently bite. I try not to be giddy about having lunch with Drew... no. Andy. I force myself to push thoughts of the past out of my head. Least of which is how I can ever forgive myself. After all we've lost and how I left, I could have never expected that he would ever want to see me or forgive me, either.

Yet somehow in the last ten minutes, my life has taken a decided turn. Worse, I can't get my mind off of him. In all the time since I saw him last, I've worked hard at forgetting and trying to move on. I step carefully forward with nervous anticipation. The fact that I haven't been with anyone of consequence since *him* scares me. To allow myself the vulnerability of placing my heart on the line freaks me out. But the possibility of breakfast with him stirs a hunger within me that food can never fulfill.

When I get a text back, **Dinner with the possibly of breakfast**, with a winking emoji, I wonder if I have any right to the grin that broadens across my face.

TWO
Past

---◆---

MY ROOMMATE, JENNA, LEANS AGAINST the doorframe. I catch her out the corner of my eye. She knows my rule—no interruptions while I'm writing. My nose zeroes in on my computer screen and fingers fly across the keyboard. What feels like a thousand plus papers I have due the first month of this semester is the reason behind the rule. Jenna doesn't speak; she just occupies space. Unfortunately, she's enough of a distraction that I lose my train of thought and start typing inane crap.

"Okay. I give up. What do you want?" The question is half born from frustration, the other in jest.

She crosses her arms over her chest, determined to tell me something. "I have news." An indecent grin grows on her face like a weed.

"News?" My face pinches into a frown.

"Remember my brother's friend that was at the party last weekend?"

"I guess." Truthfully, I don't have a clue who she's talking about, but I need to get back to the paper that's due tomorrow. Besides, Ben mingled with a ton of people at that party. I almost glance away but she's quick to respond to keep my attention.

"You have to remember. He's adorable. Tall, sandy blond, blue eyes. His name's Drew?"

Her face lights up as if she's an entertainment news reporter with a breaking headline story.

"And?" Because honestly, as much as I'd love to chat, all the work I need to do trumps guy talk.

"He wants you. *Bad.*"

I pause for a second at the way she added that last part. Then I shake it off.

"Is that what you interrupted my train of thought for, crazy girl?" Smiling, I throw the pencil that's tucked in my ear at her.

"Hey!" She laughs because she thinks I'll give in. "Drew is hot. Smokin' hot. As sin on a graham cracker."

"Okay, one, I don't have time for Smokin' Hot Drew. And two, what the hell is sin on a graham cracker?"

"A s'more. That's what. And he's better than that. And you know how much I love s'mores."

I shake my head because Jenna has always been boy crazy. Lucky for her, she's been successful at meeting the right guys.

"As tasty as he sounds, I'm far too busy these days. I have to maintain my grades to keep my scholarship." I turn my attention back to the computer and try to remember what I was about to type.

"Jeez, Cate, all you do is study and write. I practically had to drag you to that party on Saturday. I swear if it hadn't been for Ben being in town, you never would've gone."

I roll my head around, trying to ease the stiffness in my neck. "You know why I can't take a break. If I lose my scholarship, there goes my tuition money. As it is, I can barely afford what the scholarship doesn't cover. My parents warned me about my financial situation when I decided to go to school here." She stares at me like she's forgotten. I sigh. "It's all on me." Finally, I spell it out, hoping she remembers. "My family doesn't have money like yours does. That means I have to keep my grades up. I almost screwed all that up with dickwad."

Jenna frowns. "Jeez Cate. One little break won't kill you."

"Yeah, I went to the party, didn't I, and got wasted. I don't remember half the things I did. Besides, last time I gave my attention to some guy it almost cost me. I learned a huge lesson that time. Remember?"

"Yeah, but I thought you were talking about the way …"

I have to stop her. That is one memory that needs to stay buried. My palm flies up in the air as I groan. "That was a fucking catastrophe all around. I mean, I tried to sleep with the jerk and you know how that went."

She runs over to me and hugs me. "I'm sorry. I know he hurt you."

"Yeah, even worse, it was humiliating," I mumble into her shoulder. "Not only that, my grades crashed. I can't go through that again. I'm taking extra classes and working double time to make up for that semester. So no. Graham cracker sin can't be an option right now. I wish it could be different."

Jenna pulls her hair out of an elastic band and twists it up in a messy bun, wrapping the band around it again. "After all the time you spent ogling him and chatting it up with him on Saturday, I thought that maybe you were interested."

Scrunching up my face, I say, "Um, yeah, those details are totally sketchy to me."

"You're positive then?"

"I wish I could, but studying comes first. Now scram so I can get something done."

She sidles out the door and I resume my work. But now I have to conjure up some BS because the old thought choo choo has chugged right off the tracks. This sucks. After about twenty minutes, I get up and decide to go for a run. Running always helps my brain reconnect. I tie my shoes and charge out the door. Forty minutes later when I get back, there's a lovely bouquet of flowers on the counter.

"You got a delivery while you were gone," Jenna announces with a smirk.

I rest my arms on the counter and stretch my calves as curiosity has me leaning toward the little white card that reads, *Cate Forbes*. "From who?"

"My guess is they're from Drew, that's who," Jenna says, moving closer to face me.

"Right." I laugh because I know my best friend. "You bought them and are pretending they're from Drew, didn't you?"

Jenna actually has the decency to look appalled. With fingers at the hollow of her throat, she says, "Seriously. You think I would do that?"

"Yes, I do." I nod at the same time.

"Damn. You don't think very highly of me, do you?"

"Yes, I do. I love you, in fact. But when you set your mind on something, deviant Jenna comes out in full force."

She rolls her eyes and giggles. "Okay, so I did *not* send the flowers, but now I wish I had."

This is confusing. "You really didn't?"

"I'll pinky swear if you want." She holds out her finger.

So if she didn't, then that Drew dude must have. I walk back to the flowers and with hesitant fingers reach for the little card that came with them.

"It won't bite, you know." Jenna's sarcasm reaches me from across the room.

I grab the card and read it.

I would love a chance to take you to dinner.
Drew McKnight.

"What does it say?"

Perplexed, I mumble, "Oh my. He's asked me to dinner. And these are beautiful. I've never gotten flowers before." I lean in to inhale their fragrance.

"They are and when did he ask you out? And don't frown. You know my mom says that's a sure way to create early wrinkles."

This whole flower thing has me completely shocked. No one has ever done anything so sweet like this for me before. "No set date, just that he'd like to take me."

"Oh my god."

"Don't get your panties all wet over this." I say that but in reality, I'm the one getting nervous.

"You swear you don't remember him? He was with my brother the entire night. And the two of you had a cozy little chat going."

Grabbing her arm, I squeak, "No I don't remember! Help me, Jenna! I was hammered. I barely remember seeing Ben." The night is fuzzy at best. "Wait a minute. If he's Ben's friend, how old is this dude?"

"Ben's age."

"What? That would make him what? Twenty-seven?"

"Yeah, probably."

"Jeez. That's like gramps. No way can I go out with a man that old."

"He's in his second year of residency. He's a doctor." She says it like she's dangling a golden carrot in front of my face.

"So? That's supposed to make him datable? I don't care if he's the President of the United States' son. He's too old for me. He's probably ready for a wife or something. I'm trying to finish school not start a family."

"Damn, Cate, calm down. It's not like he's twenty years older than you. It's seven. That's it. Lots of girls our age date guys seven years older than they are."

"Oh yeah? Like who."

"That Scarlett chick from our English class freshman year. She did."

"Yeah, and she's slept with almost every guy at Purdue. She keeps the Boilermakers running strong. She singlehandedly kept the entire fourth year mechanical engineering guys in blow jobs that year."

"Pure conjecture."

"Pure? That's not a word I would use in the same sentence that had anything to do with Scarlett."

"Damn, are you hardheaded. Just go out with him. One date. If you don't like him or you think he's too old after that, then fine. You don't ever have to see him again."

When I put some thought into it, there must have been some kind of spark between us for me to have spent time with him at the party, even if I was a little wasted. That's not the type of thing I normally do. My style is to stay clear of all guys.

"Okay… I'll do it. Give him my cell number. But please don't give me a hard time if it doesn't work out, especially since he's friends with Ben."

"No worries on that, my friend."

Later that night, I'm running through my to do list on the number of papers I have to write and how many will require a significant amount of research. Having a double major is not much of a picnic, but I couldn't make a choice between accounting and journalism, so here I am, writing my ass off. But honestly, I love it.

When my phone rings, I answer it without looking at the caller ID. I figure it's my mom. She usually calls at this hour because she knows it's the best time to catch me.

"Hey, Mom."

A crazy sexy voice answers, "Um yeah, this isn't Mom. This is Drew…" When I don't respond, he adds, "McKnight."

Shit. Drew. Flower and date man. Gramps! "Oh, hey. W-what's up?" I stutter. This weird nervousness settles over me because I can't remember anything about him and suddenly I feel terrible about it. But if he's half as good looking as he sounds or as Jenna says, I might be in trouble.

"Jenna gave me your number." His voice is warm and breezy and makes me remember just how long my lady parts have been neglected.

"Yes! Thank you so much for the flowers. They're gorgeous. That was very sweet of you," I add.

"You're welcome. I, um, didn't know how else to get you to agree to a date."

Now I feel bad. It makes me feel bitchy that he had to go to those lengths. "Oh, I didn't ..."

"No worries, Cate. I was only giving you a taste of my good, old-fashioned, southern charm." I sense a smile behind his words and immediately feel better.

"Well, it worked. How could I possibly say no to flowers?" Did I just flirt with him? I need to pull it together. He's putting a huge dent in my no dating wall and I need to remind myself that I don't have time to date.

"Are you occupied on Saturday?"

Occupied? Who asks if someone is occupied? I have to stifle a laugh.

"Let me check." Of course I'm not, but I don't want him to think I'm the loser that I am. So I let several seconds pass before I answer. "No, I'm free." The words slip out because Jenna's right. I have been spending way too much time on the computer. One night of harmless fun won't cause me to lose my scholarship.

"Great! I'd love to take you to dinner."

"Nice." I pause because I'm smiling. I bite my lip to stop it from growing. This isn't good. "I can meet you," I toss out.

"No, I'll pick you up. Is seven okay?"

"Seven is perfect. I can text you my address."

"Not necessary. Remember, I sent you flowers? Ben was kind enough to give it to me."

Shit. What a dumbass. "Oh, right."

"The truth, Cate, is I actually helped Ben move Jenna in."

"Oh." This surprises me. "I didn't know."

"Do you like Italian?"

15

"I like everything, but Italian is my favorite."

"Excellent, Italian it is. And it'll be fairly casual."

"Sounds great." I'm getting ready to end the call, but something stops me. "Can I ask you something?"

"Sure."

Taking a deep breath, I take the plunge. "Why me? Obviously I'm only a junior in college and we don't really know each other, other than the party."

"When I pointed you out to Ben at the party, he gave me an earful and I was even more intrigued, so I sought you out. After our conversation, I knew I wanted to get to know you better."

I chew the tip of my pen. "Our conversation?"

"Yeah. How we talked about Charleston."

"Um ..."

His chuckle is dark with an intoxicating kick like whiskey going down the first time. "You don't remember it, do you?"

"I'm not gonna lie. I don't. I'm sorry. I blame it on the alcohol."

"Like the song, huh?" He laughs. "We talked about how funny it was we never met, even though we were both from Charleston and you were Jenna's best friend and I was Ben's. Ring a bell?"

My hand automatically reaches for the back of my neck and rubs it. Oh my god, why can't I remember this? I'm never drinking again. "No, and I'm beyond embarrassed to admit it."

He laughs again and this time the sound sends warm shivers down my spine. Wow! That's never happened before. Warm shivers.

"Cate, don't worry about it. Want to know what else you told me?"

"Oh god. I'm not sure," I croak.

The deep reverberations of his chuckle make my belly tighten. What is it about him? And I can't even remember what he looks like, dammit!

"It's not that bad, really."

"Okay, what?"

"You wanted to know what a guy like me was doing at a party like that. I said I was hanging out with Ben. Then you wanted particulars. I told you what I did and you whispered in my ear that if I were a gynecologist, you'd never come to my office for a visit for fear you'd embarrass yourself during the exam."

Jesus Christmas. I cover my face with a pillow. I'm way past mortified and don't know what to say.

"Cate, are you there?"

"Uuuggghhh," I groan. This is worse than I expected.

"It was pretty damn cute, I have to say."

"Did I do anything else that will warp my life forever?"

"Nah, just some things about me being sexy, but I can't recall the specifics."

Translation—he doesn't want to embarrass me any further.

"Sexy? I called you sexy to your face?" The heat in my cheeks will probably melt my skin off.

"You did and turned every shade of red when you realized you said it out loud."

I try to speak again, but my words are muffled because I've buried my face in the pillow again. I sit up and decide to just put it out there.

"So now the question remains—why do you want to go out with a girl who made a fool out of herself the first time you met her?"

"To be completely honest, Cate, I found your frankness refreshing—especially in a beautiful woman like yourself. Even in your slightly inebriated condition, you were witty and sexy. If I could've talked you into going home with me, I would have. However, Ben would've killed me."

My mouth curves into a huge grin. "Yeah?"

"Yeah."

My body heats with his admission. And this is just a phone conversation. What the heck will he be like in the flesh? "Well then Drew, I look forward to meeting you again."

"Great. And Cate?"

"Yeah?"

"I promise not to act like a *gramps*. See you at seven on Saturday." The humor in his tone is unmistakable.

I'm going to kill Jenna. Very slowly and painfully.

Saturday at seven sharp, my doorbell buzzes. When I open it, I look up into the most beautiful pair of cerulean eyes. They crinkle at the corners when he smiles, and then I get the whole picture.

Drew is in no way a gramps. He is definitely smokin' hot. Sin on a graham cracker, in Jenna's words. And in mine—a hot fudge sundae, with whipped cream, and a cherry on top, plus chocolate cake with buttercream icing.

Thick wavy sandy brown hair that's been kissed by the sun caps his head. It's messy like he just ran his hands through it, but it makes me want to sink my fingers in and play sexy time. In a very bad way. High cheekbones, a nose that's neither too small nor too large, and lips that make me swallow before drool runs out of my mouth come together to create a beautiful face. Perfect teeth gleam as he continues to grin. This is no average college boy that stands before me. And I'm speechless. How in the hell could I have forgotten a face like this?

"I take it you approve?" Even his voice is perfect. The southern drawl I miss so much living here in the Midwest has me breaking out in a huge grin.

"I'm sorry. I just wanted to see if looking at you would help me remember." That's not true and I'm pretty sure he knows it.

He chuckles as I sneak in several more peeks at him. He's broad-shouldered with a wide chest that tapers down to a narrow waist. My hormones rage like a teenager as I salivate for a look underneath his button down shirt. I'd love to see if he has a six-y or an eight-y. I'm also curious to see his V because I'm damned sure he's got one. He wears dark jeans that ride low on his hips as they mold to his body. I'd like to ask him to pirouette so I can inspect his ass, but I refrain.

"Well?" His crooked grin only adds to his appeal.

"Okay, I'm busted." I raise my hands in the air. I've always been shy about what I want, and only tell Jenna the truth. I guess what I thought were surreptitious glances weren't quite as secretive as I intended them to be. What the hell has gotten into me?

He throws back his head and offers me a hearty laugh.

Needing a quick recovery, I sputter, "I thought it only fair, since I was over served at the party and didn't remember meeting you. I'm sure you had ample opportunity to check me out, so I figured I'd take my chance now."

He dips his head and says, "I hope I don't disappoint."

"Not in the least." I roll my lip under my teeth. If nothing else, I'm strongly considering a one-night stand. That's definitely not my style but damn, he's worth it.

He dampens a grin and I can tell it's a struggle. "Well then, Ms. Forbes, are you ready to take your chances on dinner with me?" he asks as he offers me his arm.

"Indeed I am." I grab the small purse with my phone and keys before taking his arm.

After I lock the door, we head off toward a Toyota 4-Runner. It's not the newest model, but not an old one either. It's extremely clean, unlike my unorganized and messy Honda Civic. Please don't let Drew be a neat freak. If he is, he might end up hating me and ending this before we even have a beginning. Oddly, I have a feeling I might be disappointed if that's the case.

"So, Jenna tells me you're dual majoring in accounting and journalism."

"That's right. And what else did Jenna tell you about me?" I nudge him playfully.

"Don't blame her. I pestered the hell out of her for days. She was pretty reticent at first until I just wore her out. I should warn you. I can be like that."

"Oh, not one of those!" I feign shock. It has the desired effect; he laughs.

"Yeah. I had the greatest teacher. My mother."

"Hmm. At least you've given me a heads up."

"So?"

That one word has me laser focused on his lips. It takes me a second to blink back up to meet his eyes.

"Yeah. Dual major. At first I was solely business, but I wasn't into it. Then I discovered accounting and love it. And I've always had a thing for writing so I figured maybe I could parlay the two into business journalism or work for a large corporation and do business writing. I don't know yet."

"Sounds like a plan to me." His smile is warm and I'm finding it easy to talk to him. I thought I might have to force conversation. Yet I'm vomiting words like I have the stomach flu.

"Or a half-ass one, like my dad says. He thinks I'll end up with some menial job somewhere." I laugh and shake my head, thinking about my family.

"Yeah, well parents can either be most resourceful or the biggest hindrance when it comes to this type of thing. You should follow your heart."

I grin. Not many people see my logic when it comes to my

majors. Tapping his arm, I say, "Thanks. That's very nice to hear because even Jenna thinks I'm crazy. She gives me a hard time because I'm always studying."

"It's good to be driven, Cate. Not everyone is like that."

I smooth my dress over my legs. "I wouldn't necessarily call it driven. It's sort of a must." I explain the deal about my parents and my scholarships.

"Ah, I see. But that sort of makes you even more motivated. The way I see it, you could've taken the easy road and gone to school where they wanted you to. But instead, you chose Purdue, and are working hard to stay here. It's your choice, right?"

"Well, yeah. When you put it that way, I guess so." He makes me feel good about the fact that I have to study hard. Everyone else, including my best friend, gives me a hard time about it.

I look at his profile as he drives and see his lips curl into a smile. He's nothing like I expected. What had I expected? Some older dude. And why? I don't know. Seven years from now I'll be his age. Will I consider myself old? I shake off the thought because I see how ridiculous I was being.

"What has you so quiet over there?" He glances over at me before returning his focus to the road.

"Honestly?" I should feel silly but I don't. He seems good natured.

"Yeah."

"A couple of things. One, you get why I have to spend so much time studying. Everyone else gives me crap about it. And two, I was thinking that twenty-seven isn't exactly old."

"Ah, so maybe not gramps then?" He looks at me and winks.

I shake my head. "I can't believe Jenna told you that."

"Don't blame her. Like I said, I'm persuasive. I had to know why you were so opposed to going out with me. Then I thought it was funny. Old man McKnight here."

It is comical when he says it like that.

"Well it was partly because I don't date since I need to keep my grades up. So you and Ben are close?" I ask.

"Yeah. We've been close since kindergarten."

"It *is* funny that we're all from Charleston, isn't it?"

"Yeah, but it's even funnier that you don't remember our conversation about this," he says, grinning.

My hands cover my face. "Oh lord. I'm so embarrassed about

that. And sorry. I can't believe how stupid I was, too. So, tell me what I missed."

"Only that Ben and I have been friends since kindergarten, like you and Jenna."

"That's so crazy!" I slap my knees. It's strange enough that Jenna and I, both Charlestonians, are here at Purdue. Most southerners never leave the south. Ever. Unless they have a very compelling reason to do so, such as marrying a millionaire, getting a job offer that pays millions, or you get the picture. And southerners rarely go to college at a northern school unless it's for a degree in something that they cannot get at a southern school. But really? Is that even possible? So how did Jenna and I end up at Purdue? Because her brother Ben went here and LOVED it, and for four years that's all we heard. So Jenna persuaded me to visit with her and, I must admit, I fell in love with it too.

"So, why have I never heard of you?"

He raises one hand. "No idea. Look what you've been missing all this time." He laughs and there are his pearly whites.

No shit. I'm going to wring Jenna's neck the first chance I get. And when I think about it, why hasn't she been lusting after Drew all this time? She never talks about him. Never.

My stupid filterless mouth spews forth, "Why hasn't Jenna ever mentioned you? Seriously, after all these years I would think I would've heard about you."

His face turns the prettiest shade of pink. It goes all the way up to the tips of his ears.

"Well, our age differences might have something to do with it. Gramps, you know. Think about it. Ben and I were in high school when you and Jenna were in elementary or middle school." And he winks. Then his expression turns somber. "But I was in a serious relationship until over two years ago."

"Ahh. Sorry, I didn't mean to pry." Now that makes sense, but I want to stay away from the rebounder.

"Yeah, I dated her in college and pretty much figured we'd get married, but she didn't. She ended it during my third year in med school."

"Oh?"

"I'll be honest here. I took it pretty bad. So, yeah, that's probably why."

"I see." I do some calculations in my head. "So if it's been way over two years, would that be considered a rebound?" Oh, shit. Did I just say that out loud?

"Rebound? You think I'm on the rebound?" He parks the car and I glance up to see the restaurant.

"I, uh," I suck some air through my teeth, "I didn't mean for you to hear that. I was calculating the time in my head."

He swivels in his seat and nails me with his eyes. I'm pinned in place by those damn blues of his. They are really something. "I'm not on the rebound. I couldn't even talk to a woman for months. Almost a year to be precise. Then I went out on a few dates, and stopped altogether. Just wasn't ready. But eventually, I moved on. When I let it all go, I realized we weren't a match. Our wants out of life were way off base. When that happened, things sort of fell into place. It's been over two, almost three years since the split and I'm happier now than I've ever been. So no. I'm not on the rebound, Cate."

"Thank you. You didn't have to tell me all of that."

"No, I didn't." He says it graciously. "It is strange though, us being from the same town, and never having met. Plus the fact that I'm best friends with your best friend's brother makes it even weirder. It did require some sort of an explanation. I'm glad I told you. So, shall we go in and eat?"

"I think we shall."

He walks around and opens my door, like a true gentleman.

"By the way, did I tell you how great you look tonight?" he asks.

"No."

"My bad. You look amazing."

"Thank you." I glance down at my outfit, a black knit dress that skims my body. It isn't special but it highlights my assets and I've always felt sort of pretty in it.

"I have to tell you something. That night I saw you at the party, all I could do was stare at you. After our little conversation, I decided to make it my goal to get you to go out with me. Thank you, Cate, for helping me out."

"Helping you out?"

"Well, yeah. You helped me attain my goal," he says as he waggles his brows.

"Um, do you have any other goals that involve me?" I ask. I don't dare tell him I've already set some of my own. And they aren't the kind I like to share.

"Yeah, but I can't disclose those yet. Maybe later, after a glass or two of wine."

I lean into him. "Hmm, you have me hanging in suspense, Drew."

"It's all good, Cate."

Dinner is delicious. It's the best Italian food I've ever had away from Charleston and New York City. Drew orders for us both because I can't make up my mind. I finally tell him to surprise me. When the food arrives, there's so much of it I laugh. I'm sure we'll be bringing boxes of it home, but Drew eats like he has a bottomless pit for a stomach. I'm impressed.

"Where does it all go? To your toes?"

"Yeah. About that. I run a lot and lift weights so I'm always hungry."

Now I really want to see his V. Maybe even lick and bite it. I've never seen one in real life. For that matter, I've only had pseudo sex once, and it was with that dickwad I used to date last year. He tried to repeatedly stab my vagina with his penis one night and it was so horrifying, I made him stop. He ended up calling me all kinds of awful names like cockblocker and frosty cunt, so I broke up with him while lying in my bed naked and sobbing. It was the most humiliating moment of my life. I still have nightmares over that incident. And dickwad—not even close to having a V. His abs bore a closer resemblance to a bowl of Jell-O. He was kind of cute in the looks department, but after his asshole move in the bedroom, every time I saw him after that, I swear he turned into a trollface. I still pray a horde of killer bees descends on his peen and stings the hell out of it. It's no less than he deserves.

"What in the world are you thinking that has put that scowl on your face. I hope it's not me?"

Good lord! "Oh, no!" My laugh is shaky. "It's definitely not you. Actually, it's nothing, really." I rub my arms as I glance at the napkin on my lap. Why did I have to think about that dreadful night?

"Come on, Cate. You looked like an assassin from one of those Jason Bourne movies a few seconds ago."

"I did?"

"Yeah. Spill it." His grin is disarming.

"No. You'll think I'm awful." The last thing I'm going to do is tell him about dickwad.

"Only if it involved me," he says.

"It didn't but I can't tell you. It's of a highly personal nature."

"Well, I hope to god I never put that look on your face."

"I hope you don't either. Let me just say it had to do with killer bees."

"Killer bees. I'll remember that. On another note, how about some killer dessert?"

As long as it has to do with your V, sure. "Okay. What are you having?"

"Their tiramisu is the best."

"Wanna share?"

"Nope. I'm too greedy when it comes to sweets."

"I love an honest man. Make it two then." The waiter takes our order and when they are delivered, Drew was right. It is some kind of tasty. But I bet his V is better. Why am I being such a horn dog tonight? I'm on my second spoonful, and his dish is empty. His arm extends across the tiny square table and he dips his spoon into mine.

His dessert thievery makes me laugh. "Damn, you really are greedy."

"Sorry. I'm surprised my teeth aren't the size of giant Chicklets. I have an enormous sweet tooth."

"Eat away." Why am I flirting?

He waggles his brows again and says, "I'm hoping to."

I nearly spit out the bite of tiramisu I've just taken. He turns a bit pink again, which I find most charming, and says, "Sorry. That was a bit inappropriate."

I swallow to avoid choking, and reply, "No. I don't mind inappropriate. You just caught me by surprise." By the time I'm ready for another bite of my dessert, I find my dish is empty. He gives me a guilty look. And for some reason, I want to pinch his cheek and tell him it's okay. How weird is that? I'm usually not a giggly, pinch the cheek kind of girl. Now that I think of it, I'm normally not a share my dessert kind of girl, either.

"I'm sorry I stole your tiramisu."

"It's okay. You did me a favor."

"How's that?"

"I didn't need all those extra calories."

"Oh, god, please tell me you're not one of those?" He sits back and inspects me.

"One of what?" I'm truly baffled.

"The rabbit eaters. Girls who eat like rabbits."

"No, I couldn't survive without pizza. You can probably tell."

"I can tell you look perfect to me."

Uh huh. They all say that when they want to get in your pants.

"You don't believe me?"

"No, I believe you. But come on. Most guys are only interested in one thing."

"True. But Cate, I'm not most guys."

I laugh. "Now that's an original line."

"Shit. That was a bad one, wasn't it?"

"Not the worst I've ever heard." We both chuckle.

"So, Cate Forbes, are you up for going out for a drink with me?"

"Yeah. One question. Where do you live?"

That adorable smile reappears and he says, "Indy. But don't worry. I booked a hotel room for the night. I was thinking we might be out late and I didn't want to deal with the hour drive."

That was sweet. "Where are you staying?"

"At the Union."

"Cool. Then let's hit it."

We decide on a club called Chuckie's. On the way, Drew leans toward me and asks, "Cate, since you're not twenty-one, are you going to be able to get in the clubs?"

I wave my hand in the air. "No worries. I'm a resourceful college student. I have a fake ID."

"I figured as much, since you were Jenna's friend."

When we arrive at Chuckie's, we head straight for the bar. Drew orders us a couple of drinks—a vodka and soda for me and a vodka and tonic for him—and hunts for a place to hang out. He grabs my arm and leads me across the room to a small table close to the dance floor. "I'm surprised we found this."

"I know. Score." I fist bump him and then we clank our glasses. The music blares as people dance and I scan the room, checking to see if I recognize anyone.

I don't spot anyone and focus on Drew's gorgeous eyes instead. He stares at me like I'm interesting. It's not a bit awkward. No one's ever made me feel special before, but when he looks at me, that's exactly how I feel. I grin, then sip my vodka and soda.

"If you keep watching me, I'll think I have something stuck on my face."

He folds his arms and leans on the table to get closer to me. "I'm trying to be good and not kiss you like I want to here in front of everyone."

"Maybe I want you to kiss me," I say brazenly.

He's about to call my bluff when the next thing I know, the waitress places two shots in front of us. Drew pays and I pick one up.

"Did you do this?"

The side of his mouth curves up in a sexy grin. "Guilty. I knew you liked vodka so I figured a couple of lemon drops might be fun."

"I love lemon drops. Are you trying to get me drunk, Drew McKnight?"

"I'm trying real hard to get *you*, Cate Forbes, by any means possible."

I don't need vodka, because I'm drunk on him. He's easy to be around and I'm so comfortable with him, as if we've known each other for years and not hours.

"Here's to lemons, vodka, and um, drops!"

Drew's wide grin has me grinning right back. Damn, the guy is just too gorgeous for my own good. Or is it for his own good? We clink our tiny shooters and drink them. It goes down far too easy. Then *I Gotta Feeling* by The Black Eyed Peas comes on.

I fly out of my seat, feeling unabashed. Running to the dance floor like a loon, high on life and Drew, I start shaking it up. The alcohol has loosened me up and I decide to put on a little show. Drew sits and I dance just for him, swinging my hips and spinning around. I wobble a few times, but correct myself, giving Drew a thumbs up, showing him it was a move I did on purpose. He laughs, and gives me an air fist bump. When the song ends, I shake my hair and head back to our table.

"You're quite the prancer, Cate."

"Yeah, it's one of my secret talents. You're a lucky guy, Drew. Most people aren't aware of this hidden ability." I lean close to his ear and say, "I'm the stealth dancer."

"Ah, is that so?"

"Yep. I have moves."

"I'm sure you do, but I have to share something with you."

"Yeah, what?"

"I have secret moves, too, Cate."

"Ah, I bet you do."

A slow song plays and Drew takes my wrist, spins me, and says, "Like now. How about a dance, twinkle toes?"

I'm out on the floor and in his arms before I can think about it. And it's nice. No, it's perfect. His arms hold me close, much closer than any average acquaintance. The fact is, I'd like to move my hand off his shoulder and tangle my fingers in his hair instead. He smells nice. Not too strong, but fresh and clean, and I'd like to tuck my face into the base of his neck and snuggle right here on the dance floor. My hand rests in his, but then he changes things. He shifts his so that our fingers lace. That tiny movement makes my stomach muscles clench, and I find that I desperately want him to kiss me. I lean back so I can look at him only to find him staring at me. There is no laughter on his face, only serious intent etched around his eyes. The song suddenly ends and we stand there, stuck in each other's gazes as a faster paced one begins. Drew doesn't speak, but leads me off the floor with his arm over my shoulder. When we get back to the table, he says, "Thank you for that dance, Cate." He leans in and kisses my cheek.

We drink and dance some more. And I have way too much fun. So much fun that Drew practically has to drag me out of there. Luckily he drove his car to the Union parking garage after dinner and we walked to Chuckie's from there. Now we have to walk home. I love being with this man. I don't want the night to end. And I tell him.

"This is the best date I've ever been on."

"And to think you called me gramps." His elbow nudges me.

"Who knew gramps was so sexy?"

It's late September and the night has gotten chilly. My arms hug my middle, and Drew's arm is draped over my shoulder. But I want more. I want both arms to be around me and I want to taste him. So my devious mind goes to work, and I pretend to stumble on an imaginary something or other. It works beautifully. He reaches for me, hands on my hips, to stabilize me, and we stand facing each other. My arms circle his neck and he dips his head until our lips graze against each other's. It's not enough for me. I want more of Drew McKnight. I want all of Drew McKnight. But I'm not the most experienced so I let him lead.

He leans back and whispers, "Tell me this is okay."

"It's way more than okay."

His mouth presses to mine, tentatively at first, testing the waters. His lips, which are soft yet firm, nip at mine, and then his tongue peeks out. He runs it along my bottom lip and I open my mouth. Suddenly, we're kissing. Aggressively kissing. He pulls my body up against his, arms wrap tightly around me, his head slants, and the kiss deepens. He explores my mouth as his body presses fully against mine. I feel his hardness and strength through the thin fabric of my dress. My body becomes a live wire—goosebumps erupt from my neck to my ankles; my belly clenches; my nipples stiffen; and for the first time in my life, I get wet. From a kiss. Holy sexy hell.

We're moving. Drew lifts me up and we're moving as we kiss. I'm not sure where, and I don't care, as long as he doesn't stop kissing me. When my back hits something, we stop. Every time he takes a breath, he nips my lips, making me want more. Then one hand slides down to my hip and squeezes as he grasps me tighter, pressing me to his body. He jerks his mouth away from mine.

"Fuck. Cate. Catelyn. Cate, Cate, Cate." A litany of Cates.

Then his mouth is back on mine for only a second and I moan in protest when he pulls away. The thought occurs to me that this is more than a mere kiss. My body tingles and my knees are weak. My fingers sink into his shoulders so I don't crash to the sidewalk. This is something poems are written about and erotic novels are penned over. I am wet between my thighs and the only things he's touched other than my face are my mouth and hip. Once more his lips find mine and passionately kiss me, tongue sliding against mine, turning my stomach into a knotted frenzy and making my head spin. This time when he stops, it takes me a second to collect myself.

"Come to my room with me. Please. We don't have to do anything you're not comfortable with. I swear. I just want to hold you. And stare at you. And wake up with you. And maybe I sound like some pussy whipped bitch, but I'm not ready to send you home."

My brows must hit my hairline and I giggle. Only because I'm drunk—drunk on his kisses. I hate giggly girls, but the idea of him being a pussy whipped bitch makes me die laughing.

"Yes. Okay, I'll come. But I won't fuck you," I blurt out.

"No. No fucking at all. Not one tiny little bit of fucking. I solemnly swear. Scout's honor. God, you're so fucking beautiful." This man is perfect. He's like my dream guy. And to think I almost didn't go out with him! I wasn't looking for this but what a huge mistake that would've been. He links our hands and we walk back to his room. I hope this is real and not the alcohol making me feel this way. I stop for a second and pinch my arm.

"What's wrong? Did a bug bite you?"

"No. I only wanted to make sure I wasn't dreaming." And in an instant, his arms wrap around me, his mouth hovering over mine.

"You're not dreaming, Cate. This is the real deal." And he kisses me again, stealing every bit of my air away. When he finally breaks the kiss off, I run my fingers over his lips.

I shake my head to clear my thoughts. "I don't know what I was thinking."

"What do you mean?"

"Why I didn't jump at the chance to go out with you? What the hell was wrong with me?" Then I realize I'm sounding stupid and I've said the words out loud. I need to shut my mouth before I scare the poor man away.

"That's why I had that goal, Cate."

"I have a confession to make," I say, as we start walking again.

"Yeah?"

"I tripped on purpose. I wanted an excuse to touch you."

He stops, and faces me.

"Seriously?"

I nod and he kisses me again. "I knew when I saw you at that party, we were going to click." Soon, the Union looms in front of us and I'm suddenly nervous. What if we get naked? Oh, no! I haven't done any muffin-scaping. No shaving or waxing. Nada! I look like an overgrown grizzly down below. Oh fuck! What am I going to do? This is so unexpected; I never imagined we'd get past dinner! Maybe I can sneak into the bathroom and use his razor. But then I look at his face and remember he's sporting a bit of scruff, so I doubt he even brought one for the night. Shit-doodle.

"What is it? Please don't say you're having second thoughts. I promise Cate, we can just sit and talk. I only want to spend time with you."

"I know. I trust you, Drew." And oddly enough, I do.

As my thoughts travel back to the possibilities, it comes to me. I can say I don't get naked ever on first dates. Yes. That's it. Perfectly reasonable and acceptable. We make it to his room and he asks if I care for something to drink. I ask for a water. In minutes, one is in my hand, which I greedily drink.

The way he stares at me, I'm guessing he knows I'm nervous.

"You have regrets, don't you?"

I shake my head. "It's not that."

"Please tell me. I don't want anything to weigh on your mind."

My stupid, stupid mouth blurts right out, "I look like an overgrown grizzly below the waist."

"Huh?"

I suppose being a man, he just doesn't understand. So I raise my index finger and then aim it directly between my thighs.

It's obvious when the light bulb goes on because he smiles. Hugely. "It's fine. I didn't plan on us getting naked, anyway."

Okay, so I just told him my deepest darkest most humiliating secret—well almost most humiliating—for nothing? I embarrassed myself to death, for no purpose whatsoever? I want to crawl in a hole and die. I do the only thing I know. I grab the nearest pillow and bury my face in it. The most beautiful man I've ever met, with the most gorgeous eyes on the planet, sits before me, and I just told him that my muffin looks like Sasquatch. This goes down as the most humiliating moment of my life, replacing the dickwad. I will never live this down. Ever.

THREE
Present

───────◆───────

LIVELY MUSIC AND MY LIVELIER coworkers, fill the lounge. But I see and hear none of it. I stare into the mirror on the back of the bar wondering whose reflection I see. I barely recognize the woman staring back at me with the vacant eyes. Drew... *Andy* is here in town. It's been three days since I saw him and I can't get him out of my head.

"Cate, you're too quiet. This is a celebration. We've completed the Caine account. Maybe now we can sleep for more than four hours a night." Daniel grins and puts a tumbler to his lips. "At least until our meeting next Monday to discuss our next project."

He laughs at his own joke as Mandy strolls over with two drinks in her hand. She leans down to whisper in my ear. "I'm not sure what's going on with you tonight, but you will celebrate."

I take the proffered drink feeling like a daisy downer. She lifts up her glass and my team of coworkers all raise their glasses. Not wanting to be the odd man out, I do the same and plaster a smile on my face.

"To us and especially Cate. Without her last minute save we all might be in the office reworking the project," Mandy announces.

"To Cate," everyone toasts.

"To the team," I counter. "There's no I in team. We all put in the hours and we all will, hopefully, reap the rewards."

"Here, here!" comes a chorus of cheers.

I have no idea if we will get bonuses for completing the job on time other than the day off we were given. Still, a girl can hope. I toss back the shot with no idea what kind of liquor it is.

The burn hits my throat and I feel the cinnamon taste not only in my mouth, but in the tears that form in my eyes. It's a Fireball! When my eyes pop out of my head, Mandy thumps my back as if I were choking. I keep my mouth closed for fear I will breathe out fire like a dragon.

"It'll put hair on your chest," Mandy chirps. Her honey brown curls bounce as if she's unable to contain all the energy she has inside her. "At least that's what Dad told my brothers when they had their first taste of alcohol."

"I'm pretty sure my esophagus will never be the same," I croak.

"Here. Have another?"

My expression freezes as I give her a *you're crazy* stare. "You're kidding me, right? Or maybe you're just trying to poison me."

She tosses her head back and barks out a belly laugh. "Cate, I swear we love you. I know you're worried because you're the newest member of the team and you might feel as though we're intimidated that you pulled this one out of the crapper. But honestly, everyone is happy you're here. Happy clients mean we all have jobs. So take another for the team."

She's right. No one has ever made me feel unwanted at work. Worry has clouded my thoughts. What she doesn't know is that it's Drew, or rather *Andy*, that has me rattled. Seeing him after all this time brings to the surface so many regrets.

I pick up the shot and this time I'm ready for it. I clink her glass and chant, "To the team," before I drink it down.

Mandy's sly glance at me makes me suspicious. "There is one other thing you should know."

"What's that?" I dab at my eyes, hoping the moisture the Fireball caused doesn't mess up my makeup.

"Daniel has a crush on you."

While I almost choke, Mandy's gaze remains steady on me.

"You like him?" I ask, confused.

"No." She violently shakes her head. "It's just—he's sweet. But super cute," she amends. "And I've known him forever and I feel sort of protective over him. So don't break his heart."

She taps my shoulder before she walks away and I blink rapidly, unsure of what just happened.

"Hey." I glance up and Daniel stands before me. "Mind if I sit with you?"

"Sure." I shrug, trying not to let Mandy's comments make things weird between us. Still, I'm nervous about what he's about to say. I take the last of the shooters and drink it. He smiles but sighs and I watch as he gears himself up to say something.

"Take another shot with me." The words burst out of me because I don't want to have to turn him down. Mandy's right about one thing. He's cute in that nerdy superhero way. With his dark hair and black-framed glasses, I have to wonder if he has on a blue and red leotard under his suit. Or maybe that's the alcohol talking. Before he can answer though, I order another two rounds. The drinks start to go down easier, especially after the fifth one.

I've managed to stave off any dating topics and only traded smiles. I thwart any opportunity on his part to speak by shouting toasts to everyone, from our boss to the janitors in the building. But now I've run out of excuses.

"Cate, I was wondering—"

The music stops and Mandy's voice booms out of the speakers. "Cate! Where are you, girl?"

Feeling unsteady myself, I can still tell she's been drinking much more than I have because her words are slurred.

"Wait, that's me," I say pointing to myself. I frown when I notice it's harder for me to communicate than it should have been.

"Cate, Catieeee, come sing with me," Mandy croons.

The crowd begins to chant my name and I glance up at Daniel. My eyes feel heavy. Yet, this is the escape I've been searching for.

"I gotta go. But I'll see you later."

I sway a little when I get to my feet and Daniel's hands are there to steady me. In fact, he helps me navigate the crowd.

"You have nice hands and nice teeth. I like a man with good teeth," I absently say.

Daniel shakes his head. "Be careful up there, Catie," he teases as he helps me up on stage and it feels like old times. I think of Jenna and I miss her terribly. She is planning a visit and what will I tell her about Drew... I mean *Andy*. That's going to take a bit of getting used to.

Mandy is cracking up before the song even comes on. When the popular tune begins, I know the song automatically. I sling an arm over my friend as we begin to sing enthusiastically. Daniel is our only coworker who managed to snag a spot up front. With lights bearing down on us, I have no one I know to focus on and I end up serenading Daniel so my semi-embarrassment won't cause me to puke. Unfortunately, the song Mandy picked isn't quite the message I'd wanted to send. The crowd's enthusiasm urges me on.

I know I just met you,
And this is crazy,
But here's my number,
So call me maybe!

Sometime after karaoke and a few more rounds of shots, I've forgotten the mess I'm creating. Daniel is by my side the whole time encouraging me not to drink but not stopping me either. By the time we make it out of the bar, we're hot and sweaty. Daniel is flagging us a cab while trying to keep Mandy and me on our feet. The frigid air should have been a balm, yet I can barely put one step in front of another.

"Catie, I'm so glad you moved here," Mandy slurs. "The office was so dull until you showed up." We finally stumble to a stop near the curb.

I place my arms on her shoulders needing her to focus on me as I tell her how I feel because feelings are important. "I don't know what I would have done if I hadn't met you. It's a cruel, cruel world but you're the happiest person I've ever met. And I need happy. You're my bestest friend, but don't tell my best friend I said that. Jenna's not normally a jealous person, but don't piss that girl off. She's a scrapper."

Mandy nods because she gets me. "I promise I won't tell. We can be secret bosom buddies."

We hug until Daniel breaks it up. I want to tell him that even though I'm not into him, I'm not into girls either. His voice interrupts my swirling thoughts. Now, I'm no longer sure what was so important for me to say.

Daniel and his four doppelgangers steady us. "Come on ladies, be careful of the snow and ice."

I feel like I'm on a ship. "The boat is rocking. I think we might capsize. Where are our life vests?"

"Cate."

That voice, I know it. I spin and the world tilts.

"It's the Titanic all over again," I call out as I fall forward.

I never reach bottom. "Thank god for the life vest," I mutter. I feel it tight around me.

"Cate," the voice says again.

"Drew." I shake my head. "No, it's An— Andy now," I slur. "Not Drew, can't call you that. It's Andy."

Daniel comes into view and I'm not sure if Andy is there or not or if I'm only hearing voices.

"It's okay. I can take her off your hands. I'll get her home," Daniel says.

Somehow I regain my feet but my vision continues to swirl. *Damn four-inch heels aren't doing me any favors.*

"I like those heels," Mandy responds and I realize I've spoken out loud.

When I'm steady, I glance up into piercing blue eyes. I feel the arctic air they bring. *Andy.* I give myself a thumbs up for remembering his new name.

"You're really here."

I notice his steadying hand at the small of my back. I start to melt into him and lean up to press my lips to his when I catch sight of two guys behind him. I wave because it's only polite. As wasted as I am, I don't want to embarrass Andy in front of his friends or colleagues.

"Catie, you can stop waving now." Mandy is by my side and conspiratorially whispers only to me. By the smirks on the guys' faces, they must have super human hearing abilities. "Who are these handsome guys? Have you been holding out on me?"

"Cate, Mandy, I have a cab. We should go now." Daniel sounds way too sober. Mandy and I turn to face him.

"Don't be such a Clark Kent," I say to him over my shoulder.

When I glance to Andy, his back is turned to me. I can't hear what he's saying. When he turns around, I'm struck by just how goddamn good looking he is.

I hear Mandy introduce herself and the guys speak but my gaze is locked with Andy's.

"Cate." I blink a few times, only now putting it together that Andy was talking to me.

The two good looking guys wave a quick goodbye and walk away.

I chance speaking. "You didn't have to let them go. Superman man here," I hook a thumb in Daniel's direction, "is going to save the day and take us home."

As Andy blurs into one instead of two, I see his brows arch. "Superman, huh?"

A glance at Daniel confirms that three of him agree as their smiles beam like the girl in the toothpaste commercials.

I pat Andy's chest and when I feel the solid muscle under my palm I pat it a few more times. "No need to be jealous. You're totally Batman and everyone knows Batman is the sexiest of them all."

"Not everyone," Mandy declares. She's sounds drunk and I'm almost embarrassed for her. "No offense Batman, but I'm really into Thor. So if you are truly the Dark Knight, will you hook me up with that Chris Hemsworth look alike that just left? What was his name?" Her words sputter but somehow it all comes out coherently.

"Guys, the cab is waiting."

"Daniel, hold your horses," Mandy drawls as she shifts her focus to our coworker. "Wait...you do look like Clark Kent."

We high five it but miss. That's weird. We try again, and totally fail. I start to crack up because it's so damn funny. She shakes her head and decides to take a step in Daniel's direction. I try to follow because his face is so sour, you'd think he's swallowed a lime. However, Andy doesn't let me go.

"I'll make sure she ends up home safe," Andy declares.

Daniel straightens, his super power allowing him to morph from three into five. I can't help but comment. "You are so outnumbered," I say to Andy or no one. I'm not sure.

Andy glances down at me but there isn't humor in his eyes. When his face does that horror movie blur deal, I murmur, "You aren't Batman are you? You're something else?"

"I am something," he mumbles back. Then his voice takes on bass and strengthens. "I've got her. You can take her friend home."

The ocean starts to roll again and I lean on Andy, pressing my cheek on his chest. His wool coat is rough on my frozen cheek but I move in closer wanting to hear his heartbeat. I need to know he's alive and I'm not in some crazy dream.

"I'm not sure that's a good idea. We're coworkers and I don't know who you are," Daniel says.

Andy's voice sounds muffled though one ear and clear out the other. "Cate and I..., we have history. I guarantee she's safe with me. I'll get her home."

Information I need to share gives me the strength to stand on my own once again. "Yeah, we're going to have dinner and catch up on old times. I mean new times. And we're planning to have breakfast." I laugh before I become thoughtful. "I haven't had breakfast in a while," I say absently. And in an even softer voice because I have to share this secret only with Mandy, I add, "You know what breakfast is code word for." I giggle and I can't stop it even though I hate to giggle.

"Breakfast," Mandy gives a thumbs up. Something must be in her eye because she has one closed with a weird look on her face. "Call and tell me all about it in the morning. I haven't had breakfast either and I love sausage."

She giggles the whole time as Daniel hustles her into the cab and I feel the world tilt. Andy steadies me. Then Daniel calls out, "Are you sure you're going to be alright, Cate?"

I want to nod but I'm starting to feel nauseous. "You're leaving me in good hands. He's a doctor, you know."

Daniel has lost his clones and gives me a curt nod before getting in the cab next to Mandy. When they drive off, I wonder why I feel bad about what I said. I've only been honest. But that thought leaves as another wave of seasickness fills me.

"My car is this way."

"They have cars on oceans now? I think I need some Dramamine. I don't feel so good."

We stop and Andy faces me. "How much did you drink tonight?"

I try to shrug, but my shoulders feel like lead weights.

"Did you eat anything tonight?"

Fries enter my mind first. An unpleasant gurgle in my stomach forces the images of food to back off. I shake my head and speak through pressed lips. "I can't talk about it."

"Okay, fine, let's get you home."

Andy steers me along and my feet start to ache. I stop and attempt to take off my heels, but Andy's hands stop me.

"Cate, sweetheart, it's too cold for you to walk barefoot."

"My feet hurt," I complain, but he has me standing upright again.

"It's not far, I promise."

"I don't think I can make it. Save yourself. I'll just stay here to die." I brush off his hands while trying to let gravity pull me to the ground.

Andy chuckles, then he sweeps me off my feet.

"Whoa there, cowboy. You've turned the world upside down."

He speaks so faintly, I'm not sure I actually heard him say it.

"You've turned my world upside down."

In a normal voice, I'm so sure I dreamed those other words, he says, "We're almost there."

He makes me feel like Cinderella and I'm waiting for the magic to wear off. He shouldn't be so nice to me.

"Why are you always trying to take care of me?"

He stares at me. And when he stops moving, his words are out of sync with the opening and closing of his mouth. "Because I—" Whatever direction he was going with that thought changes. "We aren't going to talk about the past, right?"

I don't answer because somewhere through the cloud of inebriation, I know that's the plan. I try to focus on making it to his car without puking on him. When we arrive at the public garage, the only thing I will remember later about his car is that it's sleek and shiny. He helps me sink into the buttery leather seat and I close my eyes, grateful I didn't vomit the whole way here.

When my lashes flutter open, I realize I'm home. It's dark and I have no memory of how I got here. What I do notice is that I'm still fully dressed and my clothes reek of alcohol. The stench makes me gag, yet I manage to stand. The fact that I sway on my feet tells me that alcohol still courses through my veins. I must not have been home very long. I have to steady myself on the wall after taking a few steps. The zing of pain in my feet alerts me that I still have my heels on. I kick them off before I walk out the room in search of the bathroom. I don't bother to turn on any lights for fear of causing a blinding headache. The first door I open turns out to be a closet. I shake my head and turn in circles as my world continues to revolve around me. I walk down the hall until finally I make into my bath.

Fumbling with my sweater, I remember the thin belt at my waist. I have a doozy of a time getting it undone along with pulling the sweater over my head. That task done, I move next to undo my skirt. I end up chasing the back zipper like a dog does its tail. Finally, I give up and yank it off. My thong is a breeze but the bra gives me hell. When I'm finally naked, I grope for the shower knob and wait for the warm water. I pull open the door and pause because something's not right. Then I remember the night with Andy and Daniel. I blink but step in the shower, hoping to clear out the confusion with the steam.

Standing there for a second, I recall Daniel's deflated look. I wonder how I'll face him at work on Monday and how I'll survive Mandy's wrath. She did warn me.

After a good scrub, I practically tumble out of the shower and I'm sure I'm forgetting something. *My teeth.* I snag the toothbrush and paste and get to work. Minty fresh breath doesn't annoy my stomach. I fumble my way into the bedroom and leave the towel on the floor as I crawl into bed. With as much trouble as I had taking off my clothes, I don't intend to waste time trying to put pajamas on.

When I blink my eyes open at some point later, there are three things I notice. First, the dreaded headache pounds just under the surface of my skull. I know I'm dehydrated by all the alcohol and need to drink some water to help ward it off. Second, the bad taste in my mouth. So much for my earlier brushing. I flick my tongue out, hoping to get rid of my cotton mouth. Third, I'm extremely warm, like I've been wrapped in an electric blanket. I cast off all those considerations and hope sleep will claim me again. I'm not quite ready to wake and no light seeps through the blinds. It's still dark out, so it's too early to get up.

Fantasy land is the best part of sleeping. I so easily slip back into dreamland. I haven't been touched in so long; I've conjured my leading man very craftily with the help of some steamy romance novels I've recently read. His hands, which I've always loved, sweep down my torso. I'm a bit mad he doesn't pay homage to my breasts, but that thought flitters away as his fingertips stroke over my bundle of nerves with perfect pressure.

"Oh my god, it's been so long," I say languorously.

"Yes, it has."

I almost jump out of my skin. My eyes fly open as I jackknife into a sitting position. There is a man in my bed!

"Drew, I mean Andy." I shake off the cobwebs because who else could it be? Besides, I would recognize his voice anywhere.

"Cate?"

"Why are you in my bed?" I'm now fully aware I'm naked. Fantasy land has morphed into reality. Despite our history, he's never been one to take liberties. I yank the sheet up to neck level.

"Actually, you're in my bed." His proclamation rocks my world.

"What?" I continue to clutch the sheet as I scoot back to lean on the headboard. That's when I notice the room for the first time. The dark furniture isn't positioned the way my more modern pieces are. In fact, the door isn't even on the side of the room it should be. So this can't be my bedroom.

He matches my position against the headboard, only he doesn't cover himself. His bare chest is there for me to peruse with my eyes and my hands if I were bold enough to do so. His muscled frame is defined ridges and hill tops that beg for attention. God, he is beautiful. I feel the moisture between my legs, which precedes the heat in my cheeks.

He takes my free hand in his and gives me a gentle smile.

"Cate, sweetheart, you passed out in my car. I had no idea where you lived. I checked your purse but you still have a South Carolina driver's license. You should get that changed, by the way."

He kisses my hand as if to put me at ease. His eyes land where I have a white knuckled grip on the sheet and he chuckles softly.

I feel stupid because he's seen the goods, yet I can't seem to let go of the sheet. Instead, I fill the silence with a hasty explanation. "I don't own a car. So I keep forgetting to change my license."

He nods and squeezes my hand. "I tried to wake you but you didn't stir. I had no choice but to bring you home, not that I'm sorry about it."

His eyes trail down my body like a caress.

"Where is home?" One glance through the partially open blinds and I know I'm not in downtown DC.

"Baltimore."

"Baltimore?"

He nods again. I could question him more about that but I have other pressing questions that need answers.

"Why am I in your bed?"

The Drew I knew was a gentleman. If he wants us to start from scratch, he wouldn't presume I'd sleep with him.

"I don't know. I put you in my spare bedroom, fully dressed I might add. I woke up to the sound of you calling my name begging me to touch you."

His eyes sweep down to my sheet-covered body and back up again. Even though I'm not exposed, I'm mortified by his revelation. Stumbling through his apartment and not finding my

40

way in the middle of the night comes back to me. I'd been in search of the bathroom, and eventually crawled into his bed naked. He'd slept through the whole ordeal until I vocalized my fantasies. I slide down and lift the covers to hide myself completely, and then I see I'm not the only one naked.

I snatch the covers back off of my head. Then have the presence of mind to cover my breasts again. "You're naked," I accuse.

"Yeah, I kind of sleep that way. But you should know that."

The problem is I know too much. This so isn't going to work. It's way too awkward for me. The past keeps colliding into the present. And even though he seems perfectly fine with it, I'm not. I roll to the side of the bed, dragging the sheet with me. I don't look back as I stand, covering my bare ass, and skedaddle to the bathroom where I left my clothes if drunk-memory serves. By the time I come out, fully dressed sans my underwear, he has pajama bottoms on and is holding a glass of water and a bottle of Advil.

In one hand, I hold the balled-up thong I'd felt too gross to put back on after showering and plan to toss in my purse once I find it. He hands me two pills, and I drink them down with the glass of water I take from him.

"Thanks."

"Not a problem. I would drive you home." He glances at his watch. "But I'm due in the hospital in a half an hour. I guess I overslept."

I wave him off. "No, it's fine. I'll call a cab."

He shakes his head. "No need. You can drop me off at work and then use my car. I won't need it. Come back later tonight and we can have dinner. Then I'll take you home."

"I can't use your car. What if you suddenly need it?"

He steps forward and cups my chin. He rubs my cheek with the pad of his thumb. In his beautiful eyes I see all the memories we made together. The way he clenches his jaw, I know he's fighting back the words to remind me of everything we shared.

"I'm going to be at work all day. I won't need it. And I know we are starting fresh, but we know each other better than this. Take my car, and come back tonight. In fact, you can pick me up at work. It will give you the excuse you'll need to have dinner with me."

He presses a kiss to my temple before walking away, leaving me to chew on his words. I watch him lift a pair of pants that are slung across a chair in his room and pull out his car keys. He takes my hand and uncurls my fingers, placing the keys in my palm and closing my hand around them.

"Give me a few minutes to shower," he says before disappearing in the bathroom.

I clutch the keys and stop myself from following him into the bathroom. It would be so easy to join him. It's harder to stay rooted to my spot and not simply slide into the routine of us as a couple.

Long minutes later, I think I've barely breathed the whole time. The keys bite into my palm from the strength of my clutched fingers. He steps out with a towel around his hips and the slight pain in my hand is forgotten. He's still damp with beads of water trickling down his back as he heads into his walk-in closet. I close my eyes and am immediately assaulted with fantasies of him lifting me with his powerful arms and taking me against the tiled shower wall. Clearly it's been a while, I tell myself as I blink my eyes a few times trying to dispel the images.

When he walks out, he's wearing a set of green scrubs. It reminds me of old times. He walks up to me and smooths my unruly hair back. It's probably a bed head mess. I didn't bother to glance at myself in the mirror when I got dressed.

"Come back tonight. I'll fix you dinner."

He's always been one to ask for what he wants. I waver while considering my minor freak after waking up in his bed.

"No breakfast." As much as he lights my fire in a big way, I can't. "I'm not ready for breakfast."

His indulgent grin makes me feel silly for even bringing it up.

"No breakfast. Not until we're both ready for breakfast. But maybe a snack."

His brow arches in question and I stare at his lips. My gaze must have lingered too long because he assumes my answer. His lips radiate warmth and security as they press against mine. For so long I've missed this. I've missed him. He pulls back and I almost wish he'd taken it deeper.

"Just dinner," he whispers.

I roll in my lower lip and sigh. I have no idea how he doesn't hate me or why he hasn't moved on. He's a great catch and easy on the eye. Women have to be banging down his door, which makes me jealous just thinking about it. Then again, despite our pact for a fresh start, nothing between us can ever be uncomplicated. But I haven't felt this way in a long time. I close my eyes for a second before meeting his. I take the plunge. "Dinner, then."

FOUR
Past

———————◆———————

JENNA GREETS ME WITH A GRIN as I walk into the apartment from class. It's Friday afternoon and I'm more than ready for the weekend to begin.

"What?" I ask. Her sly smile tells me something's up.

"You have a present waiting," she replies in a sing-songy voice.

My excitement amps up ten levels. Her tone indicates it can only be from one person. I'm seeing him tomorrow so I'm nearly shaking to find out. "Where is it?"

"On the counter."

I head over there to find a box that's wrapped up in colorful paper with a pretty bow. My greedy fingers tear into the paper, shredding it in the process. The box is no match for me. When I lift the lid, I break out in a giant belly laugh. It's a huge, cute, furry Sasquatch with a note attached.

I'm sorry, but when I ran across this, I simply couldn't resist.

Can't wait to see you.

Yours,

Drew

Jenna looks on with a smirk. "Do I dare ask?" She reaches for my new fuzzy friend as I still laugh.

"Oh, god, I'm not sure you want to know."

"Right. Like you're getting out of this one."

I should've known better. So I tell her about my confession to Drew on our first date.

She straightens and crosses her arms over her chest in exasperation. "Please to god tell me you did not share that with him."

I cover my face with my new furry friend. "I did. I had a few drinks and I sort of overshared. What can I say?"

"So, let me get this straight. You told him you looked like a grizzly?" Her face says it all. It's all screwed up like she bit a lemon.

"Kind of. That was at first. Then I said it was more like Sasquatch."

"Really, Cate? You sure know how to set the mood."

Now it's my turn to make the face. "It gets better. That was after he said he had no intention of getting naked and sleeping with me."

"Oh, now that's a double fuck. And he actually asked you out again. I'm impressed. What the hell were you thinking?"

I rub my brow. "I already told you! My mouth ran away from me."

"Okay. Rule number one. Do not drink to a point that on your first date with a guy you allow yourself to tell him shit like that."

My head hangs down. "I know. I didn't mean to. But it just sort of happened. We were having so much fun."

"Clearly. He must have too. Why else would he be taking you out again? He bought you a stuffed Bigfoot, Cate!" Then she turns to me with a serious look. "Have you waxed?"

"Yes! I'm all muffin-scaped now."

"Who did your waxing? I hope you went to the right place."

Now I know she's going to kill me. I squeak out, "I did it."

"What do you mean you did it? No one does their own waxing!"

In all the years I've known Jenna, I have never seen her look so furious.

"Well, I did. I was trying to save a few bucks," I admit.

"And I'm trying to save you from humiliation. You probably look like Halfsquatch." She plucks her phone out of her pocket and thumbs through her contacts. "Here's the number of the salon I use. Call them to have your waxing done properly." She rattles off the number.

Then I start to think about it. She may have a point. I really couldn't see down there when I was doing it. Maybe I did leave a bunch of hair. That would be awful. Worse than awful. It would be a muff-tastrophe.

"Okay. I'll call them. Just so Louise can look pristine."

"Who the fuck is Louise?"

I hold up my index finger and jab it toward Louise.

"Jesus C. You named it Louise? How did I not ever know that?"

"It's a private thing."

"Whatever. I have to go. Just make sure you get *Louise* taken care of."

She closes the door behind her and I call the salon she uses. When they tell me their prices, I almost croak. That isn't in my budget unless I skip paying my electric bill for the month. So I hit the number for the cosmetology school I use for my haircuts, wondering if they do waxing. When they tell me they do, I ask their price. I'm excited to find I can afford it. They tell me they can take me in twenty minutes, so I dash out the door with barely enough time to make the appointment.

The whole session turns out to be embarrassing, with two strangers getting a bullseye's view of Louise. And Louise is rather shy. Their pitying stares at my do-it-yourself-wax-job-gone-bad make me think I have a tree sprouting between my legs.

When I get home, Jenna is there. She looks at me kind of funny. "What's wrong with you?"

"I don't know. I went and got waxed, but my butt cheeks feel weird—like they're stuck together. Is that normal?"

"What? Your butt cheeks are stuck together? No, that's not normal. Who did your waxing? Everyone at my salon is usually great."

I give her a sheepish look.

"Well?"

"I went to the cosmetology school," I confess.

She looks horrified. "You did what?"

"I couldn't afford your salon," I cry out. "It was way out of my budget."

"Okay, let's stay calm here. So your butt cheeks are stuck together, huh?"

Then she chuckles, but it turns into a howl.

"Stop. It's not funny. My unders are crammed up there now, too."

She slaps her knee with this news and snorts.

"Wh-what? Oh my god! You have a wax-wedgy!"

I throw a pillow at her. "Stop! What am I gonna do?"

"Let's Google how to get the wax off."

Jenna pulls it up on her computer, and using some special oil, my butt cheeks are freed from their waxy prison. Right as we finish, my phone buzzes. I look down to see Drew's name. Thank god he didn't call an hour ago. I would've been mortified.

"Hey Drew."

"Cate. What's a gorgeous girl like you doing on a Friday afternoon?"

Getting all my hairs yanked out by the roots and freeing the cheeks of my ass, so I can be smooth if you happen to run your hand down my pants tomorrow.

"Oh, nothing very exciting. Trying to do a little studying before tomorrow."

"Yeah, about tomorrow."

My heart plunges. I know he's going to cancel on me, and I've never felt this way about someone canceling a date.

"What?"

"I was wondering if you'd mind very much if I came up early."

"Early?"

"Yeah, like in the afternoon. Would that be okay?"

"That would be great." My belly suddenly warms. "I'd love that." I wish he would've said tonight.

"You're sure? I don't want to wear out my welcome or anything."

Like that could ever happen! "No I'm positive. And the invitation is still open for you to stay here if you'd like. I hate for you to have to pay for a hotel room. And Jenna doesn't mind."

"I was going to ask you that. If it's okay with you both, then I'll take you up on your offer."

"That'll be fine. Great actually." Oh my god. He's going to spend the night here! I end up squeezing the phone so hard; it pops out of my hand and drops to the floor, lost in those lusty thoughts. I have to scramble to pick it up. "What's that?"

"So is lunch time too early, like say one?"

"Not at all. That's perfect. Oh, and thanks for my Sasquatch. I'll sleep with it tonight." I laugh.

"I never thought I'd be jealous of a stuffed animal."

"Strange things happen in life, Drew."

"They certainly do. So tell me how your week's been."

"Crazy. What about yours? I don't know much about what a doctor does."

"I spend a lot of time at the clinic seeing patients. Then I have hospital hours and rounds. It was a good week. But I want to know about you. What do you like to do in your spare time?"

I laugh. Hard. "When I get any, I run. That's pretty much my go to. I like to squeeze a run in whenever I can, although I don't do it as much as I'd like. It's weird, but it helps me think. If I ever get writer's block, a run usually breaks me out of it."

"I knew we'd have something in common. I love to run, too."

"Yeah, I remember you mentioning running that night at dinner. You lift weights, too."

"Do you?"

"No, sadly."

"Do I sense your face scrunching up?"

How in the hell did he know that? "You got me."

"Why not weights?"

"I hate to count."

"Cate, that makes no sense. You're majoring in accounting."

As soon as he says it, we both crack up. "I can see it now. Cate Forbes, the accountant who hates to count. Want me to make you a sign? It could say, 'Cate Forbes, CPA. I Hate Counting'!"

"That really is bad, isn't it? I'm going to suck."

Suddenly, we're both quiet, but then his voice comes to me and he says, "Uh, I could say something to that comment, but I think I'll refrain."

Again, I get those warm shivers and goosebumps erupt all over my skin. "Hmmm. I'm not sure what to say now."

"Then let me do the talking. Can I just say I'm really looking forward to seeing you tomorrow?"

"So am I."

"I'd better go. A text just came through from the hospital."

"Okay. I'll see you tomorrow. And be safe driving."

"Always. Have a nice evening, Cate."

I stand there, cradling my phone.

"If you could only see the smile on your face," Jenna says, interrupting my thoughts. "My girl Cate, I do believe you have it bad for that man."

Do I? I'm not sure because I have no comparators. I can't count dickwad. He never evoked deep feelings, other than humiliation. There have been others that I've dated, but none of them even stick out as memorable. It sounds like I'm a loser, now that I think of it, but it's only that no one ever captured my attention. Not until Drew.

"He certainly has my attention, I'll give him that much."

"Will you give him more? I've never seen you interested enough to be concerned about your girlie bits. In all honesty, Cate, I wondered a time or two if you batted for the other team."

"What?" Oh my god! I can't believe she said that.

"Don't get mad about it. But damn, you get hit on all the time, but never take anyone up on it."

She does have a valid point. "I don't because none of them interested me. Well, there was dickwad."

"Yeah, and I thought after him, since that was such a disaster, that maybe he pushed you to the other side."

I can't believe Jenna thought that. "Why didn't you ever say anything?"

She picks up a chunk of her hair and twirls it. "I figured you were trying to work it all out."

"Let's get one thing straight. I'm a man fan. Until I met Drew, I never ran across anyone that fired me up. Maybe I'm too picky." That's what I've always thought anyway.

She shoots me a sly smile. "Well, Drew has certainly stoked the fires enough for you to buff Louise up."

"Okay, no more Louise talk. That's something only for me to know."

"You like him a lot, don't you?"

"Yeah. I had more fun on that date than I've ever had with anyone."

"Including me?" She winks.

"Different kind of fun, Jenna."

Drew arrives at exactly one. He looks better than good dressed in jeans and a t-shirt. When I open the door, the first thing he does is wrap his arms around me and kiss me. I love the feel of him against me.

"You look beautiful."

I'm wearing jeans and a long-sleeved top. It's nothing special, but he makes me feel that way. "Thanks. You look great yourself."

I lean in for another kiss. "Did you bring your stuff up?"

"No, I left it in the car. Let's go. I want to take you to this place I love. I brought lunch."

"Oh, okay." He suggests I bring a jacket or sweatshirt. We hop in his car and take a drive out into the country. It's the first week of October so the weather is cool. It's a lovely day and Drew drives us to a really neat old timey covered bridge. He pulls off the road and in the back of his car is a backpack that has our lunch.

"I picked it up from this great deli in Indy. Downtown Indianapolis has great cafés and delis. One thing I love most about the place. I hope you like sub sandwiches."

"I love everything. I'm easy to please, Drew."

We walk a bit and find a great place to plop ourselves down. He spreads a blanket and hands out the food. He's right. The subs are great. They bake their own bread every morning, he tells me. While we eat, he talks about medical school and how he didn't know what type of doctor he wanted to be.

"How did you know? About being a doctor I mean?"

He shrugs. "I just did. Ever since I was a little kid."

The sun's rays are streaming through the trees and they create a halo effect around Drew. His hand brushes through his thick waves, pushing them back off his forehead, and I'm struck at how his face looks like it's been painted. His brows form perfect arches over his startlingly blue eyes, and they sparkle as he speaks. It's then I realize I could gaze at him for hours on end.

"What?" he asks.

I shake my head, smiling. "Nothing. You are lucky. Not many people know what they want out of life. And you knew at such an early age."

"I know. I do count myself as one of the fortunate ones. At first I thought I wanted to do sports medicine. Orthopedics. But then during med school, I did my first rotation in oncology and I was hooked, just like that." He clicks his fingers.

"It doesn't scare you? Working with cancer patients?"

"No. Why?"

"Like maybe you'll get close to them? I can only imagine how my heart would get broken." I rub my chest, thinking how it would ache.

"Ah, I see where you're going. I look at it from a different perspective." He reaches out and brushes the backs of his fingers across my cheek.

"Which perspective is that?"

"Cancer isn't what it used to be. There are so many different treatment options and sometimes patients can live years with it. So I look at it as a way to prolong or extend lives or cure the disease. And if I get close to the patient in the process, then that makes it all the more special. Mind you, I'm still in my residency. I have to do a fellowship in oncology before I'll be able to practice it. And then if I want to specialize, it may be another year after that."

He must be brilliant. Not only is he hot, he's kind, smart, and sweet, too. I stare at him with what I imagine is a goofy assed smile on my face.

"Can I tell you something?" he asks.

"Sure."

"I worked long hours this week and traded today with someone so I could spend it with you. All week, you're the only thing I could think of, Cate." He grabs my wrist. "Come here."

We're facing each other with our legs crossed. I'm not sure I know what he means.

He pats his leg. "Right here. I want you on my lap so I can kiss you."

I unfold my legs and move over to his lap. I don't want to smash him, so I climb on top and wiggle around until I'm properly seated. I finally look up at him and he wears an amused expression.

"You won't crush me. I'm a fairly large guy, Cate."

"But I'm not some tiny petite thing either." Almost before the words leave my mouth, he pulls me against him, his mouth landing on mine. My fingers thread through his hair, something I've been dying to do since he walked in my apartment, and he does the same to mine.

Drew's kisses are mind blowing. I don't know if it's because I'm not very experienced or because he sparks the fire down below. Either way, I heat up. And not just my mouth. Things get seriously hot between my legs. My belly tightens with a need so forceful I end up squirming around on his lap, trying to quench the burn. There isn't a way to do it so I end up wrapping my legs around him and pressing myself against him. Am I dry humping him? Crap, I need to rein this in. I pull my mouth away from his and it takes enormous effort.

"Everything okay, Cate?"

He seems so unaffected by it all. "Um, yeah. Fine. Good." My voice is all breathy.

He leans in for more kissing. I lean back so he can't reach.

"Did I do something wrong?"

"You did everything right. Too right, I think." I bow my head because I don't want him to see my heated cheeks.

"Then why avoid my kiss?"

I only shake my head.

"Please talk to me, Cate. I don't read minds and if I did something to offend you, I need to know."

I'm aggravated now. "I'm not offended, just all horned up here. I was practically dry humping you." Oh god, did I say that out loud? Of course I did. Me and my big mouth.

"And what's wrong with dry humping? It's damn sexy. I want you to dry hump me." He grabs my hips and squeezes me. "If I knew you better, I'd strip you naked and fuck you silly right now."

"Oh, god, why don't you know me better?"

He throws his head back and laughs. Before I know it, I'm laughing with him. He's so easy to be with.

After we stop with the laughter, he says, "Don't ever shut me out. I don't like guessing games. Hell, I hate any kinds of games. Just tell me. I love how you're frank about things. Don't ever change. Now can I kiss those sexy lips of yours some more?"

"Is that all you want to kiss?" I ask.

"No. Before too long, I will be kissing every single inch of you." He doesn't smile. He only pins me with his incredible eyes. They're so intense right now, I can't break the connection.

"Good. I can't wait. I hope I don't have to wait too long."

"No, not too long. But not today. I'm kind of old-fashioned in that regard."

Disappointment rushes into me. For the first time in my life, I feel like I'm going to be the pursuer.

"Hey, don't look so sad," Drew says. "I promise, I'll make it worth the wait."

"Yeah?"

"Oh, yeah." And then his lips are on mine again, doing what they do best. Turning me into one dry humping maniac. That night Drew takes me to dinner. We end up at a steak house at his insistence. I feel guilty because it's a lot of money.

"Will you at least let me impress you a little?" he asks. He swirls his wine in his glass before he drinks it. I take a sip of mine and it's delicious. He ordered for me because I'm clueless about ordering wine.

"Okay. But you don't have to try. You impressed me the first time you walked through my door."

"Ah, well that's good to know. It's burgers and fast food from now on for you, then."

I bite my lip to stifle a laugh. I need him to know something. "Drew, it doesn't take much to make me happy."

His smile disappears, and he grabs my hand. "I can see that. I want to make you happy, Cate."

"You do. I'm happy when I'm with you."

A grin spreads across his face. "I want to ask you something. Would you like to come to Indy next weekend?"

"You'd want to put up with me for the entire weekend?" I'm curious about where he lives, who he hangs out with. Of course I'd love to go.

"I do have a slight confession to make. I have a short shift on Saturday. From six to noon. Would that be a problem for you?"

"Not at all. I could actually get some studying done."

He gives me a megawatt smile. "Yeah? Really?"

"Yeah." I grin back at him.

"There's something else. On Saturday afternoon, I have a hockey match."

My brow creases when he says this. Hockey. I know nothing about the sport. Where the hell did he learn to play?

"I can tell you're not interested, are you?"

He misinterpreted my silence. "Oh no, that's not it at all. I was trying to figure out where you learned to play. Growing up in Charleston, I mean ice skating wasn't exactly common."

"You're right. I didn't pick it up until Purdue. Promise me you won't laugh when I tell you this." He has the most serious look on his face.

"I promise."

53

"I took figure skating lessons when I got to college. I loved hockey so much and wanted to learn to play, but I knew I needed to learn how to skate first. So I sucked it up and took the lessons. It was awful. A ton of little girls and me on figure skates. Learning how to do the Salchow, Lutz, toe loop, and the Axel. Fun times. I busted my ass like you would not believe. But I learned. And when I was proficient, I joined a hockey league. I was still crappy, but I improved over time and now I'm fairly decent."

"Hockey." I'm amazed that he plays.

"So, do you think you'd want to come to my game?"

When I think about Drew all fitted out in his uniform, I grab his arm and say, "I wouldn't miss it for the world. But I have to tell you, I know nothing about hockey."

"I can teach you. It's pretty basic. A lot like soccer except it's faster."

"Yeah. Okay, then next weekend it is. I'll drive up on Friday."

"Perfect."

Our food arrives and it is delicious. The steaks are perfect. No wonder he wanted to eat here. The dessert menu is drool worthy and we both order chocolate soufflés, which melt in our mouths.

We end the evening back at my place. He walks around to let me out of the car and while he's helping me out, he bends down to kiss me. "I can't ever remember enjoying myself so much, Cate."

"Neither can I."

He takes my hand and we walk upstairs. Jenna is out so we plop on the couch. I turn to him and say, "I want you to sleep with me tonight."

"It might be too much of a temptation."

Is he for real? What kind of guy says stuff like that? Most of them do anything they can to get in your pants.

"I promise I'll be good," I say with a wink. "Besides, if Jenna brings someone home, it'll be less awkward for you."

"Does she do that a lot?"

"Not sayin'." I hold out my hand to him and he takes it. We walk to my room. It's not very big, but it holds a queen-sized bed. Admittedly, my room is pretty girly looking. I point to the bathroom so he can brush his teeth and use the restroom if he wants. He goes inside and shuts the door. While he's in there, I undress and put on a t-shirt and a pair of boxers, my usual sleepwear. When he emerges, I trade places with him. I quickly wash my face and brush and floss my teeth. After I finish, I join him and he's under the covers.

"How many damn pillows do you own?"

Laughing, I say, "No idea. Ten?"

"Eighteen. I never thought I'd get them off the bed."

"I usually shove them to one side." I scoot under the covers and find him shirtless. Nice.

"Cate, are you on any birth control?" I'm startled by his question.

"No. I've never taken the pill, if that's what you're asking."

"Yeah, that's what I'm asking. If we get to the point of intimacy in our relationship, would you be opposed to it?"

"Not at all. Why?"

"Curious. I've never had sex without a condom, but I sure would like to with you."

I find it odd that he was with the same girl for all that time and they never got to the point in their relationship where they trusted each other enough for him to go without a condom. I look up at him to find him gazing at me. I thought he would be smiling, but he isn't.

My big mouth blurts out the question that's in my head.

"Yeah, I suppose it should've told me more about the way she felt. She's the one who didn't want me to go without, and I was faithful."

"Oh. I'm sorry."

"Don't be. It's old news."

My mouth decides it wants to spew even more intimate information about me. "Drew, I've never really had sex before. Not all the way sex." I thought this would be embarrassing, but it isn't.

He's a mixture of confused gestures. He nods, shakes his head, then finally says, "I don't understand what that means exactly."

So I explain about dickwad. "I guess in the end, he could never really penetrate. It wasn't for lack of trying. He was … really awful … blamed everything that went wrong on me, and it was an all around bad experience." I shudder at the memory. "He was just a dickwad."

He moves closer and strokes my arm. In a gentle tone, he says, "If it's any consolation, I'm glad—not that he treated you so badly but that you never actually had sex with him. If we end up having sex, I promise I won't be a dickwad, Cate, and I'll make it as good as a first time can be." He gives me an understanding nod.

What other sweet tricks does this guy have up his sleeve? "Are you for real?"

"I'm not following."

"Everything about you. Most guys would be tearing my clothes off, but you're more concerned about making me feel good when we do it. I've never met anyone like you before." I place my hand on his chest, hoping he doesn't mind, because I have this pressing need to touch him.

His hand covers mine. "I hope that's a good thing. I want everything to be right for you."

"See, that's what I mean. You always say the right thing."

"No, I don't. I'm on my good behavior right now because I'm trying to impress you. But can I tell you it's taking everything I have inside of me not to roll you underneath me and do all sorts of dirty things to you?"

"Drew?"

"Yeah?"

"I swear to god, I want you to do dirty things to me."

He takes my hand and kisses it. "I will. Only not tonight."

"Drew?"

"Yeah?"

"Can you give me some idea when this magical date will take place so I can do other things until that time?" His body shakes with laughter.

"How about next weekend?"

"Really? You mean it?"

"Yeah." He faces me and says, "I mean it. Now you promised you'd behave. You're not exactly making this easy on me."

"Okay, but if you think this is easy for me, I need to let you in on a little secret. It's not."

"Good. Then we're even."

"I need to tell you another secret."

"Okay, what is it?"

"I waxed Sasquatch for you. She's all nice and smooth, like a baby's butt. Guess you'll have to wait until next weekend to see it."

I think I hear him groan.

"Drew, are you okay?"

"Yeah Cate." His voice is all hoarse though.

"I had fun tonight."

"Same here."

"Can I get just one little kiss?" I ask.

"Only if you promise not to dry hump me. That would be my undoing."

That makes me laugh so hard, I actually snort.

FIVE
Present

———————◆———————

THE CAR DRIVES LIKE A DREAM, or maybe I'm just used to subway trains and taxis these days. As I take in a deep breath, I catch his scent and think again of seeing Andy naked under the sheets. He was hard and ready. I can't deny I was just as ready for him.

Only the dull ache is still there. The memories of that long ago day are ever present. How can I forget the past, even if I want to?

My phone chimes, but traffic is still a bear. I let the call go to voicemail until I realize it might be Drew... Andy. It's so hard to think of him by this new name. I fumble in my purse and almost rear end someone. Wouldn't that be great? Calling him to cancel dinner because I totaled his car wouldn't be the ideal way of starting fresh.

Thank goodness for fingerprint recognition. I unlock my phone with a touch of my thumb and sneak a glance at the screen as traffic is stopped in front of me. Jenna.

I reach to turn the volume down on the radio and accidently hit an extra button.

A sultry voice cuts the song off and says, *"Bluetooth recognized. Would you like to sync this phone?"*

"Yeah right," I say flippantly.

"Bluetooth accepted."

"What?" I ask out loud, surprised the car understood me. A pop up box appears on my phone and draws my eye. I hit okay to allow my phone to pair with his car, even though when I'd spoken out loud, I'd been kidding. I like new techie stuff, so I test the waters.

"Call Jenna."

Calling Jenna. Home or work?

"Mobile," I say instead.

The phone rings through the audio system and I'm entranced but focused on the road again.

"Hey you. I just called."

"I know. I'm driving."

After the words pop out of my mouth, I realize my mistake.

"Driving? Did you buy a new car? I thought you didn't want to have one."

"No, it's a friend's. What's up? Why'd you call?" I ask brusquely, scrambling to divert our conversation away from the car. I'm just not ready to talk about Drew yet.

"I can't call you?" The way she over dramatizes her mock offense gets a laugh out of me.

"Of course you can. You know I didn't mean it that way."

"No, really, I'm just checking on you. Last we talked you were going to happy hour with your coworkers. I'm so hoping you met a man and ended your dry spell."

I can see her scolding look in my head as she speaks.

"Will every conversation always make it back to my sex life?"

"I don't know there, Sasquatch, but I'm hoping you at least did a bit of landscaping."

I sigh. "I keep it up now, Mom," I say dramatically. "Thanks to you for forcing me to get that little wax job, I've been traumatized into keeping up my maintenance on Louise."

Shuddering, I laugh at the memory as her cackles echo through the car's sound system.

"Seriously though, did you meet someone?"

"Happy hour was a no go," I admit. "My coworker hit on me, though."

See, it wasn't totally a lie. I just edit myself. I need to tell Jenna about Drew in person.

"Oh, do tell."

I give her the details that I can remember ending with Daniel hailing us a taxi.

"Daniel looks like Clark Kent. Sounds promising."

"Sounds more like it's never going to happen. I can't date a guy at work. If things go south, it would be too awkward. And then one of us will have to quit and I like this job," I say, spitting out a diatribe of words.

She sighs. "When I get there in a few weeks, I will so get you laid if you haven't already managed to find a hit-it-and-run guy by yourself."

"Hit-it-and-run?"

"Yes! You need a good one-nighter before you'll be ready for any man. Otherwise, if you're into a guy and screw him after a dry spell, you'll scare the poor guy off with cling wrap moves."

I laugh and she follows.

"Speaking of which, what's going on with you and a certain guy?"

"Shh, we shall not speak of it. I am working on something. But I have to run. Duty calls. I have to take mother shopping. Chat with you later."

She's definitely hiding something, but I don't press her because I am, too. Once I get into DC, it's slower going. They have red light cameras, speed cameras, and I wouldn't be surprised if they have overhead cameras to determine if a driver is holding a phone in their hands while operating a vehicle.

As I turn into a public lot a block from my building, my phone buzzes again. I wait for my turn to get a ticket before I answer.

I see the name on the display just before I say, "Hello."

The whispered response is so faint, I say, "Mandy, let me call you back. I'm going to lose this signal."

"Don't call," she whispers loudly. "I'll call you back in ten minutes."

"Okay," I say, taking the ticket. The call ends so abruptly, I don't know if I lost it or if she hung up right away.

I find a sweet spot next to a wall and large enough that anyone who parks next to me can open their door wide and not ding Drew's car... Andy's.

In my tiny apartment, I plunk my purse down on the small bistro table in my makeshift eat-in kitchen slash dining room.

My phone rings before I can take another step. I answer and immediately I'm assaulted with Mandy's demand for information.

"Tell me what happened last night."

She's still whispering, so I assume she's hung over.

I head back to my room with the phone tucked between my shoulder and ear as I begin to take off my day-old clothes.

"Nothing, happened, we drank a lot and sang karaoke. Why?"

"Why?" She squeaks.

I toss my skirt in a pile in the closet and put the phone on speaker as I remove my shirt.

"Yes, why?" Because I'm at a total loss. She sounds like the zombie apocalypse occurred.

"How did you get home?"

I drop my shirt in the same pile.

"I got a ride with a friend. You and Daniel got in a cab and left. That's the last I saw of you. Is everything okay?"

I'm starting to feel awful even though I have no idea what's wrong.

"No, he's here!"

The bed sinks a little, which shows the quality of the mattress I purchased through a website when I moved here in such a rush. Future note—never buy a bed online.

"Who's there?" I ask as I head for the bathroom and check the state of my hair.

I'm brushing it when she says, "Daniel. Daniel's still here."

Pausing, I'm not sure what she plans to say next, but I hold my breath after I ask, "Is that a problem?"

She's quick with her words but it sounds like she's hiding in her bathroom from the faint echo I hear despite all her quietly yelled words.

"He's sleeping in my bed."

I haven't been to her apartment so I can't visualize. "Okay."

"Okay?" The one word comes out sounding more like *are you crazy*. "He's not dressed and there is an empty condom wrapper on my night table."

My jaw drops before a smile covers my face and I do a fist pump. *One problem solved.*

"I guess you liked him more than you let on."

"I do not," she says a little too quickly to be the truth. "He's a friend. He needs someone, which is why I tried to set the two of you up. So why is he in my bed and not yours?"

Unable to stop myself, I let out a laugh and can't help but tease her. "I think he's where he's supposed to be. You guys make an adorable couple."

Her next words are still soft but she manages to growl them. "I would hate you if I didn't already hate myself."

"Mandy," a male voice calls out. It sounds downright sexy over the phone. *Go Daniel.*

"I have to go."

"Call me later," I say before remembering my plans for tonight. She hangs up quickly and I hope she didn't hear that last part. Now, I'm starting to look forward to Monday, especially when the awkwardness will have nothing to do with me.

I turn on the shower. What Jenna said takes over my thoughts and has me worried. Although I don't have plans to sleep with Andy, *I got his name right this time,* I do want to make sure I'm groomed, just in case.

The agonizing part will be what to wear. So I decide to do that now rather than wait for later. He says he's going to make dinner. I end up deciding on a flirty top that hints at cleavage and my most comfortable pair of jeans. I toss a pair of clean underwear in my purse, then I sit on the couch to try and take my mind off everything by watching some TV.

I close my eyes to rest them, only to wake to the alarm I set just in case I nodded off. I rush to get ready and pay to get his car out of the parking garage. Leaving DC is just as slow as it was coming in. Luckily, I gave myself enough time. I have to circle the block of Andy's hospital a couple of times before he flags me down.

"Hey gorgeous, how was your day?" he asks as he gets into the car.

Oh, I don't know. I considered using BOB while thinking about you but decided to wait it out. "Nothing much, watched a little TV. How about you?"

"Another good day."

"How is that?"

His smile doesn't quite reach his eyes. "No one died on my watch."

Talk about sobering. "How do you continue to do it?"

He pauses for a long second and I know he's considering the question. "It's that child you cure and see for a routine visit years later and he's still cancer free. It's the Mom with a family of five whose kids still need her. It's hope that I can make a difference and

even if it's just one more day that they live, that's what drives me."
His passion is overwhelming and heartwarming. I can't help the
tear that spills from my eye. He's there with the pad of his thumb
wiping it away.

"I know it's crazy for me to think we can forget about all those
yesterdays, but I believe that running into you is a sign from
somewhere. Cate, I need you not to give up on this. Cancer will
always be a part of my life. I want you to give me a second chance
to see if you can or even want to be a part of my life, too."

I say nothing as he's forced to give me directions back to his
place. I hear him speak as I drift on a void of grief. Cancer will be a
part of his life. As much as I have unresolved feelings for him, I'm
not sure I can live that life.

He steers me into the garage under his building and somber
vibes fill the empty spaces between us. After I park, he steps out of
the car, giving me the full view. I saw him when I picked him up,
but I'd been focused on the traffic around me and not on the
gorgeous man in blue scrubs. I'm struck by the impossible man and
his impossible life. I'm torn between the two knowing I have to
take one with the other. Already caught up in seeing him again after
all this time, I stand there and stare like an idiot.

"Are you checking me out?" he jokes.

Deflecting, I say, "You remind me of a smurf."

He chuckles and leads me toward a door where he pushes the
up button for the elevators. "I'm not sure how to take that unless
I'm Handsome Smurf or Sexy Smurf. I do know in all that blue,
there is only one girl. Smurfette."

Teasingly, I say, "Exactly. What girl wouldn't want a harem of
guys whose only choice is her?"

His brow lifts in a sexy arch. "Harem?"

Feeling sheepish, I give a helpless little shrug. The door opens,
and we enter. I'm suddenly feeling self-conscious. After he presses
his floor number, he turns to where I've flattened myself on the
back wall. A faint smile appears on his face.

He stalks forward and says, "I've always wondered something."

My body is on high alert for an invasion I'm not completely
sure I'm ready for. "What's that?"

Breathy—that's how I sound. No way he hasn't picked up on
that I'm practically panting with need. He cages me in but doesn't
touch me. My arms are limp at my sides, unable to fight the desire

that's overtaking me. The reflection in the mirrored walls shows his incredible ass in those scrubs. I didn't think the shapeless clothing could be so damn sexy.

He licks his lips. "Forgive me in advance."

Before I can respond his lips meet mine. His tongue breaches the seam between my lips, penetrating my mouth and my soul. The bag I hold drops to the floor as I begin to lose all muscle control.

He tastes of spearmint. And I know he's been chewing gum again. Why? Because I know things about him others might not. This isn't the first time we've been overcome with lust.

I'm about to raise my arms. But before I can make that decision, he steps back. His eyes are storming and churn with need.

"Sorry. I shouldn't have done that. It's just..."

He trails off while bending to pick up my bag for me. When he glances up, his head is eye level with Louise and I feel myself clench in desire. Jenna is right. I so need to get laid.

The elevator chimes and he stands up. He holds out the bag and all I can manage to do, besides take it from him, is smile. I have to let him know some way that everything's okay. If I try to speak, it will sound ridiculous because my brain has been reduced to the age of a toddler at the moment. I'm not even sure I can verbalize three letter words.

When we enter his apartment, all I can think about is how well he worked my body the last time we were together. *Cate, get your shit together*, I chide myself.

"You've been working all day. Why don't you go take a load off? I brought dessert." I hold up the bag with an *I'm desperately trying to keep it together* smile. "I need to prep it so it can be ready right after dinner. I can also play Sous Chef if you want. I may not be a master chef, but I'm good and slicing and dicing."

His eyes are still sultry. I would pay a million dollars to hear his thoughts. "I could use a shower. The hot water will loosen my shoulder muscles."

He stretches his neck this way and that and I find myself behind him. I press my fingers in where I know he aches. He's standing so I can't exactly get it right since he's so much taller than me.

"That's nice."

"Uh huh. Why don't you sit down and I'll try to loosen you up before your shower. It will be more effective that way."

He turns around and captures my hand. "I think it would be

more effective if you join me in the shower."

I raise my other hand and use a finger to give him the naughty boy wave. "Not so fast. You haven't made me dinner yet. I'm not that cheap of a date." I wink at him.

He laughs. "Mom always told me it never hurts to ask."

"True, but no dice."

Turnabout is fair play, I think to myself. Memories remind me I'd been the one begging him to be with me.

He nods and heads to his bathroom alone and without my offered massage.

Later, he studies me from across his table.

"I'm glad you have an appetite. I would hate to have leftovers."

I toss my napkin at him which goes nowhere. "Are you trying to tell me something?"

"Only that you look really great and I'm having a hard time trying to play it cool."

Drew… Andy is a patient man, or at least he was early in our relationship. It seems as though he's lost that patience now.

"Such the flirt. Are you ready for dessert?" I stand to gather the dishes.

"You don't have to do that."

"Of course I do. You made one of my favorites, chicken parmesan."

"Seriously," he says and begins to stand up. I try to stop him and end up in his lap. "Well, I should have tried this earlier."

He kisses me again and it feels so natural to be with him like this. Reluctantly, I pull back.

"Let me get dessert."

He sighed. "You're killing me, Cate."

That goes both ways since his arousal is evident as I sit on his lap, and I know my panties are soaked.

"You'll like it."

He levels a stare at me. "Cate, nothing would taste better than you. You also have to know that I'm harder than a teenage boy copping his first feel. I'll respect you if you want to wait."

His honesty is one of the qualities I admire most about him. This isn't our first date either. I won't violate a dating rule if I sleep with him. However, intimacy changes everything. Feelings will collide in unexpected ways.

"I want you, too. I just don't want to rush anything."

Without waiting for a response, I put the plates in the sink so I can wash them before I leave. I have no intention of letting him do any clean up. As it is, he tidied up as he cooked. So there is only a pan and pot to wash along with what we've just used.

I pull the couple of pints of ice cream I brought from my place out of the freezer and reach in the refrigerator for all the fruits I diced up while he showered. I even have sprinkles and whipped cream ready to go. Grabbing two bowls I find in one of the cabinets, I head back to his dining area. It's larger than mine and fits his table for six. I wonder how often he has guests. Hell, I don't know how long he's been in the area. He stands to help when his phone buzzes.

He helps me settle everything on the table before he answers the call.

"Hello."

I can only hear a faint voice on the other line.

"Yes, this is he." He pauses. "Okay... Sure thing... alright... Bye."

I know his news is bad when he gives me the sorrowful eyes.

"I'm sorry, Cate. But I've been called in."

I wave off his apology. I know what to expect from his line of work.

"No, it's okay. I'll call a taxi or use the Uber app to get a ride home."

He steps in my space, anchoring me in place with his light grip on my arms.

"Don't leave." He practically begs me with earnest eyes. I'm transported to another time and place when words much like these passed between us. "I shouldn't be too long. We can have dessert and catch up. Then I'll drive you home."

A part of me knows I should leave. The guilt I feel is like an opaque screen between us obscuring the light with shadows and doubts. However, the other part of me is desperate to stay. "Okay."

An easy smile forms on his lips before he gives me a *there's more to come* kiss that I greedily accept. "I'll be back sooner than you think."

He's back in scrubs as he walks out the door. I stand alone in his place and a curiosity bug hits me. Should I explore it? A memory surfaces of the commercial when a girl in her date's bathroom decides to look in his medicine cabinet and everything comes crashing down. I opt to clean the kitchen and store the fixings for making our own sundaes back in the refrigerator and freezer. Finished with that task, I sit on his couch and turn on the TV. As time lingers, it becomes harder and harder to remain alert. When I wake, I'm not in the living room. The sun is bright and I'm fully dressed on a bed I don't remember. Even the furnishings aren't mine, or the ones I remember in Andy's room. The body wrapped around me, though, is familiar.

I turn and Andy's eyes are open. "Morning," he says with a somewhat chipper smile. "I'm sorry I got back so late. I wanted to wake you, but you were so cute on my couch. I brought you in here then I guess I didn't want to sleep alone."

His smile dips and I know whatever he dealt with hadn't been good. "What happened?" My hand reaches out to find his.

He stares at me as if he doesn't want to say it and I already know. "I lost a patient."

I blanket myself around him knowing how hard that is for him. "I'm sorry."

He squeezes me tight and we hang onto each other as if for dear life.

"Miracles don't always happen," he adds.

We say nothing for a long time. Again, I'm confronted with how I'm not really sure I can do this. I can't imagine how he can think so, either. I'm not that same person I was.

"I should get home. I have…" I wave a hand around as I sit up and disentangle myself from him. "Laundry and grocery shopping to do." I push at bed hair while he yawns. "And you should get some rest. I really can take a cab."

"Absolutely not. If I have to let you go, at least give me a little more time with you."

"Andy—"

"Cate, please. I can see it in your eyes you're ready to run."

"I'm not." It's a lie.

"Give it some time. Look, I have a benefit to attend next week. I was going alone but I have a plus one."

He doesn't have to say that the benefit most likely has something to do with cancer. It's all too much, too heavy, too hard. Yet I find myself wanting to give in to the hope on his handsome face. I know how good I feel when I'm with him and how I want to feel that again.

I turn a reluctant smile his way. "Okay, I'll be your plus one."

The benefit, however, turns out to be more than I ever planned on.

SIX
Past

---◆---

JAYSUS, WHAT A WEEK. SEVEN papers. Not to mention two quizzes and one exam. When Friday hits, adrenaline-laced excitement fuels me. I'm heading to Drew's and can't wait to see him. Jenna has helped me pack. Brand new sexy bras and thongs that Jenna helped me buy. Check. Sexy nightie that Jenna strong armed me into. Check. Several cool outfits. Check.

The drive to his apartment only takes about an hour and ten minutes. I texted him right before I left so he's waiting for me when I pull up. The man is one hot god. He opens my door, reaches in my car, unhooks my seat belt, and lifts me out. "I've missed you, lovely Cate." Then he kisses me. Not a sweet whisper of a kiss either. This is an all out, panty dropping, toe curling, body melting kiss. My arms coil around his neck as he deepens it further. He hitches my body against his and when he does, I wrap my legs around his hips. This is a first for me. I've never done anything like this before, nor have I been so passionate in public. Well, I take that back. We were pretty damn steamy on our first date, but it was late and alcohol-laced, so I'm giving that a pass.

"Mmmm, you taste incredible," he says. "I've been waiting for you all week."

"Same here." I knit my fingers in his hair. He reminds me of the beach in the middle of the summer, the way is hair is streaked with gold. Bright blue eyes catch mine and he flashes me a sexy grin.

"How much luggage do you have?"

"Just one bag is all and some hanging stuff."

"I'll carry you and the bag and you get the hanging stuff."

"Deal," I say.

He opens the back door and leans in to grab the hanging clothes. Then he hands them to me as he walks to the trunk. I pop the lid and he reaches for the bag back there.

"What'cha got in here? It weighs a ton!"

I laugh. "Everything but the kitchen sink. But my backpack with my books and computer is in there."

"Damn. I was wondering." He kicks his cracked door wide open and we enter his apartment. It's nice and tidy, and decorated in manly brown tones. We walk straight to his bedroom, where he deposits my bag on the bed and hangs my clothes in his closet. Then he carries me back to the kitchen and asks if I'd like a glass of wine. "I thought we'd eat here tonight, if that's okay."

"That's perfect. Are you going to cook?"

"Me?" His face is a mixture of mock horror and distaste. I can't help but laugh. He sets me on the counter, spreads my legs, and wedges his large body in between them.

"Who else is in this room?" I look around, messing with him. "Do you have a secret chef hidden in one of your cabinets?"

"No, but I do have a secret chef. He works at the local pizza parlor." His tongue pokes the inside of his cheek as he tries not to laugh.

"Hmmm. Pizza. I see you're trying really hard to impress me. It is one of my favorites."

He drops his head so his mouth is right next to my ear. Warm air blows across my neck, causing me to break out in goosebumps. "Huh uh. Not quite yet. That trying really *hard* is going to come *after* we eat."

My mouth forms a perfect O as heat rises from my chest to the top of my head. I'm sure my face is as red as the apple I spy on his counter.

His lips barely touch me, but they feel like they burn right through me. Following a path around to the hollow at the base of my throat, he dusts me with kisses until he arrives at my bra. I'm wearing a V-neck sweater. With his head down, he lifts his eyes, asking permission. With one nod from me, he continues as he slips one finger between the fabric of my bra and my breast. My nipple reacts like it's never been touched before. It springs to life, hardening into a spiky peak. I want his mouth there, sucking me. Should I tell him? I don't want to sound like some shameless slut. But maybe he wants me to sound like that.

"Drew?"

"Yeah."

"Would it sound terrible if I told you I wanted your mouth on me instead of your hand?"

Blue irises lock with mine. His pupils dilate telling me I've hit a mark. He wants me as much as I want him.

"No. It wouldn't. Cate, I want to undress you and put my mouth on you everywhere. But maybe we should eat first. If we don't, we probably won't eat at all. You are all I've thought about all week."

"O-okay." He's right. "Pizza then?"

"Actually, I was kidding about that. I'm going to cook for you." He gives me a kiss before releasing me. Then he walks over to the refrigerator and starts pulling things out. Chicken, a variety of vegetables, some sauces in bottles. He glances at me. "Can you guess?"

"Stir fry?"

"Nice!"

In no time, the meal is ready.

"Cate, there's a bottle of Chardonnay in the fridge. Will you grab it along with two wine glasses out of the cabinet next to the sink?"

I find said glasses and the bottle of wine and carry them to the table. Drew plates up the food and we sit down to eat. He watches me take my first bite.

"This is delicious."

"You like it?"

"Yes, it's really good." Surprisingly so. I expected it to be average, but this is extremely tasty. And I tell him so. "You're really good in the kitchen."

"Wait until you see me in the bedroom."

I nearly spit out the bite of food I just took. He slaps his knee because he thinks he's hilarious.

I raise my brows. "I had this impression that you were above the twelve year old mentality, unlike most men."

"Oh, Cate. How could you have been so wrong about me?"

71

And he gets this puppy dog look on his face and I immediately die laughing.

"So then, a man of many talents."

"I'm afraid you'll have to find out for yourself." Now he's not kidding. His tone has deepened, becoming almost hoarse. He leans in and says, "I have thought of almost nothing else other than being with you. In every sense of the word. But say one word, Cate. One word, and we don't have to do anything, but sit and talk. This is entirely your call."

I set my knife and fork down and look at him. His eyes are as clear as the sky on a spring day. They bear no humor; only honesty and caring, truth and sincerity. Reaching for his hand, I take it in mine and look at it for a long moment. Long, perfectly formed fingers attach to a strong, firm hand. Not calloused, yet not soft either. I bring it to my lips, pressing a kiss on his knuckles.

"I know you would never do anything to me I didn't want. But I'd be fooling myself, and you, if I told you I had no interest in being with you. I've pretty much thought of nothing else all week, too. It made studying for my exam and quizzes damned hard. And I almost wanted to write erotic journalistic articles because of you. You have occupied my waking and sleeping thoughts for a week now, so I can't wait to be with you, too, Drew. In every way."

He turns his hand around to hold mine. "Well, then, are you finished eating? Because after that, I'm finding all I want to do is to see you naked."

I push back my chair and stand. He does, too. He tries to stop me from picking up my plate. "Leave it."

"No. This will be gross if we do."

We hurry and clean up. While we do, he touches me, my arm, my cheek, nothing overtly sexual, but it's all so completely intimate that when we're done, he turns to me and our mouths collide in a crushing kiss. It's a combination of sweet and hot at the same time. Then I'm moving backward as he walks us to the bedroom.

My bag still sits on his bed and he asks me if I need to use the bathroom. I would love to brush my teeth so I say yes. I root around in my bag to find what I need, but when I get behind the closed door, my nerves barge in. My hands shake as I load my toothbrush with toothpaste. What if he doesn't like me? What if I'm not up to his standards? What if I'm so inexperienced I'm a gigantic disappointment? Oh, god, where is Jenna when I need her?

I need a serious pep talk right now.

"Cate, is everything okay?"

Shit! "Yeah. Be out in a second." My plans for the sexy nightie are trashed. I can't delay this any longer, so I open the door. There he stands, the corners of his eyes drooping with concern.

When I was a kid, I used to love it in the summers in Charleston after a huge rainstorm. When the tide is unusually high, there is shallow coastal flooding and when storms dumped a couple of inches rain, small swimming pools would be everywhere. I feel like my bones have melted into one of those pools.

"Cate." He calls out again. My name rolls off his tongue and sounds husky. "Are you sure?"

I rub my sweaty palms on my jeans. "About us? This? Yes. I've never been more sure of anything. I'm just a little nervous, if you want the truth. And it's me I'm unsure of, not being with you."

He reaches out, placing his hands on my shoulders. "Don't be. I fall asleep thinking of you and wake up doing the same. You have nothing to fear, I promise."

Glancing down at the floor, I stare at his bare feet. He must've taken his shoes off while I was in the bathroom. I shake my hands because for whatever reason, they tingle. "Drew, don't say that. Remember dickwad?" I cross, uncross, then cross my arms again.

He puts his hands on them, stopping my repeated motions. "Hey, I want you in the here and now. Not with him." His eyes have darkened. Is it with anger?

"It's not that I'm with him. It's that I'm unsure of my ability to ..." This is awkward.

He shuts me up with a kiss. And it's not just any kiss. His hands are on either side of my face as his tongue pushes through the seam of my lips. He pulls me against him as he deepens the kiss. He goes for broke here and succeeds. Everything I worry about flies out the window as my arms wind around his waist. I pull him into me and moan. When he lets me go I protest.

"I want you to undress me and then I want to do the same to you. Is that okay?"

I nod.

My hands shake as they pull at his shirt. Their clumsy movements succeed, with his help, in freeing him. I run my hands over the rigid muscles of his torso, across his hips and down to the waist of his jeans. I'm all thumbs, so he has to assist with the zipper and button. Getting his pants off isn't that difficult. Maybe I'm losing my anxiety or my coordination is returning. My eyes drop down and I can't help but notice the erection straining against his boxers. It shocks me so that I immediately look away. He smiles.

"I think I've lived in this state since we met. You only have yourself to blame."

I don't really know how to answer that so I do nothing except stare. He picks my hands up, covers them with his, and we both finish the task of removing his boxers. It's difficult not to ogle what blatantly juts out in front of me. I can't help but touch him. I've always thought cocks were weird looking appendages. Hell, so are vaginas, for that matter. But take a cock for instance. I've seen pictures of them when they're soft, and they're funky looking things with a sack attached behind them. And when they're hard, some of them curve, or are super skinny or whatever. Drew's cock is what I would call perfect. Not too big and not too little, but if a cock can be called pretty, his is.

He interrupts my cock-thoughts. His thumb and forefinger grab my chin and tip it so I'm forced to look at him. "Now it's my turn."

My palms, which are still sweaty, need a wipe on my jeans, but I don't want to give that away. He knows I'm edgy. Hell, he can probably hear my damn heart race. It sounds like a freaking jackhammer to me.

He pulls my sweater over my head and stares at me in my bra. Then he sits on the bed and opens his thighs. Pulling me between them, he unbuttons my jeans. Now I stand in bra and panties only. Good thing I took off my socks and shoes in the bathroom.

"Your skin is perfect." He runs his fingers from my neck to the top of my panties. "Unhook your bra for me, please." I do as he asks and watch his face. His eyes roam my body but I thought they'd zero in on my breasts. They do for a moment, but then ultimately land on my own eyes. "You undo me, Cate."

His finger moves to the top of my lace panties. He runs along the top, but doesn't dip any further than that yet. "Is this okay?"

"Yes." My voice is unsteady and I don't sound like myself.

"You look sexy enough to eat and I'm going to eat you, Cate."

"I know. I want you to."

"I'm going to take your panties off now." He pushes them down my legs and I nervously step out of them. Then he takes my hands and places them on his shoulders. A fleeting thought about how smooth and tidy Louise looks pops in my mind. But it's gone with his next words. "Spread your legs for me. And by the way, your pussy looks beautiful all smooth, but I would have liked it any way."

When he touches me I want to cry out but I watch in fascination. I bite my lips because I don't want to make a fool out of myself. A hot wave sweeps into my belly as he strokes me back and forth and then rubs me in a circular motion. I'm sure I'm dripping. Now I know why he put my hands on his shoulders. When he stops, I cry out. "No!"

"Shh, hang on." He lifts me and sets me back down on the bed. At first I don't understand why, but what he does next gives me my answer. He spreads my legs and his mouth teases the inside of first one, and then the other thigh. "I've been dying to do this. I want to hear my name when you come, Cate. I want to have your taste on my tongue when you come for me for the first time."

Oh, god. When his tongue trips over my nub, I almost scream. And here I thought his fingers were awesome. What the hell did I know? Louise is going to do a happy dance. But the thing that grabs my heart the most is when his eyes seek out mine over the skyline of my body. His lids flutter as though I'm the finest delicacy on Earth. He hums against my skin and I'm transfixed by the fact that he derives as much pleasure from this as I do.

I'm jolted out of my trance when he adds a finger and hits that mystical g-spot all my friends talk about. He presses and rubs it as his tongue continues to dance circles around that tiny bundle of nerves and I feel everything tightening, tensing. My arms stretch wide as I clench the comforter between my fingers. I can feel every breath he exhales across my flesh and it only heightens where he licks and sucks. And then it happens. It starts in the arches of my feet and spreads up my legs, fanning out across my body. My first Drew-gasm.

"Oh god, Drew, Drew, Drew." It's all I can think or say as I come all over his mouth and hand. And it's extraordinary. My hands move to grasp his hair and I'm unaware of anything as my world narrows down to the intensity of my climax.

When it finally ceases, my fingers still fist his hair. I release it as soon as I come to my senses. Poor guy. And he never said a word about it.

"Wow. That was … did they teach you that in medical school?"

He shakes his head, chuckling. "No, we didn't have an Oral Sex elective. But Cate, you were beautiful." He crawls up and lies next to me, resting his weight on his elbow. A hand travels up and down the curves of my body. "I want you more than I've ever wanted anything." He pauses and stares at me with so much reverence I'm almost afraid of what he might say. "I know I already asked you this. But are you sure you're ready for this? Say the word and we don't have to go any further."

I don't have to think about it at all. I've been ready to lose my V card since dickwad. He just didn't get the job done and until I met Drew, the right one hadn't come along. I'm not sure where this relationship will go. But I know he will make this experience something I'll want to remember, not forget.

"Yes, I'm ready. I want you, Drew. Now. Please." And I do.

He reaches in his nightstand and comes out with a condom. I watch him roll it down his shaft and it's hot. Totally hot.

"Can I do that next time?"

He grins. "Absolutely." Turning serious again, he asks, "Would you like to be on top or bottom? Top will give you more control and could possibly make it better for you."

A case of extreme self-consciousness attacks me so I try to hide my nakedness with my arms. Top is way too exposing for me. How could I possibly do that? "I-I can't be on top," I sputter.

He pins me with his eyes. A hand covers mine and he loosens the near death grip I have on my arm. When his fingers lace with mine, he gently tugs, and my arm relaxes. "You don't have to be on top, Cate. It was just a thought. I want this to be as good as it can get." He moves over me, hovering, and rests on his forearms. "If I haven't told you this, you are so beautiful, lying here with me. Being with you, like this, has consumed me. I know this may suck for you, but let me know if you want me to stop at any time. I'll go slow, but there's no getting around the hurt."

I put my hand on his cheek. "Drew, I'm not worried about the pain. It was a little awkward for me being naked, you know…" I trail off. "Let's just get it over with." My stomach's knotted with anticipation but I want this first time to be behind us already.

His eyes droop. "I don't want this to be like that."

I immediately regret my words. "That came out all wrong. I just want the painful part to be over with."

"I don't want to hurt you at all."

"But you might not be able to help it."

His hand moves between us and he rubs me a bit. Then he pushes himself in my opening. A little at a time he enters me, and then he stops. His forehead creases as he strains to hold himself in check. I can tell it's difficult for him.

I want to get to the good part, but I know this part has to happen first. I've heard friends talk about it. So I'm as prepared as I'm going to be. "You know the Nike slogan?"

He looks at me like I'm nuts. "Yeah, why?"

"Just do it, Drew."

His mouth curves up.

"Go on," I urge.

One hand reaches under me and I already see the apology in his eyes. And then he thrusts. No, it's more like a serious ram. Once, twice and then he's in. And holy motherfucker it stings like fire. He stills and I know it's because I've turned into marble. Frozen in time. I can't move. I just want to lie there until the pain goes away. He makes all these little calming noises, but I don't hear them for a second or two. I bite my lips to keep from howling. But then the pain eases off and after another minute or two or three, it finally slips away. I slowly come back to my senses.

"Deep breath, sweetheart. Come on. Just one," he says.

I breathe. And my body relaxes. I do it again and I feel better and better.

Then I notice he's rubbing my face, my forehead, and pressing tiny kisses all over me.

"You better?" he asks.

"Yeah. I am. Do you think you can move?" When he starts to roll off of me, I stop him by grabbing his face and I smile. "No, not that kind of move. I mean move inside of me."

"You're sure?" he asks tentatively.

Still smiling, I say, "I'm very sure."

His lips skim mine. "You don't hurt?"

"Not now."

He starts to test the waters. And while I have to say I'm not completely pain free, it's more soreness than actual pain. So I tell him.

"Thank god. I was afraid I'd really hurt you."

I shake my head. "I'm good. For a minute there, it wasn't great, but now, I'm fine."

Slowly he increases his pace until he moves in earnest. He lifts his body a little, but only enough to slide his arm between us. Then I feel his fingers on my clit and everything intensifies. Throughout all this, I can't help but watch him. Even though the sensations I'm experiencing are awesome, observing him is a sensuous journey in itself and I respond to that, too. Before long, I am caught up in everything—Drew, the sounds he makes, the way he looks and feels against my skin and inside of me, and the way he reacts to me. And before I know what's happening, I'm tumbling, falling as I orgasm and he calls out my name as he follows.

My hands are molded to his ass and I didn't even know I'd put them there. I release the pressure on them and smooth my hands over his cheeks, then I roam up the wide sea of his back. His muscles tense beneath my fingers but my eyes dig into his, bright blue with deeper striations. They remind me of the ocean on a clear spring day. "Kiss me, Drew."

He does, beginning at one corner of my mouth, playing with my upper and lower lip. His tongue darts in and out of my mouth. He's an artful kisser, doing all sorts of lovely things with his tongue. All of a sudden he rolls over and I'm on top.

"I want you this way, next time. I want to see you ride me, Cate. With your head thrown back and your hair tumbling all over the place. Tell me I didn't hurt you too much. I know you already said it, but I need to hear it again." He takes my hand and kisses each fingertip.

"At first it stung more than hurt, and then it went away. But then … I had an amazing orgasm."

"I could tell. I felt it when you came."

"You did?" This fascinates the hell out of me. "Tell me."

"You squeezed me. In sequences. Like a song keeping tempo." What a nice way to put it.

I'm riding on a post sex high and I love how I don't feel awkward with Drew like I did with the dickwad. It feels so good that I can just be honest about how I feel.

"I love the way you sound when you come." I'm sure my face is pink when I say this.

"Hmmm. Then I'll have to come more often, won't I?"

He makes me feel empowered that I could get him there. Still, I'm a bit shy when I say, "I suppose so."

"But right now, I need to pull out of you and get rid of this condom, even though it's the last thing I want to do."

"Right. I guess it's the smart thing to do." I shimmy off him and let him up. And I miss him immediately. I hear the toilet flush and the water running. Then he's back with a smile, a glass, and something in the other hand.

"What's this?"

"Ibuprofen. I don't want you to be sore."

"Thanks." I swallow the pills.

He pulls me back on top of him. "I'd like to make you come again and again, but I don't want you to be any more sore than you already are."

"I think you're making a bigger deal out of this than is necessary."

"No, I'm not. Besides, I have to get up early for my shift." He rubs my back and I purr.

"Okay, I'll give you a pass then."

"Cate, you need to go use the restroom."

"No, I'm fine."

"No, sweetheart, you do."

Lifting my head so I can look at him, I ask, "Why's that?"

He cups my cheek and says, "For a couple of reasons. One, it's a great idea to do that after sex. It prevents bladder infections. I could give you my professional explanation, but I don't think you need that right now. And two, when you get to the bathroom, you'll see why."

And then it hits me. Blood. Fuck! How embarrassing. He sees my reaction and says, "Don't you dare be embarrassed by this. It was beautiful and amazing and I wouldn't trade it for anything. Now go before I take you myself."

Scrambling out of the bed, I scurry into the bathroom and when I look at my thighs, I screech. In less than a few seconds, the door busts open and he's in there with me.

"Can I just tell you something? A little blood goes a long way. What looks like a whole lot on you there, is only a little bit. Calm down and why don't we get in the shower?"

I shake my head and say, "Okay. But let me use the bathroom first and then put my hair up."

He walks out and I use the facilities. Then I call him back in and he enters while I'm twisting my hair up in an elastic.

He turns on the shower and when the temperature is right, we get in. He squirts some shower gel in his hands and rubs them together. "May I?"

"Yes." How can I say no?

Before I know what's happening, he spins me around and pulls me back against him. "You're so gorgeous, Cate." Then, soapy hands dip between my thighs and gently wash me. He slides them all over and back between us, all around to make sure all the blood is washed away. Then he turns me back around and lets the shower rinse the suds away. He lathers up again and washes the rest of my body.

When he's finished, I say, "My turn." I mimic everything he did. It's kind of funny because when his back is to me, he's so much taller than I am, I feel like a little kid. But my hands reach around and take hold of his erect cock. His arms stretch out to brace himself on the wall. I work the lather all around him, and he moans. This may turn into something way more than a shower. As I turn him back around, the look on his face has me moaning, too.

"Drew."

"Cate."

"I want you."

"No. You'll hurt too much tomorrow."

"I should be the judge of that. Not you."

"Not in here. No condoms."

I look up at him, and then down at his erection. My mind is made up. I drop to my knees and put my mouth on him. He's large, but not ridiculously huge like you read about in those romance novels. His cock doesn't jut out and reach his chest, meaning it's not eighteen inches long. No, thank god. I would run screaming from this shower if it did. But it is large and thick. Just perfectly pretty. A nice tawny shade with a lovely mushroom cap on top. And he feels like velvet.

Blow jobs are not my specialty. In fact, I've only ever given a couple. So I decide to stop and tell him if I'm doing something wrong, he needs to tell me. Or if there's something he wants me to do, to tell me that, too.

"Just put your pretty mouth on me, Cate, and lick and suck. And leave the teeth out of it. Well maybe a little bit of teeth."

With his erection back in my mouth, I do what I think *I* would like if I were a man. Apparently, I'm right. Because he thrusts his pelvis forward to meet my rhythm and starts talking.

"Oh god, Cate. So damn good."

My tongue decides to take a trip down cock road. So it roams from base to tip, up down, up down. Faster, faster and then I put the whole thing in my mouth, sucking until I take it all and he sucks air in through his teeth. Then he makes this groaning sound and I decide to play with his balls. I squeeze, like I'm pumping, but softly, gently. And he starts calling out my name again.

"Cate, Cate, Cate, Catelyn. Catelyn." The last time he says it really long and drawn out. Then he tries to back away from me. "I'm gonna come."

Isn't that the point? Why is he backing away?

"Catelynnnnnnn!" And he comes. "Ah, ah, ah," he repeats. Guys really do love their head.

When he finishes, he touches my cheek in the most loving gesture. Next thing, he picks me up and kisses me. "This shower was supposed to be all about you. And look at what you did. You sucked me off until … well until I lost myself. You weren't supposed to let me come in your mouth."

"Why not? Isn't that the point? To come?"

"Oh, Cate." Then he laughs. We rinse again, then get out of the almost cold shower.

After we dry off, we get back in bed. Drew turns to me and asks, "Were you pleased tonight?"

"Is that a trick question?"

"No. I don't want you leaving here not feeling like you had the best sex of your life."

Now I laugh. "Drew, I had the only *real* sex of my life and it was great. And if you'd let me, I'd be humping you right now."

He smooths a hand down my hair. "You're a mess."

Wide-eyed, I glance up at him. "You think so?"

His smile is playful. "Yeah."

"So you liked Louise, did you?"

With a puzzled look he asks, "Who the hell is Louise?"

"Sasquatch's neighbor."

At first he mouths, *What the fuck*. Next, laughter reverberates off the walls. Finally he says, "Louise is one in a million, Cate."

"Well, Louise wants me to tell you she is ecstatic she finally got to meet you."

SEVEN
Present

———————◆———————

I WANT YOU TO LEAVE THIS room now and go home, but I don't want you to come back after you shower. I want you to say your goodbyes to me right here, right now.

A fine sheen of cool sweat covers my entire body when I'm jarred awake by the impact of the dream. The echoes of his voice make it more real than anything else. The wetness on my ears alerts me that I've been crying too. I sit up and fight the urge to hide under the covers from my past. I know why I'm starting to dream that moment. I only wonder why it's taken several days for it to show up.

Later as I press my head to the chilled tiles in the shower, the memories still linger. I let the remnants of the tears spill as I try to wash away my sins. It isn't until I get to work that the memories are finally shoved back into their proper place, deep in a recessed closet in the back of my mind.

It's early and I watch in fascination when Mandy skulks in with large sunglasses on and her head hanging low as if she's hiding from the paparazzi. I push away my keyboard as she comes into my office, leaving the door open behind her.

"What am I going to do?" she asks as she drops into a chair and covers her face with her hands. I can't help the laugh that escapes me. "This is so not funny."

"It totally is," I say much to her annoyance.

She glances up from where she hangs her head on the edge of the desk. She removes her sunglasses and stares straight at me. "I don't remember a thing."

I arch a brow. "And?"

"And, he remembers everything. I had to fake an appointment to get him out. He wanted breakfast. Can you believe it?"

My laughter relieves some of the pressure I've been feeling all morning. "Admit you like him."

Everything on her face widens. Her mouth and her eyes take on a ghostly impression as they mimic saucers. "I so do not."

"You do," I say chuckling. "You so have it bad."

"I don't do relationships," she says with a vehemence I almost believe.

"Morning." I glance up to see Daniel framing my doorway. He aims his next comment to Mandy's back. "Morning, beautiful."

I'm not sure how she does it, but Mandy's eyes grow ever larger in a cartoonish way. I just stare not wanting to give anything away. Slowly, she turns and I can see a hint of the smile she gives him.

"Morning, Daniel. We should—"

He cuts her off and pulls a hand full of daisies from behind his back.

"Daniel," she chokes out, obviously surprised and touched by his gesture.

Instead of looking at her, he moves aside as the office manager strides in carrying a vase full of long-stemmed pink roses. She heads directly toward me and places them on the only corner of my desk that is clutter free.

"These are for you. You must have an admirer," she says before she strides out as breezily as she came in. She gives a quick nod of good morning to the two other people in my office on her way out. Daniel glances down and I feel bad that my flowers have taken the wind out of his sails.

"Daniel, they're beautiful," Mandy says getting to her feet. She takes the small bouquet of flowers from his hands. "I'm going to find something to put them in."

Then she is gone. Daniel gives me a half smile before exiting. I'm left to pull the small white card from my own bouquet. Inside it reads…

To Cate,
The most beautiful woman I've ever laid eyes on.
I'm sorry our evening didn't go as planned. I look
forward to our plus one date.
A

The note is hand written and not typed. I recognize his attempt at a non-doctor scrawl. His scribble is actually really nice. I send him a quick text thanking him for the flowers before I dig into work.

Late that afternoon, I'm pulled into a meeting. I stop short when a man standing at the head of the conference table turns. He could have been on the cover of any magazine.

"Cate," my boss says changing my focus. "This is Ted Caine."

I face the man again, who wouldn't win any awards for height. He moves to stand in front of me. He's about my height in the flats I'm wearing.

He extends his hand and I give it a quick but firm shake. I can't help but notice how soft his skin is. His suit screams money so I'm not surprised his hands are as smooth as a baby's butt.

"Nice to meet you."

My boss jumps in. "She is the associate I was telling you about." Ted steps back and I catch him giving me a serious once over, but he's back to business before it gets awkward. My boss holds his hand out for me to take a seat. "Ted has been a client of ours for years," he announces proudly. "He's recently acquired a company and has engaged us to assess their accounting department for best practices. He would like you to head up the engagement."

Me? Why had my boss been telling him about me?

"He was impressed with you finding the mistake on the quarterly 10Q filing and fixing the problem so that it still went out on time."

Our team busted our ass to ensure we filed that quarterly comprehensive report of financial performance of the billion dollar corporation to the Securities and Exchange Commission, timely and accurately. Which was why we'd gotten drunk the other night in celebration. That was his company? I'm dumbfounded.

"Yes," Ted answers as if I'd asked the question out loud.

He shifts in his chair and the light hits the crown of his head. I notice there is a bit of salt mixed in his thick peppery hair. He takes charge of the meeting and begins to tell me his plan. "I would like you to go in and get a feel for things. The caveat is that I would like you to do it under the radar. I would introduce you as a new hire."

"Why, may I ask?" I'm curious regarding the subterfuge.

"We've done all the due diligence. Everything checks out on paper. Now that the deal is done, I need to know if changes need to be made. I find most employees are scared of change, especially when new management comes in. They fear for their jobs. I need to know if their policies and procedures are up to my company's standards. The best way to find out is from the inside."

After talking it through, the decision is for me to start work at his office on Monday. That way he has time to set me up with my fake employment. As Ted leaves, he shakes my hand and holds it just a little longer than socially required. And his stare leaves me to believe he's interested. I might have been flattered because he's a very attractive man. However, all I can think about are the flowers on my desk from Andy.

The rest of the week passes with Mandy mum on the status of her and Daniel. Andy's been silent as well. His schedule has been crazy and we haven't had a chance to talk much at all aside from nightly texts. Some are sweet and some make my toes curl.

On Friday, I get an e-mail from Ted's office regarding my assignment starting Monday. I get the location of the office and where I need to report to get my security badge. I set up a calendar invite on my phone so I'm prepared.

That night, after a hectic day, all I want to do is kick up my feet and watch a movie when I get home. Instead, I'm pulling out a dress I picked up during a hasty lunch shopping trip.

The color of the dress, bright violet, is a little out of my comfort zone. However, according to Mandy, the silk gown with its sweetheart neckline and fitted bodice with a twist makes me look heaven sent. I have to admit, it subtly hugs my curves with its A-line silhouette, and I feel pretty. I'm standing in front of the mirror when my phone buzzes.

"I'm here. Should I park and come up?" Andy's sexy voice croons out the other end of the phone.

"No, I'll be down."

I end the call and check my hair. Thanks to YouTube videos, I've managed to put my hair in an updo with a few tendrils of hair loose to frame my face. My makeup is subtle but there. I stick my phone in my clutch and head downstairs.

Andy's managed to find temporary street parking at the curb. My wool coat flutters open as I make my way over to the car, barely negotiating the lingering ice patches and managing not to fall on my face in my heels.

Before I can open the door, Andy's there. His hand on my shoulder shouldn't have given me goose bumps considering he hadn't touched me skin to skin. But it does.

"Hey, gorgeous."

He kisses me quickly before he opens the door and I slip in the car. It's toasty inside and I'm grateful because I'm rethinking the wisdom of wearing peep-toe shoes.

"It's not too far," he says while pulling out. "I'm sorry I haven't had a chance to talk to you much this week. My rotation has been brutal."

"Don't worry about it. That's the life of a doctor."

He sighs. "Sometimes I wonder why I chose this profession, especially when I see what I've missed all week."

He glances at me and I feel the warmth of his gaze before his eyes are back on the road. And he hasn't lied about the venue being close. We are at the entrance of the historic Willard Hotel in no time.

A valet opens my door shortly before Andy arrives with a helping hand. The line of cars ahead and behind us is impressive, along with the men and women with more bling than I can imagine.

My bargain find that had been a previous season's designer dress starts to pale in my eyes as we make our way to the coat check near the humongous ball room. But Andy's eyes nearly pop out of his head when he sees me without my coat.

He runs a thumb over a spaghetti strap as he leans in and says, "You are stunning."

My cheeks flame scarlet for the second time that night. "You're looking good yourself." And he does. His tux, although classic, fits him as if sewn on his body.

He takes my hand and leads me away from the direction of the ballroom. I wonder for a millisecond why we stop in an alcove.

"D— Andy," I correct mid-squeal. His sudden boldness takes me by surprise as he backs me into a corner.

"Cate. You are going to kill me tonight. I've barely thought about anything else except seeing you tonight. Then you wear this dress and all I want to do is tear it off of you."

He doesn't ask as he presses his mouth to mine hard. As he kisses me, I fear the tiny scrap of fabric between my legs won't hold the moisture I feel pooling from his kiss alone. His hand leaves my hips and rounds to the small of my back. I have the urge to hike up a leg and ride him right there, not caring people could walk by. Actually, the idea thrills me and I know I will have to go to the bathroom to mop up the moisture so I don't mess up the silk of my dress. When he presses into me further, his hard length wedges perfectly against my sweet spot forcing me to moan.

"Jesus, if you keep making noises like this I'm going to carry you caveman style upstairs to one of the rooms."

"Why not here?" I breathe. I'm teasing, but at the same time I'm daring him to do it.

He groans and steps back. I watch in fascination as he adjusts himself. He follows my eyes down to his man parts and then his eyes darken with heat.

"You're not playing fair."

My life has changed, and I'm not the same person I was. "I'm not playing at all." I hold his cerulean blue gaze letting him know how serious I am.

"Later," he promises.

I nod in agreement.

"Wait." I pull a compact out of my clutch to fix my lipstick. Then I step forward and wipe at his mouth, trying to remove the remnants of my *smudge proof* lipstick. I think I need a refund. Andy decides to play with fire and sucks my thumb in his mouth.

I shake my head, pulling my thumb free. "You said later."

He steps up behind me after I turn to make my way out. He stops me from moving forward with firm hands on my hips. "I have to be honest with you. When I finally get inside you again, it will be hard and fast. I've waited too long to have you in my bed again. It won't be sweet, but I can promise you'll love it."

I step back, pressing my ass against him. I'm completely turned on. "Give me your worst then."

The sound that comes from his throat reminds me of a growl as he slides his hands down the sides of my hips before he walks us back to the ballroom. The man's touch sets me aflame each and every time. My mind wanders to how he touched me last week at his house before I stopped him. I have to focus on the many guests of tonight's gala with fortunes to burn in order to turn the lust part of my brain off.

The philanthropists attending this event must have included men and women with net worth rivaling the assets of some banks, the way they ooze money in their couture outfits and diamond-encrusted jewelry.

A woman in a modest dress with a clip board stops us before we've made it too far. I'm busy trying not to look at Andy's ass, so I take in the room instead while she chitters in a hushed tone.

Above, chandeliers spill from the ceiling in graceful tear drop shapes. A railing circles the room, giving the impression of a second story. And the walls' trim and chairs are the color of gold which is fitting for the amount of affluence that is in the room.

"Your table is over here." I overhear her tell Andy.

We walk in a maze between round tables to one near the front. A podium is set up not too far from where we are.

"I forgot to mention I may be a guest of honor tonight," he says with a mischievous smile.

Before I can question Andy's whispered words, a woman in a Grecian dress of white and gold floats over as her flowing golden hair follows her.

"Drew! I'm so happy you were able to make it."

She's taken his arm and turns him to completely face her.

"Désirée," Andy barely gets out before she air kisses both of his cheeks.

"You are so handsome. And you'll be fine tonight. My sister would have said so herself."

Her words seem genuine, yet she sounds so fake. I can't help but feel sorry for her needing to try so hard. Then she plasters herself to him as her voices hitches on her next statement. "I know she would."

I watch as Andy's hand slowly comes up to pat her back. I'm hoping his hard on is gone or she'll take it as a good sign. It takes several seconds before he's able to disentangle himself from the woman.

"Désirée, I like you to meet Cate McKnight, my date for the evening."

She doesn't bother to hide her surprise. "Oh, Cate McKnight," she repeats as if she might know me. Woman to woman, I know her thoughts. She pulls it together. "I thought you were coming alone."

His smile is broad and I watch her disappointment grow. Andy steps back so he can slide his hand around my waist. "I was able to convince Cate last minute to join me."

There is calculation in her eyes, so I'm ready for what she's about to say.

"Are you related—?"

I cut her off before she gets any further. "No, we're not related."

She knows damn well we're not. Disdainfully, she glances over my dress. No doubt she's determined it's not straight off the runway. Then, her eyes land on my naked ring finger. Satisfied, she smirks. The fact that she now believes I don't have a permanent claim to Andy as mine pleases her.

"That's too bad. I was hoping some of his family would come to celebrate in his honor," she says haughtily, dismissing me. She turns her attention back to Andy. I begin to think only a ring on my finger would get her to back off. She smiles stunningly at him and for a second I think she's probably a better match for him. They come from similar backgrounds, I suppose. "Well, I can't wait for your speech."

Speech? I give Andy a look but try not to appear too surprised. I don't want Miss Stick Up Her Butt to have any more reasons to think less of me.

She gives him another smile and saunters off with a sashay in her step that begs men to watch. Andy gets points for not noticing. Yet, he doesn't explain the speech thing. He has us circle the table to find our name cards. When we do, I know my name is on the list; I want to rush over and tell her. But I don't.

"Speech, huh?" I ask after he pulls out my chair and helps me sit.

"Yes. Sorry about that. It's not that big of a deal."

But Andy is a bigger deal than he lets on. People keep stopping by and talking to him. I feel foolish as I'm introduced over and over and then ignored because of who Andy is. Andy is a good guy and tries to include me, but I sit and fiddle with the place card or my phone to pass the time.

"Don't look so glum, dear. These things are all a game."

I glance over to an older woman who could be my grandmother, although she's more regal than mine. The diamonds in her ears and on her fingers prove that.

"Ignore that Désirée. She's a bore and no competition to you, my lovely girl. That man can't keep his eyes off you." Her eyes shift to my left as she speaks. "Well, I think there is someone else who also has his eye on you."

I glance up and see Ted Caine. For a man at least ten years my senior if not more, he's sexy in a James Bond sort of way.

"Drew, nice to see you."

Andy turns to me and begins to introduce me yet again, but Ted leans down to pick up my hand and place a kiss on my knuckles.

"Nice to see you again, Cate."

Andy glances at me. I plunge forward in my greeting to hopefully explain without explaining.

"You too, Mr. Caine. I received an e-mail from your office and look forward to working on the project."

His eyes twinkle and dance over me. "Let's not talk shop here. Work can wait until Monday."

I smile then and turn away, hoping to avoid any more conversation. Ted is attractive but he's practically my boss. Plus, Andy is the one that pushes every one of my buttons.

"I see you've met my date, Cate. However, I think they are about to begin," Andy says, politely dismissing the other man. I glance up to see Andy's jaw tense as if he's speaking through gritted teeth.

Ted nods and sits at a nearby table when, of course, Désirée appears at the front.

"I'd like to welcome all of you to the first annual Davenport Cancer Research Fund benefit. As you all are aware, I lost my sister to this deadly disease two years ago. But it was a young resident who was on duty one day over six years ago who spotted something so tiny it might have been overlooked. He gave my sister more time. Even with experimental drugs and radiation treatments, we were not able to save her. But we were able to extend her life, so she and I could travel and see the world together while she was still relatively healthy. That young resident found the incurable early on. Only this disease had already claimed my sister. And time was against us. Still, before she died, she asked me to do this. She wanted me to continue the fight even though she was gone. She wanted me to thank the resident that gave her time to say goodbye to everyone she loved. She gave me this."

Désirée pulls out a sheet of paper and begins to read a letter that makes even me wipe at my eyes. By the time she invites Andy to come up and say a few words, you can hear the sniffles throughout the room.

I want to hear Andy speak, but Désirée has other plans. She plops herself in his vacated chair. "He's really great isn't he?"

"He is." I face the podium not wanting to miss his speech.

"He's never mentioned you."

Glancing back, I shrug, not planning to play this woman's game. I switch my focus back to Andy, knowing what she is up to. I wish Jenna were here. She would have told her off by now. I'm not so bold, at least during Andy's speech.

"I mean, just yesterday when I was at the hospital and he practiced his speech with me, he never said a single word about you."

Points for me, as I maintain a smile. "Funny, he hasn't mentioned you either." I almost throw in a bit about us spending the night together even though nothing happened. However, I know she will say something else to one up me. I'm really not sure I want to know if Andy has slept with her or not.

Andy's speech is short because when she goes quiet, the room erupts with applause. She smiles at me as she stands to give Andy another hug. Only she leans up and presses her mouth to his. His eyes are wide and he glances at me as he steps back trying to be polite. She is back at the podium introducing someone else as Andy sits. He dabs at his mouth with a napkin while I wonder just what was between the two of them.

He moves to take my hand, but I manage to put it in my lap without making a scene. I'm not exactly pissed at him. He didn't initiate the kiss. However, I feel blindsided and it would be disingenuous on my part to pretend I'm okay with how this night has gone so far. He sighs and we listen to several more speeches before food arrives, which seems backward. The few events I've attended, you ate and then the talking occurred.

I pick at the food and I'm grateful when the servers appear to remove the plates. Afterward, when more people come to talk to Andy, I excuse myself to the restroom. When I come back, I head to an atrium to get some air instead of going back into the ballroom. A few people are mingling and I rest my hand on rails when a voice has me turning around.

"Long night."

I turn to face Ted. "You can say that."

"Ah," he says tipping his head back a little. "Désirée has her sights on your young man. I can't say I'm unhappy with it. I'm glad I'm out of her crosshairs."

He winks then laughs with a jovial sound. I'm left unsure of exactly what he means.

"She knows what she wants." That's the best compliment I can give. I'm not totally sure who she is to him and don't want to offend one of my company's best clients.

"That she does."

We stand there in silence for a bit before he flags down a waiter and grabs two flutes of champagne.

"A toast," he says. "To Désirée."

I have no idea where he's going with this so I reluctantly raise my glass.

"May she never get what she wants, at least when it comes to men."

I raise my glass a little higher and then I drink deep.

Ted starts to tell me stories about her amorous pursuits. After just one, I know he isn't one of her fans. I'm practically doubled over with laughter as he tells me about this one guy's girlfriend tossing red wine all over Désirée and her white dress when she finally had enough of her chasing her man. That's when Andy finds me.

"I've been looking for you."

Ted glances between us. "Well, it was fun talking to you, Cate. I'll see you Monday."

I nod, feeling a little tipsy.

"So you know Ted?" he asks awkwardly.

Again, his jaw is tense and his jealousy is cute. But I have my own questions.

"Not as much as you know Désirée."

He lets out a suffering breath. "Cate."

"You know, I'm tired. If you're not ready to go, I think I'll take a cab home."

He studies me and I hold his gaze.

"No need for a cab. I brought you and I'll take you home. Let me just say some goodbyes before we leave."

He takes my hand and won't let me go as much as my heart needs him to. Instead, I want to melt, with his fingers interlocked with mine. This man means more to me than I want to admit, which is why I'm so hurt. I know my anger is irrational. Andy is a gentleman. Désirée, on the other hand, is a viper and I shouldn't let her ruin my night. Only she already has.

After the farewells and so sad you're leaving earlys, Andy helps me into my coat. While we wait for valet, he says, "Désirée is a friend."

"Oh, I know," I say sarcastically.

"Cate—"

"Don't worry. I know she's into you and maybe you're not into her. I get it. But she heard your speech and I didn't. Hell, I didn't even know you were giving one."

"Why didn't you hear my speech?" he asks puzzled.

"She was too busy telling me about how much time she spends with you and how you practiced your speech with her."

"Cate—"

"Andy. I don't want to fight. I just want to go home."

The valet appears and after an exchange of a tip, Andy drives me back home without further conversation. As if lady luck loves him, he puts the car in park in a space out front. I go to open the door and he reaches for my arm. "I'm sorry about tonight."

I give a weak smile because I am too. When he leans in to kiss me, I move out of range. "You have some lipstick here." I dab my thumb at the corner of my mouth to direct him.

The lipstick is a ruse, but I made my point. While he's looking in the mirror, I'm out of the car. Again, my anger is illogical, I know this. But the thought of Andy with other women makes me physically ill. And Désirée has thrown that idea in my head, even though I have no right to be upset. I'd been the one to leave. I'm the one that ran.

If not for the text from Jenna reminding me that she would be in town next week, my prospects for the upcoming week might have been bleak. But Jenna is always full of adventure, and her visit this time is no exception.

EIGHT
Past

———◆———

THE BRIGHT SUN AWAKENS ME. I reach out my hand and all I feel is a cold, empty bed. Then I remember. Drew had to work this morning. Sitting up, I check out the clock and see that it's nine fifteen. The covers are tangled up around my legs so I kick them off and get up. That's when I notice it—blood on the sheets. It makes me wonder if Drew saw it when he woke up. And then I remember last night when he told me to go to the bathroom. *Gah.* Now I'm positive he saw it.

I yank the sheets off the bed, determined to get them washed and back on by the time he comes home. Once they're in the washer, I hop in the shower. Remnants of blood rinse away. I had no idea there would be that much blood. But then my cheeks warm as I think about all the amazing things his mouth and body did to mine. I'm sure if I looked in a mirror, I'd be wearing a dreamy expression. My fingers explore the region between my legs, testing to see how sore I am, and I'm happy to find it's not as bad as I thought it would be. I quickly finish up and wind my hair in a towel. Since Drew won't be back until after noon, that will give me time to get some studying in. Dressing in a pair of jeans and a long-sleeved top, I let my hair air dry and pad into the kitchen to make some coffee. That's when I spy the note.

Cate, Catelyn, My Catie ...
What should I call you? I'll decide by the time I get home. I hope your sleep was as great as mine and I only have you to thank for it. I believe it was all due to the greatest night of my life. Make yourself at home and I'll see you around twelve thirty.

Yours,
Drew

What a sweet note, but if he calls me his Catie, I'll have to kill him. That'll remind me of my grandmother and that's not going to work. Then I read it again and get a stupid grin on my face. He says it was the greatest night of his life. Does he really mean that? Why would he say it if he didn't? There's only one person who can help. Once the coffee is brewing, I call her.

"What is it that can't wait until eleven?" she groans.

"Drink too much last night?"

"Grrrr. What do you think?"

"I need advice."

"Okay."

I read her the note and tell her just the tiniest bit about our night.

"Is that what you woke me up for?" she asks.

"Yes! This is important!"

"He meant every word. He's not fifteen, Cate. If all he was interested in was knocking off a piece, he would've found some local chick and taken care of it. He wants *you*. Quit being so needy."

"Yes. Right. Got it. Okay, thanks. Go back to bed."

Click. The line is dead and Jenna is gone. But I'm still unsure of myself. And I guess it boils down to the fact that I don't see why he wants *me*. But I pick myself up and go with it. What the hell, right? I may as well enjoy it while it lasts.

Grabbing a cup of coffee, I open his cabinets in search of a bite to eat. They're fully stocked with everything. I opt for a banana. That should hold me until he gets home. About that time the washer buzzes, so I toss the sheets into the dryer and then pull out my computer to start work on another paper that's due this week.

Before long, I'm in my stride, and my phone vibrates. It's a text from Drew.

> **Drew: Good morning gorgeous! How did you sleep? And would you like to go to lunch?**
> **Me: Slept great and I'd love lunch.**
> **Drew: It's a plan. I'll pick you up. 12:30. Glad you slept well. <3**

Aw, he sent me a heart. That was sweet. I get back to work, but soon the dryer disturbs me. Groaning, I get up to pull the sheets out so I can make up the bed. As I do, I'm happy to see the blood came out. With the bed all made up, I get back to my paper, and my phone vibrates again. Jeez! I'll never get anything accomplished.

> **Jenna: Call me!**

"What's up?" I ask.

"I'm awake now."

"And?"

"So? Did you do it?"

"Yes. I already told you that."

"And?"

Now she's interested. "It was fabulous. He was fabulous. What more can I say?"

"That's it?"

"Yep."

"Cate! I want details!"

"I'm not giving you any."

"Oh my god! You are really in deep!"

"What's that supposed to mean?" I'm puzzled by her comment.

"It means, my dear girl, that if you didn't care about him, you'd be spilling all kinds of information. But as it is, you're keeping everything to yourself."

I digest what she says and I'm flabbergasted to find she's right. Jenna and I ordinarily share everything from how a guy kisses to what his ass looks like in jeans. But with Drew, I am as tight lipped as I've ever been. Holy shit!

"I can tell by your silence that I'm right, huh?"

"I, uh, I'm not sayin' yes or no."

I hear her peals of laughter over the phone. She knows me like no other.

"Cate, it's okay. Drew is the best. I wouldn't say it if I didn't mean it. And honestly, he's almost like my brother so I'm pretty sure I don't want the finer details."

"That's good news because you won't be getting them."

She laughs some more. "Go have fun and be sure to take serious notes on hockey. If you continue to spend time with him, you will be watching it a lot."

Now it's my turn to chuckle. "Aye, captain. I'll see you tomorrow."

When I check the time on my phone I see it's eleven thirty. I decide to fix my hair and makeup so when Drew gets here I'll be ready to leave. Then I look at my pitiful paper and sigh. I'm not even a quarter finished and I'd planned to knock this one out this morning. I hop back on it and it seems like minutes later I hear the key in the lock, and there he is, a vision in green scrubs.

"Hey, sexy writer," he says as he walks in the door.

"Hey, sexy doctor."

He sets my computer aside, pulls me to my feet, and kisses me. "I've thought of nothing else all morning. You are a huge distraction, my lovely Cate. Which, by the way is what I shall call you. That or Catelyn. Catie won't do."

"Thank god. I was going to tell you no on that. My grandmother calls me her little Catie. Every time I hear that I think of her."

"Yeah, not good. I love Catelyn. But Cate, it's perfect, too."

"Your choice."

He kisses me again. "I kept thinking all morning how great it would've been to be lazy in bed with you. Are you sore?"

I swear to god, if my eyeballs weren't attached so well, they'd be rolling down his living room carpet. "Um, ah, no," I squeak.

"Sorry. Did I shock you?"

"A little." *Hell yeah!*

"Yeah, I guess I get used to asking patients personal questions and I should have a better filter. Sorry."

Maybe I look like a bug about to hit a windshield or something because he starts to laugh. Then he folds me in his arms. "It's okay, Cate. Don't be embarrassed. I was only asking for selfish reasons." Then he leans back and has this super cute expression on his face.

I can only nod.

"So, lunch then?"

I nod again. It appears I've lost the ability to speak.

"Good. Let me get out of these first," he indicates his scrubs with his finger, "and I'll be ready in a second." He ambles into the bedroom. When he returns, I'm still standing in the middle of the living room, like a moron.

He does a double take and asks if I'm okay.

"Uh huh." I take him in. Jeans, long-sleeved shirt. Nice. Very nice. Damn, he looks good in jeans.

He grabs my hand and off we go. "Thai okay?"

"Love it."

Then he tells me about his shift. All routine, according to him. I glaze over because I'm still trapped in how he looks in jeans. And I want him. After we order, he starts talking hockey. He explains the rules of the game and how it's a lot like soccer. I'm familiar with soccer because I played it when I was growing up and in high school. He tells me about the players' positions, and the major differences.

"It's so fast and the puck is so small it's hard for me to follow sometimes," I say.

"You get used to it when you watch it enough."

"I don't understand that icing stuff."

"It's only a game delay. It slows down the play."

"I think when I watch you today, I'll be confused. It might help if we watch some games together."

Drew barks out a laugh. "Don't worry. You'll have plenty of opportunity to do that."

"Isn't all that equipment heavy and cumbersome?"

"Not heavy, but cumbersome. You get used to it, though."

"What position do you play?"

"I'm a right wing. It's like a right forward in soccer."

"Gotcha. You're fast then?"

"Fairly. Keep in mind this is amateur. I'm not that good."

"Listen, if you can stand up on skates, I'm going to think you're awesome."

"Just wait. I always have bruises somewhere. You'll see me bust it like crazy."

"Drew, just don't get your teeth knocked out."

Later that day, as we're on the way to the hockey rink, I'm a bit nervous. He told me to bring a jacket because it gets chilly inside.

When we walk in, his arm is thrown casually around my shoulders. We run into another couple. It's a teammate and his wife. "Sam. Caroline. Hey, this is Cate. She's up for the weekend," he says as he introduces me.

We all greet each other and the guys head off to the locker room.

Caroline looks at me. "Want to find a seat?"

"Sure." So we wander up to the stands and get a seat right behind the thick Plexiglas partition right next to the box where the players sit.

"It's nice to see Drew with someone. The hockey ho that's been hanging around here now will maybe get the message."

"Oh? Hockey ho?" I laugh.

"Just wait. She'll be here wearing his number. You'll see."

"That's just icky."

"It is. She wraps herself around him, too. He does everything to get her off him, but she will not leave him alone. Now she's going to have to. I can't wait to see the look on her face when she finds out he's here with you."

"Oh, maybe that's bad, though."

"What do you mean?"

"Think about it, Caroline. She sounds batshit nutty. What if she tries to stab me or something?"

"I don't think she's that psycho."

"I hope not." I'll just stay close to Drew after the game and hope for the best.

A few minutes pass and Caroline elbows me. "There she is." I look toward the door and a bleached blonde walks in. Her boobs are the size of summer cantaloupes and her lips look like they got stuck in my mom's Dyson vacuum cleaner. What the hell? Does she have a frequent buyer's card at the local plastic surgeon's office?

Caroline starts laughing. "Exactly!"

"Did I say that out loud?"

"You did."

"Oops. I need to be better at filtering my thoughts."

"No, you're right. She's a freak show. What's wrong with people?"

"I've got nothing for you on that."

She shuffles up the stands, and I mean shuffles. When I see

99

what's on her feet, I get why. She's wearing five-inch spiky heels. Holy shit. This is a hockey game, for Pete's sake. Her jeans are so tight, I'm afraid they're going to split down the middle. And when she wobbles up the steps, she drops something, bends down to pick it up and the crack of her ass shows. Oh, for the love of everything. *Cover up the crack!* Then I start to think of that ... that thing chasing after Drew and I get tickled. And it hits me so hard I start laughing. I laugh until I cry. Then Caroline starts laughing and we know we're both making spectacles out of ourselves, but we can't seem to stop. It's like when you're in church and you know you're not supposed to laugh, but the harder you try not to, the more you do. The next thing I know, I'm snorting and the FreakShowHockeyHo is watching us. OhMyGod MakeUsStop!

Finally—finally!—the guys skate on the ice and that breaks it up for us. We both wheeze for a while but we do catch our breath.

"That was way too good to pass up, right?" I ask.

"Oh, I can see it now. You're gonna have a heyday with this one. He's gonna have to tough it out, yeah?"

"Oh, yeah."

HockeyHo is only a few rows away from us so we need to cut off our chat. Then she gets up and waddles down to the glass, which is right next to us, presses her melons against it and yells out Drew's name. I cup my hand over my mouth and snort again. The back of her midriff tank top has number seventeen on it—Drew's number. She turns toward us for a second and I see the number is on the front, too.

Caroline leans into me and says, "Told ya." I can only shake my head.

Then HockeyHo yells, "I'm pulling for ya, Drew. Show 'em what ya got!" And she gives her melons the old one two.

I pull my phone out and snap a photo. I can't resist.

When the team finishes warming up, they skate into their box and Drew and Sam look up at us. Drew has this sheepish look on his face as he shrugs. I laugh. Then something comes over me and I yell, "I'm pulling for ya, Drew!" And I whistle. That's my claim to fame. I can whistle really loud with my fingers. He looks at me and blows me a kiss.

HockeyHo's eyes bulge to match her melons. She looks at me, then at Drew, and back at me. Then she yells, "I said it first, Drew."

I put my hands over my face, double over, and die laughing. I spread my fingers and can see Drew's shoulders shaking with laughter.

Honestly, and it's sad to say, I don't know who I watch more during the game, Drew or HockeyHo. They are each entertaining in their own diverse ways. HockeyHo is acting the garish team cheerleader. And Drew is spectacular on the ice, to my uneducated hockey eyes. He is graceful, yet aggressive, fast, and accurate with the puck. He has underplayed his abilities, as I knew he would. It amazes me that a man from the south who didn't grow up skating could master this sport in such short time. I'm not sure if Drew's team is just that good, or if the team they're playing is just that bad, but they trounce them eight to zip. Drew scores five goals and gets three assists. And I'm impressed.

His ear-to-ear grin at the end of the game says it all. I'm jumping up and down with Caroline, cheering and yelling, HockeyHo long forgotten. When they emerge from the locker room, showered, and in their street clothes, he picks me up and kisses me.

"You were awesome!"

"I had some fan help!" he says. Then he looks at Sam and Caroline, "See you guys later."

They both wave and Caroline says, "Cate, I hope to see you again soon."

"Me too. It was really great talking with you, Caroline. Maybe next game then." I wave bye as we walk to Drew's car.

"That was so much fun. I loved watching you. I can't believe how good you can skate. I mean you were everything out there." I bump his shoulder with my fist.

He tosses his stuff in his trunk and as I'm getting ready to say something else, he grabs me and his mouth slams onto mine. Hands delve into my hair, and he wraps his other arm around me pulling me tight into his frame. God, can anything feel any better? Oh, yeah, when we're sexing it up.

My hands tuck under the waistband of his jeans. I have a need to get naked with him. He must feel it, too, as he deepens the kiss. I moan in response because I want him with everything I have as my blood flames through my veins. My sex throbs and I realize I am rubbing myself against his thigh. I slip one hand further down the back of his jeans and mold it to his perfect ass. *Damn.* I love his ass. Now I know why. All that skating has made it this way.

He pulls away and stares, not saying a word. He traces the outline of my face, nose, and lips. It's nearly unbearable. My throat is thick with desire.

"Drew, I—"

In a husky voice, he answers, "You don't have to say a word. I know. Let's go to dinner. I need food and then you. In the worst way."

"Yes."

Dinner is at a small local restaurant. They know Drew because he apparently does carryout here a lot. We hurry through the meal because both of us keep making innuendos about being in bed together. That's all either of us want.

We're tearing each other's clothes off as soon as we walk in the door. I've never experienced this before but I don't want the feeling to stop. When we're both down to our unders, he puts one arm under my knees and sweeps me off my feet—literally.

"How one girl has managed to occupy almost my every waking minute, I have no idea. But you have done a damned fine job of it. I'm glad you're here and we're about to get in bed."

His voice is gruff with lust. He sets me on my feet and slides his boxer briefs down. His erection leaps out, as though it's been waiting for this moment. I want to feel it so I reach for it.

"You're so soft, yet hard. Such a contrast." My hand tightens on him.

"Not too much, Cate."

"Did I do it wrong?" I glance up feeling like a chastised puppy.

"No. God, no. I just want you too much." Arms reach behind me and unhook my bra, then slip my lacy thong off. "You're so unbelievably sexy. This is why I can't think of anything but you."

He kisses me again as his hands find their way to my sex. His fingers are gentle, yet purposeful. And he knows how much pressure to apply. I'm moaning as my fingers sink into the muscles of his shoulders. I have to hold on because my legs want to crumple.

He pulls his hand away and says, "Let's get in bed." When he pulls back the covers, he asks, "Did you wash the sheets?"

"Yeah," I say.

"That wasn't necessary."

"Yes, it was. They were messy." It's an unpleasant moment for me and I cringe.

His hand slides under my chin so he can look me in the eye. "Like I said last night, don't turn something beautiful into an embarrassment. It was perfect, Cate. I couldn't have asked for anything better."

His lovely words expunge my awkwardness and I lunge at him. Just as I'm about to kiss him, the corner of his mouth turns up and he throws me backward on the bed. Air whooshes out of my lungs as he brushes his lips over mine. Then he begins to work his way down to the apex of my thighs. Muscles tense as air is vacuumed from my chest. For a moment, I forget how to inhale. The anticipation of what's about to occur, coupled with the fever in my blood makes me manic by the time his lips and tongue graze over that tiny bundle of nerves. I'm torn between wanting him like this and wanting him inside of me. But before I can think about it further, he does that thing with his finger, inserting it in just a bit, and I don't need to make a decision at all. My back arches as I latch my fingers onto his hair and come all over the place, calling out his name. When he starts to glide up my body, I jerk him toward my mouth so I can kiss him. I want to absorb this man into my soul, crawl inside of him and stay there forever.

"Cate, are you sure you're not sore?"

"Just a tiny bit tender, but I'm good. I want you, Drew."

"Why don't you get on top? Then you control everything."

"O-Okay." I'm a bit nervous about this. I've never done this and I'll feel so exposed.

He rolls on his back and reaches for a condom. I watch him put it on and it makes me want to put my mouth on him. When he's ready, I bracket his thighs with mine and he holds out his hands.

"For a little leverage."

He places them on his hips. "Find your rhythm and I'll match it."

I nod, take a hold of him, and insert the tip. Then I inch down on him. It aches a tiny bit, but it's okay. I keep going, and slide back and forth until he's seated all the way. I stop a second, allowing myself to adjust to him. I make the mistake of catching a glimpse of his face. His lips are barely parted but it's the deep cerulean of his irises that grab me. "Oh, god. You're sexy." A different ache replaces the one I had before.

"Fuck." He lifts his hips against me, and I move in sync with him. "Not anywhere close to you." He slides his teeth over his lower lip and bites down. Oh, hell, when he starts to play with my breasts, I know I'm not going to last long. This isn't good. But maybe it's his plan.

"Tell me if I'm doing this right, Drew." I need to know if I'm pleasing him.

"Fuck, Cate. What do you think?"

I toss back my head, riding the sensations, before I straighten and manage to say, "If it's anything like how I feel right now…"

His eyes turn molten as his hand moves to my clit. *Oh, good lord.*

"I, I won't, can't, I'm going to come."

My head drops back and I reach for his sack behind me. When I squeeze his balls, he immediately reacts by sitting up and pulling me close. As I climax, he kisses my cries of pleasure away before he follows me over that ledge. Whoa! That was incredible.

"Don't move. Let me kiss you," he says.

Feathering light kisses across my forehead, cheeks, and then my mouth, he moves from one corner to the other. Then he drops to my neck, where he runs his tongue up and down one side. This is good. The hot kind of good. His teeth and lips join in and he traverses to the other side and repeats his actions. I'm nothing but a squirmy heap when he finishes.

"I know you can't, but I want you again."

"Who says I can't?" His eyes dance with mischief. "I may not be able to orgasm, but you can."

"Please hold me close like this." I want to feel all of his skin on me.

He does and proves his theory by rocking his hips into me as my eyes widen in surprise. I clutch his biceps and try to match his thrusts.

"Cate, wrap your legs around me."

His authoritative voice makes my body involuntarily clench.

"Oh, that's nice." He's so deep now.

"Now put your arms around my neck." His slight commands turn me on.

"Oh, okay." We're so tight. Touching everywhere. I grind myself against him, trying to find that perfect contact.

"Here, let me …" He slips his hand between us and I feel his finger touch me.

"Ah!"

He laughs. "Too much?"

"No. Just surprised me."

He presses and rubs in a slightly circular motion. And it's so good. I'm hanging on that edge.

"I'm almost there. Can you come?" I ask because it's only fair.

"Let go, Cate. Don't worry about me. I just want to watch."

I lick my lips and nod. His gaze locks onto mine. His eyes are gripping. But then so is his body as it brings mine to another spectacular climax as I cry out his name.

"Jesus, Cate. Watching you come is a damn thrill." He still plunges into me, slowly though, taking his time, running his hands all over my boneless body.

In an instant, he flips me on my back and brushes my hair off my face.

"Beautiful Cate. I could make love to you for days." He rolls to his side and puts his hand on my hip after he pulls my leg over his. "Are you good? Still not too sore?"

"I'm great."

He smiles. "You are indeed."

"Drew, I, uh, I'm not on birth control. Remember?"

"I do. Are you worried about the condom?"

"Yeah."

"I'm still hard so it's still on."

I feel my cheeks heat. "Okay."

He's still moving in me as he watches me closely. "I'll stop if you want."

"I want you to go on forever," I confess. "I just don't want a baby."

He laughs as he pulls out. "No baby." Then his face gets serious. "I'm going to marry you some day, Catelyn Forbes. And then we'll have babies."

When I open my mouth to speak, he says, "No, wait. I know this is entirely too soon to talk about this kind of stuff. You don't really know me, much less love me, nor do I you. But I have this weird feeling about us. And it's strong. And when I say marry you some day, I'm not talking about tomorrow. But mark my words."

I'm speechless. There isn't a thing I can say to that. The truth is I have a strong and weird feeling about him, too. And I haven't been able to put my finger on it. Maybe he just did for me.

"Have I weirded you out?" he asks.

I smile and shake my head. "Not really."

Lying next to each other as we are, it would be hard to lie. "I believe you." His mouth catches mine and he sears me with another kiss.

It isn't until the following afternoon I have the will to force myself to leave. Papers and exams call me back to school but Drew is tempting.

"Go. You have two degrees to obtain."

"I do. You already have yours and I'm still working on mine," I say.

"Don't worry. You'll have it before you know it." He blankets me in his warmth and his lips find mine one last time. "This is going to have to hold me until next weekend."

"We'll figure it out," I tell him.

"Of course we will. Be safe driving and call me when you get in."

The week is like double over-time. Since I didn't get much done at Drew's, I have my work cut out for me. Drew calls on Tuesday and wants to know if he can drive down to spend Wednesday night.

"I want to say yes, like more than you know, but right now I'm underwater. I have three papers due and an exam on Thursday. If you come, I won't get my work done." I hate telling him no. There have been few times in my life I've hated missing out on things because of studying, but this ranks as number one.

"No worries. I understand. Cate, I was there once. Don't ever feel bad about telling me this."

"Okay," I say with some relief, but admit, "You sure make it tempting though."

"So, Friday or Saturday then?" he asks.

"Friday night. Your place. Do you have a hockey match?"

"I do. Saturday again. But at night," he says.

"Cool."

"Hey, I gotta run. I'm at work and I just got a text."

"Okay. Call me later."

At least I have an awesome weekend to look forward to.

NINE
Present

———————◆———————

RIDING THE SUBWAY MONDAY morning is a mistake. I'm used to walking the few blocks to work, which is how I decided on the location of my apartment. The work site I'm headed to is about ten blocks away. And even though I can walk it, I don't want to arrive in the form of an icicle. I can cab it, but I thought I'd be adventurous and try something new and out of the elements.

The morning rush is unforgiving. The push and pull of people careens me forward and eventually catapults me up to the sidewalk, where I'm spit out like a wad of tobacco. I'm not familiar with DC yet, so I spend a few moments trying to orient myself. When I find my bearings, I make my way into the steel and gray building.

After a tango with security and a salsa while trying not to get mushed into the elevator, I make my way to the reception desk on the floor I'm directed to.

"Mrs. McKnight?" The woman asks brusquely. The severe bun at the nape of her neck seems to be the cause of her forced smile. It makes me wonder if she suffers from frequent headaches wearing her hair like that. TooTightABunitis.

"It's *Ms.* McKnight, actually."

She frowns and I wonder if it was a good idea to correct her and earn a place on her bad side. She glances away from me, not rolling her eyes, though I can tell it's a struggle for her not to. She presses a button on the phone.

"*Miss* McKnight is here." She clicks a button with a perfectly painted nail and focuses on me. "You can have a seat. Someone will be with you."

I acknowledge her stern tone wordlessly and take the seat she indicates. A short time later, a tall, slender man with black-rimmed glasses, and reading papers smashed to his face, blindly comes toward the reception area as a brunette follows closely on his heels.

"Yeah, yeah, that's fine. Just go with it," he says animatedly to the brunette.

She nods and scurries off.

"Cate?" the guy asks when he comes to a stop in front of me.

He holds out his hand. I take it and give it a quick shake.

"That's me," I say brightly, unable to risk a glance at the twenty-something receptionist who acted more like my mother.

"Jeff," he says and adds conspiratorially, "And don't mind her. She's a bit of a bitch. She likes to think she's like the gate keeper in World of Warcraft."

I have no idea what that is but am grateful I'm not the only person she probably doesn't like.

"Follow me and I'll show you to your desk and introduce you to the team."

We end up in an area filled with cubicles, which are like mini offices with moveable or knock down walls. They are tall enough to give you privacy while sitting, but when standing, I can see the vast number of them that spread throughout the large open room. Through one of the openings, I spot a woman filling a banker's box with stuff. She lifts the heavy cardboard box onto the desk using the nifty handles on the sides.

Jeff pauses and waits. I have the uncomfortable feeling that I'm replacing this woman.

"Don't worry. She isn't being fired or anything. Rumor has it she's dating the boss. Because of a non-disclosure agreement, she can't confirm or deny that. But she can't work for him because of it."

The dark haired woman glances up and she's beautiful. If the rumors are true, I can see why any man would want to date her. She flutters her eyes before hefting the box and exits without a word.

"Bye Miss Thing," he mutters at her back. To me, he says, "So this is your seat. And I'll be the one to train you."

He holds out a hand like he's a game show host. I sit because it's easier than the alternative.

"You log in this way." He begins to show me what to do and produces a paper with all the pertinent information. He pulls it from somewhere in the middle of a stack of papers he holds. I'm surprised by his organization. A while later into our training session, a voice startles us both.

"Ms. McKnight, I found these at reception and was told they weren't delivered to you by mistake."

Jeff and I turn as one. I'd seen the small vase full of purple and lilac flowers when I'd walked in. I wonder if they hadn't been delivered because the woman I'd replaced had still been in the office or if the hateful receptionist is paying me back. For all I know it's both.

I take them from his awaiting hands. "Thank you Mr. Caine."

"It's Ted."

The weight of the smile on his handsome face is almost too much to resist.

"He's no cuddly bear, I tell you," Jeff mutters quickly. "Quite the opposite, to be exact."

"Jeffery, just because we're related doesn't mean I can't fire you." Jeff rolls his eyes. "Please give Cate and me a moment."

Jeff's lips purse and he wisely says nothing as he heads out of my cube.

"Thanks for the flowers," I say.

"Everyone gets them." Jeff's disembodied voice passes through the thin walls.

Ted sighs. "Yes, it's company policy to make all new employees feel welcome."

"Some more than others," Jeff's voice croons.

Ted's jaw tightens and I want to stop Jeff because he seems like a really nice guy and I don't want him to lose his job over warnings to me.

"I hoped I could take you to a welcome lunch today."

Jeff's voice is clearer and I realize he's standing in the cube behind me leaning over. "I'm afraid she can't. We're taking her to lunch as a department."

Ted is barely holding back his anger as he says, "Tomorrow, then." He manages to make it sound pleasant before he tips his head to me and walks off.

Jeff sighs loudly and several other heads pop up all around me.

"He is so dreamy," a cute blonde in glasses breathes.

"I know, he is," says a woman with a thick Latina accent.

"I would so do that," from another woman whose caramel skin makes her hazel eyes stand out in her pretty face.

"You are full of crap," Jeff says to the last woman. "He hit on you and you turned him down."

She shrugs. "My man would kick my ass."

Jeff shakes his head. "Back to work, people."

Everyone, including the two guys who say nothing, disappear again behind the brown walls.

"This desk is cursed," Jeff says. "Don't fall for him. Promise me. I don't need to lose another employee."

I don't have time to ponder that because Jeff switches back to business, like he's bipolar, as he makes his way over. We spend the day reviewing everything thoroughly. I'm impressed at his managerial skills. He seems to uncover my skill level and run with it. I learn more than I expect about their process in that single day. Except for the informative lunch, where the office dirty laundry is aired in a maelstrom of names I will never remember, I feel like we've accomplished a lot.

By the time I get home I'm beat. Too lazy to cook and too hungry to wait for take out, I make a salad with all the fixings. I'm just about to dig in when my phone rings.

"Jenna," I squeal.

"Hey Love Bug, has Louise gotten a fix yet?"

I sigh. "Really, that's what you lead off with?"

"I'm guessing that's a no. No worries, hun. We are going to a masquerade ball when I get to town."

"Friday?" I ask unable to contain my excitement to see her. I miss her like crazy.

"No, Saturday, but I swear, you will get laid."

"I'm not having sex with a stranger, Jenna."

"Stranger, smanger, baby Jesus in a manger. Have you done anything I suggested dating-wise? I researched all the ways to meet new single people in DC and you do nothing with that golden information."

"No," I murmur.

"Not even Match.com?"

"Of course not, and do not ask about those hook up apps."

"What's wrong with Swiping Left?" she asks while barely containing her laughter.

The app she refers to has potential dating partner's profile pics show up on your screen. If you liked what you see, you swipe right to see if that person also likes your picture. If you don't like how they look, you swipe left. It seems too mean for me. Someone with low self-esteem might be pushed over the edge if they swipe right and that person swipes left.

"So many things," I say.

"Whatever, you will find the man of your dreams at the masquerade ball."

"What's so special about this ball? Other than spending way too much on a dress I won't ever wear again."

"What's so special? All the movers and shakers of the city will be in attendance. There will be so many eligible bachelors there. You're bound to meet someone. And don't worry about a dress. I have that covered."

By the time we get off the phone, I'm actually pretty excited. Not so much about meeting a man or dressing up and seeing celebrities, if what Jenna says is to be believed. I can't wait to see her. I think about Andy in a tux and how he looked the other night. I check my phone and he hasn't called. I ponder texting him but decide maybe it's for the best that we don't have further contact. We have too much history for us to ever work.

The next day, Jeff manages to wiggle me out of lunch with Ted. Easy when it's his assistant who calls while Jeff is sitting at my desk.

"I have to go to a meeting," Jeff sighs. "The vultures are here."

"Vultures?"

"The auditors. They're like a Rottweiler with a bone. They latch onto to any one mistake and make a huge deal about it."

For the first time, I feel bad. Here I am, one of those auditor types, spying on these good people. When they find out what Ted has contracted me do, they'll hate me. I barely know them, but they've made me feel so welcome.

"What's wrong? You look like you've seen a ghost."

"An auditor," I jest.

He laughs. "I'll be back in an hour if I'm not torn to pieces."

I sit staring at the computer wondering how to handle

everything once the truth comes out, when I get a call from Mandy.

"Oh my gosh, he won't leave me alone. When will you be back?" she asks.

"When you admit you like Daniel." I'm relieved she's able to take my mind off my current problem.

"He wants to hang out this weekend. That's so code for let's have sex. And I can't even remember the last time."

"At least one of us had sex."

She gasps. "You didn't have sex with doctor drop dead gorgeous?"

"First, I thought you didn't remember anything from that night."

"It's slowly coming back," she admits.

"And second, it's so not cool to mention doctor and dead in the same sentence." I laugh.

"Oh right, yeah, no good. How about Dr. McDreamy?"

"I think I've heard that one before."

I hear a tapping on the other end. "I'll think of something."

Changing the subject, I say, "In the meantime, have you ever heard of an annual masquerade ball with all the important people of the city?"

"Oh my gosh, yes," she gushes. "A former friend of mine went one year and met a lawyer she ended up marrying. I heard she has three kids now."

"You heard? She didn't tell you?" I cautiously ask.

"She ended up marrying a lawyer," she reiterates, making it clear what the problem is. "Now with all her society events, she doesn't have time for us little people. Anyway, are you going?"

"Yes," I begin.

"Promise me you won't marry a lawyer and forget about me. Or just take me with you," she begs.

I snort and have to cover my mouth. I fear the people around me heard. "I would take you but I'm the plus one. My friend has the invite and she's taking me."

"Well, pack some condoms in your purse. I hear it gets a little wild."

I'm still thinking about Mandy's comment on Friday after I get home from work. Jeff has given me a thorough view of Ted's company's accounting system and practices. It's good and he and his team seem to know what they're doing. I set up a meeting with

Ted's office on Monday morning after filing a report with my boss. I'm going to have to bring muffins, donuts and coffee as peace offerings and maybe take them all to a fancy dinner to make up for my ruse.

There is a knock at my door and I'm pumped. Since I wasn't sure when I would get off of work, Jenna agreed to take a cab to my place when she lands.

"Jenna," I say throwing open the door. Only it isn't Jenna. "Andy."

Confused, I just stand there. Since he hasn't called all week, I've assumed he's given up on us.

"Cate," he says before leaning down to take my mouth in a possessive kiss.

He pulls back and I dumbly say, "Andy," again like my mouth is on repeat.

His smile widens into a smirk. "Cate."

With an arm around my waist, he dances me back so that the door can close behind him.

"Andy, I'm so happy to see you. Come in," he mocks.

"I'm—" I start but I'm unable to finish. Jenna will be here at any time and I'm not ready for her to find out about him. She will have so much to say, none of it good.

He pulls back to stand straight. His arms are gone and I'm suddenly chilled by the cool air created between us.

"I can go." His face is so serious and I know that things are already messed up between us.

"No, it's not that. You didn't call all week. I assumed—" I waved a dismissive hand between us.

"I didn't call, but you didn't either. I planned to wait you out and not push. But when I want something or someone, I don't play around. I want you, Cate. I can't get you out of my head. I think I said your name at least twenty times this week by accident in multiple conversations. I had to see you."

"It's just that—" I try again but his lips are on mine.

He pulls me close and I feel his need pressed against me.

I practically swallow his tongue as I give him entrance. He tastes of coffee and hazelnut. I find myself on my toes wanting to get closer.

He obliges me by scooping me up under my butt. He turns and walks me over to set me down on my Ikea bistro table. It's not expensive solid wood and I worry it won't hold us both if he has what I have in mind.

He manages to untuck my blouse from the skirt I wore to work. I hadn't changed yet, not knowing what Jenna might want to do tonight. His hands brand my sides. I want them to move north and touch me where I ache. I push at his coat on his shoulders. He takes the hint and lets it fall down his arms and to the ground.

"Fuck, Cate, I need you. I love the feel of you."

That one word makes me go cold. *Love.* It's as if he's reached into my chest and fisted my heart in his hands. *Love.* It's a dirty word in my book and brings me back to the past we both promised to leave behind. But it's there. I remember with aching clarity all the reasons why he should hate me and I should hate myself.

He pulls back and focuses on my face. "Cate." He says it so soft it almost sounds desperate.

"I can't." My voice breaks on the word and I feel on the verge of tears.

"Don't do this." He sounds calm but I hear the anger behind the words. And he has every right to be angry. "You're going to run aren't you?"

He steps back without bothering to wait for an answer. I cover my mouth with my hand, fearful of the sob that's banging at the back of my closed lips. I say nothing because only pain will spew forth. He reaches down to gather his coat and when he stands I can see the bulge there for the taking. But it's too late. He turns and heads out the door. It rattles when it closes making me jump. I'm about ready to release the sob when a knock comes at my door.

I run to it, hoping I can straighten things out. When I open it, I realize my mistake.

A wide-eyed Jenna points a finger down the hall. "That guy looks a lot like—"

Her words trail off when she turns and gets a good look at my face.

"Honey, what's wrong?" That's when my floodgates open. "Was that—?"

I shake my head. "I can't. I can't talk about it right now."

She walks inside, drops her suitcase, and I'm immediately engulfed in a fierce hug.

"We don't have to talk about it tonight. But we will talk about it before I go," she declares. "Tonight, wine and ice cream. Plus—"

She steps back and from her massive purse she pulls out a DVD. "I bought this."

Proudly, she holds up a copy of the latest installment of the Magic Mike series. It could have been sixteenth or seventeenth, for all I know.

"We can watch this on mute."

"On mute," I sputter, wiping at tears.

"What they're saying is not important." She laughs. "Let's just get drunk. Tomorrow, you get laid."

So despite everything, she isn't giving up her pursuit of happiness for Louise.

TEN
Past

❖

"CATE, I HAVE A SURPRISE planned for you this weekend. Are you game?" The excitement in Drew's voice is contagious.

Laughing, I say, "As long as it's legal, yeah."

"Oh, it's legal, sweetheart. The weather is supposed to be gorgeous. Highs in the high seventies and lows in the mid-fifties. It will be perfect for what I have in mind. I'll come up tomorrow night and we'll leave on Saturday morning. You're not squeamish are you?"

Squeamish? What does he mean?

"You mean like seeing blood and stuff? You're not going to make me look at icky medical stuff, are you?"

I have to hold the phone away from my ear because his laugh is ear-splitting. "No medical stuff. This is all fun."

That's a relief. "Okay, then no, I'm not squeamish."

"Great. I'll see you tomorrow. Can't wait."

It leaves me puzzled over what he has in store.

The next night, Drew pulls up, his car packed with all sorts of things. I peek in the back asking, "Whatcha got in there?"

"Stuff for our little trip tomorrow."

"Where are we going?"

"You'll find out." We walk inside arm and arm. Jenna is on the couch so we're stuck chatting with her. We end up ordering pizza and eating dinner together. Finally ... finally we head to bed.

"I didn't think I'd ever get you to myself," I say, as I pretty much attack him when my bedroom door closes. His arms wrap around me and he's a willing partner.

"I've missed you, Cate. You are a sight for my greedy eyes. But we need some sleep because we're getting up to catch the sunrise in the morning."

"Huh?"

"The sunrise. Tomorrow is a nature day for us."

Nature day? What the hell does that mean? I had plans to wallow in the bed with my sexy boyfriend and he wants to what—watch the birds and bees in the sunrise. What the hell?

"Don't look like that. You're going to love it. Just wait. Lift your arms." When I do, he strips me of my shirt. Then he helps me remove my jeans. When I'm down to my unders, he tells me to get in the bathroom and brush my teeth. As I'm brushing, I keep trying to guess where he's taking me. I come up with one huge blank.

When I come out of the bathroom, I fully intend to interrogate him, but he stands here, shirtless in his boxers and wearing the cutest smile. All my questions evaporate.

"My turn." He disappears and I ogle him as he goes. I climb into bed and wait. When the door reopens, he's smacking his lips and he reminds me of a cute little kid.

When he slides under the covers, my eager hands reach for him but he grabs them and kisses them.

"Cate, honey, you know if we start we'll never wake up before dawn."

"What in the world is so blooming important that we have to get up so early?"

"I can't tell you." He stills my roaming hands. "Showing you will be so much better."

Damn, this better be worth putting off sex for the night.

"Okay. Then kiss me goodnight, oh secretive one."

"You'll love it, I promise," he says as he presses his lips to mine.

"I won't love it nearly as much as I love having you inside of me."

"Damn, woman, you drive a hard bargain."

"Um, I think you have that backward. You're the one *driving* the *hard* bargain."

He pinches my butt and says, "Smart ass."

Curling up along side of him, I lay my head on his chest and the next thing I know, he's shaking me awake.

"Cate, come on. Get up and shower."

"Huh?"

"Up. Shower. It's time."

"What the hell time is it?"

"Five."

"Shit."

He drags me out of bed behind him, and we hit the shower. While I'm drying my hair, he tells me he's going to pack for me since he refuses to tell me where we're going. I find that unusual, but he's seen me pull clothes out before so he knows where I keep everything. Since it's only one night, I don't worry too much. In record time, we're out the door.

We drive to a local diner and grab breakfast to go—bacon and egg sandwiches and coffee. Then we hit the road. It's still dark out and I pester Drew about our final destination.

"You'll see. You don't have much longer to wait."

About twenty minutes later, we pull into a state park and drive through the entrance.

"A state park?"

"Yep." It's all he says.

He drives a bit before he parks the car. "Come on," he says, extending his hand. I follow him along a trail that leads to a wooden bridge. The bridge crosses a narrow river and on either side there are steep rock formations. It's quite beautiful even in the pre-dawn gray light. I'm sure when the day is bright, it's spectacular.

"Have a seat, my lady." Drew indicates a place on the side of the bridge so I sink down and sit. He does the same. "Now watch over there." He points over the rocks and we wait. About fifteen minutes later, the sun inches up over the horizon and its rays cast the rocks in an orange-red glow. At first, it's not noticeable, but when the sun gets to a certain point, it makes the rocks look like they're glowing. It happens so fast and lasts for only a minute or two, if we weren't here at precisely the right moment, we would never have seen it.

"Oh my god! How did you know?"

"By sheer accident. I literally stumbled upon it camping one day. It's really something, isn't it?"

"It's phenomenal. I've never seen anything like it! Thank you for showing this to me." I scoot my butt around to face him and notice he's not watching the sunrise at all. He's staring right at me. My body heats and my stomach flutters as that familiar sensation begins to grow within me. But then his words cause my heart to trip all over itself.

"Cate, it's nothing compared to you." His hand reaches for mine as he leans in to kiss me. Before my brain goes to mush, all I can think is Drew McKnight is all kinds of amazing.

We stay wrapped up in each other until the sun is high and the day is brighter. When he helps me to my feet, I can't help but observe his impish grin. "So what do you have up your sleeve now, mister?"

He winks. "You'll see."

We walk back to the car and after a few minutes of driving we pull into the ranger's station. "Stay right here. I'll be back in a second." He hops out and jogs inside. A couple minutes later, he gets back in the car. We drive around and soon we pull into a parking place that's marked as number twelve. It has a gravel square, picnic table, campfire ring, and now I figure it out.

"So, hot shot, I take it we're camping?"

"Yep," he says eagerly as he pulls the car to a stop. When he turns to me he still wears his boyish look. "How do you feel about it?"

"Hmm. You know, I went to camp as a kid and loved it, but I've never tent camped. So I'm game. But I have a question. Is this one of those tests?"

Confusion furrows his brow. "What do you mean?"

"Well, I've known guys who've tested girls before by taking them places or doing things they loved and if the girl didn't love it then that was it."

"So, you're asking me that if you don't love camping, am I going to end it with you?"

"Pretty much," I say, with a slight frown.

"Cate Forbes, do you really think that little of me?" He looks crushed. "Because if you do, I've done a terrible job of showing you how I feel about you."

I suck in my breath at his words. I can't let him feel like this so I blurt out, "No! It's just my inexperience, I suppose." Now I feel shitty for asking him that.

"Hear me now. If you hate camping, we will never do this again. That's not to say *I* won't, but you won't have to endure one more night of it. Understand?"

"Perfectly. And thank you. So you really love this, huh?"

His smile returns as he says, "Oh, yeah. Just wait." He starts pulling out all this gear from the back of his 4Runner and who knew? There is so much you need when you camp. After a while, I stop asking him what things are because I don't want to be a pest.

The day has warmed up significantly, and Drew has shed his sweatshirt, so now he wears a short-sleeved t-shirt. He's putting up the tent and I stare at the muscles in his arms as he works. I've never really focused on them before because I was always lured in by his abs and pecs, but damn, those arms are amazing, too. They ripple as he grabs this and that and I find myself licking my lips over and over. But what I really love is when he has to raise his arms and his shirt exposes that sexy strip of flesh. It gives me all sorts of ideas and makes me want to fall to my knees and take a nibble here and there. I think I'm going to love camping.

"Hey Cate, can you hand me that hammer over there?"

"Yeah, sure."

I find said hammer and then stand behind him as he pounds in the stakes. Only I don't watch him do that, because now I'm riveted on his ass. He's wearing my favorite jeans. They mold to his cheeks perfectly and I want to drop to my knees and bite him.

"Cate? Cate? Cate where are you? Helllllooooo?"

"Oh, sorry. What do you need?"

"I need help with the fly."

"Really? You need help with your fly?" Excitement surges through me.

He rolls his eyes, something he never does. "No Cate, not *my* fly. *The* fly. It covers the tent to protect us if it rains."

"Oh," I answer in a small voice, feeling disappointed and slightly stupid.

"What's wrong?"

"I kinda got excited about helping you with your fly," I answer.

As a smile forms on his face, his eyes dance with wickedness. He drops whatever he's holding, takes one giant step to reach me, and suddenly I'm enveloped in his arms before he kisses me. And it's some kind of kiss. Rough, demanding, and completely unlike gentle Drew. He manages to unzip the tent without letting me go. We crouch down, and crawl inside.

"Now you can help me with my fly all you want."

My hands fumble with his zipper as I go to work on his jeans and I feel his hands doing the same on mine. A question pops into my head.

"Is anyone around us?"

"I don't know, nor do I care."

"Can they see through this tent?"

"No, but they can hear."

Good to know. I finally get his pants pulled down enough for his cock to make an appearance, and all I want to do is lick it. So I do. He tastes so good and feels like velvet on my tongue.

"Cate. That's so fucking good." He strokes my hair in sync with my mouth. The faster I move, the faster his hand moves. Then he stops my movement. "I want inside of you."

I rise up and he roughly tugs off my jeans, freeing my legs. He grabs a condom out of his pocket and puts it on. "Ride me, Cate. I love to see you on me." I love to ride him as well, so I oblige us both. I sink down onto pleasure I've only known with Drew. There isn't anything sweet about what we do. It's hard and relentless as we lose control with one another. When our mouths slam together in a searing kiss, our hands join, and the brief slowness turns quick and rough as we soar to our peaks. His kiss swallows my groans and we both climax, Drew right after me.

"Jesus, what the hell was that?" I ask, when I can form a coherent sentence again. I'm still on his lap as we stare at each other.

"Damn awesome, that's what." He runs his nose along my neck and plants a dozen kisses there. "Every time with you is …" He slowly shakes his head as if to form words. "You never disappoint, Cate."

I can't stop the wide grin. It feels empowering that I can move a man the way it seems I've moved him. "Can I just say that so far, camping is pretty cool?"

His body rumbles with laughter. "I'll have to remember that line about the fly. That was priceless."

My grin turns into a megawatt smile. "Okay. The truth is I'd been checking out your ass. I can't help that you have such a fine ass."

"My ass? You're joking?"

I shake my head. "Why would I joke about your ass?"

"My ass, huh?" He shrugs.

"It's a damn fine ass."

He bellows a laugh. "I guess we should finish setting up camp."

"Probably." I don't object, because he's doing most of the work and I love watching him.

The day is filled with hiking to a gorgeous waterfall. By the time we make it back to camp, it's time to get dinner going.

That night he cooks salmon in a cast iron skillet that he puts on the grate the camp provides, over the wood fire. He tosses a couple of potatoes wrapped in foil into the fire beforehand, and has premade a salad.

"I can't believe this. It's restaurant worthy. I figured we'd be eating hotdogs or burgers on the high end. But this salmon … it has that smoky flavor from the fire."

"Yeah, it came out pretty good."

"So you've been camping your whole life?"

"Uh, Eagle Scout here." He gives me the salute.

"Eagle Scout? I'm impressed. You never cease to amaze me. But they didn't teach you how to cook salmon in Eagle Scouts."

He's laughing now. "No, this is my own invention. Every summer a group of us go camping and fishing and we try to out do each other in the cooking arena. This is actually a test dish for me. I've never done it before but I figured it had to be good."

He starts putting the graham crackers, marshmallows, and chocolate out for the s'mores. My mouth waters. "You ready?"

Licking my lips, I say, "Yeah."

He hands me a stick and a marshmallow. I load it up and start the roasting.

The fire crackles and our marshmallows are finished. We assemble our dessert and I take a bite. Marshmallow gushes out and smears all over my chin. Drew looks at me and shakes his head.

"These things tastes so good, but they are a mess." Then he leans over and licks the gooey stuff off my chin. "Mmm, I think you taste better than the marshmallow."

When he pulls back after not kissing me, his eyes crinkle at my confusion and longing. Then I realize he's teasing me and we laugh.

"How come you didn't get any on your chin?" I ask.

He shoots me a sly look and waggles his eyebrows. "Cate, I'm an Eagle Scout, remember?"

I almost spit out my mouthful of s'mores. Then he stands, stokes the fire, and puts another log on it. I love to watch him take care of this stuff. It's so ... manly. And sexy.

"Um, Drew?"

"Yeah?"

"I have to pee."

"Okay. You have a couple of options. The camp has restrooms. They are a fair walk from here, or you can pee in the woods."

"Pee in the woods? Aren't there critters in there?"

"Yeah, they have to have a home, Cate."

"So, like pee in the woods. What if I'm peeing in the woods, and a snake jumps up and bites Louise?"

He clamps his lips together and it's so obvious he's trying his best not to laugh. I let him know. "Don't you laugh at me, Drew McKnight. I'm scared to pee in the woods and I hate snakes. Louise does too."

"Louise loves my snake, Cate."

I punch him in the arm. "That's not fair. This is real. I have to pee and I'm afraid."

"Right. I'll go with you and ward off any wayward snakes that might be thinking of jumping up and biting Louise. How's that?"

I narrow my eyes at him. "What about other varmints, like rats and 'possum?"

He slowly inhales and clamps his lips again. Then he stands, holds out his hand, rifles through a bag, and pulls out a roll of toilet paper. He turns on a flashlight and leads the way into the woods.

When he finds the perfect spot, he says, "Here." And turns his back while I squat to pee. But in my haste, I do something really stupid. I yank my jeans down and leave on my unders, so I pee my pants. "OH NO!"

"What?" he spins to face me.

"I just peed my pants!"

"How'd you do that?"

I explain and he drops the flashlight as he doubles over laughing. Now we have to hunt the flashlight and I'm stumbling around trying to get my jeans off without getting my pee on them.

"So you peed on your 'unders'? I'm not sure what's funnier. You peeing on yourself or the fact that you call them unders."

"Oh, yeah, that's what my mom calls them so I just sort of inherited the term."

"I see. So, unders then."

"Yeah. Shit! Did you find the flashlight?"

Laughing, he says, "Yeah."

I get straightened out and decide to walk back to the tent bare-assed so I can clean myself up appropriately. Drew laughs all the way back and I can't blame him.

"Can anyone see me like this?"

"I don't think so. Besides, the water spigot is behind the tent so it blocks the view. Here's some soap and a washcloth if you want to clean off."

"Thank you for being so prepared."

"Eagle Scout."

I grumble and become the speedy cleaner-upper and am back in my jeans in no time.

"I cannot believe I did something so dumb."

"Uh, I'd have to agree."

Sometime in the middle of the night, I wake to hear all kinds of noises—growling, scratching, and other creature sounds.

"Drew! Something's trying to tear up our tent!"

"Huh?" a sleepy Drew asks.

"There's something outside of the tent trying to get us! Wake up!"

"It's nothing. Probably a raccoon. Go back to sleep."

He conks back out, leaving me to fret, awake. Of course, the giant, man-eating animals threatening to shred our tent and eat us alive resume their activities. I know there are dozens of them right outside of that flimsy piece of fabric that affords me zero protection from the monstrous beasts. I pull the sleeping bag over my head, as if that will help. But the noises grow even louder.

"Drew! Wake up! I think there's a grizzly out there!"

He sits straight up in the tent and his head wobbles around like one of those old timey bobble headed dolls. I think he's still asleep. So I grab his arm and shake him.

"Waaakkkeee uppppp! There's a bear out there!"

"What are you talking about?"

"Something is trying to eat us alive!"

One hand rubs his eyes. "Jesus. Cate, nothing is out there, other than pesky raccoons or maybe skunks."

"SKUNKS! WHAT THE HELL!"

Immediately, I scramble for the tent exit. Only there's a problem. I'm still zipped in my sleeping bag, and it's one of those mummy styles that narrow at the feet. In my crazed state, I try to stand, but end up taking a three-inch step and face plant in the dirt right outside the entrance to the tent. Now, I'm frantically trying to get up and run from the so-called grizzly bear or skunks that threaten to eat or stink me to death. My arms flail and I can't do anything because of the stupid sleeping bag. Two arms grab me and haul me backward into the tent. I'm a mermaid out of water, wrapped in downy fluff, thrashing around like a madwoman. That is until a strong and sexy body traps me under it, grabs my chin, and plants a searing hot kiss on my lips. Heat replaces panic, and my arms stop flailing and find their way around his neck, fingers winding into his thick waves. What's that mewling? It's only after he lifts his mouth off mine that I realize it's me.

"Much better," he says. "There is no bear, sweetheart. You're perfectly safe in here with me. What do I need to do to prove it to you?"

"I-I don't know. I'm really scared."

"I know and I don't want you to be. Let's have a look around outside. Would that make you feel better?"

"Maybe," I say, my voice squeaking.

"Okay. Let's go."

We get out of our sleeping bags, put our shoes on, and he grabs the flashlight. Then he does a thorough inspection outside of the tent and we don't find a single thing. He turns to me, tucks a tendril of hair behind my ear, and says, "Honey, this is their home. The little creatures live here in the woods. Many of them come out at night to eat. They live on plants and things. They won't hurt you, I promise. Sometimes they make noises when they feed and it sounds like they're growling, but they're not. They're more afraid of you than you are of them. Would you be afraid of a rabbit if you saw one?"

"No."

"Then you need not be afraid of these, either."

"But a skunk?"

"Won't bother you unless you threaten it."

I hang my head, feeling rather idiotic.

He puts a finger under my chin, saying, "Hey, you didn't know.

This is your first time out here. It's okay. Let's go back to bed." He takes my hand and I feel comforted, and not chastised. Wrapped in his arms, I fall into a deep hard sleep. By morning, I wake up surprisingly refreshed.

My stomach lets out the biggest roar and Drew chuckles in response. "I guess that's my wake up call. Time to feed my girl."

"Are you going to cook again?"

"Oh, yeah. You are getting the full camping breakfast."

"Is there anything I can do to help?" I feel pampered but bad that he's doing all the work.

He looks at me earnestly. "You can tell me you're having a good time?"

"Last night freaked me out, but I'm honestly having a good time with you."

He smiles, then proceeds to make coffee, bacon, eggs, and pancakes.

"I can't believe you did all this." I say around a mouthful of pancakes in syrup. "It's so good."

"Eagle Scout." That grin of his makes me want to kiss him.

I shake my head at him. Then I say, "Thank you for putting up with me last night. I guess that's what you meant when you asked me if I was squeamish."

"Sort of. That, and if you minded getting dirty." He reaches over and wipes my chin. "Just a bit of syrup you got going there."

"Jeez. First the marshmallow, and now this."

"You look cute with stuff all over your face."

"Just what a girl wants to hear."

"Okay. How's this? You're sexy enough to lick, Cate."

Oh, boy. "And will you follow through with that?"

Asking wasn't necessary. Drew always follows through. He scoops me up and zips us back into the tent. Later that morning, we pack up and head home. Well, head back to my home. Once there, Drew walks me to my apartment. He sets my bag down and holds my hand.

"All week I look forward to our weekends together. I had a great time."

I fall head first into his blue irises. "I did too. Peed-on unders and animal noises excluded. I'm sorry it's over."

"I didn't mind either of them." He pushes strands of wayward hair behind my ear before cupping the back of my head to kiss me.

This time the kiss is slow and I feel something tighten within me. And it isn't just my hormones. I feel it in my chest. This man has turned out to be everything I never thought I could have. As the emotions well up I feel something pool in my eyes.

When he pulls back to look at me, his expression turns into concern.

"What's wrong, Cate?"

I shake my head afraid of what I might be beginning to feel. "Nothing. I think something got in my eye." I'm not lying—the unshed tears still burn there.

His eyes focus on me and I smile. He leans in and blows across my eyes. "Better?"

I blink back the tears and nod. "I'm going to miss you. I wish you lived closer."

"I'm going to miss you too, my camping girl." He licks his lips and pauses as if he wanted to say more. "Next weekend?"

I nod, not strong enough to admit I'm falling hard for him. I can only hope that if he doesn't feel the same, I don't break when I hit bottom. He presses a sweet final kiss to my lips before he turns to leave.

"Next weekend," I say more to myself as he walks away.

ELEVEN
Present

———————◆———————

ROLLING OVER IN BED, I encounter a wall of pillows.

"Hey," Jenna's says, her head popping up on the other side of the wall. "I'm not ready to get up."

Her whine makes me smile because I've missed this girl so much. Only my grin turns into a frown as my head throbs. I can't remember how much wine we consumed last night. My confusion doesn't stop the playful jab that comes from my mouth.

"You talk in your sleep. You know that?"

"I do? What did I say?" she asks anxiously.

"Something about Brandon."

Her faces lights up. "Don't mention that name when we meet Kenneth tonight."

"Who's Kenneth?" My nose wrinkles up.

She waves a hand in the air as she falls behind the pillows to hide herself. "I met him at the country club a few months ago. I don't get to see him often. He lives here most of the year, but his family home is in Charleston."

"You haven't told me about him."

She doesn't come up to face me. "You know. It hasn't been serious, just a few hook ups. I think he's smitten with me. He comes from all the right stock. Still…"

I decide not to press her. She hasn't mentioned him before, but

I'll trust what she tells me.

"You kick, you know? That's why I have these pillows here."

"I do not," I whine.

"You do too. I swear I might have been better off on the couch. At least I wouldn't be black and blue."

I almost believe her until she bursts out laughing. I toss a pillow at her.

"It would be stupid for one of us to sleep on the couch when I have this queen-sized bed." I push up to my feet, not really ready to get up for the day.

Our conversation, like my brain this morning, drifts from topic to topic.

"If you wear those to bed, I know now why you aren't getting laid."

I glance down at my oversized tee-shirt and fuzzy sleep pants with tiny pigs printed all over them.

"What's wrong with pigs?" I ask.

She sits up and as I make my way toward the door to go to the bathroom, I add, "Ducks aren't any better."

She starts making quacking noises and I have a nostalgic moment. It's so strong I have a wild moment of wanting to move back to Charleston so I'll have more moments like this.

"Don't go all lezzy on me. Don't get me wrong, a little girl on girl action never hurt anyone. But you're looking at me like you should look at dick."

I feel my mouth turn into a pout as I change course and throw myself at her. "I missed you so much," I say as I land on the bed and crush her in a hug.

"Okay, okay, I missed you, too." She squeezes back and then I let her go. She sits up and props herself against the headboard.

"I know you told me everything last night, but we really didn't talk about it. I'm still mad at you for not telling me until now."

I sigh and glance at my cuticles, which suddenly need my attention.

"Don't you mutter at me," she says.

I can't remember saying anything.

"You ended up in bed with Drew and you say you didn't do the dirty with him. And the way you were all disheveled at the door. I would have sworn you had sex with him if you hadn't said otherwise. And you wonder why Louise is rusty."

"Louise isn't rusty. Sex is like riding a bike."

"In your case, a rusty bike, considering how long it's been."

I fall back into the wall of pillows. "What am I going to do?"

"I can't answer that for you. Part of me thinks that he's obviously still crazy about you and you would be crazy not to jump at that chance."

"How can I? Why doesn't he hate me?" I bury my face in my hands.

"Hun, he may be able to blame you for leaving. But he knows damn well why you left."

I press the heels of my palms into my eyes. "Every time I look at him, the guilt, it hurts."

She lets out a heavy sigh. "I haven't said this before because you had too much going on then. And you didn't need advice like this. But you need to forgive yourself. You did what you thought you had to do. He's obviously not mad at you. And it can't be easy for him either. If he's willing to give it a shot…"

"He wants me to call him Andy, like that somehow wipes the slate clean and gives us a brand new start."

"Drew?" she asks. I nod and she adds, "When I saw him I swear it was like seeing a ghost."

I glare at her. "Too soon?" She wears an *I'm sorry* expression.

"A ghost, really?" I wave a hand.

"I'm sorry, Cate. Drew – Andy—what the fuck, he's here now. You have to decide what you want and maybe going out tonight is the answer."

"How is that?

"There will be plenty of men—"

I cut her off. "How will that help?"

She holds out a hand. "Wait. Plenty of men, rich men—"

"Money doesn't move me, Jenna."

"Will you let me have a word?"

I sigh, then nod.

"If you keep an open mind, and you meet someone that interests you, then you know you're ready to move on. If you keep hiding out, how will you know if he's the answer or not?"

She has a point. "Fine, but I'm not sleeping with anyone."

"You don't have to."

"What? You're giving up your love quest for Louise?"

"I'm not giving up. I'm giving you a pass for tonight. Plus, I have a feeling the man of your dreams will be there tonight."

"Are you saying that because Drew won't be there?"

"I'm saying it because I have this feeling in my gut. Plus it doesn't hurt tomorrow is Halloween. Something's in the air and tonight's masquerade ball is a grown up version of a Halloween party. Lots of tricks and mischief. Time for you to give up some of your treats."

Her eyes spark to life and I know that look. I groan. I also know if I don't get out of here, she'll make plans for us to go to the spa or something. So I get to my feet and make a beeline for the bathroom. As I shower, I think she's right. I haven't given anyone a real shot since him. And maybe it is time for me to spread my wings and find out if this bird is ready to fly.

A few hours later after coffee and breakfast at a café near my apartment, a delivery arrives. A woman artfully carries several bags into my apartment.

"What's this?" I ask Jenna, hiding behind the closed door of my bedroom because I don't want to ask in front of the impatient looking woman.

"It's the Belfour treatment," she says like that's the answer to everything. When I fold my arms over my chest, she flutters her lashes and sighs. "Kenneth is providing my dress and yours although he doesn't know it yet."

That's Jenna for you. She's going to stick the guy with the cost for my dress too. "Jenna, I can't."

"You can because if you don't go, I don't go." She shrugs like that's the end of it.

Only it is, because protesting doesn't work. I'm forced back into the living room as the woman unzips gorgeous dress after gorgeous dress from individual garment bags by well-known high end designers. There are shoes and clutches as well, specially selected for each outfit. There is even lingerie. The woman, whose nose couldn't be any higher in the air, finally leaves after showing us everything and promising to pick up whatever we don't want the next day.

"Come on, pick one and then we can check each other out."

I point to the bags. "No, you first. This is your day, Cinderella. Your fairy godmother just left."

Her mouth purses. "I'm not Cinderella at this ball. I have my Prince and it's time you find yours, or at least one to try out for the night."

"Fine, but Cinderella doesn't pick first. Her evil step-sisters get the best dresses."

She looks aghast, pointing at herself. "I'm evil?"

"Yes, yes you are." I laugh. "You're the one that wants me to get dolled up and laid by some stranger as long as he can get to my glass slipper."

"Well, true."

She makes a fuss spinning around and leaving the room in a flourish with all the bags. She tries on the gowns and settles for a royal blue dress with lacy appliques that hide certain body parts while revealing skin in a way that is going to make Kenneth's jaw drop.

"Here, try this one."

She hands me a pure white dress. It isn't the one I would have picked, but she reminds me that Cinderella doesn't get a choice. So much for my big mouth. The gown dips low in a plunging neckline. If not for a sheer piece of fabric across the middle, I would pop out of it. Still, I won't be able to wear a bra and by the clingy look of the dress, I might not be able to wear underwear either.

After getting into it, I know I will have to go totally bare underneath the dress. When I walk out, Jenna excitedly claps. "That's it. That's the one."

"I haven't tried on anything else," I complain.

"You don't have to. Your body is perfect for it."

I hate to admit it, but the dress is stunning. There are no price tags, but I know the dress costs a pretty penny based on the store name printed on the business card the woman handed us before she left.

After changing back into our own clothes, we walk down the street to one of my favorite restaurants and eat a light lunch. Jenna's afraid if we eat too heavy we might be too bloated to fit our dresses well and I have to agree. The fabric on both is unforgiving. Every curve and rut will show.

Later, I shower and spend an hour flat ironing my hair to add some curls as Jenna helps me create a half up and down do. I can't help but feel like a princess when a limo arrives to pick us up. The ball is at a place I am unfamiliar with, so I'm glad for the ride. We are ushered out in red carpet style fashion, and even stop to pose for pictures before we enter. I recognize the Speaker of the House, who stands behind us. Although that is kind of cool, I wonder if all the men will be silver foxes or if some younger guys will make an appearance tonight.

Inside, a pleasant melody plays and some people dance as others mingle. But it's too quiet and I can't put my finger on it.

I slip on the white mask trimmed in silver with a feather plume on one side that was in a separate bag inside the garment bag for my dress. Jenna slips on her royal blue mask covered in black lace.

"Jenna," says a man with striking features and hair dark as midnight.

"Kenneth," she says with a squeal and practically leaps into his arms.

They only have eyes for each other for a moment and I kick myself for not asking more about him because I've only been caught up in my own life.

"Kenneth, this is my best friend, Cate McKnight. Cate this is Kenneth Belfour."

He takes my hand and kisses it. "Cate, I've heard so much about you."

I catch his accent and smile. I nod because I don't want to lie and repeat what he said. Before I have a chance to say anything, a stern looking woman in a server's attire appears. She puts her finger to her lips.

Kenneth appears amused, but cordially nods, and places a finger against his lips in acknowledgement. I turn to Jenna with wide eyes when I finally get why it's so eerily quiet despite the music. No one is talking. Jenna shrugs. I shake my head to let her know we will talk about it later. How did she expect me to meet anyone if we aren't allowed to talk?

A man walks up next to Kenneth and points at me. Kenneth smiles and gives the thumbs up. The guy takes my hand and kisses it. Seems to be the thing to do. I find myself dipping in a curtsey. He gestures to the dance floor and I agree because Jenna and Kenneth have conveniently disappeared.

At first the music is classical and we dance like we are at court in front of a king. I almost wish I'd known what kind of dance would have been required so I could have taken lessons. However, as the night wears on, the music changes into something a bit more contemporary. My partner is relentless and I begin to tire of being on my feet. Thank goodness, my stomach growls are absorbed by the beat that continues to pick up with more heady sounds. Jenna's salad choice for my lunch has fled the building and I'm starving.

I'm about to request a break when another man appears. His salty but more peppery hair is distinctive. That and Ted's mouth are a dead giveaway as to who he is. He nods at my partner and the guy nods back before stepping away. I'm not given the chance to agree or disagree to the hand off before Ted sweeps me away. He seems to favor the formal way of dancing as he sweeps me across the floor in contradiction to the music. I wonder how I don't stumble or step on his toes as he leads me through complicated steps. When the song ends, I shake my head.

Either I'm dizzy from him or lack of food and water. I gesture with my hand like tipping a glass to my lips as I glance above at the large chandeliers that dot across the room.

He nods, takes my hand, and leads me to a table with drinks and finger foods. A line of waiters appears in front of him with several trays of drinks and hors d'oeuvres. They take his attention off me for a second. As hungry as I am, I cram a cracker with some sort of substance on top into my mouth like an errant child.

When he turns back amused, I know I'm caught. I cover my mouth and chew quickly. He hands me a flute of champagne and I immediately drain it to clear my throat. We laugh before being hushed by the noise police. They seem to be everywhere. After a warning from a librarian looking woman, he winks at me conspiratorially after she wanders off to scold other party goers. He picks up a different cracker type thing that is topped with caviar. I allow him to place the bite size portion in my mouth. I chew while he waits for my reaction. For a second my eyes roll back as I want to moan at how good it is, but I know better. The noise police aren't far away. He reaches out toward me with his thumb poised to wipe something away from my face. Only an arm tangles from behind me and grabs me around my waist. I'm scooted to the dance floor leaving Ted looking on wide eyed. I wipe at my mouth fearing I won't have another chance.

The music changes from contemporary to a timeless melody. I recognize the beat of a tango immediately. Although I've never danced one, I'm led expertly in the movements as I catch sight of my dance partner. I'm so surprised my mouth must hang open the entire time. He dictates every move I make and we must look amazing, because I can see people nearby watching. His mask doesn't hide that lush dirty blonde hair and I'm lost in blue eyes that take me places I'm not sure I can recover from. He dips me just as the song ends with his mouth hovering over my neck for long seconds until he places a gentle kiss on my throat. Clapping ensues and he rights me on my feet. I'm left to watch as he disappears into the crowd, leaving me standing alone. However, as I search for him, I spot two guys that seem familiar from that drunken night out on the sidewalk with Mandy over a week ago. I'm pretty sure they're his friends. They stare at me like they know the depths of my sins.

Embarrassed, I turn away and head toward the food table where I snatch a glass of wine. I guzzle it and grab another. I open my clutch in search of my phone. We may not be allowed to talk, but no one said we can't text.

Me: 911

Jenna: What's the trouble?

Me: He's here.

Jenna: Who's here?

I don't get to answer before Ted appears. I slip the phone back in my clutch as he takes a third drink from my hand and offers me what looks like bruschetta. Silently, he tells me to eat something before I drink too much. He's taking care of me. And maybe that's what I need for the night.

Thankfully, Ted's attention is silently taken away from me as a woman walks up and steps into his personal space. I pick up another glass of wine and drain it before slipping into the crowd of people. I have no business with Ted. My head is miles away from making the right decisions tonight.

On the dance floor, I start to lose myself to the warm buzz that percolates in my brain from a couple of glasses of wine. I move without care to the Latin beat in the middle of a crowd, trying to forget what it felt like to be in Andy's arms. He came and left and I try to find peace in the music. If he wanted me, he would be there.

The next song begins with an erotic trumpet solo that's sad yet sexy all the same. When the drums set in, the beat begins to pick up and my hips move on their own accord. I see several guys watching me, including Kenneth's friend and it only spurs me on. I

135

raise my hands in abandon as I shimmy and slowly bend at the knees swaying my ass in a suggestive way that makes one guy bite his lip. In the back of my mind I hope that Andy sees me and wishes he hadn't walked away earlier. I continue to play with fire as I give good eye contact with a few of the men. Jenna is right. One of them is really cute. Maybe I should give someone else a try.

A man's possessive hands land on my waist. Even though he is behind me, I already know who they belong to. I have no idea how we ended up in the same place at the same time. Maybe fate. But I don't allow myself to think anymore. Thinking so far hasn't won me any prizes.

The melody carries me away to a tropical place where everything happens under a forgiving moon. His lips land on my neck, and I combust in raging heat. I rub against him, hoping he feels the fire he stokes within me. His hands move over my abdomen to press me further back into him. Then his magic fingers glide up and he's seconds away from cupping my breast. I don't care that we are dangerously close to appearing as though we are making love in front of everyone there. I want him in a bad way.

We continue our private yet public dance and capture the attention of the crowd. Lost in the beat, several couples around us have taken their dances to another place that isn't a ballroom. We are no longer the pioneers in changing the mood of the party to something much more seductive. As the sultry beat drones on, I long for four walls and a bed. I miss the fire of passion that this man can create in me.

It's the finality of the music with its mournful tones that remind me of the past. I want to stay there with him, but pain is like a lance in my chest. It has me running away as the song ends on a trumpeted chord. I don't look back for fear I might turn around and run back to him. I make it out onto a balcony breathing in frosty breaths. Despite the chilly night, the air is hot with desire and I'm gasping for breath. I hold on the frozen railing looking down as the DC's foot and car traffic continuously pass despite the late hour.

Why can't life be simple? I want to give up control and just feel, but I'm afraid to lose myself again. The pain nearly killed me before. I'm not sure I can do it again.

I hear the faint click as the terrace doors are shut. A quick glance over my shoulder and I see curtains on the window paneled door segment us from the crowd inside. He approaches from my blind side. A warm body, hotter than the sins I run from, presses to me. I begin to face him, but his hands are on my throat and chin, directing me to face forward, his message firm and clear.

He hasn't uttered a word, but I know his touch. His other hand snakes across my right fabric-covered breast and manages to undo the body tape on the left that holds the material secure to my skin. He slips his fingers under the fabric to caress the left breast. Just the briefest contact causes my nipple to peak. He nuzzles the back of my head as he presses his hardness against my bottom. I find myself pushing back. It could be the wine, but I'm tired of fighting. I need this more than I want to admit.

The music floats in through the seam of the door and I find myself grinding against him along with the tempo. He shoves a leg between mine and spreads them. His possession is all encompassing as his hand moves lower from my breast. I wonder how long he's been watching me tonight. Could his intense desire be born out of jealousy?

The slit in back of my dress plays an important role when his hand slips between my thighs and cups me as if to brand me. He easily parts my bare folds and isn't gentle when he thrusts two fingers inside my core. I can feel the wetness flow down onto his hand as he pumps into me a couple of times.

My head falls forward and I grip the railing tighter, the coldness forgotten as I allow his invasion. The cars on the street down below don't matter. I want to feel for the first time in far too long. I moan and suddenly his fingers are gone. His middle finger reappears to silence me first before gliding over my bottom lip. A second—maybe two—then he slips the digit into my mouth, forcing me to taste my arousal on his *fuck me* finger. I don't even care as I wrap my lips tight around it before he pulls it back out.

He bites my neck, not hard enough to break skin, but enough to send early warning shocks through my center. He takes hold of my throat again as he works what I think might be his zipper. He lifts my leg with a hand underneath my knee and positions me. I'm surprised when his length bumps against my opening and I feel that he's somehow managed to protect himself and me from what comes milliseconds later.

Rewarded for all the time I waited for this moment, I gasp as he pushes into me. His hand comes up from my throat to cover my mouth as if the noise police will show up. He fills me in a way I didn't think I would remember. I bite his finger—none too gently— when it gets too close to my teeth. He doesn't make a noise. He continues to move in me, forcing the railing to make contact with my clit in a way that starts the countdown to my orgasm.

With a hand to muffle my cries, he wedges himself deeper inside me with every punishing stroke. He bends me slightly forward and the angle allows him to hit that spot that shoots off my first orgasm like a firecracker. He isn't done. He rolls himself inside me to stroke my g-spot over and over until I'm building for another explosion I'm not sure I can handle. His hand leaves my mouth and somehow he has my dress parted so that he's able to cradle my center and move the pad of his thumb over my clit as he continues to fill me inside. The scream that escapes my throat is muted by the note the trumpet hits in the crescendo of the song.

Then he is gone, leaving me to almost crumple to my knees. The force of both orgasms weakens me to the point that gravity begins to pull me down. He spins me around and I get a flash of hot azure eyes before he guides me to my knees with his larger than life cock in front of my face. Condom gone, two fingers that still taste of me are there to open my mouth as he guides himself inside. He sweeps my hair aside as I give into his silent demand. I hollow my cheeks and tighten my lips around his thick length. Even at this angle, he can't fully sheath himself in my mouth.

I swirl my tongue as I bob up and down him. His grip tightens in my hair almost painfully and it's not long before I taste the effects of his orgasm shooting to the back of my throat. I see the muscles in his jaw clench as he muffles his own sounds of pleasure. I swallow everything before he finally pulls out. He neatly tucks himself back in his pants before drawing me to my feet. He spins me around and dusts me off.

At first, I'm too afraid to face him. My lips still tingle from everything we just did. Then I hear the patio doors open, and I turn around. I'm too late to say anything; his dark blond head has already been swallowed by the crowd. I stand there wondering what the hell just happened. I'm literally shaking when I pull out my phone. It takes a few times before I'm successful at texting Jenna. There is no way I can stay. I feel the wetness on my legs. The lighting might be dim inside the ballroom, but I imagine my white dress isn't as pristine as it was when I walked in. I'm going to catch a cab home and text Jenna that. I dare not make a move until I get a chime back signaling I have an incoming text.

Jenna: Wait for me.

Me: No. Stay. I'm going straight home. You have a key.

I'd given her one in case she wanted to stay out with her guy and come back late.

Jenna: Are you sure?

Me: Absolutely. I'll catch a cab.

Jenna: Text me when you get there.

Me: I will

The party is in full swing. I'm not the only person who's being naughty and uncaring of peeping eyes. I worm my way through the hedonistic crowd. Mandy was right about this party. And what I've done isn't me. I don't have sex in public places. To top it off, he left without so much as a goodbye or even a thank you for the fuck. We were alone. He could have broken the 'be silent' rules if he wanted.

Still, he'd never been like that with me before. How much did I really know about him anymore? Maybe there's a reason behind the new name. I would have never guessed he would have come to a party like this. Then again, who am I to judge? I'm here.

I push through the doors where two large men in suits stand on either side. I hit the elevator button and pray I will be alone. Luck is on my side and I make it down to the lobby without another soul getting on. I'm practically running to the street with my hand raised for a cab when a cool voice calls out.

"Cate."

I turn and Ted is standing in front of an open limo door.

"Do you need a ride?"

I almost say no, but I find myself nodding.

"Come," he says waving me over.

TWELVE
Past

———◆———

ON THURSDAY, IT'S BECOMING CLEARER that I may have to push my trip to see Drew back to Saturday. I know if I go on Friday, I won't get any work done and I have two papers due on Monday. It kills me to do it, but I force myself to make the call.

Drew's cheery voice answers, "You're just the person I was hoping it would be."

My spirits sink even further with his words. His smiling face pops into my head and the image makes my craving for his hands on my body all that much stronger. "I hate to be the bearer of bad news, but ..."

"That damn but," he says with a chuckle. "What's up?"

"School. I'm underwater with my writing. I know if I come tomorrow I won't get done what needs doing, and I have two long articles due on Monday. I'm going to have to push back coming until Saturday."

"Hey, Cate, no worries on that. You have to do what's important and school is important. Understand?"

"Yeah, but I want to see you, too."

"And you will. Just a day later than previously planned. And don't worry, I'll make up for it," he says. I can almost see him grinning.

"Oh yeah? Tell me."

"Hmm. I don't think so. Have I ever told you how much I adore your neck? That should keep you guessing." His deep chuckle sends shivers up and down my spine.

"You're not playing fair."

He laughs again. "I know but when did I say I played fair?"

I rifle through my thoughts for something to latch onto, but come up empty. "Did I ever tell you I fight back?"

"You did now."

My mouth turns up at the corners.

"But Cate, I play hockey, remember? I know how to fight really dirty."

Oh my god. The way he says, "Really dirty," makes me want to jump his bones. Like right this second. How will I ever wait until Saturday?

"Um, Cate, are you still there?"

I swallow the huge heated lump of desire that's knotted up my throat and croak out, "Uh, yeah. I'm here."

"Good. Because I like the turn this conversation has taken. What I think I'd like to do is put you in my penalty box and perhaps punish you."

"P-punish me? How?"

"Mmm, I'll have to let you think about that for a while."

Holy shit. What is he talking about here?

"So, Cate?"

His deep sexy voice has me all worked up. "Yeah, Drew."

"What time do you think you can be here on Saturday?"

"Sin. I mean six."

A salacious chuckle hits my ear. "Hmm. That's the time my game starts."

"I'm talking six in the morning."

He roars with laughter. "Eager, are you?"

"I would probably call it something else, Drew."

"Oh, and what would that be?"

"I'll have to let you think about it for a while."

His laughter rings out over the phone.

"Oh, and Drew, just so you know, Louise is all hot to see you, too." In a breathy voice, I add, "Be ready for me at six on Saturday." As I'm moving the phone away from my ear, I can hear him still laughing.

Friday is nothing but constant work. But the good part of it all is that I accomplish what I set out to do so I can go to Drew's with a guilt-free conscience. I pack a bag at night so all I have to do in the morning is take a quick shower and go. I set my alarm for four forty-five, and fifteen minutes later, I'm on the interstate. An hour later, I pull into Drew's parking lot. As if on cue, he stands in the doorway of his apartment, waiting.

Wearing faded jeans with the top button undone and nothing else except his mussed up hair, he looks good enough to eat.

"You didn't even give me a chance to knock," I say.

"I figured you'd be on time. You said six and it's six." His mouth curls into a sexy smile so I stand on my toes and kiss him. He palms my ass and lifts me so we're the same height, and kisses me back. "Is this everything?" He's referring to the small bag I'm carrying.

"All except for the couple of things I have hanging up, but I can grab those later."

"Good," he says as he kicks the door closed behind him. Then he starts peeling me out of my clothes. "These were in the way."

"I noticed. But what about you?"

"Not a problem." He unzips, tugs his jeans down, and is nice and naked underneath.

"I like," I say as I run my hand over the ripples of his torso. But I don't linger because there is something else that begs for my attention. "Mmm, I *really* like."

"Not nearly as much as I do." Abruptly, he picks me up and throws me over his shoulder as I squeal. "I've been waiting far too long for this, Catelyn."

His bedroom is mere steps away. He tosses me on the bed and follows me down. Kneeling, then sitting back on his heels, he says, "I'm too impatient for much right now." Ecstasy is soon mine because Drew is right. He's impatient. His tactic is to make me come and he achieves that with a stellar performance.

Kissing Drew is a sexual experience in itself. I love the magic of his mouth and tongue. It's like stepping into a fairy tale, one that's all sparkly and filled with fantastical enchantments. My body becomes something completely different when he kisses me.

While inside me, he moves his hand between us; I know it won't be long.

"Cate, I'm not going to last much longer."

Thank god. "Neither am I." I cry out his name. He pulls out

and I wonder what's happening until I see him come all over my belly. Only then do I realize he didn't have a condom on. *Shit.*

It takes me a while to catch my breath, but when I do, I want to chastise him. He beats me to the punch. "I got so wrapped up in you, I forgot the condom. Thank god, I remembered to pull out."

Rubbing my forehead, I say, "Uh, you know that's not one hundred percent."

"Cate, it'll be fine. You won't get pregnant. But I would like for you to go on some type of birth control. Are you willing?"

"Of course. I just haven't had the time."

"I understand," he says. "If you'd like, I can call the residency clinic here today to see if they can fit you in."

"Yeah?"

"Sure. They open at seven thirty."

"On Saturdays?"

"Yeah. They have Saturday hours."

"Okay."

"Stay put. Let me get a cloth to clean you up."

He hops out of bed and I get to admire the fine view as he walks. By the time he gets back, I'm half asleep. He cleans me up and I drift off, curled up beside him.

The next thing I know I'm waking up to the smell of bacon wafting in the room. Lifting my head, I find myself alone in the bed. After a speedy trip to the bathroom, I borrow one of Drew's T-shirts and pad into the kitchen where the bacon aroma has my tummy rumbling for a taste.

"Good morning sleepy head," I hear his voice coming from behind me. I turn to see him with a mug of coffee and his computer on his lap.

Yawning, I stop to stretch. "What time is it?"

He moves the computer, stands, and I'm in his arms as he answers, "Ten. I thought you might need the sleep."

"Ten! I never sleep this late!"

"Must've been that amazing lover you encountered this morning."

Just to keep that cocky attitude of his in check, I say, "Naw, I think it was all that damn studying I did this week."

His hangdog expression has me giggling. I ruffle his hair, saying, "Of course it was that amazing lover I encountered." Then I kiss him. "And where can I get some of that bacon? All that lovin' has made me famished."

"Right this way, pretty lady." He takes my hand and guides me to a seat at the counter.

"Have you eaten?"

A guilty expression clouds his eyes. "Uh, yeah. I've been up since seven thirty. My hunger overruled my desire to wait. I'm sorry."

"Don't be. I'm sorry I slept so late."

He starts pulling things out of the cabinets. "Would you like some eggs?"

"You know, bacon and toast would be great. And some coffee, please."

After passing me a mug of java, he pops some bread in the toaster. When it's done he butters it and asks me if I want jelly on it. I decline. Then he hands me a plate with the toast and a pile of bacon on it. I sip my coffee and delight in my toast and bacon.

"I wish bacon was a healthy food option," I say, biting into a piece of the stuff.

"That would be nice, right?"

"It's the best." I polish my plate clean and stick it in the dishwasher when I'm finished.

"Oh, you have an appointment today at one. Is that okay?"

My brow furrows because I'm lost. What kind of an appointment?

"Remember? Birth control?"

"Oh, damn. Face palm. I forgot. Yes, that's great. Thanks for pulling the strings for me. Do you know who I'll be seeing?"

"Not really. She's a friend of a friend."

"Nice. So, what's our agenda today?"

"Other than your appointment and the game, we're open. Anything you want to do?"

I waggle my brows and he chuckles.

"Yeah, why don't we wait for round two until after your appointment? They'll most likely do a gynecological exam on you."

Oh. This is weird. It's not something I would normally discuss with my date, or with a guy for that matter. My cheeks heat up.

"Cate, I know you feel awkward about this, but you don't have to. It's not something I ... I guess what I'm trying to say is dealing with this type of thing isn't uncomfortable for me so I don't want you to be uneasy about it. I know I take this all for granted and it may be asking a bit too much of you."

Damned right it is. This is freaking weird. Can I stick my head under the sofa right now?

"I can tell I'm making matters worse. I'll just shut up."

Good idea. "I think I'll shower," I say. So I can wash all remaining traces and evidence of you away now. Jeez. Why did I consent to this? What the hell was I thinking? Ok, Forbes, get it together. This is a hell of a lot better than a baby, right?

When I turn to walk to the bathroom, a pair of arms snatches me and I find I'm caught against what feels like a concrete wall. Drew's head drops down next to my ear, and he murmurs, "Please don't be shy about this. It's all normal stuff. Your body is beautiful to me, all the tiny pieces of it." Then he nuzzles me with his nose before releasing me. He's right. This is silly. He's seen all the tiny pieces of me, too. There isn't any reason for me to be shy now.

Turning in his arms, I loop my hands behind his neck and smile. "It's going to take some getting used to is all. I've never openly discussed this stuff."

"I get it. Now go shower and we'll figure out what to do today."

While I shower, I decide I want to see Drew's hospital. I'm interested in what he does every day. So he gives me a tour and then he takes me to the clinic early so he can show me around because he sees patients here, too. "You really like it here, at this hospital and all, don't you?" I ask.

"Yeah, it's worked out great for me."

"And you never considered going back to Charleston for school or residency?"

"You know, I did for a time. But then I had an awesome relationship with my professors in med school here and everything was sort of set up for me, so I thought why ruin a great thing?"

Mulling this over I have to ask him. "So how will this work for your fellowship? You say you want to do oncology, right?"

"Exactly. Maybe then I'll go back to Charleston. They have a great oncology program and then it might be time to spread my wings. With oncology nowadays, all the major cancer centers are linked one way or another so it's not like it used to be."

"That makes it better for greater opportunity then."

"Yes!" he answers.

By now, we're getting close to my appointment time so I suggest we head to that department. When I'm finished, Drew is

145

waiting for me.

"How'd it go?"

"Great. I have a prescription for the pill. The doctor said it was the best option for me. Can you drop me by a pharmacy where I can also get refills back at school?"

"Sure."

He takes me to one of those chain pharmacies and as soon as we verify it won't be a problem, I get my birth control.

We leave and on the way to the car, Drew pulls me into his side. "So, when can you start on these?"

"I'm supposed to wait until after my next period."

"When's that due?"

"This week."

I am awarded with a beaming smile that makes me melt. Right then, my stomach growls.

"Hmm. Someone's hungry."

Damn stomach. "Yeah, I guess so."

"Let's eat. I'll need some food and we won't eat dinner until after the game."

He takes me to a cute little pub downtown. The hostess seats us and makes doe eyes at Drew the whole time. During lunch, Drew's phone rings, and when he checks it, he doesn't answer. But he also doesn't say who it is. I wonder why. I want to ask him but I don't want to be nosy, either. Then our waitress keeps stopping by and the only way she could be any more obvious about her attraction toward him would be if she actually drooled at our table. I want to say something clever, but I don't want him to think I'm jealous. It's times like these I wish Jenna were in my hip pocket.

He must finally notice that I'm sort of pouting because he asks, "Is all okay over there?"

"Fine." My clipped tone indicates otherwise.

He sets his fork down and looks at me. "Did I do something, Cate? And don't make me try to be one of those mind readers, please."

Shit, he's right. I can't very well blame him for the way others treat him. Smiling, I say, "No, I'm fine. Truly."

"You're sure? Because a minute ago you looked like your beer had kerosene in it."

"I'm sure."

He lifts my hand and brushes his lips over my knuckles. It

happens at exactly the time our mooning waitress shows up. She shoots me a dirty look and in turn, I fire off a smug one at her. Then I lay my hand over his and say loud enough so she can hear, "I think we should have dessert at home."

"Is there anything else I can get you or will a check be all?" the waitress asks as she glares at me.

"Oh, I think we're quite finished here," I say sweetly. "Aren't we, honey?"

"Yeah." Drew puts some cash on the table and he stands.

"You aren't going to wait for the check?"

"This is more than enough. Let's go!"

Eyes as blue as the sky on a crisp fall day stare at me and he's completely erased all of my insecurities about him with that single, encompassing look. A hand extends out to me and I take hold of it. It takes everything I have not to throw myself at him and kiss him.

We walk arm in arm to his car and by the time we get home, my hand is in his pants and we act like two teenagers making out in the car. "Cate, I ah," and that's all he says before he sinks his hands in my hair and kisses me. We both pant and claw at each other and I think it's me who suggests going inside.

"Good idea." He gets out and rushes to my door, where he helps me out as well. Then he all but drags me to the front door. I stop and think about a quote I read somewhere, sometime about it not being the journey but what you did along the way. And being with Drew reminds me of that. I want to remember every single second of the time we spend together because being with him is that fabulous. I want to inhale his touch, his embrace, his kiss, his beauty, every tiny thing about him. I want to engrave them into my brain so every minute detail is committed to memory, because one day, when I'm old and senile, I want to be able to rely on those memories and pull them forth and with a smile, be happy they were all mine.

His mouth is against mine when he asks, "Whatever put that satisfied look on your face?"

"Thinking about you."

Without moving his mouth, he says, "Well, let me add to it then."

"Be mine and Louise's guest."

He doesn't refuse my offer.

A couple of hours later, we sit in the parking lot of the ice rink.

He turns to me and smiles, but then his face becomes serious. "Jesus, Cate, don't look at me like that."

"Like what?"

"Like you'd give me the world with your body right here and now."

I wasn't aware I was staring at him like that. But it's true. I would do exactly what he said, without compunction or hesitation, if I could. And I never imagined any guy would ever make me feel like this. Whatever we have going on between us is getting deeper. On the one hand I love it, but on the other, it scares me to death.

He must see that it frightens me because the next words out of his mouth soothe me. His voice is low when he breathes them. "Don't. Don't let it scare you away. You are the one person I want to explore. Let's explore us, Cate. This is the real thing. I know it is." His mouth crashes into mine, bruising it, and taking my breath away. He's right. I can't deny this—whatever it is between us and I can't push him away, nor do I want to. This may be our one chance in a lifetime to find our own chunk of happiness.

"I won't let it scare me, Drew."

"Good. Now kiss me for good luck."

When we enter the ice rink, I instantly spy Caroline. She's sitting in the same area we sat last time. She sees me, too, and waves. Drew tells me he'll catch me after the game.

"Cate, I'm so glad you're here!" Caroline says, when I take the seat next to hers.

"So am I. Do you think they'll win?"

"I hope so. Sam's been talking about this game all week. I'll be glad when it's over."

I can't help but laugh. Then I look up and see HockeyHo entering. "Oh my." We both giggle.

Caroline sucks in her breath and I raise my brows. "Would you look at that?"

I cough to cover my bark of laughter. "What the hell? It's getting close to Thanksgiving. Does she not realize we don't live in Florida?"

"Guess not," Caroline sputters between giggles.

HockeyHo is wearing a bikini top festooned in feathers.

"Maybe she thought the shirt with Drew's number on it wasn't enough." I'm just fascinated by her brazen behavior.

"Oh, dear. Check out her hat."

She's wearing one of those straw cowboy hats and on the front is pasted a sign that reads, "I'm in love with Drew McKnight." Then on her ass she has written, "Drew's #1 Fan."

"Have you seen her ass?"

Caroline is doubled over. "She won't give up. I give her credit for perseverance."

"Yeah, or just pure stupidity."

The guys take the ice and HockeyHo goes crazy. I can't help but roll my eyes. Drew looks up at the stands and he appears to be quite mortified when he sees her. I give him a thumbs up. Sam punches him on the arm and the rest of the team starts giving him hell. Poor guy. I have to feel sorry for him. But dayam, that chick is a kook.

During the game, HockeyHo plasters herself and her double D's that threaten to pop out of her bikini top against the glass and it looks like she's dry humping it. Where do people like this come from? I'm at a loss.

Drew plays magnificently, and HockeyHo plays the part of the hooker cheerleader. Unfortunately, I'm so caught up in her, I miss one of Drew's goals. Damn her! When the game finally ends, Caroline and I run down to where the team is and congratulate them. Drew leans over and kisses me. HockeyHo is not happy.

Caroline and I wait near the entrance to the locker room, but HockeyHo sidles up to us. I'm not sure if she thinks she actually has a chance with Drew or not. It's embarrassing to watch her. The guys funnel out of the locker room at last and when Drew spots her, he is reluctant to move. I make it easy on him and run into his arms.

"Babe, that was awesome. Congrats on another win." He lifts me up and kisses me, and not just a shorty either. When he releases me, I say in his ear, "Just keep talking to me all sexy-like, so she doesn't get a chance to butt in."

His hand is in my hair, but HockyHo, having no couth, butts in anyway.

"Hey Drew. How about let's go out to celebrate?" HockeyHo is definitely slow on the uptake.

"Huh? No, I'm going home with my girlfriend and we're going to have sex." Then he whispers to me, "Sorry, but I think it's gonna take everything I've got to get rid of her."

"I don't think a woman who dresses like that is ever going to take the hint."

"You're probably right."

Then HockeyHo says, "Well, next time then," and sashays out of there.

We all can only stand and stare at her. What else can we say?

Finally Sam asks if we're headed to dinner and we all decide to grab a bite to eat at a local restaurant the team frequents. Some of them are already here when we arrive and Drew introduces me. It's fun to watch the guys banter about the game. But I notice that Drew doesn't hand it out as much as the others.

Caroline and I sit together and I ask about it. "Do they always act like this?"

"Oh, today isn't as bad as usual. Most times they are like twelve-year-olds on the playground at school. It's ridiculous. I give Sam a hard time about it. It's nice to have another girl around, let me tell you."

"It must be the testosterone thing."

"Yeah, but consider yourself lucky. Drew is better than most of them. I think he's much more modest. But the others—when they bring a date, oh god, it's awful. You would think they were playing king of the mountain."

We share a good laugh.

"It looks like you keep Sam in control, though."

"Oh, you better believe it. If he starts acting like one of them, I have to jerk a knot in his drawers really fast. Once, I went out of town to visit my family in Michigan, and when I came back, he had reverted to being a Neanderthal. It was ridiculous. He was in the doghouse for a week. I do not put up with that crap at all."

Drew pops over to us and asks, "What has you two laughing so hard?"

"You guys and the way you act," I say.

"What's wrong with it?"

"It only reminds me of Mikey Farrell in elementary school." Then I explain that Mikey was the class clown who was constantly getting sent to the principal's office.

The look on Drew's face is priceless. Then it morphs into something completely different. His gaze becomes hot and smoky; he rips my chair away from the table, puts his hands on my sides, and lifts me out of my chair. "Does this remind you of Mikey Farrell?" And his lips crush mine in an intoxicating kiss. I'm so shocked by his actions, my mouth opens, and he takes advantage of the opportunity by sliding his tongue into the cavern of my mouth. In the background, the inevitable catcalls can be heard, but they barely register as I wind my arms around his neck.

"Get a room!"

"Take her home, bro!"

"Do her! Do her!"

He finally releases me and says, "We need to get out of here."

My head spins from his kiss and I can only nod. I glance to the left of his shoulder to see Caroline giving me the thumbs up.

"My purse," I say weakly.

"Got it," is his response.

Giving Caroline a small wave goodbye, I let Drew lead me out of there. We're half-naked by the time we get home and I'm glad we make it safely. That would be difficult to explain if we had gotten into a wreck. I need to ditch the underwear so these times in the car make it easier on us.

THIRTEEN
Present

━━━━━━━━━━◆━━━━━━━━━━

ANOTHER PAIR OF EYES MEETS mine as I slide into the limo. I don't have a chance to ask or choose another seat as Ted sandwiches me in and closes the door.

"Where should I drop you?" he asks.

Flustered, I spout off my address, wondering how I can move from between Ted and the woman I remember packing up and leaving the first day I was at his office. She sits with her legs tucked beneath her. The black dress she wears blends into the interior of the car but it's the sparkling studded choker she has on that draws my attention. I don't remember seeing her at the party. And that piece of jewelry is so spectacular, I know I would have remembered.

Ted informs the driver of my address by pushing a button on a console near his seat. When he turns back to me, his smile is warm and inviting.

"The party a little too much for you?" he asks glancing down at my dress.

I follow his eyes to my once immaculate white dress which now bears crease marks and looks slightly less perfect than when I put it on.

"I'm just tired." A part of me worries I smell of sex even though I don't detect anything myself.

The woman next to me has no notion of personal space. She crawls over my lap and presses her face to Ted's. I'm so uncomfortable with half her body still suspended over mine that I try to push myself back into the leather seat.

"Now, Pet," he says, but I don't glance in their direction. I'm sure my cheeks are super-heated much like the core of a nuclear reactor. "Sit over there and be a good girl."

Is he kidding? But no, she does exactly as he requests. Pulling back, she sits up before moving to the seat perpendicular to ours on all fours like a cat.

"She's not here to play?" the woman purrs.

I feel Ted's eyes on me but I refuse to look at either of them. I feel like I'm intruding on something that is totally out of my league.

"We're giving Cate here a ride. That's it."

I can practically feel her pout by the little mewling sounds she makes. Dear god, is this the Twilight Zone? I don't realize I've moved, putting more space between us until Ted asks, "Comfortable?"

Chancing a glance at him, I nod. "Sorry, I probably should have taken a cab. I didn't know you had company."

His lips slyly curl. "It's really no trouble at all." He winks, then adds, "I enjoyed dancing with you tonight."

It's an odd thing for him to say with his date or companion sitting right across from us.

"It was a fun evening." I wish again I'd cabbed it.

When the limo pulls to a stop and I see my building through the window I'm grateful that I live in the city near most everything.

"Thanks for the ride," I say as Ted exits and helps me out of the car and onto the slick sidewalk.

He walks me all the way to the front entrance. He takes my hand and kisses it. "Lovely Cate, I'm sorry Pet made you feel uncomfortable. But I'm glad I got to spend more time with you. Until Monday."

He kisses my hand again before he walks back to the limo. By the time I make it up to my apartment, my phone blows up with texts from Jenna.

Jenna: I'm so mad. I'm headed back to your place.

Jenna: I can't believe him.

Jenna: I'm mad at both of them.

The texts are coming in so fast. My own reply keeps getting derailed. I have to wonder if I'd hit a dead spot and the texts are finally showing up on my phone. Finally, I get my text off to her.

Me: I'm home.

Jenna: Good. I'm on my way up.

I've barely placed my bag down when I hear keys rattling in the door. Jenna bursts through like a hurricane. She halts when she sees me. "What happened to you?"

"You first," I say because she must have left right after me. "Why are you here and not with Kenneth?"

She sighs and plants herself on the sofa which lets out air much like her own sigh. Another reminder—never order furniture online without sitting on it to test it out. I sit on the opposite end and face her waiting for her to spill her guts.

"Everything was going great until Brandon texted me. I thought it was you, so I didn't hide my display when I looked at it."

I can tell she's worried because she begins to bite her nail, a nasty habit that only shows its head when she is stressed, which isn't often.

"Okay, we need to back up a little. Who is Brandon anyway? I thought your mechanic is named Brandon."

"He is," she says glancing heavenward.

"So why is your mechanic texting you on a Saturday night?" I ask, staring at her pointedly.

"That was Kenny's question." She tosses up her hand like it's ridiculous. "He also wondered why I had a picture of Brandon sitting on my couch as his profile picture on my phone."

"And?" I ask because I happen to agree.

"And Kenny has no reason to be jealous. Brandon and I are just friends. We talk. There can't possibly be more. Can you imagine me bringing Brandon home to meet my parents? They'd freak just at the sight of his tattoos. It's just that he listens to me, you know." She stops to catch her breath. When she begins again, her first words sound like she's reading the opening line of a novel. "It began one day when the laws of the universe conspired against me. My car was in for an oil change. And he insisted on getting coffee for me and me getting my shit, as he says, off my chest. And we…"

She waves her hand grasping for a word. "Clicked."

My brows rise and she begins to back pedal.

"As friends. I don't know what Kenny has to be jealous of. Kenny's going places. One day he'll be a Senator like his Dad and I'll be his wife. He's exactly the kind of guy I should be with."

When Jenna gets like this, it's best not to argue. I don't agree so I change the direction of the conversation.

"Let's see this picture of Brandon."

Hesitantly, she pulls her phone out of her clutch. As she scrolls, I can tell when she's reached the picture. Her whole face lights up. She hands it over. There, with a smirk that spells bad boy, is the object of Jenna's affection whether she wants to admit it or not. "He's hot."

She shrugs and I take in the flop of dark hair and sleeves of tattoos. The boy has a face that would make girls lift their skirts, that's for sure.

"You like him," I say, because it's not really a question based on her body language.

She sighs again. "I'm in like with him," she finally admits. "Now it's your turn. What did you do at the party, because you look like Louise finally got hammered and not in an alcohol way?"

At least she admits she may have a thing for this Brandon guy. So I tell her about dancing with Kenneth's friend, then Ted. "He was there," I whine.

"Who was there?" Her face is screwed up with confusion.

"Andy."

Her jaw drops … and stays there.

"Exactly. One minute I'm dancing with Ted, the next I'm doing the Tango with Drew. Then there is this freaking sexy song and I'm on fire. I want him so bad, so what do I do? I run."

"Not again," Jenna sighs.

"I couldn't help it. My heart was on fire and it hurt from all the pressure. I swear I wanted him and hated him in the same moment."

"And then what?" Her eyebrow lifts in question.

"I let him screw me on the balcony. Who does that? It was hot and dirty and freaking right out in the open where anyone could see."

A giant puff of air whooshes out of her lungs. "Whoa. Sounds more than hot." She raises her hands toward the ceiling and grins.

"Thank baby Jesus, Louise finally got serviced."

I grab a pillow and toss it at her. "It's not funny. He gave me the best orgasm I've had in ages and walks away. Why would he do that?"

She purses her lips and I can tell she thinks I should know the answer. "Oh, I don't know. To teach you what it feels like to be the one left standing when someone runs away from you?"

I close my mouth and drop my head. "So this is my fault."

She moves over and wraps me in a hug. "I love you, Catie Bear, but Drew..." When I give her the evil eye, she corrects herself. "Andy has to be fed up with all this running you do."

"So I'm wrong."

She pulls back and glances at me. "It's not a matter of being wrong. You need to decide what you want. You need to forgive yourself and give him a chance or move on for good. You can't keep hiding away and not going out because you're afraid to love him or anyone else."

"I need some wine," I say, because she's right.

"I need some ice cream. So let's have both."

After filling our bellies as we teasingly man-hate, I toss and turn so much during the night that Jenna ends up sleeping on the couch. When morning comes, we spend the rest of our day together down on the National Mall and that's not code for shopping. We take selfies making it look like the Washington Monument is in our hands and we give Abe the he's looking good eye wink in our selfie with him. It's so hard when we grab an Uber to take her to the airport. I glue myself to her until she promises another visit soon if I just let her go.

The other reason for the Uber is that I've decided to go see Andy at work. He has rounds at the hospital today. Thanks to Jenna's detective skills by calling his office and feigning an emergency, the call service gives up his location. God, I love that girl.

The Uber ride to the airport and then to see Andy is a bit long, but I realize it's something I must do. Andy is a great guy and I'd be stupid not to take this second chance with him.

Channeling my inner Jenna, I manage to find out where the Oncology Department is from the person at the information desk at the hospital. More importantly, I procure a visitor's badge so I won't be accosted by security as I roam the halls. It is a matter of a tiny lie about surprising my brother, the doctor, on his birthday that does the trick.

I'm excited as I exit the elevator. I think about pulling Andy in a supply closet and having my way with him. I'm practically vibrating with need as I finally make it to the cancer ward when it hits me. I have to stop because it feels like something has a vice grip on my heart. I can't breathe. All it takes is to see a female patient with a hairless head to be reminded of just where I am and all the memories flood back. I lean against a wall wondering how Andy does it. How can he stand to be here? It hurts me so much and I know he wants to help people beat this nasty disease. I know that. I steel my spine and control my breathing. *This is part of the package, Cate. If you can't deal, you need to walk away from him.*

I conjure an image of Andy in my head. He's worth it, I tell myself three times then I straighten and begin to walk. There is a gaggle of nurses animatedly chattering at a nurses' station I pass. They remind me that it's not all death and total destruction of the heart on this floor.

"She's with him right now," I hear one of them say.

Gossip is a fact of work life, I think. I should call Mandy and see how her weekend went with Daniel. I have to remember that even with Jenna not in town, I'm not alone.

As I turn a corner, a flash of movement down an alcove catches my attention. I have to cover my mouth to stop the gasp of air from escaping. The wild cap of dirty blonde hair above a blonde sporting a ponytail is enough for me to make out Drew with his lips attached to another woman. I don't waste time as my feet squeak on the tiled floor. I run and this time it's with good reason.

On the sidewalk outside, a blast of frosty air hits me. Snowflakes begin to fall and I try to decide if I should set up another Uber or just take one of the taxis waiting at the curb. I am downtown and cabs are plentiful. I head over and get into the first one in line.

"Where are you headed?" An older guy who reminds me of my Dad asks.

"DC."

"Whoa, lady, that'll cost you. The Marc and Amtrak train station is only a few blocks away. It would be a lot cheaper."

I could catch a train to Union Station, and then take the subway home. I have a feeling none of the cabbies will want to make the trip and it might be faster than waiting for an Uber to show up after I book it. "Take me to the train station then. And thank you for the tip."

"No worries. We're heading into the holiday season soon. We all need to save our pennies."

I nod, grateful for some friendly and honest people. Luck is with me. An Amtrak train will arrive in minutes. The ticket is less than twenty dollars, which is a steal. The ride gives me time to wonder what's changed about Andy. He's clearly not the person I remembered, but then again, neither am I. That night, I barely sleep and make it to Ted's office feeling ragged.

"He will see you now," his admin advises. Her perfect smile is a little too perfect to be real. However, my brain is sleep deprived and I can only hope to get through this meeting without making a fool of myself. My words are a jumbled mess in my head. My points all seem pointless.

"Cate," Ted says halfway to the door to greet me.

I let him take my hands and I give him a professional shake.

"Have a seat."

His office is massive and the row of windows behind his desk give a perfect view of the Capitol. His desk looks heavy and made of solid wood. As he sits, he looks every bit the commander and chief of his domain. I plant myself in a chair that's more modern than the desk and set my bag on the floor. I admire the artwork splashed around his room, and I mean that literally and not figuratively. Each canvas boasts a splash of abstract art. However, the longer I stare I start to see shapes and maybe objects within the chaos.

"You like art, Cate?"

I snap my head in his direction. "I'm not an avid art lover but yours is so unusual it catches the eye."

He nods. "They are done by a local artist. I was lucky enough to persuade her to part with them."

I can imagine his persuasion and decide not to ask any more questions.

"So," he begins. "I received a copy of your report. It seems you believe Jeffery and his team are doing a good job."

"I do."

"And you weren't swayed by your fondness for them?"

"No sir," I said beginning to feel like a scolded child.

"Sir? Cate, I'm not that much older than you. Call me Ted."

"Of course. Ted it is."

"Your only recommendation is to have a set of written policies and procedures."

I nod.

"Great. According to your boss, you also majored in journalism. I think you would be perfect for documenting that process."

"I—"

"I've already worked it out with your boss. We will be seeing more of you here."

I shut my mouth. As much as I balked about writing in school, I do enjoy it. "Okay," I say enthusiastically. "However, I do wonder if I could borrow the team and a conference room." I hold up the shopping bag. "I brought a peace offering. I know they will be upset when they find out why I was really here."

He nods. "I think Jeffery is going to miss you. He's raved about how wonderful you are. He'll have to start the interview process over again."

I want to know about the beef between him and Jeffery but don't ask. I begin to get up.

"Cate, just one more thing."

I sit back down.

"I hoped you could help me out. I would like it if you would join me Saturday evening for a charity event."

I open my mouth to speak but close it again. I take a moment because I'm tired and I'm not sure I've heard him correctly. He clasps his hands and smiles as if he can read my mind.

"What about..." I begin, but realize I never learned the woman's name.

"Pet."

I nod.

"She'll be out of town visiting her mother this weekend. But Cate, I really like you. I won't beat around the bush. I want to get to know you better."

"But I work for you," I blurt.

"Technically you don't, and not even for appearances' sake anymore. I'm contracting you out to write policy and procedures that are already in place. So there is no ethical reason we can't go out."

A flash memory of Jeff's warning about Ted and the sight of

Pet on the seat in the limo give me pause. "You seem like a decent guy, but I'm not in the business of dating men who I know are seeing other women."

He steeples his fingers. "Why don't we see how the night goes? I'm not opposed to putting an exclusive label on a relationship for the right woman. And we don't have to put pressure on ourselves for the night. We'll just see how it goes with no expectations."

Jenna's advice floods my head. *If you're not going to date Andy, then give someone a chance.*

"Okay."

His grin is wide and I can see him calculating his win. I almost backtrack on my agreement.

"Don't worry about something to wear. You're a size four I'm guessing, a thirty-six C in the chest, and a seven or eight shoe."

My mouth drops. He's dead on. "Size eight shoe."

"I have your address. I'll have something sent over on Saturday morning."

I think about Jenna and Kenneth sending her clothes. Is that how all wealthy men operate?

"I can find something on my own to wear."

He shakes his head. "Let me for springing this on you at the last minute." I nod. "Then let's go inform the team they had a spy in their midst," he says conspiratorially.

I groan and he laughs.

The rest of the week breezes by. I spend part of the time at his office and I'm forgiven by Ted's accounting team, but I can see the hurt and mistrust in some of their eyes. Ted e-mails them part of my report which gives a glowing review and eases some of the tension. By Friday, I almost accept an invite to hang out with Mandy but I haven't been sleeping well, so I decline. She makes me promise I'll go out with her next week when I inform her of my date for Saturday.

Andy hasn't called and I'm not sure that's a blessing or a curse. He's obviously moved on but it hurts more than I thought it would.

Saturday comes with a winter mix falling from the sky. Undaunted by the weather, my clothes for the evening arrive as promised by Ted. I stare at the beautiful things he's sent. The dress is black, classic, and simple, but quite stunning on. The forgiving fabric won't show the lacy La Perla bra and panties that are included. The garter belt and thigh highs are a surprise, but then again Ted seems very detail oriented. However it's the red-soled heels that make my heart flutter ... until I reach the rectangular box. Inside there is a ribbon choker with a large onyx stone that dangles from it. The stone is crowned in tiny sparkling black jewels. There is also a matching pair of understated stud earrings. I don't want to be dazzled by his wealth of gifts, but it's hard not to. I probably have enough time to go out and find a dress of my own.

"Jenna, what should I do?"

Her voice is filled with humor. "Let him spoil you. He can afford it. Otherwise, he wouldn't do it, Cate."

What he spent is probably nothing to him. So I dress and fix my hair in an understated, yet elegant do, so it won't compete with my outfit and jewelry. By the time I get to Ted's limo, I feel pretty.

"Cate, you are exquisite."

"Thanks. You're look very handsome yourself." And he does. He's classically dressed in a tux with a white shirt and it suits him. "I have to say I'm a little hesitant to wear this jewelry."

His finger brushes the stone and I have a moment to wonder if he'll touch my skin. He moves his hand and the moment is gone. "They are expensive but not so much as you would need a body guard to wear them. And it's my gift to you. Don't argue. I can already see it in your eyes. I wouldn't have done it if I didn't want to. And there are no conditions on the gifts. I don't expect anything from you tonight. We're just two friends out on the town."

Hardly, but I won't say anything. He isn't a struggling college graduate. He's a billionaire and whatever he's spent on me is probably what he spends on a good bottle of wine.

I change the subject. "Are you going to tell me where we are headed?"

His eyes twinkle. "I hope you like the ballet. We are headed to see the Nutcracker opening night. All proceeds benefits one of my favorite charities for kids."

The ballet and the Nutcracker to boot. It reminds me how close we are to the holidays. I couldn't have imagined that it would be a star studded night. We pose for pictures on a red carpet. I feel mystified how my life has changed in the last couple of weeks. This marks the third event I've been to where celebrities in attendance are not by chance but expected.

"Cate," a woman calls. Before I can stop her, Désirée is air kissing me. "Wow, Ted, you look very dapper this evening."

Ted obliges her and gives her the two air kisses I neglected to give the fake woman.

Her grin turns megawatt and she aims it at me. "Drew and I missed you last night at the White House Press Dinner. Now I see why he didn't bring you. Oh, and I must get a picture of the two of you."

My hand comes up to block the picture but she beats me with her tap on the phone. I'm too late as her thumbs furiously move across the screen. "Young and in love. Short and sweet for InstaGram don't you think?" She winks before striding off.

I groan. I have no doubt she's posted the picture more than just there. I don't know what I should worry about, the picture or the fact that Andy was out with her last night.

"Shall we?" Ted holds out his arm, clueless about my inner turmoil.

I accept his arm, giving into the night. Ted seems like an okay guy. Andy is obviously out of the picture. It's time I move on, take back my life, and enjoy it a little.

We end up in box seats alone. The ballet is spectacular. After, we have a late dinner. Ted is cordial and our conversation easy. He doesn't leer at me or make suggestive comments. I begin to think Jeff's dislike of the man has nothing to do with Ted at all.

"Why don't you get along with Jeff?" I ask.

He sighs and uses the napkin to blot his mouth. "Truth?" he asks. I nod. "This will sound somewhat arrogant but there is no way around it. Simply, Jeffery was interested in a woman who was more interested in me." Shocked, I feel my eyes reach my brows. "Don't look so surprised. Jeffery is a bit on the sweet side but he's into women."

He laughs at my open mouth. We end the night with Ted regaling me with tales of Jeff's escapades Ted's caught him in. None involve work and I get that Ted is professional and wouldn't give me information about his employees that is work related.

When the limo stops in front of my building I can honestly say I had a good time. Ted, again the gentleman, walks me to my door with my arm in his.

"I had a lovely time Cate. I hope you did too."

"I did."

He takes my hand and kisses my knuckles. "I would kiss you Cate, but I don't want to scare you off, as I'm sure Jeff has done his best to do. And maybe some of what he's told you is true. But I can make this an experience of a lifetime for you, and who knows what the future would bring. I'm headed to France for the holidays after Christmas and through New Year's. Maybe you would consider joining me."

I'm too stunned to say anything. He leans down and presses a kiss to the corner of my mouth, just missing my lips. I watch him walk away and get back into the limo. When he drives off, I try to decide if I should be worried about what little Jeff has actually told me. He hasn't said much but implied many things. I turn to head inside when I hear my name.

"Cate."

I swivel around so fast I sway, catching myself. What I find is Andy closing his car door and walking toward me. I didn't hear an engine cut off, so I wonder if he's been waiting for me all this time. He looks distressed, still in his scrubs. His hair is disheveled and his face sports scruff. He stops a few feet away from me as his eyes drift the length of my body and back again.

"God, you take my breath away." His words are smooth but the sadness in his eyes takes away from his compliment. "You went out with Ted Caine. I saw the pictures."

"Andy." The word leaves my mouth on the wind, drifting away as if we are two ships passing in the night.

"Did he kiss you?" The anguish in his voice is palpable.

I shake my head no, unable to speak for fear my voice would break.

He comes forward and cups my frosty cheeks with his hands. His warm lips against mine take away the chill in the air. When he pulls back, I find myself reaching for him but he steps out of my reach.

"I want you to be happy, Cate. I always have. You're the one woman that's made me want to change my life to make you the center of my universe." His eyes are filled with so much emotion I'm captured in them. "Maybe fate is wrong or my interpretation of it. I won't chase you anymore. I'll leave you to be the Princess Ted can make you be." He glances at my dress which can partially be seen through the opening in my wool coat. "Maybe it's better this way."

My heart knocks in my chest. Being this close to him brings back all the feels that had me falling for him in the first place. I don't understand his words and why he's so upset with me. He's the one who moved on. Yet he's here. I watch, unable to move, unable to breathe, as he briskly walks away. He's gone so fast he's almost reached his car as I feel his name on the tip of my tongue.

FOURTEEN
Past

———————◆———————

IT'S ALREADY NOVEMBER AND THANKSGIVING is bearing down upon us. And then finals will be here. It's hard to believe I've been seeing Drew for almost two months. The difficulty in believing it is every time I'm with him, every weekend we spend together—and we've haven't been apart much at all—is better than the last.

As I'm thinking about him, my phone lights up and it's him. The simple fact of seeing his name causes my heart to stutter. Right now the sixty miles that separate us seems more like a thousand. Then I'm thankful he's not any farther than that.

"Hey," I answer with a grin.

"Hey, back atcha. Question. Are you going home for Thanksgiving?" Drew asks.

"Yeah, are you?"

"Uh huh. I'm leaving Wednesday but I have to be back Friday night because I work that weekend."

"Oh, that's not good."

I can almost see him shrug. "Naw, it doesn't bother me. It's the life of a resident. I have to pay my dues. Next year will be better."

"You have the best attitude," I say. "I'm leaving Tuesday and I'll be back on Sunday."

"Cate, I'd like to invite you over to meet my parents on

Thanksgiving Day. Can you come? We could work it around your family's schedule."

Holy crap! Meet his parents! This is serious stuff. Am I supposed to reciprocate?

"Um, yeah, we could do that. I can ask my mom what time we're doing our dinner and all."

"That would be great. You all will love each other. I just know it." The smile in his voice warms my skin.

"Drew, if they're anything like you, how can I not?" And that is the truth. They raised this man to be who he is—kind, honorable, trustworthy, and considerate of others. What's not to love? "And I'd like you to meet my family, too." Where the hell did this come from? I haven't even told my mom I'm dating anyone. *Shit!*

"I'd love that. But I'll meet them when I come to pick you up."

"Oh, right. I didn't think about that. My family is crazy. I'm just warning you."

"Crazy as in craaaazy? Or crazy as in haha?"

"Uh … both. Ask Jenna. She can give you the scoop."

"I want you to give me the scoop," he says.

I cringe as I say, "Yeah. Okay. Well, my mom can be awesome, but she can be very cantankerous, too. And Dad, he's sort of a hypochondriac. So, I'll apologize in advance because when he finds out you're a doctor, he's going to hit you up for all kinds of medical advice on his so-called diseases."

Drew only laughs at my Dad.

"Hey, laugh now, but just wait. They'll drive you fucknuts. I love 'em to death, but at the same time, they make me batshit crazy. You know?"

"Yeah. Sounds like my Aunt Edna. God, that woman is as sweet as they make 'em but loony as hell."

"Maybe we should invite Aunt Edna over. She sounds like she'd fit right in my family."

"What about your siblings?"

"My little sister doesn't pay them any attention. She's too selfish and my brother gets doted on because he's the star athlete."

"What sport does he play?"

"All of them. But not hockey. No hockey in Charleston, you know."

Drew chuckles. "Yeah, true."

"I'm surprised my dad let any of us play sports. He's such a worrywart about us getting hurt."

"Overprotective?"

"You wouldn't believe it if I told you. I had to beg for roller blades. He told my mom to only let me skate on the grass! Of all things!"

"Hmm. I've often wondered how I would be as a father."

This conversation is turning into something a little deeper than I expected. "Oh yeah?"

"I think sometimes I'll be like your dad. When I see kids coming into the clinic all banged up, it makes me curious. What about you?"

"I haven't given it much thought, to be honest."

"Do you want kids, Cate?"

"Yeah, I guess so. Someday."

"Good. I was hoping you'd say that."

Why? Does he want kids right away? What's his deal here?

"I want to have kids someday, too, but not for a while."

Thank the lord! "Yeah, a long while," I laugh. "Hence, the birth control." Hint hint.

"Sounds like someone is pretty career minded."

"Hell yeah. I haven't worked my ass off in school not to use this double degree. I'm hoping to see it pay off here soon."

He sighs heavily into the phone. "Oh, Cate, have some confidence in yourself. Of course it's going to pay off. Take a look at yourself. You are a brilliant, talented, clever, woman. You have a very bright future ahead of you. You are going to dazzle your prospective employers, mark my words."

His words make me glow inside. "Drew, you make me feel so good about myself."

"You don't need me to do that. Seriously, Cate. You're the total package, if you would only see it for yourself."

That night I tell Jenna about our conversation.

"You're meeting his parents? At Thanksgiving?" Her sly grin tells me more than her words.

"What? What does that mean?"

"Drew McKnight isn't one to take girls home to meet his parents, that's what."

"And how do you know that?"

Jenna gives me one of her looks and says, "I'm his best friend's sister, remember? I know a lot more about Drew than you think I do."

"Oh, yeah," I say in a puny voice. "Shit. This is a major deal, right?"

"Oh, I'd say it's a seriously major deal." She grabs her phone and starts texting a message. A few minutes later she receives a response. Jenna grins as she hands the phone to me. It's from Ben.

Ben: WTF! Drew is taking Cate to meet the P's! How did I not know this????? Major shit going down at the McK's crib.

"Oh no! Will I be on display or something?"

"Or something? Hell yeah. And you know his mom, right? Big Charleston society in all the major circles and all that. I'm talking money, Cate. Did I tell you?"

I'm going to fucking kill her. "No, you did not tell me. How the hell could you leave something like that out? What the hell is wrong with you?"

At least she has the courtesy to look chastised, though knowing Jenna, she doesn't feel the least bit that way at all. Then she lets out a gurgle of laughter. "For all of Letty's money and the circles she runs in, she adores Drew and is the sweetest woman you'll ever meet. I promise you'll love her and she'll love you because you're not one of those simpering bitches that always pants after her son."

"Letty?"

"Mary Lettington Standford McKnight."

"You're joking. She's one of those Standfords?"

"Yep," Jenna says, with a satisfied smile. "Hence, Andrew Standford McKnight."

"Jeez. Thanks for the warning."

"I really do think the two of you will get along perfectly."

"Well, did I tell you Drew started talking about having kids?"

That shut her up for a minute. Then she suddenly looks like the cat that swallowed the canary. "I knew you two were perfect for each other. You need an older guy. That's why all the guys you were meeting weren't getting your panties wet, but one date with Drew and BAM. You were so done. I think I hear wedding bells in your future."

"Oh, miss fortune teller, let me fill you in on a little secret. I think I hear wedding bells in your future too."

"Funny, Cate. But I'm serious. You have to admit it. He is

perfect for you. What more could you ask for?"

I have no answer for her, because she is absolutely right.

"This is moving too fast, Jenna."

"Okay, I can see why you might feel that way. But it's not fast at all. You've been seeing each other for about two months now. And Cate, Drew isn't some young dude that has no idea what he wants out of life. He's got his shit together and is going places and so are you. But, don't worry. You're not going to do anything until you graduate, so sit back and enjoy the," she clears her throat in an exaggerated manner, "ride." Then she slaps her knee and howls with laughter.

"Don't quit school. Your comedy routine needs work," I say drolly.

Two weeks later, I find myself pacing in the foyer of my parents' home. Drew should be here to meet my family any minute. My fifteen-year-old sister skips down the stairs and says, "Nervous about the new boyfriend? Catelyn's boyfriend's coming to visit." She sings it loud in an obnoxious voice.

My mom yells from the kitchen, "Are you sure he doesn't want any leftovers?"

"I don't know Mom. You can ask him yourself." She's asked me this a dozen times already. Then my thirteen-year-old brother ambles in, looks at me, shrugs, and walks back out. His earbuds are in so he couldn't give a crap about me or Drew.

"Do you think Drew would have time to chat with me about my family history of colon cancer?" my dad wants to know.

"No, Dad! He's not here to discuss your health matters and he's not your doctor." We've been through this at least ten times today. This is going to be torture. Why did I agree to this? I should've just met him at his house.

A motion outside catches my eye and I look in the driveway to see him pull up. Should I open the door or wait for him to knock? I'll meet him on the porch to warn him.

I run outside, straight into his arms.

"Hey," he catches me before I have a chance to blurt anything out, and presses a light kiss to my lips.

"Oh, I missed you," I say instead.

"I like that greeting."

He looks like sunshine on this gloomy day and I've never been happier to see anyone before. I want to cling to him and never let him go, but I can't because I'm sure we have an audience.

"Listen, my family is insane."

He laughs.

"No, I'm serious. I just came out to give you a quick warning."

"I see. Well, let's go meet the insane Forbes family then." He winks and we enter the den of craziness.

My family stands in the foyer like a troop of soldiers, ready for inspection.

"Mom, Dad, this is Drew McKnight. Drew, my parents, Bob and Lydia Forbes, and my brother and sister, Shannon and Eric."

Greetings are exchanged, but my sister appears to be drooling over him. She stands there, mouth open, dreamy eyed, not speaking a word. This is not her usual style.

"Shannon, you can go now," I tell her. She doesn't move. "Shannon?" Finally, I spin her around and push her in the direction of the kitchen. My mom asks Drew about five times if he wants any leftover Thanksgiving food. I want to scream, "NO, MOM, HE DOESN'T." But I don't think it will do any good. And at last, the coup de grace is my dad asking Drew about his opinion on digital rectal exams in colon cancer screening. REALLY DAD?

"And on that note, I think it's time Drew and I head on over to his place. Are you ready Drew?" I'm quite sure my face is the color of the cranberries my mom served at dinner and my expression must look like a clown's. I need to get the hell out of here.

I usher Drew out so fast it looks like we're on skates. I literally dive into his car, not giving him a chance to open the door for me. When he gets into the driver's seat, he's shaking with laughter.

"That was some kind of exit you made."

"Are you kidding me? I had to get out of there. I am so mortified by my dad!"

He only laughs. "Don't worry about it. You wouldn't believe the questions I get asked by patients. That was nothing. And he has a concern due to family history."

I bury my face in my hands. "I don't care! I told him not to do that to you." My voice is muffled.

"Babe, it's fine." He tugs the back of my hair so I'm forced to face him. The corner of his mouth turns up and his eyes dance with mirth. "I thought your mom was the funniest, trying to get me to eat. Do I look like I'm starving?"

"No." I bust out laughing. "But you put my sister in a boy-coma. I've never seen her shut up like that before. I may have to borrow you on occasion."

"Anytime," he purrs.

Then it hits me. I flash him a quirky grin and say, "You called me babe."

"I did. Is it against the rules?"

"No. It's just you've never called me that before."

"It's not a term I've ever used in the past. But when I think of you, sweet honey comes to mind, too."

"Isn't that a bit repetitive?"

"No, because honey isn't sweet enough to describe you." His gaze grabs mine and drills into me. It's intense and heated and I grab his face and plant my lips on his.

"Cate, I could sit in your driveway and make out with you all evening, but I'm afraid we'd have a captive audience and my mother would never forgive me."

Glancing up, I see four pairs of eyes peeking through the blinds. What the actual fuck!

"Oh gawd! Let's go!"

He's chuckling as he backs out of the driveway. On the way to his house I ask him to fill me in on his parents. He doesn't give me near the information that Jenna did.

"My dad is a doctor, too. But he didn't want me to go into medicine. He thinks it's a thankless profession for the most part—too many hours spent away from the family. And in retrospect, I suppose he's right because in his day, things were different than they are now. I won't say you don't work your ass off, but they have hospitalists who handle inpatient services, unlike in his day, so call is a lot better."

We pull into their driveway and, of course, their house is lovely. It's not extravagant, but it's beautiful. His parents greet us at the door. Jenna was right. Letty is very warm and gracious and I'm instantly drawn to her. Drew's father, Ray, is quiet, taciturn. I get the feeling he's not impressed with me. Drew must get his outgoing personality from his mother. Letty steers us into the den, which is a warm and cozy room, lit with a fire, and offers to get us drinks. Drew pulls me onto the loveseat next to him while his dad wanders off to get us each a glass of wine.

"So Drew has talked about nothing but you, Cate. He tells us you're at his alma mater right now and that you're a junior."

"Yes, ma'am. I'm studying accounting and journalism."

"You must be very busy," she says.

Understatement, I think. "I am and I'm looking forward to Christmas break."

About that time, Ray returns with our wine and I thank him. Drew gets his looks from his father because Ray is very handsome, but he gets his beautiful eyes from his mother.

"So Cate, do you expect to have a difficult exam period?" Letty asks.

Ray sits and stares. It's a bit disconcerting, but Drew picks up my free hand and brings it to his lips. It surprises me how affectionate he is with me in front of his parents.

"Cate will be very busy. She works her ass off, Mom."

I turn to Drew, pretty shocked that he said that in front of his parents.

"Well, son, after she's finished, you'll need to spoil her then. She'll deserve a break." I'm surprised to hear Ray say that.

"Oh, I don't know about that," I say.

Letty leans toward me and says, "Cate, honey, let me give you a little piece of advice. When a man says they want to spoil you, don't you ever refuse it, you hear me?" And she winks.

I laugh and say, "Yes, ma'am."

"Mom, don't worry. I plan on spoiling this one a lot. And I mean a lot." Then he kisses my cheek.

"I can see that, Drew."

We chat for quite a while and I have to say I feel very much at home here. Letty and I get along so well I hate to leave, and I've even warmed up to Ray. But it's late and I'd like to spend a few moments alone with Drew. So on the way home, we park at a now empty tourist area, and sit and chat a bit. He's leaving the next day on a late flight because he has early call on Saturday morning.

"When will I see you?" he asks.

"Ugh, finals start the week after next so I'm getting down to the grind."

"What are your Christmas plans? Are you coming back here?"

"Yeah, but I'm driving since I get a month off."

He takes my hand and rubs a circle over my knuckles with his thumb. "Why don't you spend some time with me before and after?"

I think about his proposition and it sounds enticing. I could stay with him for several days after I'm done with exams, then go home. And after the holidays, I could go to Drew's and return to school the Sunday before classes. "Yeah, that sounds pretty awesome. Are you coming home at all for Christmas?"

"Yeah. From the twenty-third to the twenty-eighth."

"Oh, cool. Then I could come back to your place for New Year's maybe?"

"You'd want to?"

He seems eager but then I just realized I've invited myself to his place for a date. Is that too forward?

"Yeah, I mean if you didn't have other plans."

"Cate, I only want plans with you. In fact, if we haven't said this, I want us to be exclusive. I mean I pretty much took it for granted since we're sleeping together and I knew you weren't the type to sleep around."

"No, not the sleeping around type. So yeah, I'd like exclusivity. In fact, I demand it," I say with false bravado.

"So do I." His deep voice sends shivers racing down my spine.

A thought strikes me. "Hey, does this mean we're going steady?"

That corner of his mouth lifts and he says, "Not only steady, but strong." He leans over and our lips meet. "Since we're going steady, could I interest you in some car sex?"

Giggling, I answer, "I don't know. The closest I've come to it is with you."

Even though it's dark, the light in the parking lot reflects the sparkle in his blue irises, and he says, "Since you're wearing a skirt, I thought you planned it."

"Well, if your dad doesn't mind—since it's his car." A giggle slips out.

"We won't tell him."

He helps me clamber over the center console until I straddle his lap. It's a good thing the seats recline. My skirt gets bunched up around my waist and we must be starved for each other because things progress at a rapid pace. It's all so incredible and the only thing I notice afterward is that it really is true—the windows get steamed up during car sex.

When I mention this to Drew, he says drily, "I'm glad you were so taken with my skills, that's all you observed."

"After," I remind him, "not during."

"Thanks for clarifying." He slides out and I ask him if he has any tissues. Fumbling in the console, he offers me a handful. When I move to slide to my seat, he stops me with his hands. "Stay. I'm not quite ready for you to leave here yet." His hands hold my thighs and his pants are unbuttoned and pulled down to his knees. Damn, the man is sexy.

"I want to spend the night with you," I say.

"No more than I want you to. This coming home sucks."

We both chuckle.

"You look hot as hell sitting on my lap like this." His half-lidded expression has me thinking the same of him. He grabs the tissues I hold in my hand and proceeds to wipe me, but instead of cleaning me up, it turns us both on. I watch in fascination as his dick springs to life. Not bothering to ask, I take it in my hand, lift my hips, and impale myself on it. His hands move from my thighs to my hips and his fingers sink into my flesh as he lifts me up and down, helping me, guiding me. My hands settle on his shoulders and I rest my forehead on his for a second, until he says, "Kiss me, Cate."

This is one of those moments when you think back and remember how silly it all is, but here we are, in a car for Pete's sake, having some of the hottest sex. But that's not all it is. It's the way he stares, the way he breathes my name, the way his hands hold me. And it's what's happening to my heart. Drew McKnight is tangling himself in it until I don't know which part of it is him or which part is me. And what I thought would scare me doesn't. Not one single bit. I want to fall with this man. And I want to fall hard. But I think I already have. The question is—how does Drew feel?

I don't have to wait to find out. Because we both climax shortly after, and as we sit in the aftermath, he lightly kisses me and says against my lips, "Catelyn Forbes, I love everything there is about you. I never thought there'd be someone like you. I'm not a believer in there only being one person for each of us. But I know damn well it's hard to find that perfect match. *You* are my perfect match. Please tell me I'm not alone in the way I feel."

I brush his hair off his forehead and say, "You're not alone, Drew. I love you, too."

FIFTEEN
Present

———————◆———————

MY CHEST CONSTRICTS AS I watch Andy drive away. I berate myself for not being able to speak and say something to keep him from walking away. It all feels too familiar and I have to force myself inside my building.

The elevator closes in on me, making it feel claustrophobic. The pain of the day comes back and I wonder if I can ever get past it. I miss the carefree girl I used to be, the one that could laugh and look forward to a bright future. Now the gloominess of winter pulls me into darkening clouds. Life has lost its luster and I think I might have lost the one shot I had at happiness.

When the doors open, I shoot out like a light. I wonder how I can blur the lines between the past and the future. Guilt is what holds me back. Yet the promise of love is what pushes me forward.

I strip out of the dress and jewelry. I let my hair tumble down onto my shoulders. Then I step into a cleansing shower. The guilt of walking out of the hospital room as requested, and then of running out and leaving things, presses on my chest like a fifty pound weight. I don't know how to forgive myself. I don't know how to move on. As water sloshes over me, I make a decision.

After dressing in comfy pjs, I pick up my phone and begin to type. I hesitate for a second and read over my words before I hit send.

ME: I'm sorry.

I stare at the wall a long time waiting for a response and get nothing before sleep claims me. Sunday rolls in with snow flurries. I get laundry done and begin work on the policies and procedures manual I'm writing for Ted's accounting department because I'm just that lame. I chat with Mandy and Jenna for only a few minutes each, really not up for conversation.

Mom calls and complains about Shannon. Apparently, she missed curfew. My brother has a girlfriend that my mother describes as the princess of doom in all her black, from clothes, to lipstick, to nail polish and hair. She's out of sorts and Dad now thinks he has some rare disease she can't pronounce because he has five of the seven symptoms, which are the same symptoms you get with the common cold according to her. I finally get her off the phone and take stock of my life. I'm alone with no dating prospects because I'm not going to France with Ted no matter how rich he is. I never get butterflies when I'm with him. I've had butterflies before and I can't settle for less than that.

When Monday arrives, the snow is falling in thick clumps, accumulating on the roads and sidewalks. I walk to my office because there is a delayed opening for Ted's office. Cabin fever won't allow me to stay in; I need to get out before the walls press in on me any further.

Once I get to the office, it feels like I haven't seen my desk in ages. Because the snow is coming down hard, the place is pretty vacant even as late as nine, when usually the office is bustling by this hour.

"Cate." I glance up and see Daniel in my doorway. "Do you have a minute?"

"Sure." I'm grateful from the diversion of my inner thoughts. When he sits, I say, "What's up?" as I clasp my hands on top of my desk.

"That night we all went out," he begins. "I was trying to ask you out." *Oh, boy, this is going to get weird.* "Because I wanted to talk to you about Mandy." I inwardly sigh, both relieved and mortified. I'd assumed he was into me. "I've liked her forever. Only she sees us as just friends."

Interesting.

"What about what happened that same night between you two?"

I'm not sure I should let him know I know what happened between them. Then again, he's here for advice. He has to know girls talk.

"What about it? She was wasted and tried to pull my clothes off," he admits freely. I relax because he's okay talking about it. "When I wouldn't comply with her grabby hands, she took off hers." His face reddens and he actually blushes. It's sort of cute. "I tried to fend her off because I didn't want her to regret anything that happened between us the next day. She persisted until she finally passed out face first on her bed."

"Nothing happened that night?" Mandy has no idea and she does regret what she thinks happened.

He shakes his head. "I slept in her bed only because you hear about drunken people choking and dying on their vomit. I didn't want to leave or sleep on the couch knowing I could have saved her, in case something like that happened. When I woke up, she was already up and talking on the phone to someone." That someone was probably me. "She practically shooed me out of her apartment. And ever since, she's done her best to offer up friends and relatives she wants to set me up with." His eyes are earnest and I can tell he's at a loss. "What should I do?"

I love Mandy, but she's lying to herself about her feelings for Daniel. She's totally into him but for some reason won't admit it.

"Give her a dose of her own medicine," I say with a shrug.

We talk for a little while longer before the office starts to come alive. Mandy makes her way into my office when she stops short.

"Daniel," she says and the shock is evident in her voice. I hope she doesn't think something is going on between us.

He turns in her direction before he stands. "Thanks, Cate," he says over his shoulder. To her, he says, "Morning Mandy. I was just telling Cate that I plan on taking your advice. I'm going to ask Tammy out. You know—the Tammy downstairs. She's a receptionist for the law offices."

Mandy nods and Daniel walks out after his declaration. I watch her pale.

"I can't believe he's going to ask her out. She's cute and busty but ..."

"She's not you," I finish for her.

She nods before shaking her head. "No, that's not it. It's a good thing he's moving on."

Clearly, she isn't ready for a reality check. I decide to clear her mind about one thing.

"He came in to talk about how weird you're acting. He says that nothing happened between the two of you that night."

Her eyes snap to attention.

"We didn't have sex?"

"Nope. He says you were all over him though until you passed out."

"I was naked," she says absently.

"He says that was all you. And he blushed while recalling it. I think you're crazy for not going out with him."

Just when I think I've gotten through to her, she asks, "And what about you and that gorgeous doctor?"

I chew on her words all morning long. Hadn't my words been advice I should take for myself? I glance at my phone. Andy hasn't texted me back. If he were any other guy, I would let it go and consider it a loss. But he isn't just another guy. We have history. History I'm not ready to give up on, I realize.

I pick up my phone and try again.

ME: I am sorry. I wonder if you would be up for a blind date.

I stare at my phone and wait for a reply. After a couple of minutes, I set my phone down. He's probably working and not ignoring it, I think, giving myself an internal pep talk.

Just as I start to type again, my phone rings. I'm so hopeful it's Andy, I don't bother to wait until the caller's name pops up before I grab it and place it to my ear.

"Hello."

"Sorry, huh?"

Despite his gruff tone, his voice is the oxygen I need to breathe. I say, "Truly."

"So sorry, you want to send me on a date with someone else?"

I hear people talking in the background. He must be at work. I clamp a hand over my eyes. I guess what I thought were clever words come off as an epic fail.

"No, no one else. That wasn't what I meant."

"But—"

I cut him off. "Me. I want you to be blind to how stupid I've been and give me a chance to take you out to dinner."

"Oh," he says taken aback. "That kind of blind date."

"Yes, it seems I'm not the wordsmith I thought I could be."

There is a lingering pause that crosses into heavy awkwardness.

"Cate," he begins and it sounds like regret.

No one likes rejection, least of all me. "We can go as friends," I blurt. "Just let me make it up to you."

"Friends?"

His one word question doesn't give me enough to read whether he thinks it's a good or bad thing.

"Yeah. I mean even though things were super-fast with us. I think on some level we connected as friends initially. Isn't that the basis of a good relationship?"

Another pause. I think I've blown my shot when he finally speaks.

"When would this blind date occur?"

I'm ready with an answer. "Whenever you're available."

This time the silence between us isn't so unbearable. He's hopefully checking his schedule and not thinking of a way to blow me off.

"I work late tonight. Then I start morning rotations tomorrow. Wednesday night would work because I don't have office appointments until the afternoon on Thursday."

"That works. I don't get off until six. So I could be in Baltimore by eight." I would have to go home to shower and change first.

"You work on Thursday. Why don't I come to you?"

I'm feeling more confident, so I let the short laugh which sounds halfway like a giggle come out. "Now that's not how dates work. I'm supposed to pick you up."

He doesn't join in my laughter.

"There's nothing typical about you and me, Cate." His serious voice kills the smile from my face. "Just tell me where to meet you."

Why do I have the feeling that what I hope will be a rekindling will ultimately turn out to be a goodbye? Because shouldn't he be asking to pick me up? I glance at the clock on my computer.

"Give me until noon to make a reservation, and then I'll text you the location."

"Sounds good. I have to go. Duty calls."

"Sure," I say weakly.

And he hangs up.

I want to call Jenna, but I know what she'll say. She's said it a thousand times already and it might be too late for everything. At least I'll get the chance to ask him about the woman he was kissing at the hospital and the date with Désirée. We hadn't talked about commitment. So do I really have a reason to be mad, especially when I've been the hot and cold one?

That's probably why he agreed to meet me. He wants to tell me he's seeing other people and I should too.

I make a reservation anyway at McCormick & Schmick's. It covers the gamut from steaks to seafood, so I text Andy the place and a time of six-thirty. I don't end up going to Ted's office that day. Instead, I go there bright and early the next day where Jeff is waiting for me.

"Traitor," he spits.

I stop in my tracks. "What did I do?"

"I saw the pictures of you two. You went out with him after all my warnings."

I've heard Ted's side of things. It's time I hear Jeff's. "Is your hatred for him over a woman?"

He pauses. "He told you?"

"Not much. He just said it always comes down to a woman and she was more interested in him."

He huffs, "Yes, there was a woman. But that's not the whole story."

"It never is." I let out a heavy sigh. "Look, I like you, Jeff. But your warnings were for naught. Ted was a perfect gentleman the entire time we were out. He didn't do or try anything. You have nothing to worry about. We're just friends."

"He's never just friends," and he wiggles his fingers, "with a woman," he mutters before heading to his desk.

I don't want to fight, so I don't argue. I sit and get to work. Ted drops by.

"Cate, have you thought about France?"

I glance around worried about the thin walls.

"I'm not sure it's a good idea."

He takes it well. "Fair enough. I'll leave you to it."

The calm way he walks away is unnerving, but I let it go.

By Wednesday, a case of the anxieties hits. I work out of my office and slip out early, only taking half a lunch break. I head home to freshen up and change into a snug scoop neck red sweater, slim black pants, and date heels, or what Jenna refers to as fuck-me heels. I take a cab the few blocks to the restaurant because there is no way I could have walked and survived. The weather is still gloomy and ice patches still litter the sidewalks. The shoes I wear aren't exactly made for walking.

A valet opens my cab door and helps me out. That's what you get when dinner will run in the low hundreds if not more. Andy has already arrived and the hostess escorts me to our table. He's up and helping me out of my coat. His hands are warm and they burn through the fabric of my sweater with his accidental touches. I shiver and miss his touch when it's gone.

"Beautiful as always," he says with my back to him.

I turn to face him because I hope our connection is still there. Only he's turned to hang my coat on the hook outside our booth. I slide in and wait for him to sit.

By the time he does, the waiter is there rattling off the daily specials before excusing himself to give us time to make our selections.

Andy hides behind his menu. I pick mine up and decide what to order.

"What are you having?" he asks, still masked by the menu.

"I think I'm going to go with the Chef's Choice of salmon." It's stuffed and served over vegetables and sounds absolutely yummy. "You?"

However, I already know what he'll decide. He's going for the steak, which is why I chose this restaurant. They specialize in fish and steak.

"I think I'll have the bone-in ribeye."

I smile to myself because I probably could have ordered for him. At least that much of him hasn't changed.

"You're smiling."

"It's nothing. I just knew what you'd order."

His mouth curls slightly and the knot in my stomach eases. "Am I that predictable?"

"Actually, no." I would have never predicted that he'd take me on the balcony of a masquerade ball.

The waiter arrives and we order. When he leaves, the uncomfortable silence presses between us. Figuring the mood can't get worse, I decide to get one question answered.

"I came by the hospital the other day." I pause. "The day after the ball," I clarify.

His piercing blue eyes finally focus on me and I get the feeling he's been avoiding the contact.

"You did? You didn't stop and say hi?"

His voice is guarded and the distance that's grown between us becomes palpable.

"Actually, you were pretty busy. Some might say you were even a bit tongue tied."

His eyes narrow. "You saw me."

I nod and finally just blurt it out. "You had some blonde wrapped all around you. I didn't want to interrupt."

His eyes widened. "The noise," he says more to himself. "That was you. I heard someone walking away. I assumed someone on staff caught us."

"Guilty," I say a little wanly raising a hand like a child in preschool. "Imagine my surprise especially after you... we um... on the balcony."

"Cate."

"No." I shake my head. "I should have known after you walked away and said nothing that night, you were just acting in the spirit of the party and it didn't mean anything to you."

"That's not it," he growls. I watch his jaw set. He's a little fierce when he's determined about something. "I was angry that night, seeing you there. Dancing with guys, their hands all over you." That is an exaggeration but I keep quiet. "When I hoped you felt what's between us, you ran out to the balcony. When I followed you out there, I had no idea what I planned to do or say. Then you let me touch you—"

"Your wine," a red faced waiter says, holding a bottle of merlot.

Andy glances up as the flushed waiter pours him some and lets him taste before he leaves the bottle with us.

Andy continues as if the interruption hasn't happened. "I took what we both wanted. What you eagerly let me have and I won't apologize for it."

I can't blame him. "I don't expect you to."

"But what you saw at the hospital wasn't what you thought. Nurses have hit on me since day one, but that's probably because I'm new and single. The one you saw is a little more aggressive than most. She won't take no for an answer."

"Sexual harassment," I say, but it's more of a joke.

"Exactly. I had to report her because this isn't the first time she wouldn't back off."

I sit back because you don't often hear men taking a stand on a willing woman throwing themselves at them.

"Is she pretty?"

He pauses mid-sip. "Does it matter? I'm not interested. Is that the reason you went out with Ted Caine?"

I could have lied. Instead I opt for the truth. "It wasn't to spite you. He asked and I assumed you'd moved on."

He's quick with a retort. "And you know what they say. To assume is to make an ass out of you and me."

"Fine," I say, defeated. "I could have talked to you about it." I hate how our conversation is taking a turn for the worse. "But that doesn't explain why you went with Désirée to the White House Press Dinner."

"And that's what you think?"

"That's what she said when she saw me out with Ted and took the picture to share with the world, but especially you."

"Again, you assume the worst. When in actuality, she was there, but not with me. I went with my college buddy. You remember the two guys that were with me that night I took you home? I know them from undergrad. When I moved in the area, I called them up knowing they lived here. Well, one of them is a Congressman. His date bailed on him at the last minute and he talked me into going with him."

Insert foot. I have gotten everything wrong. "How did it go? Or is that scowl for me?" I ask tentatively.

He sighs. "Both actually. I feel like all this misunderstanding could have easily been explained if you just trusted me."

"I do."

He shakes his head. "You don't. And maybe that's partly my fault for how I left things on the balcony." He at least looks a bit shamefaced.

We were silent for a moment. "And the other reason for your scowl?"

Dinner arrives in grand fashion. The orchestrated way the waiters show up with the meal and place it before us interrupts his answer. Steam billows from the plates as I smile at the waiter before he leaves.

Andy doesn't immediately dig into his food. We are warned it's piping hot.

"The other reason for my scowl is my buddy is an equal opportunist when it comes to dating and he doesn't hide it, especially now. So I spent the night getting congratulations regarding the upholding of the 14th amendment that passed several months ago." He pauses and gauges my reaction. I smile and don't show the skip of my heartbeat. He continues. "There were reporters and I spent the whole night dodging flashing cameras. And not because I don't agree with the ruling, but because I don't want to have to explain my sexual orientation to my colleagues."

I manage a laugh and finally he laughs too. We eat and our conversation lightens. He tells me stories of his friend's antics. Dinner turns out okay. I pass on dessert because I'm stuffed. I have to swat his hand away when the check arrives, but he finally lets me pay. After all, I am the one who invited him on the date.

"I know you have to work tomorrow. But can I take you somewhere?"

I don't expect it. Despite the tension loosening, we haven't exactly patched things up. We've avoided all talk of our relationship during the rest of the meal.

"Sure. Can you tell me where?"

When the valet pulls his car up to the curb, he just grins while walking to the driver's side. He does like his surprises. When he pulls up on Constitution Avenue where the lights are strung up between lamps, it doesn't dawn on me where he's taking me until we walk to the ticket booth. A lone figure waits and Andy checks his watch.

"I have a reservation."

"Yes. Drew?"

Andy nods.

"Follow me."

We walk through the gate and I can't believe my eyes. They begin to mist, overcome with emotions.

He stops at a bench and takes my gloved hands. "I know this is hard for you." He glances up to the sky before meeting my gaze. I wipe at the corners of my eyes. "I want this to work and ignoring the past isn't working. We have to confront it."

"I'm not sure I can." My voice breaks, but he's right. We can't ignore it. "There's no one here," I say.

"Just because we need this, doesn't mean you have to do it with an audience. I've booked this time only for us. You and me."

In every other circumstance this would be a swoon worthy moment, a romantic gesture that can be told to future grandchildren. Instead, I try my best to keep the tears at bay. We put on our shoes that wait for us because he's thought of everything. I realize he preplanned this as he holds out his hand to me.

"It's time to take the first step. Will you take it with me?"

I stare at the rink and all it represents. And I know if I can't trust him and walk onto the ice, it will never work between us. I gaze into his willing eyes and at his open hand.

SIXTEEN
Past

---◆---

CHRISTMAS BREAK. DREW. IT'S MORE than difficult to keep my mind on studying, but I have to. I'm almost done with finals and I need to pull this off. I'm counting on a 4.0 this semester so my head needs to be in the game. Drew acts like my coach, texting me encouraging messages every few hours. I wish he'd send me naked pictures instead. Not really. I'd never get anything accomplished if he did.

My last exam is this Friday afternoon and then I'm headed to Indy to stay with him for six days until we fly home. We're on the same flight, which will be nice. He can only stay in Charleston three days, but I'll be there for a week. I'll return to Indy and spend another week with him before I have to go back to Purdue. This will be the most time we've ever spent with each other and even though the excitement is killing me, it also has me biting my nails. This could be one of those make it or break it things. All of our weekends together have always been like vacations, but this will be more of the real thing.

Shoving those thoughts away, I refocus on my accounting. This exam is supposed to be a ball buster so I pour another cup of coffee and hit the books. Jenna is in the library so the apartment is as quiet as a church on Monday. I stay at it until two a.m., when I hear the lock turn.

"You still up?"

"Yeah," I say, stretching and rubbing my eyes. "I'm just about to call it a night."

"I had to do the same when my lids started slamming shut. My *5 Hour Energy* wore off long ago," Jenna claims. "I'm beat. Thank god my exam isn't until ten-thirty."

"Yeah. Mine's not until noon. That'll give me a couple of review hours. And then Finance on Friday and voila! I can't wait to be done."

"You can't wait to get into Drew's bed."

"Well, there is that. But I'm so over studying. I want a break."

"There is truth in that," she says.

"You're driving home, right?"

"Oh, yeah. Didn't want to be that long without a car. I'm staying the entire three weeks, unlike someone I know," she clears her throat.

"I wanted to talk to you about that. I'm a little freaked, if you want the truth. This will be the first time we've been together like this."

"You'll be fine. Drew is Drew, you know? He's easy. He's not a diva man. And you're not a diva either. You two were made for each other."

"God, Jenna, I hope so."

"I've never seen you like this before, Cate. How long have we known each other? Since kindergarten? Trust me. I *know* so. But just remember. I don't care that you have a sister, I'm going to be your maid of honor in your wedding."

I pick up a pillow from the couch and toss it at her. "You're a nut."

"No. I'm about to fall asleep on my feet so I'm off to bed. G'night."

"Night."

It doesn't surprise me to see Drew waiting on the porch of his apartment as I pull in and park. His ear-to-ear smile only heightens my excitement at being here. He's wearing my favorite faded jeans and the top to one of his scrubs. He must have only gotten home a little while ago.

"Hey you," I call out as I climb out of my car.

"Hey back. One more semester down, huh?"

"Thank you, Jesus."

"I'll second that, because you're here and I can finally get some Cate time." I'm on the porch by now and he wastes no time in reaching for me. "I have missed the hell out of you, sweet thing."

"Sweet thing?"

"Sweeter than honey and that's for damn sure. Now shut up and kiss me."

You sure can't hide the southern boy in him. When I wrap my arms around him, he stands up and lifts me off the ground. I love it when he does this, so I giggle, but he inhales it with his mouth. He walks backward through his door and takes me straight into his kitchen. His hands wrap around my thighs and I find myself sitting on the countertop. Then I spy what's next to me chilling in an ice bucket, and I let out a muffled whoop against his lips that are still nibbling on mine. He reaches behind him and pulls open the refrigerator, our lips still locked, and grabs a bowl of ruby red strawberries.

"Mmmm," I mumble.

"Not done yet."

When he sets the can of whipped cream on the counter, I know we're going to have some serious fun tonight. He unbuttons my sweater and I shrug it off. Next comes my bra. I'm sitting on his counter, naked to the waist, as he pops the champagne cork and pours.

Then he hands me a glass with a heated gaze and says, "Congratulations on one more down." We clink our glasses and sip. He takes his and pours a bit down my chest, stopping to lick it up as it makes a trail from my neck to my navel. I shiver as goosebumps poke out all over me. The points of my nipples practically scream to be licked or sucked, but he does neither. Instead, he takes the can of whipped cream and coats them with it. It's cold and gives me chills. But when he sucks and licks it off, I whimper with need.

After the whipped cream is gone, he steps back and offers me a strawberry to go with my champagne. Then he tilts my head back and feeds me one of the luscious berries, covered in the sweet, white cream. I close my eyes as I chew because it's that tasty. "They complement each other, you know." I'm not sure if he's referring to his mouth, the whipped cream, and my nipples, or the champagne and strawberries.

My hand trembles as I raise my glass to sip the champagne. "They sure do."

His blue eyes sparkle and I can tell he knows he's a tease. So I decide to run with it.

"Is this our dinner?" I ask.

"This?" He sweeps his hand over the strawberries and champagne. "Yeah."

"Oh, no. This is just our appetizer. The next course is in there." And he points to his bedroom. How exciting. I cross my legs. He sees it and uncrosses them and moves in between them. "What's the matter, Cate? Something bothering you?" His voice is deep and gruff.

"Um, no. Not at all," I squeak.

His knuckles brush the seam of my jeans and I squirm against them. "Is this what you want, Cate?"

"Yes." This time, my voice is rough with urgency.

"But, I thought you were hungry."

My fingers latch onto the collar of his scrubs and I jerk him closer to me. "I am. Starving. For you."

"Hmm. Well, I'm starving for you, too. What a coincidence. But first, I have a surprise."

Surprise? What kind of surprise? I want sex, not a surprise. Louise is dying here, not to mention the state of my panties is getting to the point where they'll have to be wrung out soon. He slides me off the counter and I practically dry hump him.

"Uh, Cate, is there something you want from me?"

"You're kidding, right?"

He only offers me one of his through-the-roof, deep, sexy chuckles, which only adds to my sexual frustration. Louise quivers.

"Give me your hand."

Oh, no. Please to god, don't tell me he wants a hand job! I'm all for that on some occasions, but right now, I just want a good, old-fashioned fuck!

"Cate?"

I place my hand in his and he escorts me to his room, where to my utter surprise, I find it lit in at least a dozen candles. On the nightstand is a vase holding an unbelievable flower arrangement containing roses, lilies, calla lilies, white carnations, orchids, and tulips. There are also two trays on his bed with covered dishes on them.

"I took the liberty of having dinner ready when you arrived. But there's a catch."

"A catch?"

"We eat naked."

"Naked?"

"Naked, as in no clothing."

"Oh. My. Goodness."

The left corner of his mouth curves as he unbuttons my jeans. The zipper follows and when he jerks them off my hips and puts his fingers inside the elastic of my thong, he grins. "This is going to be fun."

"Er, yeah," I swallow, as I watch him strip. I will never tire of seeing his muscles ripple when he moves. It's a damned movie to me.

"Cate? Cate?" He snaps his fingers in front of my eyes.

"Uh, yeah."

"Sit. I want you to taste something."

"Your cock?"

"What?" He barks out a laugh that shakes the bed I just sat on. "Not yet. I want you to taste this."

I've been so busy watching his abs and arms, I didn't even notice that he's taken the covers off our plates and put a bite of food on a fork for me to taste. "Open up." He slides the fork in my mouth and buttered lobster melts on my tongue.

"Oh, hell, that's ... that's so good," I say.

"Good. Let's get comfortable and eat."

Jesus, how can I eat with him in the bed, naked? He's such a distraction. He shimmies up to the headboard and leans back against it, and all I want to do is stare at the lean curves and dips of his firm body.

I follow his actions and find myself against the headboard, next to him, with a plate in my naked lap. The lobster is grilled and so tender, I can't believe he did all this.

"Did you cook this?"

His brows shoot up to the heavens. "No. I ordered it, because I knew if I tried, I'd ruin it."

"It's the best thing I've ever eaten."

"I can't say the same."

By now, the food has captured my attention, so I miss his innuendo. "No? Then why did you order it?"

"Because I love it and I remember you saying one time that you did too."

"But if it's not the best thing …"

"No, you are, Cate."

"Me?" I say, around my mouthful of lobster.

"Oh, yeah. You, by a landslide."

Swallowing my bite is so difficult, I'm afraid I'm going to choke. Grabbing my champagne, I take a huge gulp, hoping to help my issue, but I only end up making it worse. When my coughing subsides, I chide him. "Don't ever say things like that to me again when I have my mouth full."

"What if it's me your mouth is full with?"

"Well, that's okay I suppose." I notice his plate is nearly empty, so I move it aside, along with mine, and I climb onto his lap. "Thank you for all of this. It's truly beautiful. And very unexpected. I've never had such a wonderful dinner, and in bed no less."

"I would hope not!"

"You know what I mean, and you should know I haven't."

"I do and I was teasing."

"The flowers are gorgeous, too."

He brushes my hair off my neck and presses a kiss to it. "They all have meaning. But I'll let you look that up later. Right now, I have something else in mind."

I touch his bottom lip with my index finger. "Oh, and what might that be?"

"This." He flips me over and kisses me.

Later that night, we use the entire can of whipped cream doing all sorts of things. Drew says he planned it out for dessert. I think he just likes whipped cream and wants to see what it looks like on Louise. I have to confess. I like the way it tastes on his cock, especially with the strawberry on the end. I think I scared Drew when he thought I was going to bite the tip of him by accident. In the end, a shower was necessary because after the whipped cream, we ventured into Drew's freezer and got into the ice cream, too. I can only say that ice cream is fun, particularly on the nipples.

In the morning, I Googled all the flowers Drew had selected for the arrangement, which was so heavy I had to use both hands to carry it.

The red thornless roses mean love; white lilies mean virginity and it's heavenly to be with you; calla lilies signify beauty; white carnations indicate pure love; orchids represent love and beauty; and the meaning behind the tulips nearly brings me to tears. There are red ones which symbolize a declaration of love; the variegated ones mean beautiful eyes; and the yellow ones suggest there is sunshine in my eyes. Tulips in general also represent the perfect lover. The fact that he went through all this trouble to select these flowers tells me more than the flowers themselves.

"Drew. I ... this is so beautiful. I never knew any of this."

"I only wanted you to have something that showed my true feelings for you."

"They're perfect."

"Flowers are perfection and should be enjoyed. I'm glad you appreciate them because I intend for you to enjoy them often, Cate."

Just one more reason to love Drew McKnight.

Our six blissful days together pass like light speed and I find myself seated next to him for the flight home to Charleston. A rush of happiness steals over me. The angst I had over spending time with him was all for nothing. We were great together, like peas and carrots, as Forrest Gump would say. Now I'm dreading the stay at my parents' house for a week until I can get back to Drew's.

"Oh gawd," I moan.

"What?"

"The idea of staying at my parents' house just plowed into me."

"That bad, huh?"

"You know how nutty they are. I love 'em to pieces, but ..."

Drew chuckles. "There's always that but."

"Just wait. You didn't get the full impact at Thanksgiving. But you will. Trust me."

"Never lose sight of the fact that they love you, Cate." His face is all kinds of serious.

"You never have a bad thing to say about anyone. You are the kindest person in the world. Probably the universe."

"I doubt that."

"No, I'm serious. I've never heard you say a bad word about anyone. I don't think you have it in your nature. How do you do it?"

"I'm not sure I know what you mean." His eyes are sincere when he says it.

"Let me give you an example then. Take my family for instance. My parents, bless their hearts, mean well and I love them. But my dad is the world's biggest hypochondriac and drives me nuts with all his incurable ailments that are a figment of his imagination. You would sit there and listen to him patiently and ease his mind, while I, on the other hand, would brush him off and tell him nothing's wrong with him. That's what I mean. You have that way about you. And you don't think ill of others. There's only kindness in your heart."

"Oh, Cate, I don't know. I think you see something that's not there."

"Nope. I disagree. I've seen it with you many times. You don't have a mean bone in your body, Drew McKnight. You are too good for this world. And that's the truth. I think you were sent here to make this world a better place."

He slants his head and those intense blues of his pin me, right before his lips meet mine. "I think *you* were sent to make *my* world a better place, Cate Forbes." His fingers weave with mine and we huddle together in our seats as our plane takes off. "I think this is going to be my best Christmas ever," he says.

"Mine, too."

Our parents are at the baggage claim waiting for us when we land. Drew's parents know all about his feelings toward me. I haven't exactly been wide open with mine. It's not because I don't want to. It's just that my family isn't like that. We're not all huggy kissy like some families are. So I've decided to tell my mom over the holidays. But when it's time to part ways in the parking lot, Drew grabs me and lays a major kiss on me, in front of everyone. And since it's Drew, I do what I always do—turn into a boneless heap right there in his arms. I become oblivious to the fact that two sets of parents are witnessing this. When he finally, finally ends the kiss, and mind you I really don't want him to, he tells me in front of everyone, "See you tomorrow, sweet thing. And I love you more than hockey."

Without blinking an eye, I respond, "More than hockey?"

"More than anything." And he lays another *monstrous* kiss on me!

"I love you, too."

Then I turn around and see *The Parents*! Oh shit! His are grinning from ear to ear and mine have their mouths hanging open, jaws on the asphalt. So what do I do? What any girl in my shoes would do. I grab my parents by their arms and say, "Come on Mom and Dad, let's go home. See you tomorrow Letty and Ray." I give them all a little wave and we walk to my parents' car.

"You're in love?" my mom asks.

"That boy loves you?" my dad asks.

"Yes, now come on."

"Why didn't you say something?" Mom asks.

"I was going to tell you when I got home, but Drew beat me to the punch."

Then I'm met with silence. Neither of them utters a word until we pull into the driveway and the garage door is going up. It's my mom who speaks first, laughing, "Well, you could've done a lot worse." And then my dad says, "And a doctor. Hmph. Just what I need. Did you pick him for me?"

"Yeah, Dad, just for you."

"What kind of a doctor is he?" Dad asks.

"He's going to be an oncologist. You know, a cancer specialist."

"A cancer specialist! Why would he want to do that?" Mom asks, horrified.

"Because it's his calling, Mom. That's what drives him."

"But they all die!"

"They do not all die. What century are you living in? They've made amazing strides in cancer therapies and Drew loves helping patients. Besides, it's his career, not yours."

"Well, I don't see why he can't be a doctor that does happy things."

"Mom, he *is* a doctor that does happy things. How do you think the families of his patients feel when he cures them? I don't think they feel sad, do you?"

"No, but that doesn't happen all the time."

"All doctors have to treat life threatening illnesses, not just oncologists. And I think we need to drop this subject because it's not our choice anyway." I need to shut her down or this will go on and on for hours. She'll beat a dead horse into the ground if you let her.

My dad finally sticks his two cents in and says, "Well, I'm just glad to have a doctor in the house." And I'm sure he is. Poor

Drew.

By Christmas Eve, I'm ready to dive head first into the bottle of vodka and swim my way to oblivion. Drew only laughs at my complaints because when he visits, my parents, other than my dad and his unusual medical questions, are on their best behavior. I did have to pull my dad aside yesterday and warn him about getting into a discussion with Drew about his hemorrhoids. He kept bringing them up at breakfast, the perfect time to talk about them. So I told him if he even dared mention them, I would leave and never return home. He clamped his mouth shut and that was that. Thank god, he hasn't mentioned them to Drew yet. Or at least I don't think he has.

"So has Dad hit you up on all his ailments?"

A rumble of laughter shakes Drew. "Only a few."

"What? What has he asked you? I warned him." My scowl is fierce.

"Calm down there, oh feisty one. It's okay. I don't mind and I'm not sharing what we discussed."

"Why not?"

"It's private, that's why. Now let's talk about you." He traps me against his chest and soon I'm lost in one of his kisses. But then I remember we're at my parents' house, and I start to push him away. "What's wrong?"

"We can't do this here," I hiss.

"I'm only kissing you."

"I know, but we don't do public displays of affection in the Forbes family."

"Is that a fact? Well, guess what?"

"What?"

He runs a finger under my chin and whispers against my lips, "That's about to change, sweet Cate." Then he captures my mouth in another kiss and I give up the fight. I really don't care anymore. I'm in love with this man so why should I? He's respectable and has nothing but good intentions toward me and we're both adults. To hell with it. I feel him chuckling.

Pulling back, I look at him with narrowed eyes. "What's so funny?"

"Not a thing. I'm just happy you see things my way." As I get ready to plant another kiss on him, Shannon busts in the room, all giddy because Drew is here. She's a different person around him.

"Hi Drew. Are you staying for dinner?"

"No, actually Cate is coming to my place for dinner with my family."

"Ugh. Why can't you eat with us?" she pouts.

"Shannon, Drew's family has their big Christmas celebration on Christmas Eve. So I'm going there with him to celebrate."

She has the nerve to flash me a nasty look, like I'm a piece of dirt not worthy of her time. Drew catches it and is not happy. What happens next is a shining moment for me.

"Hey kiddo. Do you have a problem with me or with your sister coming over to my house?"

She shakes her head.

"Then maybe you should apologize to her."

Shannon wilts like a flower in the middle of the August heat. She looks at Drew with her big puppy eyes and says, "I'm sorry."

"Don't apologize to me. It's Cate who deserves the apology."

Then to my absolute shock, Shannon turns to me and says, "I'm sorry, Cate. I didn't really mean it."

I want to say, "Yes you did, you little brat." But I don't. I nod and smile instead. Shannon flashes me her perfect little grin that she uses on Mom and Dad all the time and turns it on Drew.

In a voice dipped in sugar, she asks, "So, Drew, will we get to see you tomorrow then?"

"Yeah, I'll be here for dinner."

"You will? Can I sit next to you?"

Oh, god. Not only do I have to worry about my hypochondriac dad, I now have my sister crushing after him, too.

"I think you need to check with your mom on that."

"Yeah, okay, I'll do that right now," she says, as she skips out of the room.

Shaking my head, I say, "And the drama never ends in the Forbes household."

"She is a bit much, isn't she?"

"Uh, yeah. And my parents do nothing to contain that mess. It's ridiculous the disrespect she shows them, too. Eric is fine. At least for now. All he knows and cares about are sports. My worry is that one day, he'll wake up and it'll be other things, and Mom and Dad will be oblivious to it. But Shannon sure responded to you."

"It's only because she thinks I'm cool. One day I'll be a pain in her ass and I'll have no effect at all."

"Hey, I'll take what I can get when I can get it."

"Does that include another kiss?" He laughs.

Pressing my hand against his chest to stop him, I ask, "What time do we need to be at your house? I don't want to be late."

"We're fine." He skims his lips over mine right as my mom walks into the room.

"Oh, Drew, before you leave, I wanted to let you know that dinner tomorrow will be at three." She's told him twice already.

"Thanks, Mom, I think he's got it."

"I'll be here before then, Mrs. Forbes. I can't stand to be away from my girl that long."

My mother actually blushes. For the love of god, will someone just help me here? Then she gushes, "Ah, that's so sweet, Drew."

Now it's my turn to blush, because I'm embarrassed for my mother.

"Okay, Mom, we've got to go now. I'll be back later." Clamping my fingers around Drew's bicep, I literally drag him out of the house.

As we're leaving, I hear Drew calling out, "See you tomorrow Mrs. Forbes."

Flying into his car, I slam the door closed before he has the chance. He gets in and says, "I think this is becoming a habit here."

"Oh gawd! My mother, acting like an adolescent ... no. Just no."

"She wasn't that bad."

"Yes, she was. She batted her eyelashes at you. Do you have this effect on all women?"

Drew is backing the car up but at my question, he puts the car back in park, turns to me and says, "Cate, I don't care about the effect I have on all women. I only care about the effect I have on you."

My heart seriously falls to pieces and liquefies into one big giant puddle of goo. I unbuckle my seat belt and fly across the console straight into his arms. "This is only one of the many reasons why I love you, Drew McKnight."

"Well, hell, if I'd have known that was all it took to get you to fall for me, I would've told you that a long time ago." His blue eyes twinkle and we both end up laughing. "Now are you gonna get back over to your seat and buckle up so we can go to my parents', or are we gonna sit in your driveway and make out like a couple of teenagers and entertain your family again?"

I climb back into my seat and say, "I'd like nothing better than to make out, but there's no way I'm letting my family in for that show."

"Maybe I'll have to sneak you up to my room later tonight, and pretend I'm showing you something, like I used to in high school."

"Oh, is that how you worked it?"

"Yeah, but my parents monitored my time, so I'd have to be quick."

"Hmm. I'm sure you were." Then I start thinking about it. "I bet you had a ton of girlfriends in high school," I tease. "I bet they were all over you, like ants on honey."

He shrugs and says, "I had my share of them. Except for a few, they were actually more bothersome than anything else."

Knowing Drew, he was probably too kind to tell them to get lost. "So, did you have a special one?"

"Not really. I went out with Jilly Rivers probably the most, but other than that, just, you know."

"Yeah, I know."

"What about you, Cate?"

I shake my head. "None for me. I was the one that had all the guy friends. But I didn't go out with any of them. I was too busy with school, too."

He gives me a quick glance and then his eyes are back on the road. "That's very hard for me to believe. I have this vivid image of dozens of hormone driven boys knocking your door down, trying to get to you."

"That's a good one, but far from the truth."

About this time, we pull into his parents' driveway. "Oh, no. Aunt Edna beat us here. I was hoping we'd get here first."

His descriptions of her have me so intrigued, I can't wait to meet this woman. "I swear Cate, don't be shocked or surprised by anything that comes out of the woman's mouth."

"Drew, look who you're talking to. I had to warn my dad not to bring up his hemorrhoids to you and my sister drools in your presence, not to mention my mother's eyelash batting. I live in the house of loons."

"Oh wait. You haven't seen loony yet."

And he's right. Aunt Edna sits in a chair and I do a double take at what she wears. It takes me awhile to figure it out, but I think she's taken Christmas place mats and sewn them together to create a vest. Each one depicts different scene, so she's quite the holiday image. She also wears a baseball hat encrusted in red and green sequins and other sparkly things. Under the hat her hair pokes out in various curls here and there, creating the old *I just stuck my finger in an electrical outlet* look. Red pants and black boots, similar to what Santa Claus would wear, complete her ensemble. No doubt, Aunt Edna certainly has the Christmas spirit. The only things missing are ornaments and lights. I'm truly speechless.

Drew and I have decided to exchange gifts privately, but I've brought a gift for his parents. It's nothing fancy, but a lovely picture frame. Those are something everyone can use, so after discussing it with Drew, we both decided to give the same thing to each of our families.

During the exchange, they are very gracious when they open it. Then Letty opens Aunt Edna's gift to her, and Drew pinches my thigh. "Check it out."

Inside the box is something that may resemble a purse. I'm not sure. It looks like it might have been a Clorox bottle at one time, but it was cut and holes were punched into it, and then red and green yarn was woven into it to create the purse effect. It's so hideous, I have to cover my mouth to prevent the snort that threatens to explode out of me.

Drew leans over and whispers in my ear, "What the actual fuck is that?"

That's my undoing. I bend in half and try to cover up my snort with a cough.

"Cate? Are you all right?" Drew asks.

He damn sure knows what's wrong with me. He grabs me and hauls me out of there to the kitchen where I proceed to die laughing.

"Oh my god! That was the worst she's ever given, I swear," he says.

A response isn't possible as I gasp for air. When I'm capable of pulling air into my lungs, I say, "I've never. That was awful. She reminds me of Aunt Bethany in the movie Christmas Vacation. Are you sure she doesn't have a cat wrapped up in a box somewhere?"

He starts to laugh again and says, "It wouldn't surprise me. Maybe I should check the house. Didn't I warn you? A new kind of crazy, right?"

"True, but don't ever whisper again. That's when I lost it."

We rejoin the family, me with a glass of water in hand. Drew's parents eye us as his mom winks. We share one of those looks and continue with the opening of the gifts. Ray's gift isn't quite as bad. Aunt Edna gives him one of those gigantic inflatable block pillows you use for flying. You're supposed to put it on your lap and rest your head on it during the flight. The only problem is you look like an absolute dork if you do.

Now it's Drew's turn. He unwraps his box and inside is a huge pair of Playtex yellow cleaning gloves. He's clueless until Aunt Edna pipes in.

"I heard how important it is for you doctors to keep your hands clean so I thought these would come in handy for you when you examine your patients."

This time, I shake as I hold my laughter inside. I don't dare look at Drew as he thanks his aunt, but I can tell how his voice squeaks, he's about to lose it. Just when I think we're done, I look to see a box under my nose.

"And here's one for you, dear," Aunt Edna says, as she wobbles back to her seat.

Shit!

"Why thank you! But you didn't have to."

"Aw, just open it."

So I do and inside is a hand knitted scarf by what looks like a kindergartener. *It's the thought that counts, Cate.* Unfortunately, the colors are horrific. Red, green, purple, orange, rust, a blend of clashing shades, it pains my eyes to look at it.

"Oh, it's so … lovely. Thank you so much for thinking of me."

"Why, you're welcome."

I lay the thing on my lap and hear Drew snicker, so I don't dare look at him. But as I'm staring at the scarf, I notice something else. It's literally covered in cat hair. And I mean layered in it. Now I really want to laugh. But I can't. So I put the thing back in the box and fold my hands in my lap.

"Well, I think it's time for some holiday cheer," Ray announces.

"I'll drink to that," Aunt Edna declares, and the celebration begins.

Others begin to arrive, cousins and aunts and uncles, and I lose track. By the time all are present, there are a total of twenty-four here. Everyone brings a covered dish, as is the southern tradition, and Letty handles all the meat dishes and desserts, along with the bar items. It's quite an affair.

When the dinner is over and the relatives have gone, Jenna and her brother, Ben, show up. I haven't seen Ben since the party where Drew first laid eyes on me.

Ben man-hugs Drew and says, "Glad you two hit it off so well."

"Like there was ever any doubt?" Drew asks.

"You were so damn persistent about it. Did he tell you, Cate?"

"Yeah, he did. So did Jenna."

"He drove me crazy for a while. I didn't know what I was gonna do if you hadn't gone out with him."

"We don't have to worry about that now, do we?" Drew asks, pulling me to his side.

I glance up to see Drew looking down at me, grinning.

"We certainly don't," Ben says. "And I'm happy to say you two look perfect together."

That seems odd coming from Ben. I wonder if Jenna told him to say that, but when I look at her, she's staring at Ben looking like she just swallowed a glassful of vinegar.

"Ben Rhoades, when have you ever said anything like that to anyone?" Jenna asks.

"Probably never. I'm a dick when it comes to this sort of thing. But Drew is my best friend and I happen to know how he feels about Cate. I'm happy he found her and that she makes him happy and it's about damn time."

I look on as Drew says, "Thanks, dude. That means a lot to me."

"I would've told you over the phone, but I knew I was gonna see you here so I decided to wait. And besides, I wanted to *actually* see you before I said it. I've known Cate almost as long as I've known you, so I have to say," and he does this funny thing with his hand that I think is supposed to imitate a religious blessing, "I bless this relationship."

Drew tosses an empty plastic cup at him. "You're off the ledge, dude."

"Nah, I'm trying to be serious here. I am glad you two are together. And bro, Cate here is *so* much better than Rebecca."

"Fuck. Did you have to spoil the night by bringing that up?"

That surprises even me. Rebecca is Drew's old girlfriend, the one that broke his heart. Jenna told me all about her and that Ben hated her. I look at Jenna and she's trying to mask her grin. What's so funny about that? I think it's kind of tasteless. Then I look at Drew and a slow grin spreads across his face.

"Okay, I'm completely off the trail here, lost in the woods," I say.

Drew throws his arm over my shoulders. "Ben always hated Rebecca. I defended her constantly, but then when I figured out he was right, I was ... well you know the story. I told you at the beginning when we started dating. What I find funny here is I never thought I'd wave the whole Rebecca thing away, and now, here I am with you, and I could totally give a shit about her. That's why I'm smiling and I figure it's why they are too. She was always a touchy subject around me, but not anymore."

I beam at his words. Drew always knows exactly what to say to make me smile. Our conversation moves to how long Drew is in town to how long I'll be in Indy, to when we all can get together again. Soon they depart and it's only Drew and me. I want to curl up next to him somewhere, but it's getting late and I know I need to be getting home soon.

"Yeah, I know," he says, reading my mind. "Weren't we going to exchange gifts tonight?"

"Yeah. Do you want to do it now?"

"Hell yeah. But I have to go to my room. You wanna come?"

"Is this the deal where you tell your parents you have to show me something?"

"You bet it is."

"Then I'm in."

There's a bag I brought in and I snag it before we run up the stairs and go into his room. He shuts the door behind us. His hands slide under my skirt, and glide along my thighs as he follows it up to my unders.

"Cate, I need you. I've been thinking about this constantly."

"What if someone hears? I don't think I can." I bite my lip, worrying, as anxiety gnaws at me.

"I know. We can't. We'll have to live frustrated for a while and I hate this."

"So do I. Maybe we can do car sex again?"

"Yeah, but tonight, I want to give you your gift." He walks to his closet and comes out with a ginormous gift bag. "Merry Christmas, babe. I love you."

"I love you, too, and thank you."

"Open it."

I spread the top of the bag apart and inside there are several things. First, I see a big box, so I pull it out, unwrap it, and laugh. "Oh my goodness! Will you help me?"

"All the way."

"Good, because if I put these skates on, I'm sure to bust my ass like crazy."

"Cate, I'll always catch you if you fall." His blue eyes catch mine and I know he's not talking about that kind of falling.

"Drew, I won't let you fall either. We're in this together, you know."

He leans in and kisses me. "There's more in there."

My hands dig down, and I pull out another fairly large box. I unwrap the most luxurious bathrobe known to man. On one side is soft terry and on the other side is silk. "Oh my, this is amazing. I love it."

"You do? I noticed you didn't have one."

"I do now and I absolutely love it. It's perfect! Thank you!" I lean over and kiss him.

"One more and you're done."

I fumble in the bottom and find the last box. When I pull it up, I know it's jewelry. I give him the *I can't believe you did this* face. He shrugs. "Just open it," he says.

When I do, I fall in love all over again. It's an exquisite necklace, very delicate gold filigree surrounding a center diamond. The design is simple yet elegant and I couldn't love it any more than I do.

"Cate, don't cry. It's only a necklace."

My fingers fly to my cheeks, because I hadn't even realized tears were falling. "Now that's a surprise," I say, brushing them away.

"The necklace or the tears?"

"Both, I guess. Drew, this is gorgeous. I love it."

"Let me put it on you." He takes it out of the box and puts it around my neck. "Perfect," he says. Then he pulls me to my feet and walks me to a mirror. "See?"

It's beautiful. "I've never owned anything like this. It's so pretty. Thank you for everything." And I kiss him. "Now for yours."

I hand him a prettily wrapped box. I hope he likes it. It's not as extravagant as what he gave me, but everyone I spoke with told me to go with it. My fingers are crossed.

He unwraps it and I watch his expression change from perplexed to pure excitement and joy.

"You didn't? You scored Blackhawk tickets?"

"I did. For the week I'll be with you."

He stands and pulls me off my feet, twirling me around. And then he stops, puts me down, and rubs his face.

"Stop worrying. You don't have call that night. I got it all cleared and you're off."

"What?"

"You heard me. Look on your computer and check the schedule if you don't believe me. You're good. We're going. And the rest of your present includes, if you didn't read it …"

"I did. A hotel and dinner that night. Cate, it's too much for you."

This is the tricky part. I screw up my face and say, "I know. I was gonna go halvers with you."

"That's perfect."

"But Drew, I feel terrible because you got me so much and I was only able to get you …"

"Stop that train of thought. I love your idea and the Blackhawk tickets are perfect. It's the best gift ever. Now, kiss me."

Right before I do, I say, "Merry Christmas."

SEVENTEEN
Past

———◆———

THE WEEK AT MY PARENTS without Drew feels more like a month. Without him here as a buffer, my mom is relentless with her questions. How long have you dated? How serious are you two? I know you're in love, but are you going to get married? You have to finish college. Don't think about dropping out. Seriously, Mom? Like I would actually drop out of college and forego my degrees after all this hard work. What does she think I am—a moron?

My flight back to Indy finally lands and Drew waits by the luggage claim. To say I throw myself at him is a gross understatement. I think I hear one or two "Get a room" comments. And it's true. We practically make out while we wait for my bag to arrive. Once it does, we smile at the onlookers, and Drew says in a booming voice, "Let's get a room." I can't help but giggle.

In the car, we can't keep our hands to ourselves.

"This was the never ending week," I say.

"Yeah?"

"I had Mom, Dad, and Shannon on my back constantly. Eric was the only one who was fun because we played video games together. Then I crazy missed you. You know that part, though."

His hand makes its way up to the button and zipper of my jeans and his fingers find their way inside. "Please don't start something you can't finish."

"What makes you think I can't finish?" he asks, as he slides his finger around me.

"I can't talk while you do that." My head drops back against the seat and I mewl when his finger circles my clit and slides inside of me.

"Wow, are you ever wet. Were you thinking about this on the plane?"

"Might have been. Just don't stop because I'm close already." I hear him chuckle.

Then he says, "Touch me, Cate." My hand reaches over the console and I touch him. His erection is not hard to miss.

"Looks like you've been thinking of this, too." He hits a spot that's perfect, then intensifies his motion. "Don't stop. Right there. I'm going to come."

And about then, I feel my orgasm race along my spine, down into my arches of my feet, back up my legs and center in my core until it spreads back up my spine and finally settles down. The tiny muscles inside of me stop clenching Drew's fingers and I sigh.

"That was nice to hear," he says.

"Yeah?"

"Uh huh."

Then I reach across and unzip his pants. "Promise you won't get in a wreck?"

He offers me a shaky laugh. "I'll do my best."

I lower my mouth around his cock and proceed to suck him off. The best thing about giving Drew head is the sounds he makes. They are the biggest turn on ever. Oh, that, and the way he threads his hands in my hair. And the way he feels against my tongue. Like velvet wrapped around steel.

"I'm going to come."

I keep sucking and then I squeeze his balls and his orgasm hits him. The groan he releases is enough to make me moan. When I lift my head, he apologizes for shooting off in my mouth and I laugh.

"That's the craziest thing I've ever heard. I loved it. I love sucking your cock. It's super sexy."

"It's sexy to watch, but I was afraid if I did, we'd wreck."

I zip him back up and say, "Then I'm glad you didn't."

We spend New Year's Eve quietly at home, catching up on what went on in Charleston after he left. And of course, we do other things, too. New Year's Day is celebrated by eating the traditional southern meal of ham and collards, and I make homemade macaroni and cheese. We eat way too much and fall asleep on the couch, watching football. It's Drew's choice, but I don't mind.

Mid-week, we're off to Chicago to the Blackhawks game. Drew is so excited I have to drive. All the way there, he spouts off Blackhawk stats and who the greatest players are. I'm sure I'll never remember any of this.

He has his GPS set and I'm glad for it because I've never driven in Chicago before. The traffic isn't too bad, as far as big cities go. It may be because we left at noon to check into the hotel early and spend a little time in the city. In any case, Drew doesn't pay a whole lot of attention, because his focus is all on hockey now.

When I pull up to the hotel, he's surprised that we've stopped. "We're here," I announce. The expression on his face is so comical, I immediately start laughing. "What were you expecting? Mars?"

"No, but it went by so fast."

He looks like such a little boy; I ruffle his hair and shake my head. "Let's go check in, hockey boy."

He wears a goofy grin and I smile. His eyes are bright with excitement and he looks like he wants to leap ahead of me. "Go on and run ahead if you want."

"I can't help it."

"Hey, this is your day, your gift. Go for it." And I'm more than pleased to see how much fun he's having.

Suddenly he stops and turns, pulls me in his arms and says, "Have I told you how much I love you today?"

"I believe so."

"Well, I'm telling you again." Then he plants a kiss on my lips. And my excited Drew is back again.

We get to the front desk and he bounces on his toes as he waits for the room key. As soon as we stash our bags, we're off. It's a blustery day with the wind coming off the lake, but we're prepared with coats, hats, and gloves as we walk to all the cool places to see in the little bit of time we have. Drew drags me down Michigan Avenue to all the shops and tries to buy me things, which I won't let him. Then we stop in for a mocha at a coffee shop. Soon it's time to grab dinner. We eat at one of Chicago's famous steak houses, Gene and Georgetti's. He gets the bone-in rib eye and I get the filet mignon. The food is beyond delicious. He, of course, orders the wine, which is some sort of cabernet sauvignon, and it's so yummy, I want to lick the bottle. But the place is pricey. Really pricey and I can't keep thinking about it.

"Cate, I can afford this. You don't have to worry about it."

I lean into him and whisper, "It's so high. I never thought."

He takes my hands in his and squeezes them. "It's fine. Cost is not a problem here. Can I share something that may make you feel a little better?"

"Okay."

"I have a trust fund. My mom is … well, her family is wealthy. Money isn't a problem for me. I don't want you to worry away the enjoyment of this meal. Okay?"

"But the whole point of this is it's my gift to you."

"Babe, the thought means more than anything and those tickets, and the fact that you arranged for me to have the time off, well that's better than anything. The cost of this is nothing compared to that. Please get this off your mind. I want this to be fun for you."

"Okay. But I want you to know that just because you have some trust fund doesn't mean I don't pull my weight."

"Deal. Now drink up. We're here to celebrate."

And the rest of the meal is much better now that I don't have to worry about paying for it with my tuition money.

When we leave there, we head straight to United Center. I almost have to restrain Drew. He's been here before, but it's like a shrine for him. When he walks in, he does a three-sixty to have a look. Then, when we get to our seats, he about freaks.

"Seriously? How did you know to get these seats? Most first-time buyers would go for low and center."

"Yeah, I checked with Sam and Caroline on that. I wanted to make sure."

"I knew my girlfriend was smart."

"Not me, Sam. He told me corner seats because if I got center ones, they'd obscure the corners of the ice on the side we'd be sitting on. It's what Caroline and I complain about all the time. So now I know."

They really are awesome seats. They're lower level, but high enough to give us a great view and the greatest thing of all is they're right on the curve of the rink.

He grabs my hand and we walk down the row to take our seats. Drew's thigh thumps up and down, his thrill of being here palpable. I wish I could bottle it up and sell it. I'd be a millionaire. He's so damn adorable like this—not that he's not adorable all the time, but this little boy thing has me in a constant grin.

The game begins and Drew immediately is into it. Every now and then he leans into me to explain something or to tell me about his favorite players. But honestly, I don't listen to a word he says. I'm so charmed by his elation, I glance at the ice just to make him happy, but my eyes are pretty much glued to him the entire time.

It's these special times that make my heart race, like when he flies out of his seat, yelling for his team with his arms raised. That's when I feast my eyes on that slice of skin that peeks out beneath his sweater, and I lick my lips in anticipation of later tonight, when I can nibble on his delicious abs. And it's when, even during the thrill of the moment, he bends down and plants a wet, warm kiss on my lips. I notice all the women around eyeing him and that's when it happens.

My heart swells so much it almost hurts. Pride nearly gushes out of me because that's what I'm feeling. I am so proud Drew loves me. Out of all the women he could've chosen, he picked me—the one who never thought she'd fall in love. And I'm so proud of the fact he's such a good-hearted man. He can't say a bad word about anyone because of the kind and compassionate nature of his soul. I'm so proud he's so giving of himself and even in the midst of my crazy family, he says kind things about them. But most important of all, I'm proud and honored to call Drew McKnight mine.

He turns at that very second, catches my look, tilts his head, and asks, "What?"

"Nothing."

"Oh, it's something. The look on your face tells me so."

Pulling him toward me, I confess, "I'm proud and honored to call you mine."

EIGHTEEN
Present

───────◆───────

WHAT FEELS LIKE A LIFETIME of memories flashes before me as Andy stands there with his hand held out to me. The remembrance of budding love, the sorrow of cancer—a faceless foe, even the crook of a smile for HockeyHo's antics, and back to that painful day of my leaving. As the moments pass, I blink back tears and say nothing about the hefty guilt that hovers in the background.

As Andy waits for me, I feel a tear slip through my barrier. It spills down my cheek as I raise my hand to take his. I want this man more than I've been prepared to admit. I let the pain of the past wash away with the tear as it drops from my face and crystalizes on the ice that is beneath my feet.

He takes his thumb and gently wipes away the residue of long ago hurt. Then, I'm pulled forward feeling unsteady and worried about the future. His hand feels solid in mine and I know I have to trust him with my heart. If only I can trust myself. My momentum pushes him backward to smoothly glide over the ice. I'm carried along, wobbly at first, until he's there to steady me.

His earnest eyes haven't left me once and I'm in awe of the emotions I see churning in them. The blue is as clear as the daytime sky and shines through the night that surrounds us. I'm romanced by how he is bringing me out of my own darkness through his guiding light.

"I remember the first time I saw you."

His voice breaks into my tumbling thoughts.

"You had no idea I saw you. I remember thinking that's a woman I can see spending the rest of my life with."

I smile up at him. "How could you know that?"

He hooks his hands in my coat pockets and draws me closer. "Mom told me when I met the one, I would know. And Dad backed her up. Corny, but they've been married for over fifty years. It's hard not to trust their advice."

He doesn't back down from my challenging stare and I become undone by his sincerity. I bury my face in his chest as he takes the lead in our lover's embrace. We skate facing each other across the expanse of the ice, and he makes me feel safe in his capable hands.

His words are soft when he speaks again. "I know we can make this work, Cate, if you let me."

How on Earth can something so right be so difficult? I pull back as he slows us to a stop. "Honestly, I'm surprised you did this." I glance around and wonder what woman has had a man rent out a rink for a private skate. It has to be one of the most romantic things ever. "I was so sure you'd given up on me."

His tentative smile sobers to a pensive line. "There were times I wanted to," he confesses before a lingering pause. When he speaks again, his voice lightens some from his somber tone. "I had to remember there are some things in life worth fighting for. And you, Cate, are one of those. I want you; you have to know that by now. But I can't promise I'll chase you forever. I do have some pride left."

His admission is almost honest to a fault, which is why I know I can trust it.

"I don't know what to say."

"Say you won't run. Say you're in this as much as I am. Say you want me the same way as I want you."

The determined expression on his face causes a V to form between his brows. He's in this for keeps. And it's time for me to make that leap of faith. "When I took your hand and came out here, I'd decided I wouldn't run anymore. I want this. I want you."

He raises my hand and twirls me. I'm not an expert skater but in his arms I feel like I can do anything. I spin but lose my footing and we fall in spectacular fashion.

The sky above Washington, DC is too bright with manmade lighting to have a clear view of the stars. As we lie there, I imagine what they look like.

"Are you going to get up?"

I laugh. "I thought maybe we should stay down and make snow angels. It might be safer."

His chuckle comes from somewhere deep in his chest. Before I can think more about it, he's there cupping my face and pressing soft warm lips to mine. I'm reminded again how good it can be between us. Then he stands up before me, and offers a hand up. "Come on, snow princess. There will be time for snow angels later. We should go skiing... soon."

Reluctantly, I'm up on my feet again. As we begin to skate side by side, I notice the dull heartache in my chest hasn't completely left. Yet for once, I feel as though I can breathe through it.

The magic of the night imprints on my brain as much as my heart. Lights that circle the rink along with the holiday decorations twinkle and add a sort of enchanted quality to our nighttime skate under the hidden stars. Even without a full-skirted dress and glass slippers, this man makes me feel like I stepped into a fairytale.

The night only ends because the guy comes to tells us he has to close up for the night. I find myself smiling uncontrollably when we change back into our shoes.

"Someone's in a good mood."

"Only because I'm one lucky girl."

I'm still floating on the drive home. He turns off the engine after he finds a park on the other side of the street.

"Let me walk you up."

I have no intention of letting this man leave tonight, but I only nod. We get out and I do my best to dodge the dirty gray snow that has yet to melt from the last storm. He takes my hand in his and we enter my apartment building as a unit, an unbreakable couple. Or so I hope. When we get to my door, I turn to ask him in. Before I can speak, he twines our fingers together.

"I had a great night."

My jaw drops because he sounds like he's actually going to leave. Then a sinful smirk appears on his mouth right before he dips his head and covers my lips with his. At first the gentle pressure is sweet. After one taste of him, everything changes. I reach up and tangle my fingers in his hair, trying to bring him closer. His hands land on my waist under my coat as I explore every inch of his mouth.

When his grip tightens, I feel cool air on skin as my shirt lifts. He takes advantage, and I feel his fingertips glide across my bare skin, under my shirt and around to the small of my back.

I'm breathing so hard when I pull back and say, "Please stay tonight."

He stares at me a second before he captures my mouth in a hot tangle of emotions. Then he strips the keys from my other hand that dangle at my side. Quickly, the door opens at my back. His hand steadies me as we step inside with tandem precision without a breath between us.

As the door closes behind us, I let my purse fall. He takes a step back to heatedly glance over me. I decide to give him more of a view, so I let my coat fall to pool at my feet. I kick it aside as he takes his own coat off with more care. He blindly places it on the high kitchen counter behind him that separates the kitchen from the tiny living room.

Then he steps into me and cups my chin possessively to expose my neck. He places a hot trail of kisses down toward my shoulder as I try to remain standing. When he reaches my collar bone, his hands shift. He lifts his head and his eyes are focused on me. He slowly pushes my sweater up while his hands roam over my ribcage and then over my breasts, which instantly feel heavier. Once my bra is fully exposed, he latches onto my nipple through the thin fabric while continuing to skim the sweater up my arms. When it reaches my wrist, he holds my arms there to stretch over my head as I feel myself grow wet with need.

"Please," I beg for everything and nothing at the same time.

His hot mouth releases my breast as he slowly faces me. His lips are but a whisper from my own.

"What Cate? What do you want from me?"

I squirm, trying to close my legs tight enough to create the pressure I seek between my thighs. His next move shows he knows what I want. His free hand cups me through the fabric of my pants and the heel of his palm presses against my nub just hard enough to make me needier, but not yet fulfilled.

"Andy," I breathe.

Instantly, his hand is gone and I groan in frustration. "Tell me what you want, sweet Cate."

"I want you."

"I know that," he says confidently. His words or maybe his voice ratchets up my desire for him. "Be specific, Cate."

"Make love to me."

He moves in and sucks my lower lip into his mouth. He gently bites it before releasing it with a quiet pop. "I'm afraid I can't make love to you Cate."

I'm devastated because he sounds serious. Only his hand is back. This time he uses his thumb to circle my clit before pressing it hard. I cry out as Louise begins to fire on all cylinders. Like a sadist, he pulls back just before the final countdown has ended.

"Why?" I ask in frustration.

His answer comes when his deft hands undoes my pants. It takes a second before they tangle at my ankles. I feel trapped. It should frighten me, but just like how he took me on the balcony turned me on, I am ready and willing to be at his mercy. Still, I kick the pants to the side.

He still hasn't answered me even though my heavy lids droop as I voicelessly plead with him. His hand is back and I'm not sure whether I should be embarrassed as his fingers press my damp thong against my hot skin. I don't have time to explore those thoughts. His skilled fingers easily slip the fabric barrier to the side as he shoves two fingers inside me.

"You're wet for me."

"Yes, always." I admit it, hoping for points so he gives me what I want.

I buck my hips against his thrust, ready to do anything if he would just let me come. The build up to my orgasm is quicker now because I've yet to spill over the edge. I want to curse him when he pulls them out before I can find release.

"Please," I plead again.

He groans and presses me into the wall with the full weight of his body. I feel his erection grind into me but only once. Then his body stills.

"I can't Cate. I can't make love to you."

Confused to the point of exasperation, I whine. "I don't understand. Why can't you?"

His hips rub against mine again. It's maddening when I know he wants me as much as I want him. I try to pull against his restraining hand at my wrist because I know if I can touch him, I can change his mind.

He puts some space between us and I arch my back trying to keep contact with his lower half. Only he pushes me back into the wall with a firm hand on my center as he guides my bottom to meet the wall. I moan as his touch lights a fire in me. Again, he removes his hand, but I'm encouraged by the sound of him undoing his belt.

"I can't make love to you Cate because I have to fuck you first."

I don't have time to process his words. He releases my wrist and he spins me around to face the wall. Then he lines himself up to rub against the cleft of my ass. I drop my hands to reach back and touch him, only he snags my wrist.

"No touching. Not yet."

He takes my other wrist and uses what feels like the leather of his belt to bind me as my cheek presses against the cool wall. It feels wicked and the desire in me intensifies. I've never done this before, but I feel safe with him. I know he won't hurt me.

He takes my shoulders and turns me to face him before he steps back to admire his handiwork.

"God Cate, you're so damn beautiful."

His kisses me hard and I writhe, waiting for him to make his next move.

"You're not afraid are you?"

I shake my head, unable to form words.

"Good, because I'm going to fuck you now."

His thumbs slip underneath the hem of his boxer briefs. As he tugs them down, his impressive erection springs free like a divining rod. He steps forward and lifts me with remarkable strength, using the wall like an elevator shaft. Up I go, my arms pinned between me and the wall. When I stop, I feel his tip at my entrance.

"I want you bare, Cate. I've never been with anyone else skin to skin. I want no barriers between us."

"Yes, please. I haven't been with anyone else since you."

His grin is anything but sweet. It's sinful. Then he lets gravity pull me down around him. My back pulls away from the wall as my body bows from the contact.

"Fuck," he growls.

I voice my pleasure with mewls and other nonsensical words. Managing to hold me up with one arm, he uses the other to take hold of my head and angle me for a kiss. His tongue penetrates my mouth just as impressively as he fucks me mercilessly against the wall. I'm sure I'll have bruises in the morning and I don't care.

Taking me by surprise, he pulls out and sets me on my feet only to turn me around. With a hand pressed to my shoulder, he bends me over a little before he enters me again with striking force. I'd bang my head against the wall if not for his hand holding my hips steady. I feel off balance, but the pleasure is beginning to eclipse anything else as my brain clouds, clearing any coherent thoughts.

He slips his hand around my waist and applies pressure to my clit. His other hand grabs my breast and tweaks my nipple. His shift in movement allows him to go deeper inside me at a different angle. It touches something inside that sends me shooting off like a bottle rocket. I explode and scream out my pleasure. He's relentless. The sound of our flesh slapping against each other is enough to start another orgasm building within me on the heels of the last.

"Cate, baby, are you close?"

I hear his words, but I'm in another place and can only moan in response.

He squeezes my breast before his hand comes around to my ass. His finger circles a place I thought off limits. "Oh! What are you doing?"

"You like that?" He prods a finger at my backdoor entrance and stokes his other fingers over my clit in a circular motion. "I want to have you there eventually." He continues to stroke, prod, and otherwise rock my world when he asks a different question. "Are you still on the pill?"

I nod frantically as he continues to ring my g-bell with each stroke.

"Good, I'm coming."

His words are enough to get me to detonate again as he slams into me. My toes curl against the floor boards as I try to maintain my position and not fall. A few more banging thrusts and he stills inside me. He presses his head to my back before he brings us both to a standing position. My bound hands stop my back from fully meeting his chest, but I don't complain.

Soft lips skim up my neck until he whispers in my ear, "I will never get enough of you."

The hand that isn't cupping my breast manages to undo the belt restraint from my wrists. When my arms fall free, he turns me to face him so he can take each of my wrists and rub them gently as the blood circulates. Then he kisses each one.

"Are you okay?"

I bob my head once, having no idea how I managed to stay on my feet as long as I have on rubbery legs. Finally, I begin to fall to my knees ready to give up the fight with gravity. He's there to catch me under my legs to lift me up. I'm languidly limp in his arms, sated and satisfied. I feel as though I'm floating as he cradles me in his arms. He walks me all the way to my bedroom to carefully lay me on the bed.

He places a chaste kiss to my forehead. "Wait here."

I want to tell him I couldn't move if I wanted to, but I lack the energy to say the words. When he comes back, he cleans me up with a damp wash cloth. My eyes are heavy with sleep.

"You can have a little rest. But I'm not done with you."

His warm arms wrap me in their embrace and I snuggle into the curve of his body as drowsiness descends. I feel amazing as I slip into sleep. Sometime later, I'm awakened when his cock fills me again as we lie on our sides. I'm a little sore, but say nothing as he slowly slides in and out of me in an unhurried rhythm. I'm pretty sure he hasn't come even though I have when he pulls out and raises my leg. He moves to lay his face on my thigh as his mouth covers me. His tongue takes a dive into a happy Louise as I fist a hand in his hair, overcome with the feels as my toes curl. He uses his mouth to fuck my pussy just like he kisses, long strokes and sucking my nether lips and clit until I skim through the horizon of pleasure like a shooting star.

Just as my orgasm ebbs, his cock replaces his mouth and he moves inside me again. He makes love to me this time. It's not loud or frantic like earlier. Soft moans and groans fill the room as my heart expands with need. I have no idea when we finally fall asleep. I only know when I wake, I smell coffee.

I open my eyes and shoot out of the bed when I see the time on my silent alarm clock reads seven.

"Shit," I call out. "I'm going to be late."

I scramble into the bathroom and take a quick shower. I mourn the fact that I'm washing Andy's sexy scent off me. It makes me feel branded. A feeling I haven't had in a while. But I can't go into the office smelling like sex. The water is warm and I hate that I have to rush my shower, but if I don't get a move on, I won't make it to the office on time.

There is no time to blow dry my hair, which sucks because the temperature outside is probably going to be below freezing. I comb it back and pull a ponytail holder around it. I apply a little makeup after brushing my teeth and head out to my bedroom.

Andy is there, wearing only pants. He holds two steaming mugs and extends one out to me.

I step over to grab it. "You're a godsend."

"I don't know about that," he says on a chuckle.

He's so damn beautiful and that crooked smile makes me want to jump him.

I delight in the taste of a good morning cup of joe before I set what is left down on the bedside table and walk naked over to my dresser.

"Sore?" he asks.

Mortified he notices that I'm walking a little strangely, I feel my cheeks flush. "A little, but in a good way."

I pull out the necessary undergarments and try not to squirm under the weight of his gaze as I put them on. He makes me feel naked, and not just the clothes-less kind of way. I feel like he can read my soul as he watches me.

"You should take a video," I tease, trying to hide my discomfort.

His brow quirks. "Didn't know you were into sex tapes."

"Hardy, har, har."

I stride past to go into my closet to find something to wear. I grab the first thing I see, a cream blouse, navy pants and a matching short jacket. It's professional and stylish enough to make an appearance at Ted's office.

When I put the blouse on, Andy, still shirtless, shakes his head. I turn away to sit in order to put on my pants. When I stand again, he's holding a turtleneck up in my direction.

"I think this is better."

I laugh wondering when I last wore that. It's something I should have given away long ago. "Why is that?"

He walks over and places a finger above the top button of the blouse. It lands right at the crest of my cleavage.

"You have to know after last night, I'm not sharing you with anyone else."

I glance up into unfathomable blue eyes. "I don't share, either."

I place my index finger on his pec before sliding it across his nipple.

With only our fingertips on each other, I can almost hear the crackle of sexual energy pass between us.

"Don't start something. Otherwise, you'll have to call out sick today."

I take the turtleneck from his hands and toss it to the side. "I wish I could, but I have a meeting today."

"Important?"

"Yes. I have to go see Ted." I don't think about my words until his eyes darken. Quickly, I add, "I'm working on a project for him and I need to give him the first draft."

I've been working my ass off on the accounting policies and procedures. Writing again, even though it's technically a manual of sorts and not an editorial piece, feels good.

I lean up to him and press my lips to his. "You have nothing to worry about."

He stares at me for a minute. "I trust you. It's him I don't trust."

"I trust you, too, and I can handle Ted." I sigh. "I wish I could stay."

"Let me take you to work. Maybe I should pay a visit to Ted and say hello."

Something in his words almost sounds like a threat. I can't imagine the two of them together. I don't think Ted is interested in me anymore, but male pride could have them going at it just to prove a point.

"I don't think that's a good idea." I laugh, trying to play it off as I slip on my jacket.

"Okay, but I want to take you to lunch. I'll hang out in DC today and meet you later."

I pray he doesn't run into Ted as I agree to his lunchtime plans.

On the way to the office, I can't seem to tear my eyes off of Andy as he manipulates his car through the DC traffic. It reminds me of the way he handled my body last night, and a warm flush spreads over me.

"What has you so quiet over there?"

"Honestly?"

"Yeah."

"Thinking about last night and how much I would have

219

regretted if you walked out of my life. I want this to work." I reach for his hand because I have this need to touch him. Again, I'm surprising myself.

A broad grin stretches out across his face. "That's probably the best thing I've heard in a long time. Other than your lovely sexy sounds last night. And I plan to make sure I hear those on a regular basis."

"Are you making me a promise?"

"Oh, you can count on it. Do you have an office with a door?"

The sexy cast of his eyes makes me cross my legs. My cheeks warm at the thought of office sex.

"I don't have an office here at this location. I'm working out of a cube."

"We'll have to get creative then."

His hand slides up my thigh. I playfully slap it away.

"We won't be having sex in Ted's offices," I laugh.

"Too bad, I'm sure we could teach him a thing or two."

"You are so bad."

I'm instantly looking very forward to meeting Andy for lunch today but I also hope to dodge the bullet of the two men meeting.

NINETEEN
Past

---❖---

SECOND SEMESTER IS FLYING BY. I am angry with myself because I promised Jenna I would go to Key West for spring break with her. All I want to do is spend the week with Drew. She catches me pouting on more than one occasion.

"If you want to back out, it's fine."

"I don't want to back out."

"Look, Cate, you and I have been friends since what? Kindergarten? I know when you don't want to do something. If you don't want to go, I don't want you to go. It won't be any fun dragging you around to clubs and stuff with your lower lip hanging on the ground."

"I'm not acting like that."

"Uh huh, right."

She's right and I know it. I thrum my fingers on the table as she stares at me.

"You need to decide soon, because if you're not going, I need to get a replacement."

"I'm going." This will be good for me. "I need some Jenna/Cate time."

"You sure about this? You've been stuck to Drew's side since Thanksgiving. Sometimes I think you're his third arm."

Once again, I can't argue with that. "I know, but I can't help it.

When I'm not with him, it's like a part of me isn't here."

"Jaysus. You're kidding, right?"

"No! I'm not. I wish I were." I hang my head.

"Well damn girl, there's no need to be down about it. Be happy you found your one! Not many people can say that."

"I know, but it seems like forever until I graduate."

She thumps me on the side of the head. "Get a hold of yourself, you fucknut. It's not like you're in school in China, for Pete's sake. You're an hour away from him. Of all people I know, you're the last one I thought I'd be having this talk with. You, Cate Forbes, pining away for your guy." She shakes her head. "Remind me never to fall in love. You look like a damn fool." Then she makes a funny face and pokes out her tongue and I can't help but giggle.

"It is ridiculous. I can't argue with you there. But one day, you'll see what I'm talking about. It's like something takes a hold of you and won't let you go."

Jenna gives me this priceless look and says, "Girl, you know what that is, don't you? It's the damn sex spell. Your slut gene has been activated and you've gotten a taste of that orgasmic DNA. That's all it is."

"Do you believe there's only one person on this earth for you?"

"What? Hell no!"

"Drew doesn't either, but he does think it's difficult to find one that can make you happy."

"Yeah, I'll go with that. But I think the sea is loaded with tons of fish. You just have to use the right bait."

Jenna and Drew are probably right, but whatever the case, I'm glad Drew and I found each other.

"So, Key West with me then?"

"Yeah."

"No surly Cate?"

"Yeah."

"Okay, but if you do, I swear I'll kick your ass."

And she almost ends up doing exactly that. The first couple of days I'm fine, loving the warm temps and the beach, but after day four, I'm over this place. Every day and night we do the same thing and Jenna's agenda is completely different from mine. All I want to do by this time is go home. To Drew. I want to get away from all the partying because I'm not into it at all. The sticky floors where everyone has spilled their sugary drinks, or worse, and the gooey seats, where you're afraid to sit, make me cringe to think about. And then I have to fend off drunk and horny dudes, who are kind of sad and pitiful, but completely annoying with the way they pour their drinks all over me. Each night when we get home, I immediately jump in the shower, while Jenna promptly passes out. By day five, I'm doing a mental hourly countdown until I can leave this horrible place.

Saturday morning, I practically have to beat Jenna to get her to wake up. Of course, she didn't go to bed until five a.m. Our flight is at ten, so we need to leave for the airport at eight. After four attempts, I finally get her going. When we land in Indy, Drew is waiting at the baggage claim and Jenna looks like a worn out hooker.

"Don't ask," she says as she walks straight past him and takes the first seat she finds.

"Is she okay?" he asks.

"Hung over. I had to beat her up to get her out of bed. I'm so glad to be home. I'm never leaving you again."

"I like the sound of that," he says.

"No, I'm serious. It was awful. I never should've gone. It was not my scene at all."

He turns to me and runs his finger down my cheek. "I'm so sorry. I was hoping you'd have a great break." Then his arms are around me and I bury myself in his embrace.

The luggage starts dropping and I reluctantly pull myself away. Drew collects our bags and Jenna, and we head to his car.

"I think we need to stay here tonight. Jenna's not in any shape to drive and needs sleep and so do I. With you."

"That can be arranged."

When we get to Drew's, he takes Jenna to the extra bedroom and she crawls into bed. That's the last we hear from her until later that night. Drew and I sit in the living room and catch up for a while. I tell him all about my awful week, but instead of feeling sorry for me, he laughs. He thinks it's funny that I hated the clubs and bars, and hated staying out late with Jenna.

"Why is it so funny?"

"Selfishly, because you weren't looking for other guys."

"So, you are happy I was miserable?"

"Uh, yeah." And his smile speaks a million words. Drew McKnight may have been a little jealous before I went to Key

West. But now, he's a happy guy, knowing I was miserable there. And it's my turn to smile. I lean over and kiss him. Then he adds, "By the way, I wanted to wait until you got back to share this news with you." He's almost rubbing his hands together.

"What news?"

"I've been named chief resident for next year."

"What? That's awesome! Congratulations!" Now I really lay a kiss on him. "I can't believe you've been holding this in!"

"Yeah, I know. It's been kind of hard." He's so excited; he grabs me and squeezes all the air out of me.

"Drew," I squeak, "Can't breathe!"

"Oh," he instantly releases me. "Sorry 'bout that." Then we both laugh.

"Oh my god, I can't believe this. This is so huge for you. This means you'll be able to practically name your fellowship then, right? I mean, don't chiefs carry a lot of clout?"

Never being one to boast, he says in an understated way, "A fair amount. I think I want Charleston, though. Is that okay with you?"

He's asking me as though I'm a part of his future. We've kind of hinted at this sort of thing, but this is no hint this time.

"Are you asking because you want my opinion or because you want to know if I want to go with you?"

His hand cups my cheek and all the cheer turns serious. "Cate, I'm asking because I want you by my side, wherever I go. I want you to be happy with that decision. I'm not going to choose just for me anymore."

Wow. My head drops down as I stare at my lap. This is an unexpected discussion. Not that I don't want to have it. I love Drew and at some point I figured we would have this chat, but I didn't think it would be today.

"I take it from your reaction we're traveling different roads."

I quickly say, "No, not at all! I was only thinking I didn't expect to be talking about this today. I want to be with you, too, Drew. And to answer you, I would love to return to Charleston, as long as I don't have to live with my parents."

His eyes grow dark and hooded as he says, "You won't be living with anyone but me. And at some point our kids."

I'm sure my brows shoot up to the heavens when he makes this announcement. Then he adds, "That is if you want kids. I'm willing to do anything your way, Cate."

"I want kids. No more than three, though. That's my limit."

"Fine with me. But we won't work on that until a few more years. We can practice for the time being."

"I like that idea." We get a little practice in that night, and the next morning, Jenna and I head back to Purdue. For once, I'm ready to hit the books and finish up this semester.

My birthday weekend arrives in April, and Drew says he has something special planned. On Friday, another spectacular flower arrangement is delivered. It contains all the special flowers he gave me before: roses, lilies, calla lilies, white carnations, orchids, and tulips. This time, I know what they all mean. Jenna's jaw hits the floor and I take my finger and push it back up to close her mouth.

"Fuck, are you spoiled." That's all she says.

"Yes, I am. He hasn't mentioned anything to you about this weekend, has he?"

"Not a word. Want me to ask Ben?"

"Yeah, would you?"

She picks up her phone and makes the call. I can hear them chatting, but when she hangs up, she has a sly look on her face. "Don't ask me a thing. I promised Ben I wouldn't tell you."

"That is not fair. You're my best friend."

"Yeah, but I'm Ben's sister and he's Drew's best friend. And that puts me awkwardly between a rock and a hard place. So I'm screwed either way."

"If I guess will you tell me?"

"No. My lips are sealed. When are you leaving?"

"As soon as I get packed."

Jenna presses her lips together. "Did he tell you what to pack?"

"No, why?"

"I don't know. Just asking."

"Gah, you suck."

She makes a face, runs to her room, and slams the door shut. I look at the flowers, smell them, and go finish packing. I want to take the flowers with me.

"Hey Jenna, how can I take these with me and not have them spill all over the place?"

"Got a box? Set them in a box," she yells through her door.

Looking around, I don't see anything, until she tosses one out of her room. "Here." Then her door slams shut again. Damn, she definitely is avoiding me.

When I'm finally packed, I yell through her door that I'm leaving. She runs out and squishes me in a giant hug. "Have fun, birthday girl and I'll see you on Sunday." Then she skedaddles right back into her room, as though she can't bear to face me. Weird. Shaking my head, I head to my car and hit the road.

Sexy Drew waits for me as I pull into his parking lot. It's a gorgeous spring day, and he's wearing a black t-shirt and faded jeans. He opens my car door, as usual, and pulls me into his arms.

"Happy Birthday weekend, gorgeous."

For whatever reason, I'm unusually excited to see him.

"Thank you," I bubble out. Then his warm, wet lips find mine and I sink into his embrace. My fingers weave into his thick, messy hair, and all I want to do is stand here and kiss him. But he ends my pleasure all too soon.

"Let's get your things." I pop open the trunk and he surprises me when he takes my things and instead of carrying them inside, he puts them in his car. Then he takes my hand and says, "Let's go."

"I ... where ... the flowers."

His brows crease in confusion.

"I brought the gorgeous flowers you sent."

"Ahh." He nods.

He walks to the passenger's side and retrieves them. "We'll bring them, too."

"Where are we going?"

"You'll see."

We drive downtown and he pulls up to the Conrad Indianapolis Hotel and a valet opens my door. I look at Drew and he gets out of the car and meets me, grabs my hand, and we walk inside to check in. Apparently he's booked a suite for the weekend. He's lost his mind.

Leaning in to him, I whisper, "Are you crazy? This is expensive!" He chooses to ignore me. The clerk hands him his keys and the bellman follows with our luggage on a cart. Once upstairs, the bellman gives us a brief tour of our one-bedroom suite and then leaves. When he's gone, I say, "This is amazing, but Drew, it's way too much."

"Happy birthday to the love of my life. Now if you don't stop with this train of thought, you'll kill my pleasure. Don't kill this for us, Cate."

A bottle of iced champagne awaits us with two glasses and Drew heads over to uncork it. He holds up his glass and says, "Here's to the girl who changed my life. Happy birthday, Cate."

After we sip our tasty drinks, he announces that it's room service tonight and tomorrow is a spa day for me. He's lined up some sort of body treatment, massage, a manicure, and pedicure. "And, by the way, their room service is supposed to be excellent."

I'm stunned. I don't know what to say. I suppose I look like some big goofy fool, because I say nothing. And then I start to cry. Not a full on ugly, boohoo cry. But an overwhelming type of cry. You know, the kind where you feel joy and loved.

"Don't cry, babe. This is supposed to be fun for you."

"It is," I wail and sniff. "But I've never done these things before and I'm so affected—in a good way."

He puts his hands on my shoulders and says, "Cate, look at me."

I do as he says.

"This is only the beginning of all the things I want to do for you. So, sweet beautiful thing, you'd better get used to it in a big hurry."

He's all blurred as I look at him, and I smile, though it's watery and icky, but he hugs me into his broad chest. And it's exactly where I want to be.

In the morning, I slap Drew's hands away as he wakes me.

"Don't you want coffee and breakfast before you go to the spa?"

"Grr. What time is it?"

"Nine-thirty."

"No, it's not." I stick my face back into my pillow, convinced he's teasing me.

"Uh, yes it is. There's a clock on the bedside table if you don't believe me."

Lifting my head, I take a quick look and am shocked to see he's right. "Holy hell! How did I sleep this late?"

"Want me to tell you?"

Then I remember the night before and my face warms.

"Ahh, she still blushes at the thought of sex with her boyfriend." I don't know why, but I do.

"That wasn't sex. What we did should be illegal." I think about all the things his mouth did to me, and the places his fingers went, and I'm pretty sure my face is now red as an apple.

"God, I love it when your skin flushes like that." His mouth moves to my neck and kisses me on my pulse point. "If you don't get a move on, you'll end up going to your spa appointment smelling like a freshly fucked woman. I don't mind it, but I'm not sure if you do."

Shit! I hop out of bed and make a dash for the shower, hearing his laughter follow me.

After a quick shower and some breakfast, we head off to the spa. Drew's only getting a massage and says to meet him back in the room when I'm done.

The rest of the morning and early afternoon I am pampered, exfoliated, moisturized, massaged, hot-stoned, and given the hand and foot treatment. It's amazingly relaxing and when I return to the room, I feel like a new woman.

Drew is watching hockey when I get back. He's totally absorbed since the playoffs are set to begin in a couple of weeks. But as soon as I enter the room, he turns the TV off, and I'm the center of his world.

"You don't have to do that," I say.

He gives me a look like I'm one of the Velociraptors from Jurassic World and I just stepped off the screen and into the living room. "It's your birthday weekend and I plan to be with you every moment. I can watch hockey any day of the week. Now, how was it?"

"Oh my goodness. It was like nothing I've ever experienced before."

"Okay, now you're stepping on my toes, babe. I thought I was your best." He winks.

I laugh. "You know what I mean."

"You loved it, then?"

"God, yeah!"

"Let me see your fingers and toes."

I hold out my hands while I kick off my shoes.

"Nice. I'm gonna have to play with those toes a little."

"Didn't know you have a toe thing."

"I don't. But I kinda like yours. You hungry?"

"Starving."

"Let's go eat."

During lunch we talk about mundane things, but then I turn the conversation down another lane. "I've been offered an internship this summer with a finance firm here in town. It's a great opportunity and I'd like to take it."

"Congratulations, Cate, that's great! When did this happen?"

"This past week. One of my professors told me about it and said it was a long shot, so I didn't think much about it until they called and made me the offer yesterday."

"You accepted, I presume?"

"Not exactly. I told them I'd let them know on Monday."

"Why?"

"Because I need a place to live."

He laughs. "What? Did you think I'd say no?"

I fidget with my napkin before answering. "No. It's only that a whole summer is a lot longer than we're used to, and my parents will freak at the idea of me living with you."

"Hmm. I see. So you're willing to give up a huge career enhancer because of a couple of minor glitches."

He has a way of making my objections sound silly. "I guess it would be pretty damn stupid of me."

"Look, we won't get on each other's nerves, if that's what you're worried about. I would love having you with me for an entire summer. In fact, I'll go so far as to beg you to take the damn job. Please, oh please, Cate."

He has me laughing by this time.

"And didn't you say your father thought you had a silly major?"

"Yeah."

"Well, this is your chance to prove him wrong."

"True. But they still won't like us living together."

He waves his hand through the air. "Oh, hell, they'll get over it when they find out you have free rent."

"Oh no. I can't do that. I'll pay a part of it."

He shrugs. "We'll figure something out then. But make that call Monday."

"Okay, I will."

That evening, Drew tells me only to dress in whatever is most comfortable to me. He's wearing jeans and a light sweater. A knock on our door surprises me and he goes to answer it with a sly smile on his face. In walks an entourage of people, one obviously a chef. His name is Michael and he's here to prepare our dinner. I go to the bedroom to quickly change, and come out wearing jeans and a sweater, too.

The chef prepares something, but Drew won't tell me what. And the other people have disappeared. When I ask about them, Drew only smiles and shrugs. Then he leads me back into the bedroom for a minute. "It's a big surprise birthday dinner, so if it doesn't work out exactly right, please don't hold it against me."

"Why would I hold it against you? And everything you've done so far has surpassed anything I've ever experienced, so stop." I hug him. "You're the best, Drew."

"No, you are. And you stole my line." He smacks my butt and then gets that heated look in his eyes.

"No! We can't. Michael is out there. And those other people."

"Don't worry about them." He starts stalking me around the bedroom. I can't help giggling because I feel like a little kid. Finally, I'm trapped in the corner and he pulls me by my wrists and tosses me onto the bed, where he tickles me until I almost pee.

"With everything I've ever done, all the places I've ever been, and every person I've ever met, nothing can come close to the sparkle in your eyes, or the love I feel in my soul when you look at me, Cate Forbes." His lips skim mine, teasing them, as they taste and his words touch a place in my heart I didn't know existed.

"I feel it too, Drew, when you look at me."

It's one of those rare moments between two people that love each other and I don't want it to end. But we're interrupted by a knock, and Drew offers me a crooked grin when he gets up to answer it. I hear them murmuring, but don't know what's said. Then he's back and tells me dinner will be ready in about forty-five minutes.

"Would you like some wine? And we can watch Michael cook."

"That would be nice."

So we sit at the small counter in the kitchen while Michael is busy preparing our meal and I soon become engrossed watching him. He's making oven-roasted salmon, sautéed mixed baby vegetables, and parmesan risotto. He will also serve a grilled romaine salad with walnuts, gorgonzola, and a cherry vinaigrette. It all looks and sounds delicious.

When it's almost ready, the chef nods to Drew, and Drew asks me to wait in the bedroom. I think it's sort of strange, but I don't say anything. I go in and sit on the bed, waiting patiently. About five minutes pass and Drew comes to get me.

"Okay, close your eyes for me, please, and I'll lead the way."

"We're going someplace else?"

"Just follow my lead, Sherlock."

With my eyes closed, and holding onto him, I follow. I step up and down when he tells me and finally I hear the words, "You can open your eyes now, Cate."

Grinning, I do, but then, I gasp and my hand flies to my mouth. This is one of those *I can't believe it* moments. I do a couple of pirouettes and my eyes stay saucered. One thing I didn't pay attention to was the fact that there was a terrace outside of our living room. The team of people that arrived with Michael evidently came out here and decorated it. There are paper lanterns, rose petals, candles, and twinkling lights everywhere. A small table is set for dinner and music plays from inside. A waiter is ready to serve us and it's the most perfect setting I've ever seen.

Drew holds the chair out for me and I sit. Our food is delivered and it's so tasty I keep mmming.

"You keep that up, you'll mmm yourself to death."

"Maybe, but this is really delicious."

"The hotel said I wouldn't be disappointed and they were right. Michael is excellent."

"How did you come up with this?"

"I wanted something special for your twenty-first birthday."

"You succeeded by miles. Thank you, if I haven't said it yet. You keep upping the ante."

"There is no ante." His kind eyes are earnest and intently focused on me. "I want to please you, Cate."

It's difficult to contain my excitement and I feel giddy. "You've more than done that."

We finish eating and I'm ashamed to say there isn't a morsel left on my plate. Then the waiter reappears with a small cake and candles in it while Drew sings me happy birthday.

"Thank you, Drew. I wouldn't change a thing. But oh god, it's a good thing you have another career because you'd go broke as a singer."

"Yeah, pitiful, aren't I?"

"Never that," I say conjuring up images of last night remembering how he makes up for the lack of singing skills in other areas. "But the cake?"

"Just wait."

The waiter serves us and it's an ice cream cake with chocolate cake and oreo ice cream.

"It's official. Best birthday ever," I say around a huge mouthful of creamy, yummy stuff.

When we finish our cake and all the servers and Michael are gone, I look at Drew and say, "I doubt this birthday could ever be topped."

"You sure about that?"

"Hell yeah. This was nothing but a series of awesome."

Only he strikes me speechless when he gets out of his seat, drops to his knee, and takes my hands in his. "Cate Forbes, I knew the minute I saw you that I would be asking you this question one day. You have opened up my heart and soul to a love I didn't understand, but now that I do, I never want to let it go." He swallows and I feel the tears begin to well up in my eyes. "Will you say yes to being my better half? I promise to be Louise's slave for life." I open my mouth to form the word yes, but all the air has left my lungs. "Marry me, Cate."

He has the most adorable look on his face; all I can do is hug him. I'm so surprised by everything he's managed to do, but when he reaches into his pocket and pulls out the ring box, he looks like that playful, excited little boy again. He places it in the palm of his hand and holds it out for me.

Finally, words burst from my mouth. "You don't want to put it on me?"

"I want you to see if you like it or not. If you don't, we'll get whatever you want."

"I'm sure it's perfect, like everything else about tonight."

He just holds the box for me to take. "It's all yours, Cate."

I take it, open it, and feel myself smile from ear to ear. I close the box, and throw myself into his arms again. "I couldn't have chosen anything better." My body trembles from head to toe. I never in a million years imagined I'd be getting a diamond ring for my birthday.

"You never answered me."

"Huh?"

"Will you marry me?"

"Yes! A million yesses!"

He stands, spins me around, and lets out a huge *whoop!*

"When?" I ask.

"After you graduate and I finish my residency. Next year."

"Oh, that's perfect. Can it be small?"

"I don't care if we get married in the Elvis Chapel in Vegas. I just want to be Mr. Cate Forbes." He grabs the box from me and slides the ring on my finger.

"Oh my god!" And we both start laughing. Then I sober up. "My parents!"

"They know. I called your dad to ask for your hand and for his blessing."

I put my hand over my heart thinking how sweet that is. "You did that?"

"Of course! I'm a southern boy, you know. Besides, my mother would've killed me if I hadn't."

"And your parents?"

"They know too."

"And?"

"Can hardly wait to hear your reaction. My mom helped me pick out your ring. Do you like the solitaire?"

"Yes! It's what I always wanted. Just a solitaire. How did you know?"

"Mom asked if you wore a lot of jewelry, and I said no. This is what she said to go with."

"Remind me to thank her. It's so huge."

"No, it's not. It's two carats."

"Whoa. I'll be afraid to wear this."

"Don't be. It's insured. I love you. You, Cate are everything to me."

"I love you, too, Drew. I can't wait until you're Drew Forbes." I manage to say straight faced before a laugh bursts from me.

He cracks a smile. Then his lids lower to half-staff and he says, "Let's dance."

"What's wrong?" I ask, because his mood has shifted.

"Not a thing. I'm just so damned happy you've agreed to make it official and be mine forever."

He pulls me into his arms, and it's here I want to stay. For a lifetime.

TWENTY
Present

FOR SOME REASON I STAND in the elevator glancing at my ring-less finger. I want to run, but I promised Andy I wouldn't. I've been given a second chance and I'm ready to take it.

The doors part and Ted is standing there, waiting. I step out.

"Cate, just the woman I'm looking for."

I frown and say, "Me?" I place my hand on the hollow of my throat.

"Yes, I have to reschedule our ten o'clock. I'm hoping we could do lunch instead."

I hesitate because I want to see Andy for lunch.

"I'm actually already late for a meeting. I have to run. Talk to my assistant if you can make lunch."

He steps into the elevator and is gone before I can respond. I walk over to the cube I've been using. Jeff is standing there flipping through papers. He glances up when I get close.

"What's the long face for?"

I shake my head not wanting to get into the Ted debate with him. "I think this is my last day here."

"No, come work for me," Jeff pleads dramatically.

I smile. "I'm going to miss you all."

"We should do lunch."

I give him a tight smile. "I actually have plans. However, it's not like my office is that far away. We can plan a lunch another time."

He leans in for a hug. "I'm going to miss you. I have to run to a meeting, but promise you won't be a stranger."

Then he's off and I sit at my desk and boot up. While I wait to log onto the system, I dial Ted's extension from the list posted on the wall. After a short conversation, I learn that Ted is booked solid for the day and going out of town tomorrow. His only available appointment short of something late in the evening is lunch. The project deadline is tomorrow. I have no choice but to take the lunch meeting.

Sighing, I make a call to Andy to give him the bad news.

"Hey, I'm sorry but I have to break our lunch date."

"Something came up?"

There's hesitancy in his voice. I can't get mad that he sounds as though he doesn't quite trust me. I have been running from him the last few weeks.

"I have a meeting that got rescheduled to lunch. However, that means I can probably swing leaving early. Why don't I come to your place and bring dinner to make it up to you?"

"You sure?"

"Yes, I want to see you again."

His voice is more relaxed. "Then it's a date. See you later."

"I'll call you when I'm on my way."

The meeting with Ted turns out to only be two minutes. I end up e-mailing him the document at his request. He tells me he'll be in touch if he has any questions and apologizes for breaking our lunch date. Our conversation almost seems sterile. Clearly, he's moved on after my refusal to go to France with him, which isn't a bad thing. I'm grateful we can remain cordial with no bad feelings either way.

Ted makes up our missed lunch by paying for me, Jeff and the rest of the staff to go out instead. By the time I get to my office at the firm, Mandy follows me through my door.

"You don't call. You don't write. I thought we lost you to Ted."

I turn and hug her. "I missed you too. How are things?"

She spins in a whirlwind and sits in one of the chairs in front of my desk.

"How are things? I'll tell you how things are. Daniel is dating that redhead downstairs from the law office—Tammy. And she's not good enough for him."

I sit on the edge of my desk and face her. "In other words, she's not you."

"Exactly."

"I can't say I blame him. You totally freaked after he spent that one night at your place. Then you pawned him off to other girls."

"Whose side are you on?"

"Yours, but you have to see the part you played in this."

I have that déjà vu moment of saying words that have been said to me.

"Fine," Mandy says. "We're going out Friday and finding me a new guy. And don't say no. I see it in your eyes." She holds up a finger. "You promised."

I sighed. "Fine. We'll go out for drinks on Friday."

She stands and smirks. "I see someone isn't in a dry spell anymore."

I open my mouth. She shakes her head. "Don't say a word. Tell me on Friday. It will give us something to talk about other than Daniel. Anyway, I'm glad your assignment's over. We missed you."

I spend the rest of the morning making sure my billable hours are in the system and I compose an e-mail to my boss about my two minute meeting with Ted. I currently don't have any assignments, so I'm able to duck out a little early.

At home, I take a quick shower and get dressed. When my cab arrives, I finish placing my takeout order to be delivered to Andy's. The Thai place he recommended says it will be about forty five minutes. The ride to his place is just over thirty.

I knock on his door and he opens it with a grand smile.

"Hey gorgeous."

"Hey you," I say before lifting on my toes and giving him a quick kiss.

When he asks me, "How was work?" it feels so domestic it's as if I've arrived home.

"Boring. I'd much rather have spent the day with you. What did you do all day?"

He takes my coat and my skin feels electric everywhere he touches me.

"I went to the gym, did some laundry, picked up my dry cleaning, boring stuff. I would have preferred being with you as well."

He kisses me as his hands slide down and rest at the small of my back. He pulls me closer and I can feel how happy he is to see me.

I pull back far enough to say, "I ordered dinner on the way. It should be here in about fifteen minutes."

He grins. "I can accomplish a lot in fifteen."

"Is that a challenge or a dare?"

His eyes twinkle and before I know it he's kneeling before me. I run my fingers through his blond hair liking his blue eyes radiating up at me.

We don't speak. Holding eye contact with me, he pushes my skirt up my thighs. It might have been more practical for me to wear jeans since we didn't have plans to go out. But I wanted to wear the garters because they make me feel sexy.

When my skirt is bunched up at my waist, he tugs a little at the garters that hold up thigh highs. "You know I like these."

I bite my lips because I remember all too well.

Then his mouth is on me. First through the fabric, then his breath heats my bare skin before he feasts on me. He's good, so very good and easily gets me there. I let out an unladylike scream seconds before a knock sounds on the door.

I cup my hands over my mouth as my eyes widen. My face gets hot as Andy grins at me, still on his knees. I point at him and then at the door.

He laughs and gets to his feet. My feeble attempt at angry face is a massive fail because I'm flaming hot from embarrassment.

"Just a minute," he calls out and heads to the kitchen to wash his hands. He uses the towel to wipe his face and I duck in the shadowy hallway.

I don't worry about coming out of my hiding place because I've already paid by credit card over the phone. Andy only has to give the guy a tip. When the door closes, his guffaws have me narrow-eyed. He sets the bag down on the counter and comes to the hallway.

"It's not funny," I try to say straight faced but blow it.

"There is nothing to be embarrassed about. So you like sex. Who doesn't?"

"I screamed," I say, feeling a little silly.

"So what? You're vocal about it. I like hearing you scream knowing I can do that to you."

He silences further protest with a long kiss. I can taste myself on his tongue as he presses me into the wall. His rigid cock rubs against me and I moan, wanting him inside me more than the delightful smells of the food.

I reach behind me and unzip my skirt. I let it fall to the ground unceremoniously. Andy is in the process of undoing the button on his jeans when a knock sounds at the door.

Andy frowns. "Maybe he gave me the wrong credit card copy. Stay right here."

I nod. I'm no longer embarrassed by the scream. I'm turned on to the point of not caring who sees me. Andy has a way of doing that to me. I curl a finger into my unders to take them off, ready for what's to come. A man barrels past Andy.

"Drew, my boy. I haven't heard from you for over a week. That woman has you tied into knots. And you need to get out that funk. I brought food." He holds up a bag. "And beer." He holds a six pack of Yuengling with the other hand. "We can watch the Capitals play the Blackhawks. Or I have a hook up with a set of twins who live not too far from here if you're ready to finally get laid. If we hurry, I can make that call and get them over here."

The guy finally looks up and even though the hallway is shrouded in darkness, it's clear I'm not wearing pants. For a moment, I'm the deer and this stranger is hunter. I'm not sure who is more surprised.

"Oh, you have company."

Everything happens so fast; Andy is already moving to block the guy's sight of me as he was speaking. I have a vague memory of him the two times I briefly caught sight of him. I'm pretty sure he's one of the friends Andy was with the night I was too plastered to get home by myself and at the masquerade ball.

I crouch down and step in my skirt while six foot plus of Andy hides me somewhat. I'm so mortified I know I resemble a ripe tomato. When my skirt is zipped, I step up behind Andy. He glances over his shoulder before reaching for my hand and tugging me to step forward next to him.

"Is this the one?" the guy asks. "She looks like the one we ran into twice. It's her isn't it?"

"Yes. Mitch, meet Cate. Cate, this is Mitch, one of my friends from undergrad."

Mitch is slightly shorter but broader than Andy. He's a decent looking guy with deep set dimples. However, he stands as if he has a chip on his shoulder. I'm not quite sure if he has a problem or if that's his personality.

"Nice to meet you," I say reaching out a hand to him.

Mitch just looks at it. Awkwardly, I drop my hand back to my side.

"Cate, the one that left you in Charleston. Cate, the girl you came to Baltimore to forget. Cate, the girl you just happened to run into in DC. That Cate?"

Even if he hadn't said those words, the way he looks at me says he's not my biggest fan.

"Mitch, don't start."

The guy looks dumbstruck. "Seriously? We don't hang out much since undergrad. You show up in DC needing a place to stay for a while. Dave and I get you good and drunk and we hear this whole story about a girl who up and left you high and dry in Charleston. It takes a while to get your head out of your ass and move on, only for you to run into that girl again."

I should be insulted he's calling me a girl, but everything he's saying about me is true.

"Now, she's leading you around by the balls. If your mood is shit, I know she's playing games with you. If you are in a good mood, then I know she's leading you around by your dick."

"That's enough, Mitch. What I choose to do with Cate is my business."

"No, he's right Andy," I say.

Mitch's brows shoot up into his hairline. "Andy? What the fuck is up with that?"

"Drew," I say instead. "Maybe I should go."

"You should," Mitch says.

Andy cuts in. "No Mitch, you should go."

I don't want to be the cause of problems with his friends. Mitch has a right to be angry. "No, I have work in the morning. I should leave."

"Unfortunately, nobody is going anywhere. Some freak storm that was supposed to miss us is pounding DC and headed to Baltimore to ram us up the ass. Maryland has declared a state of emergency. I'd already taken the exit off the highway when the snow started. I turned off Sirius to listen to local radio station and knew I was fucked. You're stuck with us both."

I walk over to the window and I'm surprised by the amount of snow on the ground. It has only been less than a half an hour I've been here and the roads are already coated. Under the lamps that line the street, you can see that its coming down so thick it will be nearly a white out situation.

"There's a hotel in walking distance," I hear Andy say, as I watch the snow with fascination.

"So that's how it is now. I put you up when you first get into town and you're sending me to a hotel."

"I'll pay for it."

I turn from the window. "No, Mitch should stay. I'll go to the hotel."

"No fucking way," Andy growls.

Mitch and I both stare at Andy. It's not often I've seen him angry. His stubborn jaw has nothing on the narrow eyes he gives Mitch.

"Look," I begin. "Mitch, you're right. I made some poor choices with Drew."

"You're damn right."

I breathe and let Mitch's comment go for the sake of Andy. "I don't want to be the cause of a disagreement between you two. Friends before lovers," I offer like a peace pipe.

"Bros before ho's you mean."

"Fuck Mitch, stop being an asshole. Cate's not going anywhere. If you want to stay, you're going to be nice to her. You should start by apologizing. I'm a big boy. If I want Cate to keep my balls for me, that's on me."

His words might have been comical if not for the tension that's created a wall between Mitch and him.

"I'm not wrong, so what am I apologizing for?" Mitch declares.

"You're right. I'm sorry. I'm so sorry to both of you."

I head toward the bathroom because I have nowhere else to go and I'm not crying in front of Mitch. I won't give him that satisfaction. And If I leave the apartment, I will be running again and I promised Andy I wouldn't run. I close the door and stare at myself in the mirror. I want to cry, but I won't. If I plan to be with Andy, this won't be the last time I have to deal with hard feelings. This will be only the beginning.

I straighten my clothes by glaring at my reflection. I splash water on my face before I feel strong enough to go face the music. When I open the door, Mitch is there with his fist poised to knock.

He sighs. "Cate, I didn't mean to make you cry."

I hadn't cried. He's mistaken my flush from rinsing my face, but I don't correct him.

"Drew was in a bad place after you… Anyway, you aren't the bitch I thought you were. You could have called me all kinds of assholes out there. Instead, you took it. And that takes balls. They might be Drew's that you're holding." He chuckles at his own joke. I say nothing. "All I ask is that you really consider what you're doing. Guys have feelings too. He's a good one. He deserves a good woman. If that's you, well, all I ask is that you prove it." He holds out his hand. "Deal?"

I could have been a jerk and left him hanging like he'd done me earlier. However, I want to be with Andy. Mitch is his friend and it would be better if we could at least get along. I take his hand. "Deal."

Guys are strange. After our talk by the bathroom, Mitch sits down on the couch as if the last fifteen minutes hasn't happened. Obviously knowing his way around, he's made a plate of the Chinese food he brought and some of the Thai I ordered. I say nothing and watch the guys eat and drink with the game on after they ask if I would mind. How could I say no after being put in my place earlier?

Andy has my legs draped over his lap so my feet rest on the middle cushion between him and Mitch. My thighs become his plate as he eats.

While I struggle to chew the lukewarm food, they watch the hockey game take shape on the screen. Andy and Mitch banter about good and bad calls as I continue to force myself to swallow.

"You see that Cate? We're going to pull a win out of this one."

Mitch's whole demeanor has changed. He grips my ankle as if we are the best of friends while his eyes remain on the screen. He squeezes before letting go and jumping to his feet as the buzzer sounds.

Andy looks so alive, his face serene. The contentment of having me and his friend over is clear in his expression. I like the look there, so I smile when he faces me. His eyes darken and I sense he's forgotten about the game and wants to focus on me.

"You know where the other bedroom is," Andy says as he stands up with me in his arms. "I've got rounds in the morning."

"You have to work," I say dumbly. Of course he does.

Hospitals never close.

I've already received a text from the office emergency system letting me know the office will be closed tomorrow.

He glances down at me with a huge smile on his face. "Doctor's work is never done. Why don't we go play doctor?"

Mitch snickers. "I bet all that doctor play you did as a kid influenced your job choice."

"I was good at it," Andy says with a laugh and carries me into the bedroom.

He sets me down on my feet and his face is sober. "My office will most likely be closed. However, the hospital won't. In fact, because I live closer, I might get called in."

"Like you said, a doctor's work is never done. But I didn't bring a change of clothes."

His grin widens. "Great! You can sleep naked."

He's already working on the buttons of my blouse.

"Mitch is here," I say playfully slapping at his hands.

"I locked the door and he'll probably fall asleep on the couch. I don't have a TV in the other bedroom. He'll stay out there watching Sports Center most of the night."

"Andy."

"Cate," he says taking my hand and placing it on the hard length of him though his pants.

"I don't think I can knowing he's out there."

Andy groans and lets his head fall back on his shoulder.

The idea of me screaming with his friend in the other room is mortifying. "I do have a solution," I say as I get to my knees and work his jeans down to his ankles.

I do my best to suck him to the moon and back with hollow cheeks and humming noises. I know I'm doing a good job when he begins to lose control. He fists my hair in his hands and starts to fuck my face. It's so hot, I decide to use my free hand to work out the pressure that builds in me.

"Cate, baby, I'm coming."

His release is hot and salty and I take pleasure in swallowing it as I hold in the noise from my own pleasure. He frees himself from my mouth and pulls me to stand up.

"Did you just get yourself off?"

His eyes are husky on mine. I nod.

"With this hand?" he asks as he takes my wrist.

I nod again.

He lifts my hand to his mouth and sucks my fingers.

"Fuck, you taste good."

He then picks me up and I squeal not expecting it. He tosses me on the bed and I giggle as I land, which is so unlike me. He works my skirt and thong off before spreading my legs wide. He nestles there and gets me off another two times.

"I can't get enough of you," he says before sliding his stiff cock into me. He makes love to me long and slow and I've forgotten all about Mitch.

We lay in bed wrapped up in each other as his hand strokes my hair. I finally broach the subject.

"So were you really that bad off when I left?"

His hand stills. "Cate, I thought we weren't going to talk about the past."

"I know, but..." I'm not sure how to put it. "I need to understand."

He lets out a deep breath. "I know where everything went wrong. I know my part in it. When you left, it took me by surprise that you'd left the city for good. No one would tell me where you'd moved to and you changed your phone number. I admit I was pissed for a short time. I thought what we had deserved more than you leaving that way. But I get it. I know why you did it. Why you felt like you had to do it."

I listen to the sound of his heartbeats a few seconds before I speak. "I never meant to hurt you like that."

He was silent. "Let's just move on. Nothing is solved by dwelling on a past we can't change. You're here. I'm here. We're here together. In this together."

"We are and I'm so incredibly happy."

He kisses my forehead. "There is nothing in this world more important to me than to see you happy."

The smell of coffee wakes me in the morning as the bedroom door opens.

"Morning, I brought you a cup."

I squeal because it's not Andy speaking. I grip the covers around me. Mitch laughs.

"It's nothing I haven't seen before, cupcake, and I don't poach. You're Drew's and I respect that."

He sets the coffee down. "I'm making breakfast if you're

interested."

And he leaves the room as quickly as he came in. Only he doesn't close the door. My clothes are at the other end of the room. I'm left wondering what twilight zone I've entered. Men are crazy. Instead of getting out of bed, I sit up and grab the coffee. On the bedside table, a note sits on top of some clothes.

Cate,

I had early rounds and didn't want to wake you.
You look so beautiful when you sleep, when you're awake,
and wherever and whatever you're doing.
I've left you a tee-shirt and boxers.
Mitch has no boundaries when it comes to personal space.
I won't be long. I'll be back before lunch.
Stay.
Andy

I smile and quickly get dressed under the covers before heading to the bathroom to take care of my morning routine. I glance and only see the one toothbrush. As much spit swapping as Andy and I've done, it doesn't take much for me to talk myself into using his toothbrush. Fresh breath wins out and I head to the kitchen to deal with Andy's friend alone.

TWENTY-ONE
Past

---◆---

MY ROLE AS AN INTERN is in full swing and living with Drew is working out better than I'd expected. He is as easy going every day as he was on the weekends we were together. There are never any surprises, which I love about him.

My boss, Mr. Hendershot, is great. He takes me under his wing and spoon feeds me the kind of information interns rarely get. I've landed a gem of a job. Besides the occasional audit engagement for clients who have fiscal years, I'm working on writing their policy manual in the accounting department, which gives me the opportunity to use my dual major. Mr. Hendershot is filled with all sorts of knowledge that he doles out to me like M&M's and I joyfully gobble them up. Midway through the summer, he asks what my intentions are as far as geographical locations after graduation.

"My fiancé and I will be moving back to Charleston. He is going to pursue a fellowship in oncology there."

"Well, that's a shame, Cate, because I would love to have you on board with us. But I can certainly promise you a great recommendation. You know, wherever you land, you're going to shine."

That night I rush in from work, eager to share my news with Drew. He loves hearing about my work, and he's always very supportive of everything I do. But he's not there and I spy a note from him on the counter.

Just a reminder, babe, I have hockey practice tonight.
Won't be late.
This guy looooves you!

A giant grin spreads across my face. He always leaves me the cutest notes. I hug it to my chest on the way to the bedroom to change. When I get back to the kitchen I open up the fridge and decide to make Greek chicken for dinner. Drew loves it and he will be famished when he gets home.

I get everything assembled and pop the pan in the oven. Then I make a tossed salad. While it does its thing, I decide to drink a beer and read a bit. A little over an hour later, the apartment smells heavenly and my stomach rumbles in response.

When I open the oven door, the chicken looks scrumptious. So much so that my mouth waters. Checking the time, I see that Drew should be home in about thirty minutes. I turn the oven off, cover the pan loosely with foil, and decide to wait on him. Not much long after that my phone buzzes. Checking the caller ID, I see it's Drew.

"Hey honey."

"Cate," he wheezes.

"What's wrong?"

"I got checked in the ribs and I think they're fractured. I'm on the way to get an X-ray."

"Shit. Want me to come and get you?"

"No. I'm good to drive."

"You sure? You sound bad."

"Just hurts to breathe. I'll be home soon."

"Be careful."

"Will do."

Now I'm worried sick about him driving like that. Sitting and waiting is the worst. I want to call him, but I hate to be a bother. Too many minutes tick by and my phone rings at last.

"No break but I'm bruised. I'll be home in a bit."

"That's good news. Be careful."

I pace until I see his headlights through the blinds and I shoot out the door.

246

"This is a fine greeting. I need to get injured more often."

"Drew McKnight. Don't you ever say that. I've been worried sick."

I hold his arm while he gets out, noticing him wince as he does. "Can I get you some ice?"

"I'm not sure that will help, though it won't hurt. I have pain meds, but I don't like taking them."

"Take them at least tonight. Can you tell me what happened?"

"An everyday body check. Happens all the time, but this must've caught me just right. It was weird though, because I didn't feel like the guy hit me that hard." He shrugs and says, "I guess he got my sweet spot or something."

"Know what I think?"

"What?"

"Gramps can't take it anymore." I give him a lop-sided grin.

"Oh, I guess that's what it was."

We're inside now and I ask, "Want to sit or lie down?"

"Sit. I need food with these pain meds."

"Well, lucky you. You've come to the right place. Let me fix you a plate."

He doesn't eat much, which tells me how much pain he's in. Drew is not one to complain, and he doesn't now, but he can't seem to take a deep breath.

"I'm sorry, Cate, this is excellent, but I can't eat any more."

"It's fine. I'd rather you be comfortable than force yourself to eat. Let me help you to bed."

"I need a hot shower."

"Need help?"

"I've got this."

He does hurt. Normally he'd never refuse an offer like this. I help him to the bedroom where he slowly undresses. His side already has signs of bruising.

"Yep. Black and blue popping out already," I say.

"Hmm." His fingers probe the area, and he winces.

"Stop that. You already know you're bruised. You don't need to keep poking at yourself." He favors his side as he sort of does a wobble-walk to the bathroom. Not much later, he's out and gently plops onto the bed.

"Damn, I do feel old."

"But you look like a million bucks." I wink.

"Kiss me, Cate."

I bend over him and offer him my lips.

"You're the best wife-to-be a man could ever hope to have."

"And I love you more than ice cream, Drew."

"Hmm. That's a whole lot, isn't it?"

"You bet it is. Now let those pain killers do their job and get some sleep."

The next morning, he's feeling better. Physically, anyway. But something bothers him, only he won't say what. I pester him but he tells me he's fine.

It's about three weeks later while Drew is in the gym doing bench presses, when the side he injured flares with pain. It's so severe, he has to drop the weight, and call me.

"Cate, can you come to the gym?"

I pick him up and take him to the ER. They X-ray him and tell him he has pleurisy, an inflammation of the lining of the lung. Drew grills the doctor, while I as the ignorant layperson have no idea what's really going on. They give him antibiotics, which Drew insists he doesn't need and argues with the treating physician, but they eventually convince him to take them.

On the drive home, Drew is quiet and when I ask him questions, he responds in monosyllabic answers.

"Will you tell me what's in your head right now?"

"Frustrated, that's all."

"It's fine. You'll take the medicine and you'll be fine."

He isn't. The pain doesn't resolve. He goes to one of his attendings at the hospital, and they suggest more tests. He doesn't tell me any of this until a few weeks later.

Summer is ending and my final year at Purdue begins in one week. I can't believe it. I'm ready to get this show on the road so Drew and I can get on with our lives. I move back to West Lafayette in a few days, as my internship has ended, and most of my things are packed up. Drew and I will be spending these last few days together, because for whatever reason, he doesn't have to work.

I've just come in from the store and Drew is sitting on the couch. My arms are laden with grocery bags and normally, he would jump up to help me. This time he only sits there.

"Hey," I say.

"Cate. Can you sit here with me, please?"

"Give me a minute. My hands are full." It sort of pisses me off a little that he ignores my struggles. When I have everything put up, I go into the living room and notice how pale he is. His usually tanned face has a slightly grayish cast to it and he appears ... stressed. The normally happy-faced Drew is absent.

"What's wrong?" I ask, as I sit down, taking his hand.

He scratches his neck and says, "I should be fairly good at this, but I'm not. So I'm going to tell you straight up and please forgive my bluntness."

"Drew, you're scaring me."

"Cate, all this stuff going on with me, my ribs, the pleurisy. It's none of that. I have cancer. Bone cancer. Ewing Sarcoma to be precise."

My arms and hands go numb as shock settles in. "Wh-what? What are you saying? Cancer?" My gut drops through the floor and I want to lose everything I ate today. *Cancer! Drew!* My brain spins with his words.

"Yes, cancer. I wasn't satisfied with their diagnoses, so I discussed everything with one of the attendings in my program, and he suggested a bone scan. That's what it showed. Well, it showed a mass the size of a thumbnail and then I had a CT-guided needle biopsy, and a follow up PET scan."

"And you didn't tell me any of this?" I don't even know what most of what he said is.

"I didn't want to worry you if it turned out to be nothing."

"Drew," I throw my arms around him. "I wish you had told me. I would've been there with you."

"Guess it doesn't matter now," he says as he hugs me back.

"Oh my god. How did you hide this from me?"

He doesn't answer, only shakes his head.

"So now what?"

"I guess my choice of fellowships was prophetic. The oncology fellow gets cancer himself."

"Oh, Drew." I squeeze him tighter.

"Easy there, Cate."

"Oh," I say, letting him go.

"Don't let me go, just not so tight. I need those arms of yours right now. I'm scared. For one of the first times in my life."

Now I know this is the real deal. I know I can't let the tears loose that keep trying to punch their way through. I must be strong for him.

"Talk to me, babe. Tell me what the plan is," I say, my face against his neck. *Please, God, let me be strong for this beautiful man.*

"Chemo. Then surgery. Here's the weird thing. I have a pediatric cancer. It's super rare for an adult to get this. But they may switch up my chemo a bit since I'm not a peds patient. I meet with the Oncology team Monday. I had a phone call with one of them today. They may want to do a surgical excision first. They're having a tumor board on Friday."

"A tumor board?"

"Yeah, it's where a bunch of oncologists get together and discuss a case. I will be theirs this Friday. Then we meet on Monday to decide my course of therapy."

"Are you good with this? Do we need to go somewhere else?"

"Nah. They connect with all the major centers so the treatment protocols are pretty much the same."

"Your parents? Do they know?"

"Not yet. I'm going to call them tomorrow."

"Drew, look at me." Sadness dulls his normally bright blue eyes. "We're going to kick this cancer in the ass, babe. Do you hear me? I'm going to be with you every step of the way and we're going to knock this thing out of you. I want you to understand this."

"I know. I'm with you, Cate. We're going to win this war. It's what I want to do with my life ... with our lives."

I grab his face and kiss him. "You bet your ass we do."

"There's something else. With chemo, there's a strong chance it will destroy any possibility of my ability to have kids."

"Drew, I don't care ..."

"Let me finish, Cate. I want to freeze my sperm. In the chance that it does, and I do beat this ..."

"There is no if. You're going to beat this."

"I know. So, when the time comes, and we want kids, we'll still be able to do that."

"Okay." And I hug him, because if there is a choice, I will always choose Drew.

Drew has a meeting scheduled with his oncology team on Monday, the same day classes start for me. I want to skip so I can be with him. He assures me he's good.

"Realistically, babe, what can you do? I have one of my attendings coming with me, and Mom and Dad will be here, too. It's not that I don't want you there, but you need to be in class. This is your final year."

"I know but this is your life. I'm a part of it. I want to be with you, holding your hand."

"And you will. In spirit."

I pace the living room. I've delayed my departure by two days. I don't have books or anything purchased yet. He's right and I know it. This is going to be a tough semester for me, too. I'm taking eighteen ball-busting hours.

"Come here." He calls me over to the couch where he sits. Then he pulls me on his lap. I suck in my breath and try to get up. "I'm not fragile, Cate. Don't treat me as though I am. Now listen up. We both have lives to live and I want us to be as normal as possible. Cancer sucks, no matter how you look at it. There will be times I'll need you desperately. Right now is not one of them. I have a huge support team and you're my number one. I know that. As soon as I'm finished, I'll call. But you have a job to do. When we get married in June, you need to be done, your diploma in hand, with that summa cum laude behind your name. You won't be able to do that if you skip classes."

"I love you, Drew."

"Good. Now take your clothes off, because it's going to be a few days before I see you again."

This time when we make love, it's slow and careful. Drew's eyes never leave mine, it seems. Almost like he's memorizing everything about me that he can. And as much as it's beautiful, it's frightening, too. The vibrancy of him, the way he's so full of life makes me believe they must have made an error. They must've gotten it all wrong. It was someone else's biopsy that they got mixed up with his. Then the truth bullies the fantasy aside and I know it's real. Urgency invades me and I can't seem to get enough of him. I want to drink him in, fill myself with Drew, until I can't possibly take any more. He senses it; I know it. I'm no good at hiding my emotions. His lips capture mine in a searing kiss and when he releases me, he says, "It's going to be fine. We'll make it, Cate. I know. I'm going to beat this."

And I believe him. He's so convincing and strong. How can he not?

His chemo treatments begin the following week. As his luck would have it, they are opting for the more aggressive approach. The drugs they will use are toxic. I cringe just thinking about it. Caroline, Sam's wife, is going with him for his first treatment, and then I will be there the next day, to spend the weekend. This semester is turning to shit. All I think about is being with him.

When I arrive at his apartment, he's in bed. The blinds are drawn and he's asleep. I don't want to wake him so I stand in the doorway and watch him. He's beautiful. His full lips and straight nose are profiled against his pillow and I want to bend down and kiss him, but I don't budge. The sheet is pulled down his body, exposing his torso, and I think about what's lurking beneath that gorgeous skin. How can something so ugly, so grotesque, be growing inside of all that magnificence? I cover my mouth to stop any sound from escaping. The urge to kiss his ribs nearly drives my feet into forward motion. I want to be the one to take it all away from him. Ridiculous, I know, but that's how I feel, nonetheless. Guess you could say it's my protective instinct. If I could touch every single bit of him right now, without waking him, I would. I wish I could soak him up, absorb him into me, and keep him safe there forever. I turn and quickly run away, trying to get out of there so I don't wake him with my sobs. It's so fucking hard to keep my shit together when I'm around him.

The vibration in my pocket has me digging out my phone. It's Jenna.

"Hey," I gulp.

"You okay?"

"Yeah. Just a small meltdown. He's sleeping and I haven't even woken him up."

"Why the tears then?"

"Because I looked at him lying there and …" I'm a hopeless, sobbing mess all over again.

"Shh, it's okay," she coos. "It's going to be fine, Cate."

In a shaky whisper, I say, "I don't think it is, Jenna."

"Cate, get a grip. You have a ton at stake here, particularly that guy inside. Get your shit together."

I sniff loudly and rub my eyes with my fist. "You're right. You're right."

"He needs your happy face, not some weepy-assed woman in his life right now."

"I know. I only do this around you."

"You can cry on my shoulder any day of the week, but if you ever do this in front of him, I will personally kick your ass all the way back to Charleston."

I rub my face again. "Okay. You can. I may even help you."

"Now go inside and crawl in bed with that man."

"But he needs to sleep."

"Listen to me you dork. He needs *you*! He needs you to hold him so get in that bed and wrap your arms around him and hug your body close to him. Oh, and stop in the bathroom first to make sure you don't have raccoon eyes and skanky breath."

That makes me laugh, and I actually snort. "Okay, boss."

"Now 'git'."

Sneaking in the bathroom, I fix my eyes, removing all signs of the raccoon and then brush my teeth.

Back in the bedroom, I don't allow myself to have any morbid, weepy thoughts. I undress and slide under the covers, then wind myself around Drew.

He lifts his head and smiles. "Hey, babe. You're the best thing I've seen in ages. God, you feel good." His arm hugs me tightly to him and holds my head to his chest.

"How're you feeling?"

"Just wiped out. Otherwise, okay."

"Yeah?"

"Yeah. They gave me all kinds of stuff to counteract the side effects and so far so good, other than the damn exhaustion."

"Then sleep. I'm here and will get you anything and everything you need."

"The only thing I need is you." He kisses the top of my head. "I missed you."

"I missed you more."

"Your classes?" He's always so worried about me, and how I'm dealing with all of this.

"My professors are awesome. I'm good."

"Hmm. Good to hear."

"Sleep, babe. I'm right here with you, if you need me."

"Love you."

"Right back to you." I press my lips to his chest.

I didn't think I was tired, but being in Drew's arms, close to him, must have made me relax enough to fall asleep. When I wake up, it's pitch black in the room. He's still out, so I scoot out of bed and I'm shocked to see it's after ten. I need to fix something to eat because my stomach just let out a huge growl, like Tony the Tiger. Then I chuckle to myself, thinking that's probably what I'll end up having to eat—Frosted Flakes. I doubt Drew has shopped for groceries with everything going on. But I get a big surprise when I open the refrigerator. It's stocked full of things. So I grin and go to work.

Chicken and dumplings is on the menu, along with homemade chicken noodle soup. Those are two things I can cook and cook well. My mother taught me how to make them when I was young, and they are two of my specialties. Jenna always begs me for them, and Drew loves them, too. I'm just about finished with both when he makes an appearance in the kitchen.

And did I ever fuck up. He looks green. And then it smacks me in the face. The odor!

"Oh, shit!" I turn on the exhaust fan and light a couple of candles, but the damage is already done. "I'm so sorry. I didn't think. I was hungry and figured they would be a great treat for you."

He has my favorite faded jeans on and a t-shirt and he says, "I'm just going to go and sit in my car for a minute."

Now I totally feel like a douche. "Oh, no. I'll open a window. The smell should be gone really fast."

"It's okay. I just need some air."

I fist my hands in my hair. How in the fuck could I have been so damn stupid? The man just gets massive chemo, he's bordering on nausea, and I'm in here cooking up a storm. What a dumbnut!

My first mission is to air the place out, so I open a couple of windows and burn some more candles. Luckily, everything I've cooked is done. I turn it all off and run outside to check on Drew.

He sits in his car with his head leaning back against the seat.

"Are you okay?"

"Just sweating. I got so nauseated, I was pouring the stuff."

"Jeez. Nice to know your fiancée is a moron, huh?"

He laughs a little. "It's all in the learning curve, babe."

"Thanks for not being pissed off."

"As if I could ever be that at you."

"You never do get mad at me. Why is that?"

His head is still back and his eyes are closed. He shrugs and says, "What purpose would that serve? Anger only breeds anger. I get pissed at you, then you get pissed back at me, and it turns into a vicious cycle. It's just better if I analyze my feelings and deal with them."

I'm standing right outside his car, talking to him through his window. I lean down against the frame as I think about what he says. It makes so much sense, but most of us react before we process what's happening. We don't stop and listen to what the other person is saying. "How the hell did you get to be so smart and intuitive?"

"I'm not. I'm just a thinker."

"I'm glad I fell in love with a thinker, then. And since you fell in love with a stinker, I'm going to check to see if the apartment still smells."

I see his body shake as he chuckles. "Cate, kiss me first."

Leaning in, I press my lips to his, then I run inside.

The smell leaves and Drew returns. It's good to see green man is gone.

"I think I'm gonna be one of those people who gets affected by smells. Some people are fine with it, but I can already tell I'm not gonna be one of those."

Putting my hands on his shoulders, I say, "If that's one of your side effects, I promise not to cook on your worst days."

"The weird thing is though, I feel like I could eat something."

"I made chicken soup and chicken and dumplings. Want to try some?"

He nods. "Maybe a little bowl of the soup."

I ladle up a little bit and he takes a few spoonfuls. "This is good, but my appetite isn't in full swing yet. I've always heard how quirky chemo makes you. I'm starting to get that now."

"I'm just happy as hell you were able to take a few bites. Why don't you go and take a shower and I'll fix you a glass of ice water."

He gets off his chair and wraps me in a hug as I'm clearing his bowl. "You're the best. Thanks."

The next morning, Drew wakes up and shakes me.

"What is it?" I ask, flying out of the bed.

He lies there, laughing at me. "Damn, you're jumpy."

"You scared me!"

"I need a favor."

"You woke me up out of the deepest sleep ever, to ask me for a favor?"

"Yeah." He has his old boyish grin back and the sparkle in his crystalline blues has returned.

"You know I'll do anything for you. What is it?"

"I want you to shave my head today."

"Huh? Shave your head?"

Without any sadness, remorse, or regret, he says, "Uh huh. This mop of mine is going to start falling out in clumps and I don't want the mess all over the house. I decided I want to shave it off to save myself the trouble. I have one of those barber clippers from when I used to wear my hair almost shaved. So, will you do it?"

"You trust me that much?"

He busts out in a knee-slapping laugh. "Seriously, Cate. I'm asking you to shave it all off. How can you possibly fuck it up?"

"You're talking to the person who tried, unsuccessfully I might add, to wax Louise. Remember?"

"How can I forget? But I'm not asking you to wax my head. I wouldn't dare do that."

We both are in fits of laughter now. Finally I say that I'll do it, as long as he doesn't hold any fuck ups against me. So, later that day, I watch all of Drew's gorgeous hair fall off as I work the barber's clippers over it. And when I'm done, I can't believe how damn sexy the man looks bald.

"You are the only man who looks as good without hair as you do with it."

"Aww, you're just saying that."

"No, I'm not."

"Get over here, Cate."

I climb on his hairy lap and give him a smooch. "I hope you

don't usually ask your barber to do this."

"My barber's name isn't Cate. It's George. And no, I don't. But he wouldn't mind, because he's gay."

By Sunday, Drew is back to feeling pretty good. I hate to leave, but I have to get back to Purdue.

"I'm fine," he insists. "Go. You have a shit ton of stuff to do. And don't try to fool me."

I wrap my arms around him, hating to let him go. "I'll call as soon as I get back."

"And I promise to call if I need you."

He repeats his treatments every Thursday for a total of three and then gets two weeks off. At the end of the first round, I'm at his place on a Saturday. He's watching TV and I'm writing, and I happen to glance at him. His cheeks are as pink and flushed, almost sunburned looking.

Crossing the room, I touch his forehead with the back of my hand and he feels terribly warm. He has a thermometer in the bathroom, so I go get it. A half hour later, we're headed to the hospital. One of the problems with chemo is it kills your white blood count and makes you very susceptible to infections. Chemo patients must be very cautious and if they spike a fever, they need to be admitted to the hospital. That's where Drew ends up. He has what's known as an FUO—a fever of unknown origin. And it can be life threatening. His temperature was one hundred three when I took it. I'm freaking, but don't want him to know it.

As soon as we get to the hospital, they put him on a gurney and wheel him into one of those tiny cubicles. A nurse comes in and attaches an IV line to the port they put in prior to his chemo—it's a direct line into his bloodstream that's attached to his chest. This way they never have to stick an IV into his vein. Then she draws several tubes of blood and says a doctor will be in.

An hour later, his oncologist cruises in, smiling.

"How do you feel?"

"Hot," Drew says.

"Yeah, we're doing blood cultures now, but you know how long those take. You'll be out of here before they grow anything. I'm starting you on the big gun antibiotics prophylactically. Sorry man, but you're in for the duration. We're gonna add some stuff to your regimen to prevent this, too. You'll get a room in about an hour. You need anything?"

"Can you cover my rotation for me?"

His doctor laughs. "I'll get your attending in here. We've got you, man." Then he turns to me and says, "No kissing and wash the hell out of your hands. I would prefer if you wear a mask and gloves around him, Cate. He's in a risky situation right now." He walks to a cart, grabs a box of masks and gloves, and hands them to me.

"I understand." Then he's gone.

Before I get the chance to speak, Drew says, "Go home, babe. I'm so sleepy. I'm probably gonna nap all afternoon. This fever takes it out of me. You'll be able to get your work done."

"Maybe so. I can bring you back something to eat."

"No, I meant go home home. I'm in for the week. I feel wasted. You have so much work and I know you're blowing smoke up my ass when you say things are fine. Just go home and get your shit done. Come back Friday and I'll be ready to go home. I promise."

"Drew! I can't leave."

"Cate, come here." He pats the bed so I sit. "Realistically, what can you do? And give me an honest answer."

He's right. I can't do anything for him that he can't do himself.

"See. I can hold my own dick to pee," he says, winking at me, "but if I really needed help with that, I would tell you."

I can't help the bubbly giggle that spurts out of my lips.

"And my hands would be happy to hold your dick."

"Oh, don't I know it. Go, babe. Go pack up and call me when you get home. I'll text you every time I wake up, but I'll try not to bother you. I love you more than hockey, but you have shit to do."

Guilt gushes into me. I want to stay with him, but he is so right. I have so much crap hanging over me right now, and this time away from him would help.

"I can see it in your eyes. You need to go. I couldn't be in a better place. Go and drive safely. Call when you get home."

I kiss the top of his beautiful bald head.

"Cate, don't forget, bald is beautiful."

"It sure is on you. Love you." I give him a wave as I leave and my heart squeezes as he waves back. His crimson cheeks starkly contrast the purple crescents under his eyes. He really is feverish.

The trip home is miserable. I alternate between crying, laughing, and screaming my anger out in the car. Jenna waits for me when I walk in the door.

"He's right and get over yourself. You need to be here and you can't do a damn thing for him, as he lays in the bed sleeping."

"Jenna, what if the infection kills him? His doctor wanted me to wear a mask around him."

"Precautionary. Stop this. What happened to my no nonsense, solid thinking friend?"

"What happened to her? I'll tell you what happened to her! Her fiancé got this fucking disease called cancer and it's ravaging his body! That's what happened to her!" I'm screaming at the top of my lungs and I want to break something. "And don't fucking tell me to calm down!"

"Wouldn't think of it." Jenna doesn't skip a beat as she walks to the cabinet, pulls out a bottle of vodka and two shot glasses, and pours. Then she hands me one. "Drink."

"What?"

"Drink, goddammit. You're on the verge of freaking out on me. You need a fucking drink. Down it, now."

Grabbing the glass out of her hand, I swallow it. Then she hands me the other one. "One more."

After I drink that one, she walks to the refrigerator and pulls out a bottle of wine. After pouring two glasses, she hands me one and says, "Sit your ass down."

So I do.

"How long do you think you can do this?"

"As long as it takes. I'll do anything for him, Jenna."

She shakes her head. "That's not what I meant. You need help. With him. You're driving back and forth like you're the only one in the world who can help him. You have an unbelievable class load this semester. He has a mother, you know."

"Oh, I don't think …"

"Fuck you and your not thinking. Reach out to Letty. She's probably trying to stay out of your hair. And here you are killing yourself."

"You think?"

"I know. And Drew would never ask anyone for anything. Call her. She needs to know he's in the hospital."

I make the call and Letty arranges a flight for the morning. I don't care if Drew is angry or not. The relief in her voice was worth it. Ray and I talk, too. He's comfortable with what they're doing, but sad Drew didn't call. I tell them how wiped out he was and blamed it on that. It satisfies him so he says he will give Drew a call later.

Jenna is all smiles. "Feel better?"

"I do. Thanks."

"You have to start delegating. This will be good experience for you when you get into your career. If you can't delegate, you're fucked up a tree, girl. You cannot possibly do it all. I know you're super awesome and all, but hey, you're not Wonder Woman."

"I'm not?" I ask with a straight face.

"Nah. I am."

I throw a pillow at her and then pounce on her.

"What the actual fuck would I do without you? You are keeping me in line here. Keeping my shit together."

"That's what maids of honor are for."

TWENTY-TWO
Past

———◆———

DREW HANDLES THE REST OF his chemo fairly well, with only a few little bumps. One more fever scare but it's only a low grade one where they initiate antibiotics at home and delay his next treatment a week. He loses a bit of weight, but not too much. What I hate the most for him is that his strength declines so hockey is no longer an option. Besides, he needs to work as much as he can, so his extracurricular activities are cut to almost none. His coworkers have been unbelievable in their support. They have picked up extra hours to give him time off when he needs it and the outpouring of support he's received humbles Drew.

His mom makes frequent trips during his treatment while I'm at school and goes home for the weekends when I visit. We've worked out a great schedule between us and even Drew is good with it. He likes having her there to cook for him because he's so wiped out if he works at all and too tired to do it himself. I'm happy knowing at least he's getting good meals and someone is watching after him.

At the end of February, they do a follow up bone scan and another PET scan. The news is good! The tumor has shrunk down to almost nothing, so the second week in March, they do the surgical excision. It's a rough one. They remove seven inches of his seventh rib. No one has prepared me for the chest tube and the other tubes he has coming out of him. I never was bothered much by the sight of blood, but this takes it to an entirely different level.

The nurses all hover over him, and why wouldn't they? He's one of their own. But damn, he looks awful. When I see him, I run to his mom and break down and cry. He's so out of it, he doesn't even notice I'm there.

Letty holds me, and we hang onto each other for dear life. Ray paces. It must be a terrible thing to be a physician and have your son become ill with cancer, and not be able to help him. Ray's mind must always be in doctor mode, and that has to include a prognosis with outcome data that may or may not be positive.

"He's going to be fine, Cate. You must believe that," Letty says.

"I do. Only I hate seeing him like this. I don't want him to be in pain, hurting."

"He's medicated. He doesn't even know we're here," Ray says in a comforting tone.

"How are your classes?" Letty asks, trying to divert my attention, but I don't want to talk about that right now.

"How long before he wakes up?" I ask Ray.

"Maybe tonight. The longer the better for him," Ray says.

"That's good. That will give me time to pull myself together." I sniff.

"He needs that, Cate. He needs your strength. And for you to be here for him," Letty says.

"Like I could possibly be anywhere else."

I plant my butt on a chair next to his bed and the only time I leave is to use the restroom or to get something to drink. Food has no meaning for me. He wears a clear mask over his face that streams more oxygen into his lungs, but Ray tells me he's doing really well. It's not until his lids crack open and I see him look at me that I smile. I crawl in the bed with him and hold him.

Letty walks in and sees me. "Cate, I'm not sure you should …"

"Let her be, Letty. She's fine and he needs her right now. She can't hurt him." It's Ray that speaks.

I run my hands over his head, and seek his hand out under the sheet. Lacing our fingers together, I'm happy to feel his slightly tighten against my own. And then I doze off.

Ray wakes me some time later, asking me if I want anything to eat.

"I'm fine."

"Cate, you need to eat. You didn't eat yesterday, that I can recall, and you haven't eaten a thing all day."

I didn't notice that Drew's mask is gone and in its place are those small tubes that go in his nose. When he speaks, I'm surprised. "Eat, Cate. You must be starved."

I look at him and beam. "Look who's awake!"

"Yeah, but I feel like I got nailed by an eighteen wheeler."

"Aww. That bad?"

"Yeah, but the morphine pump is good."

"Huh?"

He points to a little machine on a pole next to his bed and explains how it works. It makes me feel better that it helps him so much.

"This sure breeds empathy in me for patients who go through this. Maybe I'm going through this for that reason."

I clamp my mouth shut because I don't believe that for a second. Drew is the most empathetic person in the world. He would be the last one to be chosen for that reason. And this is what's killing me about him getting cancer. It should've been me.

Ray prods me again for my answer about food. "Okay, just get me whatever you're having."

He nods and both he and Letty leave.

"How's my girl doing?" How can he ask me that? He's the one lying in bed with his chest ripped open.

"Shouldn't I be asking you that?"

"I'm good, Cate. You're lying next to me and that's all I need."

"Honestly, Drew, you kill me sometimes. How do you feel?"

"Like I said, I feel like a truck hit me. Other than that, good. I'll be better when I know this surgery did the trick."

"Me too. Are you thirsty? Can I get you anything?"

"I'd love some ice chips. That's all I can have yet."

"You got it."

Grabbing his large water container, I wander down the hall until I find a nurse to help me. She shows me where the ice machine is and I fill up the cup and bring it back to Drew. When I spoon some into his mouth, he hums his delight.

"Never thought I'd enjoy ice chips so much."

"It's the small things in life."

"And you, Cate." He hums as I feed him more chips. "I hate I'm putting you through this."

"Love encompasses a whole lot of things, Drew. And when I fell in love with you, I didn't fall for only the good times. I fell for it all, including this. I'm here and we'll get through this. So stop with that kind of talk."

"I don't like seeing you with the dark circles under your eyes."

"And I don't like seeing you in the hospital, so we're even."

He says he's done with the ice and pats the bed, telling me to get back in. "I want to have you next to me."

"You got me." I climb back in and put my head on his shoulder. "Let me know if you need anything."

"I won't because I have you. You're it for me." Then he drifts back to sleep as I worry about what will happen next.

Ray and Letty return and they don't look so good either. She hands me a bag that contains a chicken salad sandwich and some fries. Ray hands me a large iced tea.

"Thanks." I get out of the bed to eat, but can only down a few bites. My stomach fights every swallow.

"It's anxiety, dear. I feel the same way," Letty says.

Setting my food down on a side table, I stand and pace the room. Letty glances at Ray and then says, "Cate, maybe you should go back home and take a shower. Relax. Try to get some sleep."

"No. I won't leave him. I have things here and can shower in his bathroom."

"Then why don't you do that? It might relax you some," she suggests.

After giving it some thought, I decide to go ahead and do exactly that. As soon as the water hits me, the tears break loose. The question I keep asking myself—why Drew—yields no answer. I've heard people say they've cried themselves out. I wish that would happen to me, because my supply of tears is endless. I need to buck up and pull my shit together. Drew cannot see me like this.

Finishing my shower, I put on a strong front and get dressed. When I come out, he's awake again. The groggy grin he offers me makes me laugh.

"You look like you've had too much to drink."

"Yeah, I feel like it, too."

I bend down to kiss him and he tells me I smell lots better now. Ray and Letty chuckle. "Glad you noticed," I say.

The rest of the day is much the same, with Drew sleeping away most of it. By the third day, he gets antsy and cranky. He wants to go home and I don't blame him. It seems like he's constantly getting poked and prodded by a nurse, doctor, or a medical assistant. Sleep becomes more difficult because they withdraw his morphine and transition him to something milder.

"Cate, you need to go home tonight and get a good night's sleep. Mom and Dad even think so. You don't have to stay here."

"I want to," I insist.

"I know, but I want you to go home. This is crazy. You're exhausted. You need a solid night of rest and you can't get that here. I don't want you getting sick."

He gets me to agree, so late that night, I head to his apartment. When I crawl in bed, his scent makes me sad, so I end up crying myself to sleep. In the morning, the constant buzzing of my phone wakes me.

"Huh?" I answer.

"Cate?"

"Jenna?"

"Damn! You never answer your phone! I've been trying to get you for three days. Thank God for Ben. Drew's parents are keeping him informed. What the hell is going on with you?"

"I'm sorry. I turned my phone off in the hospital so it wouldn't disturb Drew." I fill her in on everything.

"How are you holding up? And don't give me a bullshit answer."

"I'm fine," I say, my lip quivering. Then I break down and ugly cry. I mean bad ugly cry. I can't even talk.

She listens, and then says, "I'm getting in the car and heading there now."

The phone goes dead. A little over an hour later, she's knocking on the door. I let her in and she wraps me in her arms as I sob my heart out. I literally collapse on the floor in her arms. The last few days have taken their toll on me and I've hit rock bottom. My exhaustion coupled with my worry over Drew has burst the dam that held everything in check, and having Jenna there allows me to let it all go.

When the crying passes, I take a shaky breath. "Sorry. I didn't plan on that."

"What the fuck are you apologizing for? I'm the one who should be apologizing. I should've been here with you. But I tried to call and couldn't get you." She pushes my hair off my face and says, "I almost don't know what to say to you. How to make you feel better. The only thing I know is Drew is strong and a fighter. He's going to pull out of this. He has one hell of a support team backing him. And a shit ton of love behind him. Not to mention all the news is good, so far."

"I'm so fucking worried, Jenna. I've never been though anything like this. It's fucking cancer, you know? And it's a pediatric cancer so they don't really know the long term."

"He's going to kick that cancer in the fucking ass, Cate. You have to believe in that. And you have to believe in him."

"Yeah, yeah, I know I do. It's just that I love him so much and I don't know what I'll do if anything …"

"Hey, hey, none of that talk. You hear me? We're not even going to think that way. If anyone can survive this, it's Drew McKnight."

She's right. I put on my best happy face and say, "Yeah. I'm gonna hop in the shower and then I need to get back to the hospital."

"I'm going with you. Ben's coming in today, too. You need a bit of relief here."

"I'm just glad the surgery coincided with my spring break so I had the time off. I don't know what I would've done otherwise."

We get back to the hospital and the McKnights are already there. They hug Jenna, and Drew smiles at her. It's a weird time with all of us dancing around the cancer issue. Not much later, Ben walks in.

"Dude, if you wanted attention, why didn't you just say so? I could've worked something out." Thank God for Ben. We all have a good chuckle and the room seems to lighten up with his presence. Even Drew is more cheerful.

Thirty minutes later, half of his hockey team cruises in. Talk about a crowd. Ray and Letty step outside after the introductions are made, but not Jenna. She eyes every one of the guys, checking them out. I have to laugh. Knowing her, she'll probably end up hooking up with one of them.

Drew asks Ben if he needs a place to crash.

"No. I have a place. Yours." Everyone laughs.

Drew makes a fist so Ben can bump it. "You know it, bro. How long you staying?"

"As long as you need me." The intensity of their stares fills my heart with a deep love for Ben.

Drew smiles and says, "Thanks, bro. I can always count on you."

"You know it."

Drew grabs my hand and pulls so I have to sit on the bed. "Between this girl right here, my parents, Ben, Jenna, and the team, what more do I need?"

I want to scream—your health! But I clamp my mouth shut instead. I bend down and kiss him as everyone yells out catcalls.

Ben pats him on the shoulder and asks, "How much longer you in for?"

"A couple more days."

"Hey, can we take you for a spin in that thing?" Ben points to the wheelchair.

Drew laughs, shaking his head. "Only you, Rhoades."

"Dude, don't you want a change of scenery?"

"Have you seen all the shit that's attached to me?" Drew lifts the covers and Ben starts screaming in the loudest voice possible. Two nurses run into the room while Jenna and I laugh hysterically as do the rest of Drew's friends. When the nurses see what's going on, they join in.

"Which one of you is the trouble maker?" one of them asks. Everyone points to a different person and we all laugh again.

"Hey, I wanna bust my friend out of here and take him for a spin in that fancy contraption. How does one go about doing that?" Ben asks.

"You ask his nurse in a very friendly manner," she answers with a wink. She's a middle-aged woman with kind brown eyes. She's been very helpful to me over the last few days.

"Is that right? Well then," Ben checks out her name tag as he sidles next to her, "Nurse Sandy, I would very much like your kind assistance in taking my best friend here for a ride in that lovely wheelchair. I think he could use a change of scenery and give his beautiful fiancée a break. How about it?" He waggles his brows at her.

"Aww, what a sweet talker you are," Sandy says. "I'll gladly help you, if Dr. McKnight's willing."

Drew nods and they load him and all his apparatuses up for the ride. I giggle as I watch Ben's eyes widen in horror when he sees the chest tube and the pleurovac it's attached to.

"AHHHH! Why didn't you warn me?" he cries.

"Dude. Grow some balls and act like a man. And I tried."

They leave with the hockey team trailing behind.

As soon as the coast is clear, Jenna accosts me. "Why the hell didn't you tell me?" Jenna accuses.

"Tell you what?"

"How hot Drew's friends are?"

"I don't know. I guess I never paid attention."

"Figures. You fall in love and forget about your best friend."

That night, the three of us sit around Drew's apartment. He made me go home with them, saying he would sleep better knowing I was there.

Ben grabs a beer out of the fridge and says, "He looks good, Cate. A lot better than I thought he would. Except for all that shit hanging off him." Ben shakes his head. "I don't know how anyone can want to be a doctor."

"I agree," Jenna says. "About the Drew looking good part. Well, about both, actually."

I half smile.

"He told me all the tests came back good," Ben says.

"Yeah. That's why they did the excision," I say.

"He's going to be fine. I just know it." Ben squeezes my shoulder.

My phone starts to ring. It's Mom.

"I have to get this. It's my mom." We talk for about twenty minutes. She's been so great throughout this whole thing. When I hang up I promise to call her tomorrow.

Jenna and Ben are talking quietly when I return to the conversation. They look up at me with guilt written all over them.

"Spill."

"Nothing." Jenna is as bad of a liar as I am.

"Liar. I know when you're hiding something."

Ben steps into the conversation. "I shared something with her that I probably shouldn't have."

"What?"

"Cate, Drew asked me not to say anything." Ben looks really uncomfortable.

"What is it?"

"You know, this puts me in a fucked up position. Me and my damn big mouth."

"Is this something I should know?" I ask.

Ben takes a huge breath. When he does my gut twists. This is bad. "If I tell you, I betray my best friend's confidence. And where does that leave me or what does that say about me?"

"Ben, Drew has cancer. I need to know if it's something that has to do with his health. I love him more than my own life. Can you try to see past what you just told me? I won't tell him. I just need to know."

My face is wet again from tears. Jenna has her arm around me and says, "Just tell her, Ben. What more can it do?"

He rubs his neck. "Yeah, okay. He's really scared about all of this, Cate. More so than he's telling you. He doesn't want you to know that. The issue is the fact that the information on treating this type of cancer in adults is so varied. He told me if he were fourteen, he'd feel much better about the diagnosis. The other thing is the location of the cancer. The prognosis is better when it occurs in the limbs, specifically in the legs. Not the ribs. That's what else is bothering him. I think the fact that he's a doctor makes it so much worse."

When I really sob, Ben says, "And this is why I didn't want to say anything."

"She needs to know this, Ben. She needs to be there one hundred percent for Drew."

I hate that Drew feels he can't tell me these things. I'm supposed to be the one he can lean on. I'm supposed to be the one he runs to. Not Ben or his parents. I want to scream, cry, kick, yell. Something, anything to release my emotions.

"It's just not fair."

"Nothing's fair. You should've learned that by now," Jenna says.

"Jenna, don't be so harsh," Ben says.

Jenna looks chastised. But she's right. Nothing is fair in life.

"UGGGGH! Of anyone, it should've been me. Drew ... he's so good and kind." And that's when it hits me. There's a good chance he's not going to make it. It's the old saying—only the good die young that comes to mind and Drew is the best there is.

My face must reflect my thoughts because both Jenna and Ben say, "What is it?"

Jenna adds, "You've turned gray."

In an expressionless voice, I say, "He may not make it."

Jenna gasps. "How can you say such a thing?"

Ben doesn't speak.

"Only the good die young, Jenna."

"And you're going to let a stupid saying dictate Drew's life expectancy?"

"No, I'm letting the cancer do that."

"You can't! You have to fight it!"

The life has been sucked out of me. "I wish it were me. I wish I were the one sick, instead of him. He doesn't deserve this. He's never done a bad thing in his life." When they say your heart breaks, whoever "they" is doesn't have a clue what they're talking about. Broken isn't close. Shattered—no cigar. Splintered—nothing doing. Pulverized—where every tiny part is crushed beyond recognition—that's about how it feels. All the bits of my heart couldn't possibly be put back together because they are completely annihilated.

Jenna hugs me and whispers, "It's not you, Cate. It's not you. And you have to hold it together for him."

"You have to believe in miracles, Cate. Sometimes they do happen," Ben says.

The only thing I can do right now is dump more tears on my friends. How can life turn around so fast? One minute I'm on top of the world and the next, I'm at the bottom of the sea.

Time. I need to cherish it. A few short months ago I was hoping the year would fly so Drew and I could get married, but now all I want to do is freeze it. Maybe even turn it back to before he got hit in the ribs.

Ben's arm goes around me now and says, "Hey, we're here with you. If there's ever anything you need, you let one of us know."

"Yeah. Thanks. I don't know what I'd do without you two."

TWENTY-THREE
Present

---◆---

I FIND MYSELF STRAIGHTENING ANDY'S room instead of going to the kitchen where the smell of bacon beckons me. Mitch gave me hell last night in front of Andy and even though he says everything's cool, we are alone now. He may have more he wants to say.

Finally, I walk out in a t-shirt clearly too big for me and Andy's boxers rolled at the waist so they don't fall down. I decide to hold my head high and stiffen my spine.

"There she is. Princess Cate."

I'm not sure what to make of his words, so I just ask, "What are you making?"

I lean over the counter and watch him cook what I think is either the world's thinnest pancake or a crepe.

"Crepes."

"Wow," I say out loud. "You can cook?"

He nods.

"I guess the better question is—Did Andy have the ingredients to make crepes?"

"It's not that hard. All you need are flour, eggs, milk, butter, salt, and water," he says.

"Oh," I say, as he expertly flips it in the pan. "Most single guys wouldn't keep flour around."

I know Andy can cook, but he doesn't bake, or at least he hasn't in the past.

"I'm sure someone left it over."

His words sting, but when I glance at him under a curtain of my hair, I don't see any malice in his expression.

"I guess so," I mutter.

"No worries, shorty. Drew is all about you. Whoever left it is a nobody."

He's trying to smooth things over but I'm getting more uncomfortable thinking about Andy with anyone else.

I go to sit on the couch and flip the TV on. I don't want Mitch to see me rattled.

"What do you want on your crepe? I found strawberries and whipped cream in the fridge," he calls out to me.

I have no desire to eat whipped cream. It isn't like Andy constantly ate the stuff. Did he use that on another woman? I try not to let petty jealousy get the best of me. He has a right to be with anyone—or at least he did. Then I remember the ice cream sundae fixings I left here a few weeks back. That doesn't explain the strawberries.

The door opens and Andy walks in with a dusting of snowflakes on his coat. It must be really cold for them to not have melted on his way to his apartment.

"You treating my girl good?" Andy asks Mitch.

"Like a princess. I'm making crepes. Bro, you have whipped cream and strawberries in your refrigerator. Dare I ask?"

Andy's response comes so easy. "I bought ice cream and that stuff for the dessert you interrupted last night."

Mitch has no shame and only shrugs. "My bad."

Andy makes his way over to me and kisses me quickly, but not before his nose brushes mine.

"You're cold," I squirm.

"I could heat you up."

"Yeah, don't mind me. I like to watch," Mitch calls out.

Andy groans. He straightens and takes his coat off. "They're plowing the roads. You'll be able to go home soon," he calls out over his shoulder to Mitch.

Mitch puts a hand on his heart. "I'm hurt. Here I am slaving over a hot stove for your woman and you're kicking me out."

Andy laughs and I find it hard not to. "Have you heard from

Dave?"

"No, but that prick's probably got company of some variety. Has Drew told you about our friend Dave?"

"Not much," I say.

"Dave is the prettiest of all of us, or so women say. He can have any woman he wants, but he's not happy just with women. No, he mixes it up with anyone who catches his eye."

I vaguely recall the guy Mandy called Thor that drunken night and agree that Dave is pretty hot.

"If not for his self-righteous father, I think he might have given up women," he says absently. "Don't you think Drew?"

Andy shrugs.

"His Dad doesn't approve?" I ask.

Mitch laughs. "His Dad is a good ole southern boy and a Senator to boot. Dave's a chip off the old block. Kind of like me. Follow in the footsteps of our fathers, they say. You'll be successful one day… they say." He gives Andy a knowing look.

"You had a choice," Andy says. "You could have taken that fancy law degree and joined a firm."

"You're a lawyer?" I ask. It seems weird someone would go through the trouble of getting a law degree and not use it.

"I'm a Lobbyist at my dad's firm," he says with a disgusted curl to his lip.

Oh, I mouth, wanting to know more but thinking it isn't any of my business.

Now that I know the whipped cream isn't a product from any of Andy's former dates, I eat Mitch's crepe and fuss over it.

"It's really good."

"My mother is an excellent cook. She had no choice but to teach me, her baby boy." He winks. "My two older brothers showed no interest in the culinary arts."

"You're going to make some woman very happy," I declare with my chin resting on my hand as I study the guy who treated me like mortal enemy number one last night.

He shakes his head. "The only woman I'll ever love is my mother."

I say nothing because most women don't want a mama's boy, even though they say that a man will treat his wife like he treats his mother.

"He's not telling the truth. The truth is some girl broke his heart and he's never recovered."

Mitch jumps in. "She didn't break my heart," he denies. "Besides, women don't want to be treated with respect. They respect you more when you treat them like dirt." When I gasp, he adds, "Present company excluded."

"Not all women," I say feeling the need to stand up for a lot of females.

"Okay, why don't you two agree to disagree?" Andy says to keep the peace.

Mitch nods and I do too. A silence settles over us. I get up and take the empty dishes.

"You don't have to clean up after us," Andy says.

"It's fine. You've hosted us, Mitch cooked, and I'll clean."

I settle in and do the dishes while the guys sit on the couch. Andy looks tired and I realized I haven't asked how he's doing. I wonder how to bring up the subject as I watch the snow continue to fall heavily through the window.

After I finish with clean up, I join the boys on the couch. Some sports channel is droning on about basketball playoffs or something. I curl up next to Andy, needing to be close to him, when cell phones begin to buzz.

Andy gently moves my legs over to stand and walk further away, while Mitch answers his phone.

Their conversations overlap, so I don't really hear either of them well. They both end the call within seconds of each other.

"I'm out. I've got a date."

Andy glances at Mitch. "You sure you can drive in this?"

Mitch's smile is wicked. "Don't have to drive. I met this little brunette on the elevator last night. She invited me down to her place for lunch."

"You just ate," I say pragmatically.

He winks at me. "I'm suddenly very hungry. Don't wait up for me."

Andy shakes his head. "You're worse than Dave."

"Don't hate the player," Mitch says getting to his feet. "I might be back. So don't go having sex on the couch."

"I have to go into the hospital. I'm hoping Cate will come with me. We shouldn't be long though."

Mitch grabs his coat before saluting us goodbye while heading out the door.

"So, will you come to the hospital with me?"

There is hope in his eyes. He knows what he's asking of me and I'm not sure I'm ready. He may be used to walking in the cancer ward, but one experience was enough for me to last a lifetime. Still, if I'm going to be with this man, I need to get used to what he does for a living.

"I don't have a change of clothes, remember? I have heels and a skirt. I can't walk in the snow like that."

"Actually, I drove this morning which turned out to be a mistake. I left my car because they have volunteers with four wheel drive who are playing taxi. I've arranged for someone to pick me up in ten minutes. The roads should be better on the way back and I can drive us home."

I sigh with a smile. "Okay, I'll go."

He's practically beaming his pearly whites at me. He knows I like a man with good teeth and his are dentist approved.

"If you look at me like that, we're going to miss your ride," I tease.

"Are you daring me to see what I can do in ten minutes?"

He tosses me over his shoulder before I can answer and shows me just what he can do in that short time. It's a hell of a lot.

When he gets the call his ride is here, I've just finished getting dressed.

"Is your office open tomorrow?"

I check my phone. "I'm not sure. I don't have any messages from them yet. Do you know what the weather man says about tomorrow?" I haven't watched the news since I've been here.

"Supposedly, the snow will end late tonight. We will have up to eighteen inches when it's over."

"Eighteen inches?"

He nods and helps me get into my coat. We head downstairs and once we get outside the wind howls and snow lashes over me. I can't imagine driving in this weather. This area isn't supposed to be prone to snow like this. I feel like stomping my feet like a toddler that my first winter in DC area is the worst they've seen in years.

We dash over to the SUV that waits at the curb. When Andy opens the front passenger door, I'm just as shocked to see the woman driver as she is to see me.

"Hi," she says as Andy ushers me to sit in front.

I recognize the blonde ponytail the woman sports. I can't be sure it's the same nurse as the one I caught kissing him. But she does have on scrubs.

Andy climbs in the back. "Thanks for the ride, Becca."

"Yeah sure. I was on the phone with Stacy when you called in. Since I drove right by your place, I offered to pick you up."

"Becca, this is my girlfriend Cate. Cate, this is Becca. She's a nurse in the oncology unit."

"Girlfriend?" She says the word under her breath. I'm not sure she even realizes she's said it out loud. "Nice to meet you," she says with a cheery smile I can tell is forced.

She holds out her hand and for a second I'm tempted to pull a Mitch. Then again, I'm not positive she's the nurse that's been hitting on Andy. She could be another nurse interested in him, and could I blame her?

"You too," I say giving her a genuine smile and shake her hand briskly.

When it's obvious no one is going to talk, she turns on the radio. A song I recognize is playing. As I hum with the song, Becca maintains a white knuckle grip on the steering wheel. I wonder if it's because the roads are snow covered and slick or if she's grief-stricken to find out Andy's off the market. I'll keep on wondering because there is no way I'm going to ask.

The hospital isn't far. When she parks, an older Nick Jonas song, *Jealous*, starts to play. It's almost funny how fast she turns the car off killing the song midsentence.

Andy takes my hand as we walk into the building. He tries to be nice and make small talk with Becca, but her clipped answers are indication enough she's not happy.

When we reach the ward, Becca takes off her jacket and introduces me to the other nurses sitting at the station.

"Hey everyone. This is Doc Drew's girlfriend, Cate."

I get a few smiles. A few others trade glances between Becca and me. I'm starting to wonder if Becca is a former girlfriend or fling of Andy's. She does know where he lives.

"Weren't you here earlier, Doc?" A male nurse with dark hair and a round face asks, easing the tension and cutting off my thoughts.

"Yes. I'm back to see Tasha. Her mom wasn't here earlier and has asked to speak to me." He lays his coat on a chair and steps back over to me.

"Well aren't you nice? Must be the southern upbringing. Doc Chad, the ass, wouldn't ever come back in for a patient."

The other nurses laugh at the guy's comment. Andy shakes his head and steers me away from the station.

"I shouldn't be long."

We walk down a hall that isn't as sterile looking as the hospitals I've been in. The walls are paneled in a medium wood grain color and have colorful pictures of puppies and kittens on them, making the place look much more cheerful than it is. The glass fronts of patient rooms are bright with hanging blinds that can be opened or closed for privacy. The hallway is large and there are only rooms on the one side.

"Wait right here."

We stop on the opposite wall from a room where a little girl lies in bed. "Tasha" is written on a white board outside her room.

I nod and try to breathe through the anxiety. It all rushes back to me despite how everything looks different.

"Doc Drew," a nurse calls before he can enter the room.

Her hair is blonde and swings around her shoulders as she bounces over to him.

"I thought I wouldn't get to see you today. When I heard you came back, I had to come up to see you."

She reaches out, but he holds out a hand and steps back. His face shifts and he almost looks angry.

"You have to stop or I'm going to go to human resources again. I'm not interested. My girlfriend over there can attest to that if you need to hear it from someone else."

Andy points at me and I straighten. So this is the girl I saw kissing him. Then who is Becca?

Her hands fall to her sides. "Fine, you don't know what you're missing."

She spins on her nurse's shoes and they squeak in protest. She clomps off and Andy glances up at me and shrugs. I give him a thumbs up and he smiles a little. He glances away from me when a little girl tugs on his lab coat.

He kneels down to be at her eye level. I'm given a clear view of the small, pretty girl with brown skin and a bald head. She has a pink headband on with a bow. She looks so tiny compared to the IV pole she walks with.

"Doc Drew," she says in a tiny voice. "They shaved off the rest of my hair. Do you like it?"

Andy's smile couldn't have been bigger. He reaches up and touches the side of her face. "You are beautiful."

Her baldness is another reminder of how Andy is so much stronger than I am. He's ready to slay the cancer dragon, while I'm ready to be consumed by its fire.

Her eyes dip. "You think so even without my hair?"

His finger gently lifts her chin. "Absolutely." Then he leans in and whispers something in her ear.

She smiles but it doesn't exactly reach her eyes.

"Is your mom around?"

She nods. "She went to get something to eat." Her face changes immediately. "I'm not feeling so well."

"Let's see what we can do about that."

He picks her up like he's her knight in shiny armor. It's hard for me to stop the tears from spilling over that well up in my eyes.

He carries her in one arm and pushes the pole with his free hand. Just as he lays her down, she tosses her cookies all over him and the bed. He doesn't look disgusted at all. The fact is, he never even blinks, or misses a beat. He calmly reaches for a plastic basin on the side of the bed and holds her while she finishes vomiting.

Two nurses come jogging over. One has fresh linens and the other takes the girl from Andy while they remake the bed and get her cleaned up. He doesn't leave her though. He continues to talk to her with what can only be reassuring words. I can't hear them, but the way he looks at her is telling.

As they tuck her back in bed, he discreetly takes off his soiled lab coat and rolls it up. He unclips his ID credentials and takes everything out of his pockets before shoving the dirty thing into the linen cart someone brings in.

Then he sits in bed with the girl and talks to her until her mother comes in. The nurses have left and the mother isn't the wiser. I have a feeling Andy won't say anything to the mother about it in front of the little girl. I know I've hit the nail when I see him hold up a finger to her and walk out with the mother.

They talk quietly near the door and I feel like an intruder. Andy speaks softly, probably out of respect for patient privacy and so the little girl can't hear him. The mother speaks a little louder, enough so I can hear part of her side of the conversation. She's concerned that the girl can't keep any food down and "Wasn't the medication not supposed to make her little girl sick?"

I want to tell her there are no absolutes in medicine. I knew that first hand. Everyone is different and responds differently. I only hope Andy can give the girl the miracle it appears she needs.

He goes back in and talks to Tasha some more before he finally comes back to me.

"We can go now."

Tasha's situation tugs at my heart. I know I shouldn't ask, but I do anyway. "How bad is she?"

He places a hand on my back and guides me away from the rooms. Becca and the male nurse are the only ones at the station when we walk up.

"See ya Doc," the guy says.

Andy grabs his coat and waves. Becca says nothing.

I want to ask about her, but I find myself needing answers about Tasha.

"You know how things are, Cate. We thought we beat it and we're doing our best for her."

He doesn't get into details due to patient confidentially. He trails off and I'm left feeling my heart will crush inside my chest. I need to change the subject.

"Is there something between you and Becca?"

"Jealous?" He asks turning a charming smile on me, but I don't cave. He sighs. "I made a mistake when I first came to work here."

I'm not sure I want to hear the rest, considering how he begins this tale.

"She had the SUV. I had some boxes shipped to me. She offered to help me pick them up. Mitch and Dave lived in DC. She was here. I accepted and offered her dinner as payment for her help. She thought maybe I was interested. I told her I didn't date anyone where I worked. I think she's held out hope I might change my mind. Now she knows I won't."

I nod at his clinical assessment. At least he realized she was still into him. Some guys act clueless. I can't be mad at her. Not only is Andy amazing to look at, but he's a single doctor, thus a catch. If I continue to be with him, I'll have to curb the jealousy because he will always get hit on.

When we get to his car, I change the subject yet again. "Why don't you have a 4 wheel drive?"

Considering his job, it seemed like a good question.

He's buckling his seat belt when he says, "Never needed it in Charleston. And I haven't decided if I'm staying."

"Oh," I say remembering he's here temporarily.

"Hey," he says gaining my attention.

I realize I'm picking at a chip on my nail. I need a file or it will break off. I glance up and meet his eyes.

"It looks like I might have an opportunity to stay in the area." He pauses to let that sink in. "I want to make this work with you. I'm leaning toward staying here because of you."

He takes my hand and kisses my knuckles. Then we are driving back to his place. We don't talk and I think about what he says.

"I hope you'll stay. Not only for me, but for you, too," I say finally when he parks the car after a precarious drive back.

He smiles and leans over to kiss me. "That's good to hear. And this is a great opportunity, so I would stay for all the right reasons."

We stay in bed for the rest of the day before Mitch shows up late. I got a text earlier that my office is closed the next day, so I snuggle in for the night.

However, Andy's office is open the next day. Apparently DC got hit harder. In fact, I get a call from my mother that Charleston got some snow too. Andy goes into the office early, but wants to come back at lunch to take me home.

"Mitch offered me a ride," I say into the phone.

"Yeah man, we're both headed to DC," Mitch calls out in the back ground.

"Tell Mitch I can take care of my girl and to get his own."

I don't, not yet at least. "He has a point. We're headed in the same direction."

"I'm almost done. Please let me do this."

I agree but he almost regrets that decision when they call for freezing rain later in the day. He beats the next storm to roll in while the roads are clear.

"When will I see you again?"

"Saturday? I'm going out with Mandy tonight because I've been promising her for weeks."

"Saturday works. I might hang out with Dave and Mitch tonight. Dave has news he wants to share. Maybe I'll call you and I can come over for breakfast?"

He winks at our code word. "I doubt I'll be out late with

Mandy. So swing by when you're done having fun with the boys and spend the night with me. Then I'll make you breakfast."

It's my turn to wink before I kiss him hard with the need I suddenly feel. I had him in bed most of yesterday and now I must be spoiled.

"It's killing me to leave you. You better go or I'll have to cancel my afternoon appointments."

I kiss him quickly and hop out the car with the biggest smile. However, the night with Mandy doesn't exactly go as planned.

TWENTY-FOUR
Past

---◆---

GRADUATION WAS YESTERDAY. I'M OFFICIALLY done. I don't know how, but I attained two degrees and graduated summa cum laude, with Drew watching me. My shining moment is having Drew here, not getting the dual degrees or the summa cum laude designation. Funny how your priorities change when life throws a wrecking ball at your carefully constructed plans.

"I'm so proud of you," Drew says, as we put the last box in my car. I spent the last week packing up the apartment with Jenna. The moving truck is full and my dad just left. He and Jenna's dad are driving it back to South Carolina. Jenna and Ben are following Drew and me home. Drew has to fly back to Indy to finish his last two weeks there before he starts his fellowship at the Medical University of South Carolina in July. He'll have a month off because of our wedding. His department in Indy has been so awesome to him, I keep wondering if he should've stayed there for his fellowship. Too late now.

Jenna walks out and asks, "You ready?"

"Yep. Let me use the bathroom one more time." When I come out, I take a look at our building. "You know, I'm really gonna miss this place."

Jenna comes up to me and throws her arm over my shoulder. "Yeah, me too. It was a great apartment and we were great roomies." We look at each other and start crying.

Ben and Drew moan. One of them says, "Girls," and I think it's Ben.

Jenna yells out, "Shut it. We were like peas and carrots." And we sob some more.

We finally pull apart and head out of town. Drew's hand reaches for mine and he says, "Won't be long before we're headed on our honeymoon."

"Yeah and I wish someone would tell me where we're going."

He laughs. He wants it to be a huge surprise, so I'm going with it. I look at him and marvel at how awesome he looks. Strong is the first word that comes to mind. He's working out again and he looks every bit the same as when I met him. His hair has grown in, though it's not as long as he used to wear it and it's a bit wavier.

"Bathing suits, babe. All you need are bathing suits."

"What? No nude beaches?"

"Probably, but I don't want anyone seeing your gorgeous body naked. So, bathing suits."

I clap my hands together. "I'm so excited. In just a few weeks, I'll be Cate McKnight."

"Don't say another word or I'll have to pull over so we can have a quickie."

"I think I can help you out with that." I move to unzip his pants, and take his semi-hard cock out.

"Cate, it's broad daylight and traffic isn't exactly sparse."

"Just keep your eyes on the road, McKnight. And try to stay away from any eighteen wheelers."

"I don't believe you."

"Say that in a few minutes." I wrap my mouth around his cock and go to town. There's just something sexy and a bit edgy about sucking your fiancé off on the interstate. I don't know why, but it sure turns me on.

Drew moans and one hand finds its way into my hair, as he slightly pumps his hips up and down, fucking my mouth. I need to make this fast so he doesn't wreck. I do my best tongue swirling, mouth sucking, hand squeezing, blow job until Drew climaxes, groaning into the car pretty damn loud. After I lick him clean, I zip him back up and offer him a smile.

"Damn, Cate." He shakes his head. "That was great." I notice he's white knuckling the steering wheel.

"I aim to please."

"Well, you did a little more than please. Shit." He rubs his face.

"You okay there, honey?" I laugh.

"Fuck. I want to kiss you."

"Sorry. A man's gotta drive."

He looks straight ahead for a heartbeat, and then impishly says, "Yeah, but a man has a hand." And he holds it up in the air and wiggles his fingers. It gets a giggle out of me. "Lose those shorts."

Suddenly, I'm thinking what he did. It's broad daylight and traffic is thick. He reads my mind. "Oh, no way are you getting out of this one, baby. What's fair is fair."

I give a quick glance to the back seat and spy a pillow. I grab it and grin. Putting it over my lap, I tug down my shorts. "This is a fair exchange because my head was in the way. Now the pillow will be."

"Fair point."

His hand slides under the pillow and when he finds my sex, he says, "Someone was totally sexed up from that blow job she just gave."

"Of course I was."

"Shit, would I like to slide into you right now." Instead, two fingers move inside of me. He knows exactly how and where to put the pressure, but when he adds the motion to my clit with his thumb, it's not long before my orgasm bears down on me.

When he pulls out, I hand him a tissue, and then I start laughing.

"What's so funny?" he asks.

"It didn't take us long to have car sex on this trip. Gah, are we bad or what?"

"Just don't tell Jenna, because she'll tell Ben, and I'll never hear the end of it."

"I'd never tell Jenna. The only way she'd find out would be if they saw us." Then a thought hits me. "Oh, shit! They're behind us. They're gonna figure it out with my head going down and all."

Drew roars with laughter. "Yeah, you're right. They already know. I'm surprised they haven't called."

"I know why. They're saving it for when we stop to eat."

Drew and I share a glance and we both know we're screwed.

Sure enough, we stop for a late lunch and Jenna gives us her rendition of what my head looked like from their car.

"Damn, McKnight. Could you not at least wait until we got out of town? I mean we were still in fucking traffic!" Ben teases.

"Dude, who am I to turn down head?"

"Truth."

"Stop!" My face burns red, I'm sure.

"Your fault, my friend," Jenna rubs it in.

"I'm not saying another word." Drew pulls me into his side, and kisses my temple. "Don't let 'em get to you, babe. It was the best."

I elbow him in the ribs, before I even think. He winces and I immediately shrink away. "I'm good. Get back over here."

I hate myself when I forget and do crap like that. But maybe it's a good thing I can actually forget at all.

It's after midnight when we finally pull into Charleston. I'll be staying with Drew tonight because we refuse to stay apart from one another. Tomorrow I'll go home for two weeks, while Drew returns to Indy, and then we'll move into our house that he bought for us when he moves back to Charleston. It will give us time to get settled before our wedding, which is in one month.

Letty and Ray greet us with hugs. We're beat but I can't believe they stayed up.

"Of course we stayed up. We haven't seen you two since what, March?" Letty says.

"It was my surgery, Mom."

"You look wonderful, son," Ray says.

"I feel wonderful," Drew says.

"Are either of you hungry?"

Drew decides to raid the fridge and I snack on some of his findings. We chat with his parents for a bit, then head up to bed.

When we dive into the bed, Drew pulls me close and I'm almost asleep. I love the way he feels next to me. It's like I've just taken a sleeping pill.

"Cate?"

"Hmm?"

"I love you."

"Oh, Drew, I love you, too."

"I know. Thank you for hanging with me."

I lift my head to look at him. "What do you mean?"

"Cancer is a big fucking ticket, Cate. Most girls would've run away as fast and as far as they could. But not you. You're here. And you act like you're still as excited as fuck about marrying me. Like I'm fucking gold."

Tears choke the air that I try to breathe and the words that I want to say, right out of me. So I hold up my finger, indicating to him I have something to say. He knows I can't do it so he nods.

I wipe my eyes a few times and swallow, then say, "Listen to me, Drew, because I'm only going to tell you this once. I fell in love with you and that includes the good times and bad. I'm not some shallow twit that runs when things go south. I'm in this relationship for the duration, like it or not. Now you can thank me for whatever, but don't you ever thank me for hanging with you. This is the real deal. When you love someone, this is what you do. And I love everything about you Drew, the beautiful parts and the ugly parts, and that includes getting rid of the cancer."

"I never thought I'd meet someone like you. I'm sorry you have to go through this."

What? He's the one going through it!

"Don't be sorry for me. I love you and wouldn't be anywhere else. Nowhere else. But with you."

The light that glows through his bedroom window lights up his eyes and I can see the love shining in them. He traces the outline of my face, brows, lips, and then kisses me. "How did I ever luck out with you, beautiful Cate?"

"I can say the same for you, Drew. I think you're pretty damn phenomenal yourself. The truth is, I think they broke the mold after they made you."

Our house is damned awesome. It's a new four-bedroom, four-bath home in a great neighborhood in Mount Pleasant, a town across the river from Charleston. I was hesitant to buy something this large, but Drew insisted. He was so determined; I decided to go with it since it's his money. And I'm not gonna lie, this house rocks.

Drew, both of our parents, Shannon, Eric, Jenna, and Ben come over to celebrate our first night. Well, it's not really our first night because we've been here for a few days, but we're finally unpacked and settled. We cook out and have a great dinner, relaxing with family and friends. With the wedding less than two weeks away, time seems to be flying by.

"So, any late additions to the wedding we need to worry about?" my mom asks.

"Not that I'm aware of," I answer. "I pick up my dress tomorrow."

"Whatever you do, don't let Drew see it. It's bad luck."

"I know, Mom. He won't peek, I swear." I catch Jenna biting her lip, trying not to laugh. I want to throw a hamburger bun at her.

"What can't I see?" Drew asks.

"My dress. I pick it up tomorrow."

"Right. I won't peek. I'm not concerned about the dress, only what's hidden underneath it."

Letty gasps, "Drew McKnight! Shame on you! A wedding gown is a bride's pride and joy."

Drew acts chastised, but I know better. "I'm sorry, babe. Clearly I wasn't thinking. I was only being an insensitive man."

I want to snort at that. "It's okay. I'll think of a way you can make it up to me." The fact is, Drew really doesn't care about the gown. But once he sees me in it, he's going to flip. It's gorgeous. It's not what you'd call a traditional looking dress. It's a white silk halter dress that's sleek and body skimming, making it very sexy. It has a lace cover up that gives it a discreet look for the church ceremony. But, for the reception, I'll remove the lace and the dress then becomes much more revealing. At first I was hesitant to buy it, even though I loved it and it looked awesome on, but Letty, Mom, and Jenna all persuaded me to go with it. They thought it was *the* dress. Drew's eyes will bug out when he sees that cover up come off. And I can't wait.

"What's that look for?" he asks.

"Oh, nothing."

"Yeah. You've got something up your sleeve."

Jenna, Mom, and Letty all chuckle.

"Did you all do something to me? Like booby trap something of mine? I know how you girls are when you get together," he says.

Now we laugh even harder. "No, no booby traps. Go on and get out of here. You need to hang with the guys and leave us to our girl talk." He leans down and kisses me.

"Okay, but if you put dye in the shower head, someone's in for it."

"Um, Drew. Why would we do that? I use that shower, too."

"I know. But you'd rig it just so and wait with a camera so you could catch me on video."

"Cate, that's not a bad idea," Jenna says thoughtfully.

"Drew, you'd better get out of here before you give her any more ideas."

"Oh, don't worry. She has plenty. Did she not ever tell you about the time she put saran wrap over all the toilets in Ben's and my apartment?"

I look at Jenna with my brows raised.

Jenna slaps her knee and starts telling the tale. "We went to visit them for a football weekend. I knew they'd be drinking heavily so I grabbed the saran wrap from their kitchen when no one was paying attention and covered their toilets. We left and when they came home drunk that night, well you can imagine."

"Eww. That's gross."

I look at Letty and my mom. Their expressions are hilarious. We all start cracking up.

Then Drew says, "What's so foul about it is we didn't even realize it until Ben started puking."

I hold up my hand. "Stop! That's disgusting."

Jenna is snorting and holding her stomach. Now the expressions on Letty's and Mom's faces are horrific. Thank god we've finished eating. Then Jenna says, "Dessert anyone?"

We look at her and now I really do pick up a hamburger bun and smack her in the head with it. The rest of the night goes from one story to the next until we can't laugh any more. We sit outside on the deck and I'm on Drew's lap as we tell our stories. What a great way to christen our new home.

Ten days later, I walk down the aisle on my dad's arm as Drew waits to receive me, and I become Cate McKnight. It's the middle of June and for Charleston, the weather couldn't be any better. It's eighty degrees with low humidity, which is actually cool for this time of year. The breeze is gentle, though it wouldn't really matter because all of our activities are indoors. Neither of us wanted to risk dealing with a chance of thunderstorms.

As soon as I step into the aisle to make my way down to Drew, all I notice is him. Everything else fades away—the people, the beautiful flowers, the wedding party, and even my dad, who has been crying off and on for most of the day. When we get up to Drew, my dad hands me off, and I look into Drew's crystalline blue eyes as they gleam with happiness. His smile is radiant and I want this picture of him to stay forever in my mind—this perfect image stamped eternally on my soul. His hand is warm as he takes mine and his fingers fold over my shaky ones. He mouths the words I love you, and it takes all I have not to kiss him. Then he mouths, I was wrong about the dress. That gets a giggle out of me. We turn and walk up to the altar. The episcopal priest awaits us to perform the marriage ceremony and I hand off my flowers to Jenna, who flashes me a toothy grin.

It's funny about moments like this. You think you'd be so aware of every single thing, but the truth is all I can think about is the man standing next to me. The priest talks about the importance of marriage and the closeness of friends and families, but I pray about Drew's health. I ask God, since we're in His house, to watch over Drew. I'm not a particularly religious person, though I do believe. But if ever there was goodness born on this Earth, he is standing next to me. And I suppose that's what worries me the most about his cancer. I know that old saying "only the good die young" is just a saying, but maybe there is some truth in that. Maybe God really does need those good souls back in heaven with Him. But don't we need them on Earth, too?

My morbid thoughts, thankfully, are interrupted, because it's time for us to take our wedding vows. We deliberated over writing our own, but we eventually settled on letting the priest use the traditional ones. But Drew surprises me. After I'm done with mine, and he says his, the priest looks at him and nods.

Drew turns to me and says, "Cate, Catelyn, I knew the day I saw you I was finished. You caught me, only you weren't aware." He looks down and bites his lip for a beat. Then his head lifts, and his irises lock with mine. My heart feels like the wings of a hummingbird. One hand releases mine and cups my cheek. "Oh, Cate, I hope to give you the world, and I'm going to do my honest to god best. You could've run, but you didn't, which tells me everything. Now I need to tell you everything." The hand that was on my face grabs my free hand and places it on his chest. "This is yours for as long as there are beats within it. Everything I have is yours. My love, my heart, my soul, and my life, for however short or long it may be."

I can't breathe. My face is wet, and the reason I know is he wipes my tears. Then he leans in and whispers, "Breathe, Cate."

Breathe? I can't even swallow. Blink. I can blink. So I keep doing it, and he keeps wiping my eyes. Finally, the priest tells him to place the ring on my finger and he says some other things, but his words have collapsed me. I need some time alone with him. Like right now. Why did he do this to me? Here?

The priest announces that we're Dr. and Mrs. Andrew Standford McKnight and we walk down the aisle. As soon as we get to the back of the church, he pulls me into one of the side rooms. We were going there anyway to hide from the crowd, so we could take more pictures afterward. There is a bathroom in there and I drag him behind me, close and lock the door, and start sobbing.

"Jesus, Cate, I didn't think."

I throw myself at him and just cry. I need this moment to purge this out of me. "Just hold me," I say. My tears run dry and I pull away. "A little warning would've been good."

"I guess so." He looks chastened. "I'm sorry. I wanted you to know how deeply I feel so I thought ... enough said. I love you. You know how I feel. I won't keep putting my damn foot in my mouth."

"Drew, everything I have is yours, too. You know that. But your words were so unexpected."

"I know. And I was wrong about not caring about your dress. You are the most beautiful thing I've ever laid these dumb old eyes on." He kisses me. "I couldn't believe how stunning you were, standing at the end of the aisle. You are a vision."

"You think so?"

"Yes! Now let's get you fixed up again so you don't look like you've been crying. I'm sorry I made you cry, babe." He sounds so disheartened.

"You can make it up to me."

"I plan on it."

My make up bag is in here so I go to work touching up my eyes. It's not that bad because I'm wearing waterproof everything.

"How do I look?"

"Like a princess."

I roll my eyes.

"You do. Better than any princess I've ever seen. You're gorgeous, Cate. And best of all, you're my wife." He kisses me again.

Someone knocks on the door. "Hey, you okay in there?" It's Jenna.

"Yeah." And I open the door.

"Oh, god, don't tell me y'all were ... I told you he'd go crazy over that dress and ..."

I cut her off when I see Shannon standing there. "That's enough, Ms. Nosy."

Drew grins and winks at me and leads me out of the bathroom. Then the photographer grabs us and it's all about the pictures for a while. We take the church shots and then all the outdoor shots, and I'm glad because it takes my mind off of everything else.

The reception is a hit. Two things Drew and I insisted on during the planning stages were a big band, and a huge bar with anything and everything anyone wanted to drink. The rest—we really didn't give a damn about. We figured we wanted a party where everyone danced and had a great time, and the way to do that was with an awesome band and great drinks. We have succeeded. People keep telling us this is the best wedding reception they've ever attended. My feet will be killing me tomorrow, but I couldn't care less. Drew and I fly out on Monday to wherever his secret honeymoon is. I won't be walking anywhere far, I'm sure.

We don't leave the party until the very end and I hate to say goodbye to all our friends. But I'm eager to get to our hotel. We're staying in a suite in one of the hotels right here in downtown Charleston. A horse and carriage await to take us to our room. When we walk in, a bottle of champagne sits in a bucket of ice and Drew and I look at each other and make faces. The last thing we either want or need is more alcohol.

"You know what I'd love right now?" he asks.

"A wedding night blow job?"

"Well, that too, but I'm starving. I didn't eat but a bite or two. I'd love a pizza."

"Oh, me too. I'm famished myself."

He grins, grabs the phone, and starts ordering all this food from room service.

"Why didn't you order a pizza delivery?"

"I wanted variety. And I'll have my blow job for dessert. They're bringing a can of whipped cream because I ordered strawberries."

"They are not."

He looks like that little boy again. "Yes, they are."

Sure enough, when the room service man arrives, pushing a cart laden with our food, there is a can of whipped cream on it. But I don't see any strawberries. I ask Drew about it. He's a bit tipsy.

"Oh, that's right. I ordered brownie cake instead."

"That's even better!"

We dive into the array of food, from pizza to burgers, fries, and chicken wings, until we're stuffed.

"Don't forget the dessert," Drew reminds me.

"Oh, you can have the brownie thingy. I have something else in mind."

I crawl between his legs, tug his boxers down with a little help from him, take that can of whipped cream, and make an artful creation out of his cock. He'd started eating the brownie, but after a bite, got very distracted by what I was doing.

"You like?" I ask.

"Um, I love." He has his husky, sexy voice going now.

I eye his whipped cream covered cock, trying to decide if I should start at the top or the bottom, when he says, "No hands."

"Huh?"

"Don't use your hands. Mouth only."

"Is that a challenge?"

"Not really. I just want to watch you suck me off with your hands behind your back."

"Can I touch Louise?"

"Oh, no. Only I get to touch Louise."

"Hmm. Well, then. I'd better hurry it up, because Louise is getting impatient."

I dip my head down and lick the tip of his cock, swirling my tongue about the tip, sucking off the cream. "Yummy, I love this."

"Cate, stop teasing." I notice his hands clenching the table.

"No teasing. Just sucking."

And I go back to work. This really is tasty. Lick, swirl, suck until all the cream is gone and now I take him deep. He groans. Loudly. And I want this to go fast because I need some relief, too. But he has other ideas.

"Enough." He pulls me to my feet and lays me down on the coffee table, pulling off my thong. It's a sexy, white satin number. Once I'm bared to him, he takes that can of whipped cream and coats my pussy with it.

"My turn." Then his tongue starts lapping up the cream as he murmurs his pleasure. I'm thinking we'll have to buy this stuff by the case. "Whipped cream is good, but it doesn't taste nearly as good as you, Cate." My legs are spread and my feet rest on his shoulders. When he spears me with two fingers, I cry out, "Ahh."

"You want this?"

"No, I want you."

"That can be arranged, but I want an orgasm from you first." And he gets it. Or rather he gets two.

Then he pulls my hand and I'm back on my feet. He picks me up, carries me to the bed, and proceeds to make love to me. It's slow, drawn out, and perforates my heart in a way I'm sure he doesn't intend it to. But his words, "For however short or long it may be," keep coming back to me. This moment has to last forever in my heart. I don't want to feel this way—to have these doubts. I want my faith to be firm in his survival of what he faces. So I will choose to live in the moment from this point on, cherishing him day by day, hour by hour, minute by minute.

The honeymoon destination is the island of St. Martin. When we land at the airport, our driver greets us.

"Where are we going?" I ask.

"You'll see in just a little bit."

When we pull up to a private villa, Drew says, "Surprise." Then he leans over and kisses my cheek. "This is our home for the next ten days."

"This is amazing."

"Let's check it out."

Our driver unloads our bags, while a woman greets us and shows us around. The villa sits right on its own private beach, but has a pool and every amenity one could want.

The woman, whose name is Monique, tells us, "Every morning, breakfast will be delivered at seven. We will leave it outside so we won't disturb you if you are still sleeping." She beams and her face lights up, letting us know she has an inkling we'll be hanging out in bed a lot. "Then I will return at twelve thirty to deliver your lunch. You will leave me your order, yes, in the morning on the porch when I deliver your breakfast?"

We nod. Apparently there is a huge menu we get to choose from.

Monique isn't finished. "Then, at six in the evening, our chef, Pierre, will arrive to cook you dinner, if you are dining in. Again, you must give me your dinner selection at lunch, so chef can be prepared, yes?"

We nod again.

"You will find everything you need in the villa and if you don't, you just call Monique, yes?"

We nod, again. Then she leaves and we grin at each other.

"Drew, this is amazing!"

"I hope you love it."

"I do! How did you find this place?"

"Oh, this little thing called the internet. And my parents."

When our first breakfast is delivered the next morning, it consists of homemade breads and croissants, because we're staying on the French side of the island, and everything is mouthwatering. It's a good thing I don't have to worry about fitting into my wedding gown anymore because after all this tasty food, I'm sure it would be very snug.

Our views from the beach are stunning—we have a spectacular sunset to witness every night right off our terrace, so we usually sit out here with a glass of wine and take in the gorgeous scenery.

One night, as we sit together holding hands, something pops into my head. "Hey, I thought you said you didn't want anyone seeing me naked. Remember?"

"Yeah. I said that to throw you off, so you wouldn't be able to figure out where we were going."

"Really, Drew? I never would've guessed this place in a gazillion years. You outdid yourself."

"Nah, I outdid myself when I found you."

"Promise me something." There's urgency in my voice and he hears it because he sits up straighter and leans forward in his chair.

Taking my hand, he says, "Anything, babe. What is it?"

"Promise me you will fight this thing with everything you have. Because honestly, I don't want to think about this world without you in it." I'm not sure if it's the alcohol, or what, but big fat tears power their way out and I can do nothing to stop them. And this is the part I hate the worst. I'm the one who should be strong. I'm the one who should be comforting him—pushing him on. But no, he pulls me into his lap and he's my strength. His hands rub a path up and down my back while he whispers things to me and I have no idea what they are.

When the tears ebb enough for me to speak, I ask, "Is there anything you're holding back? Anything you're keeping from me?"

"No, Cate. I'm telling you everything and will always do that."

"Okay. I'm sorry I fell apart."

"Why are you sorry? You're scared. I'm scared. I don't know

how long I'm going to live."

"Don't say that."

"It's true, Cate. But none of us do. Hell, we could die in a plane crash on the way home. Realistically, we won't, but the fact is we all face death. It's the circle of life. I see it at work all the time so I think I'm a bit more practical about it than you."

"I can't let myself think that way. You're young and strong enough to beat it."

"That's what I'm hoping for. But Cate, if I don't ..."

"Stop it, Drew. I don't want to hear that."

He nods and presses his lips together. I guess he knows I've had enough of this talk. We sit for the rest of the night, me on his lap, watching the night sky over the sea. I know this talk is prophetic, or at least it's Drew's way of trying to prepare me if the worst happens. Only I don't let myself get prepared. But I'm not sure anyone really can.

TWENTY-FIVE
Present

———————◆———————

THE FORCED SMILE ON MY face is plastered there. I remember the times going out with friends who really didn't want to be with me, but would rather be hanging out with their hot boyfriends. Now I have a hot boyfriend that I'd rather be home with. But it's okay to hang out with friends, I tell myself. I can practically hear Jenna saying that I don't have to spend every waking moment with Drew.

"Cate, what's wrong? You've gone pale."

I blink. "Sorry, nothing."

I recall I have asked Andy nothing about his health. In fact, I should schedule my annual physical. Survival rate of anything improves the sooner it's found. Then I chide myself. Andy knows better than the rest of us to take care of himself. I won't ask him. He'll think I'm babying him.

"Cate."

I glance up.

"You're not even in the room. I'm telling you about Daniel."

Her lips pokes out and I feel bad. "Sorry, Mandy. I just have a lot on my mind."

"Yeah, that hot doctor. You've never really told me about how you know him, where you met. What's the story?"

The story…

"It's complicated."

There is no way I can explain the convoluted nature of our relationship. Mandy, however, folds her arms over her chest and I sigh.

"He's from Charleston, like me," I toss out, like that explains everything.

She nods and I'm glad she's accepted the simple truth of Andy and my origins.

"Obviously things are going well. You'd rather be out with him than me."

I open my mouth to protest and a male voice speaks instead.

"Excuse me."

We look up from the leatherette sofa we've commandeered to turn to face a man in a suit with dark hair and eyes staring hard at Mandy while leaning on the back of one of the chairs in front of us.

"Can I buy you ladies a drink?"

I'm about to say no, but Mandy beats me to it.

"Yes, yes you can."

The wattage on her smile has turned to super nova levels. He's quite handsome and the way the suit fits him like a glove spells expensive and not off the rack.

"We're actually having wine," Mandy explains.

The man raises a finger to a waitress walking by. "Can you bring the ladies a bottle of Domaine Vacheron 2012 Les Romains Sauvignon Blanc?"

Mandy lifts her eyebrow because the wine he's ordered isn't cheap, not to mention he rattles if off in perfect French. Then again, the bar and lounge Mandy has chosen is frequented by nearby professionals and up and coming lawyers. He takes a seat in the chair that he'd been leaning on. It's one of two high back chairs on the opposite side of a small table that separates us.

Unfortunately for me, he glances to the bar and waves over a friend who makes his way over and takes the chair across from me.

"I'm Jared and this is my friend Scott."

Mandy is too pleased and is quick to reciprocate with our names. "I'm Mandy and this is Cate."

We exchange nods and Mandy and Jared start to make conversation. It leaves me and Scott to entertain ourselves. Scott is kind of cute. He's a ginger with a warm smile. Someone I might have dated if I wasn't already involved. The key words being, I'm involved, and I don't want to have to explain that to him. It always makes the situation weird because most guys think women use that as an excuse when we aren't interested.

"So what do you do?" Scott asks a little awkwardly.

I'm flattered he's a little nervous. It only makes him that much cuter, but he's not Andy.

"Cate, Mandy."

We both glance up to find Daniel. Mandy's eyes widen before they narrow. I feel a little giddy because this is the distraction I need.

"Sit and join us." Then I glance at the two guys ready to make introductions. "This is Daniel and…"

"Tammy," the redhead receptionist supplies.

"And this is Jared and Scott," I announce.

There is only a place on the sofa next to me and another chair left in the little grouping. Daniel sits on the sofa and Tammy takes the chair next to Scott. The waitress with superb timing shows up with our wine, so Jared offers them a glass.

"Guinness, please," Daniel orders instead.

Tammy accepts the wine. The waitress is forced to go and get another glass. Jared and Scott order a couple of fingers of Scotch and we all sit there until Mandy blurts out, "Daniel, weren't you working late tonight? I thought you had a project to complete."

Music plays softly in the background, but the few seconds of silence is deafening with Mandy's accusatory statement.

Daniel shoots back, "It's not due until Tuesday. But thanks for your concern. I'm sure my boss will appreciate your diligence in making sure I meet my deadlines."

Talk about awkward. Jared and Scott glance away as if not to watch the train wreck happening.

"So Jared, do you and Scott work together?" I interject, trying to break the tension Mandy and Daniel have created.

Jared's face smooths out. He begins to speak about the law firm he works for and a pro-bono case he and Scott just wrapped up. The case is about a girl with a disease that causes bad seizures who would benefit from the use of medical marijuana. Mandy, who practically leans into Jared's lap, hangs on to his every word.

I stay quiet because I know how helpful it can be, especially when it comes to pain management and nausea, but there is no way

I'm talking about it. I'm sure if Andy were here, he would have a lot to add to the conversation. And with an MD behind his name, they would be hard pressed not to listen.

Daniel's jaw is tight and I watch as the tension between the two starts to build again.

"Isn't medical marijuana legal in DC now?" Mandy asks.

Jared nods. "It is. However, this case is across the Potomac in Northern Virginia."

Thankfully, that starts a conversation about how everyone feels on the subject. Views strongly vary one way or another and it relieves some of the strain. I'm half listening, but I pull out my phone hoping for a text from Andy. It's still early and I have nothing.

Scott makes a move and asks to switch seats with Daniel. I sigh knowing I'm going to have to give him the brush off. I hate doing that. It's insulting to him and it's embarrassing for me. I know how hard the dating scene is.

Just as Scott plants himself next to me, Mandy shoves an elbow in my side. I glare at her until she shifts her eyes somewhere off in the distance. I slowly turn and see what it means. Andy's friend, the Thor look alike, has just walked in with Mitch tagging behind him. Andy isn't with them as they sit around one of the only free tables left.

I glance at my phone and try not to let jealous and crazy thoughts muck up my head. There are a number of reasons Andy might not be with them like he said he would be. And I don't think in a million years he's cheating on me. So I finish my wine and Scott graciously pours me some more. Points scored for being a gentlemen. It's too bad I am not on the hunt for someone.

Scott asks some questions and I oblige him by answering. I even ask him questions to be polite as the legality of marijuana debate continues with the rest of our group.

"You keep checking your phone. Are you waiting for someone to call?"

It couldn't have been a better segue if I had said it myself. Scott's given me the opening I need to tell him I have a boyfriend without looking like a complete bitch. Only right then, the screen on my phone flashes.

Andy: You look like you're having fun. Should I be jealous?

I glance up and over to Andy's friends' table. He's there smiling in my direction and I feel a grin fill my face as I type.

Me: No, but if I'm in need of a rescue will you come and save me?

I glance up intending to look at Andy again but Scott is there waiting patiently for my response.

"Yes, I am," I say, just as my phone vibrates again.

Andy: IDK. I think it's interesting to watch some guy try and fail to pick up my girl.

I frantically type another message ignoring Scott completely.

Me: I'm a nice girl. I may give him a shot on principle. In fact it's rude of me to text to you while I'm talking to him.

I make a show of turning off my phone and putting it in my purse.

"I'm sorry," I say sweetly to Scott. "That was rude of me."

It's so wrong and unfair to Scott, but it makes me giddy to tease Andy. I'm curious to see what his next move will be.

"Was it someone important?" Scott asks.

I opened my mouth and words come out except I'm not saying them.

"Yeah, sorry man." His sexy voice makes my spine tingle.

Andy leans over and snags my hand. He draws me to my feet and up against him. Then he plants the hottest kiss on my lips. People around us start to make lewd comments.

He draws back, letting his hands slide down my back and over my ass before dropping away.

"You have to know it's not nice to tease," he says in my ear.

Grinning, I say, "We know the importance your mother places on good manners."

He shakes his head. "We can discuss when I get to your place."

"Promises, promises."

Mandy clears her throat. I turn to the group. "Sorry. Everyone, this is my boyfriend Drew." I purposefully don't call him Andy because I know everyone calls him Drew. Then I rattle off everyone's name and end with Scott who doesn't seem angry, but maybe a little confused.

"Are you going to join us?" Mandy asks.

"I would, but I'm here with friends and Cate's here with you. She and I will see each other later." His eyes are dark on mine and I feel the heat smolder between us. I'm sure everyone else feels it too. "However, I am going to borrow her for a second."

He glances at Mandy and she nods. Taking my hand, he walks me over to his friends and I get a sober view of Dave.

"Mitch, you know Cate," Andy begins. Mitch tips a glass in my direction. "You haven't yet met Dave. Dave, this is Cate."

Dave stands in all his California dreaming glory. His hair is that pale blonde people call sun bleached or the luck of the gene pool. His eyes are a midnight blue or so they look in the dim light of the bar. His chiseled face could easily grace the cover of any magazine.

His bear hug is brotherly and he looks over my face and pronounces, "I can see why Drew is so smitten with you. I think I could settle down if I found a woman who has your beauty."

"You're too sweet," I say.

"So they say," he says and chuckles.

His smile is sly and sexy as hell. If I'd been single, I would have drooled all over him.

"And he's lying. Dave will never settle—at least not with a chick," Mitch says offhandedly. Dave glares at him. "Don't worry. I already told her all about you and your antics."

Dave shrugs and sits casually back in his chair.

Andy shakes his head before kissing me again for good measure. "I should send you back to Scott. He looks like he wants an explanation."

A quick glance over and I see Scott's eyes glance away. I sigh. "I never led him on."

"Sure you didn't," Mitch says, dragging out the words in a flippant manner.

"Maybe if you'd get laid you wouldn't be so grumpy," I retort.

Dave snorts and Andy laughs. Mitch only glares at me, so I stick my tongue out at him. Somehow I know I can get away with this, considering what he said to me during our first meeting.

"She obviously knows you well, my friend," Dave banters.

"Oh, yeah. We're BFF's. Isn't that right, princess?" Mitch asks, a smile playing on his lips.

"You wish, hot shot," I call back to him.

Andy taps my butt. "Go get 'em tiger."

I shake my head, chuckling, but turn in the direction of my table.

As the night wears on, Scott is gracious and we end up talking politics, of all things. Daniel and Mandy trade unfriendly stares to the point they don't notice when Jared starts talking to another girl from our office who has showed up with a few other people. Daniel's redhead and Scott get in a heated debate about the upcoming election when things start to wind down. I finally stand as our group begins to break apart.

"Are you ready to go?" I ask Mandy.

She nods. We wave our goodbyes as Mandy takes a hold of my arm. "You have to introduce me to Thor first," she says close to my ear.

I sigh because I know Mandy's into Daniel and he's into her. I wave Daniel goodbye as he watches us make our way over to Andy's table. A few girls are standing there basking in the guys' hotness. One of them leaves Dave's side to make her way over to Andy and flutters her eyelashes. It reminds me of my college days when I would sit and watch the hot guys I was with, friend or more, get hit on by waitresses. I tamp those memories down, and bring myself back to the here and now. Before I move to introduce Mandy, she grabs my arm and shakes her head. Now I understand. Considering the PDA display Andy did to me earlier, I assume he'll forgive me for what I'm about to do next.

Casually, I step over and turn to conveniently trip and fall into Andy's lap. I flutter my own lashes and end up blinking a little too hard and start to laugh. "Sorry. I'm such a klutz."

Andy chuckles as he has me figured out. With a wide smile, he dips his head to kiss me.

"Subtle, Cate," Mitch says.

Catching a glimpse of the flirtatious girl, I notice she now suffers from fake eyelash paralysis. The girl's fake eyelashes freeze wide open as her face sours.

"Sorry ladies, we aren't interested … tonight," Dave says to the other girls. Out of his mouth, the dismissive words seem thoughtful and sweet. He is good. The women walk away, wondering if they should be offended or flattered.

"Cate, who is this tasty morsel you've brought over for us to sample?" Dave asks with a wink.

But it's Mitch's eyes that are glued to Mandy as if she were the

Greek goddess Aphrodite. Interesting.

"Mandy, this is Mitch and Dave."

Mandy barely gives Mitch a passing glance as she beams at Dave. Dave smiles back, looking very used to the attention.

Daniel walks by and snags Mandy's shoulder. "Can I talk to you?"

She nods and holds up a finger for me to give her a minute before she walks away. I can't imagine being Mandy right now. I'm not sure how all of it will play out considering both Dave and Mitch watch her walk to Daniel. Tammy stands alone looking uncomfortable while the two talk.

"Are you going home?" Andy asks.

I nod. "I'll see you later, right?"

Andy doesn't answer. He turns to his friends. "Dave, Mitch," Andy says, gaining his friends' attention. When they shift their eyes, he says, "I'm calling it a night."

"Don't blame you. And Cate, if Drew treats you bad, call me. I know how to make it better." Dave winks.

I laugh because I can only imagine.

"Dude, she calls him Andy," Mitch says with a chuckle.

If Mitch and I hadn't patched things up, I might have gotten mad. I know him better now and he uses words like a marine in combat. "Don't worry Dave, if Drew and I have problems, I know to sic Mitch after him."

Mandy walks up then with a shell shocked expression.

"Are you ready?" I ask cautiously.

She nods and glances back to Daniel who is busy helping his date get into her coat with his eyes firmly on Mandy.

"Andy will give you a ride," I say, because I know he will.

Mitch, who somewhere in all this has gotten up says, "I'm sure Andy," he glances at me as his mouth twitches, "and Cate want some alone time. Dave and I can see her home."

I silently ask Mandy what she thinks. Her face brightens as Dave saunters over.

"We'll make sure she gets home." When he says it, it sounds salacious.

"Go on Cate. I'll be fine."

I shake my head. When I turn, Andy has my coat. I get into it as Dave and Mitch give Mandy the princess treatment.

After we leave, I ask Andy, "Should I be afraid?"

He laughs. "They're harmless. They won't do anything she isn't on board for. Enough about them, they're adults. With you so close but not close enough for me to touch, I've been hard all night. I think I have blue balls."

As we walk through the underground parking lot to get his car, I slyly ask, "You're the doctor. Do your balls actually turn blue? You tell me if you have blue balls or not."

He takes my hand and places it on his cock. "Blue or not, I need to get you home now."

The ride is fast, but not fast enough. I consider giving him a blow job while he drives, but DC cops fill the streets with their vehicles and I don't want to waste time explaining to an officer how I was looking for my contacts down his pants even though I don't wear contacts.

We barely make it inside the door of my apartment before Andy cups my face and kisses me so tenderly I begin to melt.

"Cate, I don't think I could ever love someone as much as I'm in love with you."

The intensity in his gaze has me paralyzed. I begin to open my mouth to speak, but he's there with a fiery kiss that weakens my knees. His hands skate down to the buttons on my blouse and I'm almost ready to tell him to rip it off with how badly I want him inside me. I shrug out of my coat and toss it somewhere into the room as he makes quick work of divesting me of my top. When he releases the last of the buttons, he slowly pushes the shirt down my arms. When it reaches my wrists, he pulls the ends of the blouse together. Caged in, with my hands behind my back, I have no idea what he's up to.

"You stay right here while I worship you."

I feel the fabric tighten around my wrists right before he slides down the length of my body. His palms glide up my thighs, pushing up my skirt. Belatedly, I wish I'd worn garters tonight. Then again, I didn't have plans to see him until after I got home.

His heated breath skims my skin before I feel his tongue through the fabric of my thong. I lift a leg and lean back on the door to gain leverage to press myself against his eager mouth. He hooks a hand under my knee and settles it over his shoulder.

When he pulls the fabric apart, leaving me exposed, my other leg gives out. I begin to slide down the door. He stops my progress by hooking my other leg over his shoulder. He moves forward, so my back is as close to flush with the door as can be with my hands in the way.

"I need to touch you," I call out.

"In a minute," he hurriedly says slipping a finger and curling it to stroke my g-bell.

My legs begin to shake from the force of the orgasm building inside me.

"Andy," I breathe. "Don't stop."

He slips another finger inside and finger fucks me until I explode around him. I'm boneless as he frees my hands. He lifts me in the air and carries me back to the bedroom.

"Don't leave me yet, Cate. I'm not done with you."

After I make contact with the mattress, I hear the rustle of fabric while I explore the back of my eyelids.

"Cate," he breathes, covering me with his magnificent body.

"Please," I beg.

"Shit Cate."

"I need you, now. Make love to me."

There is no doubt in my mind I see stars as he slips into me. My back rises off the bed as it feels like heaven, like home. Nothing in so long has felt this right.

"I love you," I breathe as he begins to move.

Something breaks in my chest as he drives into me with so much passion I feel his love in every stroke. A tear falls from my eye and I know there is no turning back. This man is mine and I am his.

He doesn't ask if I'm on the pill. And had I not been, I would be ready to make babies with him. When his name slips off my tongue, it surprises us both. I call him Drew as he climaxes on a growl of pleasure. My vision explodes with a million stars.

We settle back on the mattress and he threads his fingers through mine. Tears slip out the corners of my closed eyes because my emotions are raw and I've admitted the truth I'd been holding back.

TWENTY-SIX
Past

———◆———

COMING BACK FROM OUR OWN little paradise is harsh. I shouldn't complain because life is pretty damn good. We live in a fabulous home, Drew loves his fellowship and the attendings he works with, and my new job is great. I landed an entry-level auditing position with Ernst and Young. It's not my dream job, but with my ambition and goals, I can see myself making partner one day, if not here, then another firm.

Every day, though, I find myself daydreaming of our little villa on the sea, and how Monique and the rest of the staff spoiled us. The summer ends and fall is upon us before it barely registers.

One day at my new job, a huge flower arrangement is delivered for me. I scratch my head, wondering if Drew is trying to apologize for something. But that's silly because the man never does anything to piss me off. Then I open the card and feel my heart beat a little faster as it thumps a lot louder.

Cate, Catelyn, My lovely wife,
Happy Anniversary! Two years ago you agreed to go out on a date with me
and you changed my life. Without you, I would be less than a man,
because that fist-sized thing that beats in my chest,

only beats because of you.
I love all the pieces of you with all the pieces of me.
Forever yours,
Drew

I hug his note to my chest and smile. Thinking back to that day, I laugh a little because I thought he was so old. He was twenty-seven then and I called him Smokin' Hot. And he was. And still is.

"Flowers, huh?" A voice says over my shoulder.

I turn to see my boss, Joseph, standing there.

"Yeah. They're from my husband."

"He likes to spoil you, I see."

I beam. "He sure does."

Joseph smiles and then moves toward his office. I'm in a cubicle the size of a shoebox. There are about two dozen on this floor. When I stand, I have a perfect view of the cubicle sea.

After Joseph leaves, I hear, "So, Drew sent you flowers. What's the occasion?"

It's my cube neighbor, Nan. I like to call her Nosy Nan. She knows everything that goes on here, and then some. I hug Drew's note tighter to my chest, afraid she'll be able to read it with X-ray vision or something.

"No occasion. He's just attentive."

"If I could be so lucky," she sighs.

I wonder if her luck, or lack of it, has anything to do with the fact that she sticks her nose into everybody's business. I can already hear Drew telling me to be nice, so I switch my thoughts back to the audit I'm working on.

My phone buzzes. It's Drew texting me.

Drew: Happy Anniversary!

Me: Thanks for the flowers. They're magnifigorgeous.

Drew: That's not a word, Cate.

Me: It is now.

Drew: You like?

Me: Nope. I LOVE!

Drew: Score! How about dinner tonight? FIG?

Me: Time?

Drew: Right after work to save us a drive. 6:30?

Me: Perf. LOVE YOU <3

Drew: LOVE LOVE YOU!

Dinner is awesome. But it always is at FIG, one of my favorite restaurants downtown. That night when we get home, I think the flowers were sent to seduce me, because Drew doesn't even give me a chance to get in the house.

He opens my car door, and kisses me. The silk blouse I wear magically disappears. My bra gets unhooked by the time we hit the door, and the kitchen counter becomes our bed. He doesn't give me time to think, only feel. His hands and mouth are magic, but they always are. By the time we both come, our breathing sounds like we just ran home instead of drove.

All of a sudden, Drew gets hit with a coughing spell. It's unusual and I become alarmed. Of course, anything that happens to Drew alarms me. He could stub his pinky toe and I'd freak. He accuses me of being too overprotective, but that's what happens when the man you love has been through a bout with cancer.

He finally stops, but his eyes are watery and his nose runs. "Are you okay?"

"Yeah, it was a wicked tickle in my throat. Maybe it's ragweed allergies, or something."

I hope it's the ragweed and not the or something. "Maybe. Want some water?"

"No, I'm good now."

It starts to happen off and on. Not a whole lot, but enough to send up a warning signal. It's about three weeks after the first episode, and I say, "Do you think you should talk to your doctor?"

He sighs. "My next round of scans is next week."

"Your next round of scans?"

"Yeah. They always do a six-month follow up after everything. Mine are next week."

I swallow. "And you were going to tell me, when?"

He stands and moves to sit next to me. He takes my hands and says, "I was going to tell you next week, Cate. I didn't want you to get your panties... unders in a wad over this. It's going to be fine."

"Drew, we're in this together. I'm going with you."

I see him reach for patience. "Cate, all you'll do is sit and wait."

"I don't care. I'm going with you. I think you're missing

something out of this equation here. You plus me equals us. No arguing."

He sighs. "Okay."

"What kinds of scans?"

"Bone and PET."

"What day?"

"Wednesday."

"Okay. I'll tell Joseph."

On Wednesday, we have the scans. The waiting is the worst. Only we find out really fast because of Drew's position at the hospital. The news isn't good. There's a reason for the cough. We sit across from the head oncologist in Drew's department. He shuffles the papers and looks up at us.

"Drew, Cate, I'm sorry. You have mets to the right lung."

I don't know that means. "Mets to the lung?"

Drew squeezes my hand. He sounds weary when he says, "It's metastasized to my lung, Cate."

Fuck! The lung? "How did that happen? I thought it was gone?"

The oncologist, Dr. Rosenberg leans forward and says, "Unfortunately, Cate, it only takes one cell to break away and that's what happened in Drew's case."

"So now what?" I ask.

"We have Drew up for our tumor board on Friday. Drew, do you want to attend?"

"Yes, since it's my treatment plan you'll be discussing."

Dr. Rosenberg shifts in his seat, then glances at me.

"Just say it. I'm in this as much as he is."

Dr. Rosenberg presses his lips together for a minute. "Drew, you and I have already had this discussion and I won't sugarcoat anything with you. Cate, is that how you want things, too?"

As much as it will hurt to hear, I say, "Yes."

"Okay. Drew's type of cancer is more difficult to treat in his age group. Now that it's metastasized, the odds of a cure have dropped even further. We are going to press ahead with everything we've got, but of course, part of his treatment will have to include another round of chemo and surgery. We're not sure yet if we'll add radiation. There is a possibility of some experimental drugs, but I'm not sure at this point, hence the tumor board on Friday."

My body feels numb and I can't begin to imagine how Drew

feels. Just a few weeks ago, everything seemed so great. How could it be so bad? Then I flashback to these same words I said, when his initial diagnosis first came about. I realize nothing's fair in life. Abso-fucking-lutely nothing.

Drew is quiet, as am I. Finally, Dr. Rosenberg breaks the giant iceberg of silence. "Do either of you have any questions?"

"No," I say stone-faced. The only question I want to ask is *why can't you cure my husband?*

Then he says to Drew, "I'll see you Friday at seven."

We walk out and I'm not sure what to think. But Drew, my precious Drew, does it all for me.

"Cate, look at me." He stops and takes me into a small room of some kind. "It's going to be fine. You're going to be fine."

My mouth works over a thousand things I want to say, but nothing comes out. He presses me into the hard wall of his chest and I wonder how something so ugly and horrific can be growing inside such a perfect human being.

"I'm so scared, Drew. I don't want to be. I want to be strong for you. Strong to carry you through this, but here I am, the biggest chicken shit on Earth."

"How can you not be scared? I'm scared, too. But we're in great hands here."

"Should we go back to Indy?"

He pulls my face away from him so he can look at me. "Listen up. At the tumor board on Friday, the team from Indy will be video conferenced in, along with some guru from Sloan-Kettering." A coughing fit breaks into his conversation. When it ceases, he wipes his eyes and carries on, covering up the severity of it. My heart squeezes in fear. "I think Rosenberg is also tagging some guy from MD Anderson. I can't get better care anywhere, Cate. I promise."

"Okay. If you're good with it, so am I."

Several deep breaths later and we're heading out to the car. My arm is wrapped around his waist hugging him tightly to my side.

Friday rolls around and I wait to hear from Drew. The call doesn't come until almost noon.

"Sorry, babe. I was poked, prodded, questioned, my results were reviewed, and quite frankly I'm not sure I want to talk about it." He sounds fatigued.

"Want to wait until I get home?"

"Yeah. Do you mind?"

"No. As long as you snuggle with me."

"Always."

On the way home I pick up Drew's favorite pizza and a six-pack of his favorite IPA beer. When I get home, he's lying on the couch, asleep in the den, the TV on. I almost break down in tears looking at him, because right now, he looks so robust and healthy. I can't imagine he has cancer in his lungs.

Sitting on the couch next to him, I put my head on his chest and wrap my hand around his neck. I know it'll wake him, but I don't care. I don't want either of us to ever sleep again and waste precious moments we could spend together.

"Hmmm. I've always loved waking up to you."

"I've always loved sleeping with you. By that I mean making love, and not actually sleeping."

"Funny."

"I brought dinner home."

"That's nice." He yawns. "I'm not particularly hungry, though."

I lean back and inspect him. "Did an alien beam down from space and invade Drew McKnight's body. Not hungry?"

He half smiles. My attempt at amusing him is an epic failure. "I'm sorry. We don't have to eat. We don't have to do anything. We can just lie here all night and not even talk, if that's what you want."

"Cate, that's not fair to you. You need to know the plan."

I toe off my shoes and stretch out on top of him. "Shoot."

"Tuesday morning I go in for round one of chemo. Different drugs. Same side effects."

I grab his face and say, "You good with this?"

"Yeah."

"Okay. Then what?"

"We do three rounds, then surgery. But this time we'll do bang, bang, bang."

"Meaning?" I ask.

"No time off in between."

Ouch. That's rough. That means he'll debilitate. With zero time off, it won't give him much time to regroup and gain his appetite back.

"That's rough, Drew."

"I know. They know it. But they think I'm hearty enough and it

311

gives me the very best fighting chance and I have to take it."

"Okay, I'm with you. Are the drugs as harsh?"

"Yeah, but the doses will be different and they'll add more protective measures to make sure I don't get neutropenic and such."

"Okay."

"Then PET scans and if they like the progression of the shrinkage, then surgery."

He's tempering his Greek because I understand these terms, when usually I don't. This tells me he really doesn't want to talk much more about it, and I'm good with that.

Three weeks later, Drew is down twenty-five pounds and feels like hell. I bring him milk shakes, ice cream from his favorite ice cream shop, sundaes, cake, brownies, chocolate chip cookies, you name it, to try to get some pounds back on him. But eating is a huge problem. He's nauseated all the time. The drugs they give him to prevent it don't seem to be that effective. Ben, bless him, scores some weed and that helps the most. Plus, it has the added benefit of stimulating his appetite. At first I worry it will hurt his lungs, but Drew, in his dry humorous way, looks at me and says, "What, Cate? Worried I might get cancer?"

And what can I say to that?

He finally seems to be turning in the right direction. The doctors won't even consider surgery until they can get his strength up. So Ben comes over every night and they smoke and get high. And by high, I mean completely stoned. Drew eats, and Ben and I laugh, because Drew is freaking hilarious. He comes up with the craziest shit, like telling us we're going to plant asparagus in the back yard, instead of grass. Then we'll just mow it down once a week and have dinner afterwards. Ben and I try to convince him it won't work, but he has it all planned out in his head that it will.

One night we're all sitting around, and my mom decides to pay us a surprise visit. Drew, who is stoned as hell, pulls out his pipe, and offers my mother a hit off it. Ben almost falls out of his chair, and I have to drag my mother in the kitchen and explain things to her.

"Cate, I am aware of the medical uses of marijuana. I didn't fall off the turnip truck yesterday, you know. I did smoke the stuff when I was in college."

"I didn't know that, Mom. But, uh, thanks for sharing." Jeez, talk about a shocker. I can't conjure up an image of my mom taking a hit off a bong for the life of me.

"By the way, Cate, where did Drew get his pot from?"

"Oh my god, Mom, I can't believe you just asked me that."

She shrugs. "Well you never know if you'll ever need it."

When I tell Ben what she said, he dies laughing again.

"Oh god, the picture of your mom hitting the pipe is just too good. Cate, we need to get her high with us."

"Ben Rhoades! That is a big negative."

Drew chuckles. "Oh, Cate, I think she'd get so into it."

"Most likely. You two are terrible." I shake my head at them and leave the two of them alone. Ben is good for Drew. He gets his mind off things and relaxes when Ben is around. And Ben is coming around a whole lot these days.

The following week, Drew's doctors deem him strong enough and ready for the surgery. The limbo I've been surviving in ends much too abruptly for my liking. But Drew is ready to get the dog and pony show on the road, as he says.

"Are you scared?" I ask him the night before.

"Not of the procedure itself. I've been through it once, so I know what to expect. I'm afraid they'll either find more inside than the scans showed, or they won't be able to grab it all."

"I'll be brave for the both of us," I tell him, which is a big fat lie. I'm so afraid I can't eat or sleep.

In the morning, we arrive at the hospital and things run as expected. My support team is there: Ben, Jenna, my parents, and Drew's parents. Jenna holds my hand the whole time during the five-hour surgery, and Ben never sits down. As close as Jenna and I are, Ben and I have really bonded over the last month or so. He is every bit as worried and scared as I am. I glance at Letty and Ray and my heart plunges into my guts. I can't imagine being in their shoes, having your only child go through cancer treatment like this. A sudden urge hits me and I run to Letty and throw myself at her, burying my face in her lap, my arms wrapped around her. She must think I'm a lunatic, but I can't help myself.

Her arms wrap around me and we try to comfort each other. I'm not even sure how long we stay like this, but eventually Drew's surgical team makes an appearance. Dr. Rosenberg also shows up, which is weird. This can't be good.

The head surgeon, Dr. Sherman, leads the talk. "Surgery went well. Drew's in recovery and he'll be fine. We had to take the entire lung. It was peppered with mets. When we got into the lobe we thought was affected, we decided to check further and it soon became clear that we were dealing with a more aggressive situation here. We also had to resect more bone than we initially thought. So now it's a wait and see."

"So he can live with one lung, right?" I may sound stupid, but I don't know these things.

"Oh, yeah. He'll adapt. Most people only use a percentage of their lung capacity as it is."

"Oh, okay. And what about more chemo?"

Dr. Rosenberg says, "We're going to have to switch that again, since we didn't get the results we sought. But we'll discuss that after Drew recovers. Our goal now is to get him healed up after the surgery and out of the hospital."

All of us, Ben, Letty, my parents, Jenna, and myself look like deer in the headlights. Everyone except Ray. Being a doctor, he knows what's going on. He gets it. But I don't want to ask. Because I want to bury my head in the sand and pretend none of this happened.

"When can we see him?"

Dr. Sherman says, "My recommendation is that you all go home and rest. Tomorrow morning will be soon enough. He won't wake up for hours and when he does, he'll still be sedated."

"I remember that from the last time. Can I at least look at him?"

Dr. Sherman and Ray share a look. Ray says, "Cate, he'll be on a ventilator. It might be better …"

I cut him off. "I don't care. I just want to kiss him and touch his face. Tell him I love him. Then I'll leave."

Dr. Sherman says, "That should be fine. Ray, Cate, Letty, why don't you come with me?"

He leads the way and we go into recovery. I'm shocked to see the tube going down Drew's throat, but I refuse to let it show. I place my hand on his head and my cheek next to his for a moment. Then I tell him how much I love him and kiss his cheek. Letty does the same, followed by Ray.

When we get back to the waiting room, the tears I pushed away eke past my lids, but I won't give in. Not yet. I hug Letty and Ray, and my parents. Then I turn to Jenna and Ben and ask, "You guys are staying with me, right?"

"Yep."

And we head home, where I proceed to digest everything and then break down.

"Cate, maybe they got it all."

"They had to take out his whole lung, Jenna. His prognosis wasn't good to start."

Jenna grabs my shoulders. "Stop it. Stop saying that."

"I'm hoping for the best, but expecting the worst. It's the only way I know to prepare because you can't possibly understand what this man means to me."

"She's right Jenna. And I know, Cate."

We both look at Ben and if eyes could speak a million words, his would do so right now. The grief written in them is so poignant, I automatically reach for him, and we cling to each other.

"Drew told me this was a roulette game and we all know the odds of that." Then I feel his body shaking with silent sobs, and mine does the same thing.

The next morning, we make an impressive team as we head back to the hospital. Fake smiles and chipper faces are all nothing but plastic. But Drew won't notice, because he'll be drugged out of his mind and until he does, we'll put on the best show as we possibly can.

This time when I see him with all the hoses, tubes, wires, and IV lines, I'm not nearly as shaken up. I know what to expect and I've prepared myself. His morphine pump is next to his bed and he gives me a wan smile. Thank god, they've taken him off that ventilator and he's breathing on his own.

"Hey, gorgeous," I say, kissing him. "Love your tubes. You have the best tubes I've ever seen."

"You really know how to flatter a guy." He sounds so breathless. Is that normal? I want to ask him, but I don't want to freak the hell out of him.

"It's the way I work. Is it dumb to ask how you feel?"

"No, there is no such thing as a dumb question."

"Oh, yes there is and I've heard many. But, how are you, my love?"

If I could do anything, anything at all, it would be to take his pain and suffering away right this very instant. Instead, I run my hand over his smooth head, bald from his last round of chemo and my assistance at shaving.

"Much better with you by my side."

"The only place I want to be."

"Have I told you how beautiful you are?"

"Not today."

"I just did, then. And I love you." His eyes flutter closed. I place my face next to his and kiss his cheek. Then I tell him, in his ear, how very much I love him, too. After a moment, I stand and walk out of the room so I can get my cry on. And it's a doozy.

As I'm in the hall, Ben comes out and envelops me into a hug.

"You okay?"

"Yeah. I needed to get away from him so I could cry."

"He's out of it, Cate."

"Yeah. But I still want him to see me as Wonder Woman, or something."

"That's ridiculous. He knows you're not. He knows if anything happens, you'll need the support of friends."

"Ben, has he said anything to you about not making it?"

"No. He doesn't know. No one does, Cate."

"I don't think his doctors are very hopeful."

Ben leans against the wall and stretches his arms up, dropping his head down between them. Suddenly, he slams his hands against the wall and yells, "Goddammit!"

I get ready to tell him to hush, but a nurse beats me to it. "Sir, please, this is a hospital, and I would respectfully ask you to refrain from yelling and from using that type of language. We have sick patients and their families here."

Ben straightens up and walks up to the nurse and says, "Yeah? Well my best friend for my entire life is in there and just had his lung ripped out his chest because he has cancer. This is his wife right here and I apologize to you and everyone else, but we're a little upset. Sorry for the bad language, but ..." Ben throws his hands up in the air and he turns to me as racking sobs take over him. When I see him like that, I turn into a weepy mess myself.

Jenna shows up and tells us we need to take it somewhere else. But quite frankly, I just don't give a fuck anymore. Ben and I stand there and after a time, we let each other go.

He looks at me and asks, "You good?"

"For now. You?"

"Same. Ready to go back in?"

"Yeah."

He holds out his hand and we take the next steps together.

As the day progresses, Ben and I have more than a few crying spells, but we lean on each other for support. The morphine keeps Drew's pain at bay but his head fuzzy. The thing about his breathing is freakish. He's so out of it, I can't ask him anything. Ray says it's his diaphragm and it's fine. But it's not fine. My husband is getting taken apart piece by piece and it's killing me slowly as I watch it happen. I never thought about families of cancer survivors and what they go through, but it's not for the faint of heart.

Another week passes and Drew finally gets discharged from the hospital. His spirits are up and he's eating again, too. After a few days, he says they're going to have another tumor board and he wants to attend. That means I have to take him, since he hasn't been cleared by his physician to drive.

"Do you want me to go too?"

"You can, but I doubt you'll want to because it might be all gibberish to you."

"I can sit in the corner and read a good book."

He laughs nervously.

"Spit it out, McKnight. I know when you're hiding something."

"The news won't be good, Cate." His voice is clear and strong.

"Remember, no sugarcoating," I remind him.

"See, here's the thing. They originally thought the cancer was confined to one lobe, but when they found it scattered throughout my whole lung, well, you can probably guess what I'm going to say."

My hands are fisted so tightly, my nails pierce my palms. "Don't make me guess. I need it spelled out, Drew. I'm not a doctor and don't know these things."

"The lungs are a secondary point."

"Meaning?"

"If it's there, it's most likely someplace else."

"Such as?"

"The liver."

Heart meet stomach meet floor. Stomach meet throat meet mouth. I run to the bathroom and make it just in time. After I finish my pukefest, I wipe my mouth and rinse it out. Then I think about what he said. The liver. While I'm not a smart woman, medically, I do know this. The liver usually spells out terminally ill. Drew is telling me he's terminal. Fuck. Suck it up, Cate. Get out there now because he needs you. I look in the cabinet, since I'm not in my bathroom upstairs, and thank god there's mouthwash in here. I rinse again and walk out the door.

"You okay?"

"Yeah, well, could be better. What now? More tests?"

"That and we determine if treatment is even an option anymore."

I press my lips together, doing my dead level best to hold in my tears. Nodding, I finally squeak, "And you're sure there's nowhere else we can go?"

"I'm positive, Cate. It's the disease, not the institution."

I stand there, looking at the floor, and I hold out my arms so he can walk into them and not see me cry. God bless him, he figures me out.

I drive Drew to the hospital but give him the respect he deserves and don't stay for the tumor board. He calls an hour and a half later and I meet him in Dr. Rosenberg's office. They decide another round of chemo with an experimental drug added to the protocol. This will go on for two months. If no improvement is seen, then that's it. They've reached the end of the road.

Christmas is next week and we have no tree or decorations. After moving into the house, I was all gangbusters because I knew this would be the perfect home for the holidays. There are a couple of rooms that would be great for Christmas trees, but now I'm pretty sure we won't have that.

Drew doesn't start chemo until January and I have a moment of inspiration. I get online and check things out. Then I make a call to Letty and pull her into my surprise, and then Ben. They're one hundred percent on board. My last hold out is Dr. Rosenberg. When I speak to him, he's a go, too.

So two days after Christmas, I pack a bag for us and I tell him I have a surprise. We get in the car and drive to the airport. When we get there, and he sees our destination is Chicago, he wants to know what's going on. I only jiggle my brows.

"What have you done, Cate?"

"Oh, I don't know."

The corner of his mouth curls and I can see his wheels spinning. "You haven't done what I think you have?"

"And what might that be?"

"Blackhawk tickets?"

I grin and the look I receive is like sunbeams bursting through a storm. If I could capture it on film and save it to my own personal hard drive forever, I would die a happy woman. Drew McKnight is the happiest I've seen in weeks and weeks and I know I've made the best decision to make this trip.

The three-day jaunt to Chicago is amazing and it changes Drew—if only for that short period of time. It's like we went back to those days in our sweet little villa by the sea. We are happy and nothing gets in the way of it, not even the looming monster of cancer.

Unfortunately, it doesn't last, because we have to come home. But damn, it's been so worth it.

January, chemo cranks back up and ironically, it's not as bad as the last rounds. Drew has been in some pain recently, which makes me anxious, but the chemo knocks it right out and he tolerates it well. Other than the hair being gone, which neither of us gives a shit about, he's holding his own. That's not to say all is great. He's dropping weight. It's not a huge amount. But it's a pound or so every week. I have to buy him new clothes because he can't wear his old ones anymore.

He gives me an apologetic grin. "Maybe I should just stick to sweats. With elastic, then I wouldn't have to worry about it."

"Drew! Don't be silly."

He's lying on the couch and I slide up next to him and hug him. It's sad to feel how much muscle is no longer there. It's the wasting away thing that you hear about.

"I'm nothing but a sack of bones, Cate."

"You've lost weight, but we'll fatten you back up."

"I love your positive attitude."

"Drew, you have to have one, too."

He tilts his head and stares for a minute.

"What?"

"My scans came back today." Blue eyes, overcast with sadness gut me. Shit shit shit shit shit.

TWENTY-SEVEN
Present

———————◆———————

THE LIGHT COMING THROUGH MY window is hazy and gray. Clouds thick with frozen moisture loom above DC, putting the brakes on everything as the city waits with bated breath to see if the possible storm will materialize.

"As much as I hate to say it, you should get home or you'll be stuck here with me for the foreseeable future."

"Not a bad thing." Andy tugs my back closer to his chest.

"We both know the hospital will need you."

"Maybe I need you more."

His words light a fire in my heart. I'm beginning to need him like I need food to survive.

"Andy," I begin.

He groans. "For the record, I hate that we live so far apart. I'm getting used to waking up with you. We should think about getting a place together, somewhere halfway between there and here."

My mouth goes dry. "What are you saying?"

He turns me around so that I'm facing him. "I'm saying I want us to share space. I'm saying that I need you Cate. We've spent enough time apart."

I place my finger on his cheek and begin to trace the line of his cheekbone. "No one knows we're together yet. My parents, yours, … Ben."

He sighs. "I know. Maybe we should tell them when we go home for Christmas. You are going home?"

I nod. As much as I don't want to and deal with the questions and possible hurt feelings, I have to face that reality if I plan to be with him. And I'll have to go back to calling him Drew. I'm not sure I'm ready for that either. The bubble wrap we've created around our relationship will finally pop.

"I am. When are you planning to go down?"

He shrugs. "I'm not sure. I'm asking because I thought maybe I could drive you down or back, if not both, depending on our schedules."

"I'm planning to take the week, not much more."

"Okay, I'll see what days I can get off. And there's something we should discuss later."

I rise up on an elbow. "Tell me now." Curiosity makes me feel like a kid at Christmas.

He shakes his head. "I have to leave and this is something we need to talk about. But before I go…" His hand snakes down the sides of my body. When he reaches my hip, one hand moves to my center to test the moisture levels. My climate is ripe for the taking and boy does he take me.

When he finally leaves the bed for the shower, I watch his perfect body with awe. He's always been a specimen to behold. As his backside disappears into my bathroom, I hustle out after him. By the time he leaves for Baltimore, snow is starting to fall steadily. Nervous about the weather, I wait on pins and needles until he calls to let me know he got home safely.

The rest of my Sunday is spent taking care of the little things like cleaning up and laundry because I'll be busy soon. I start a new engagement on Monday. The offices where I'll be working the next few weeks are located on the other side of the Potomac in old town Alexandria, Virginia. It will just put more distance between Andy and me. I have to seriously consider a move so that we are closer together because waking up without him bothers me, too.

The amount of snow we've gotten before the official start of winter has all the news organizations talking on Monday morning. It's one of the reasons I didn't go home for Thanksgiving. That and I wanted to spend it with Andy. It was a quiet affair, the two of us cooking a dinner for the both of us. He got called into the hospital once. He wasn't gone that long. Otherwise, we spent the weekend together and it was really nice. It made me want what he was offering that much more.

I sit in my living room enjoying a leisurely cup of coffee. Our offices are closed again today because the storm hit us head on. The federal government is closed and that means DC is practically shut down. Many businesses follow the feds as a rule for office closings because the feds rarely do since DC has an extensive public transportation system.

"You are coming to my Christmas party, right?" Jenna's voice sounds loud and clear as I'm reminded I'm talking on the phone.

"I don't know."

"You have to. It's like bestie code or something. Bring him with you."

"That's the thing. I'm not sure I'm ready for everyone to pry into the fact that we're together again," I say, even though Andy suggested we come clean.

"People are going to find out soon enough."

She is right. "Still, don't you think I should sit down and talk to everyone, not show up at a party with him on my arm? There is Ben to consider."

Jenna's sigh is loud and dramatic.

"Ben's going through his own thing right now. I think some woman has crawled under his skin and turned him inside out. I don't even know who my brother is anymore."

"Oh, is it—"

"Don't say her name and jinx it."

We laugh for a few seconds before Jenna sobers.

"Really Cate, you can't hide this. You're going to have to be honest."

"I know. I just don't want to hear everyone's opinion. And what if Ben hates us for it? He was there. He was there for all of it. He watched me walk away."

"Are you back there again? No one hates you. I thought you've given up that guilt. That's not what you need while you're rebuilding your relationship. Did you just tell me he hinted at moving in together?"

"Yes, and I don't know what to do. If I move, I'll have to get a car. It's a lot."

"You can always move back to Charleston and be close to me."

I laugh a little before I tell her the truth about something. "I can never move back to Charleston. All the old hurts and mistakes I made are there. I can never be settled there."

"But you will visit."

"Yes," I say, even though I wish I never had to.

My parents, his parents, some of our best friends are lifers in Charleston. I may not be able to call it home, but it will always be home to my family and his.

Winter-like weather continues to batter the city through early December. It isn't until the following Friday I get to see Andy again. There is a holiday party at his office tonight and one at the hospital tomorrow. I've packed a bag as I plan to spend the whole weekend with him. The Uber rides are costly but cheaper and less of a hassle than maintaining a car. However, I have started to look at cars on the off chance I decide to move in with Andy.

I'm dressed to impress in a subdued, sexy number that won't shock the doctors Andy works with, but won't age me unnecessarily either. I spent a fair amount of time with Mandy searching for the right dress.

When I get to Andy's door, his expression says it all.

"Jesus, Cate, I'm surprised the cabbie didn't kidnap you. That dress is—"

"Good?"

He nods and I lean in to kiss him. His arm snakes around my back as he draws me up against his hardening cock.

"Happy to see me?" I ask with a smirk, as I pull back slightly.

"I'm always happy to see you."

He glances at the phone in his hand. "We could be fashionably late."

"Or," I say raising an eyebrow, "We can be on time."

"Cate." I can hear the protest in his voice.

"I don't want the doctors you work with to think I'm the one causing you to be late. First impressions, remember."

"Once they see you," he says, stepping back and eyeing me up and down, "they will forgive me for being late. In fact, I'll probably get bonus points for showing up at all."

I can't help but laugh. "How about I give you some attention on the ride over?"

His brows shoot up and I give him a wide grin. He takes my bags and drops them on the table. "After you, my lady."

I giggle as he pats my butt on the way out. I love how carefree our relationship has gotten. And true to my word, I give him the promised happy ending on the ride to his office.

My palms begin to sweat as we take the elevator up. He's explained to me that with the new laws surrounding medical care for all, their office had to cut spending. The small holiday party is being held in house to save money. Less money spent on frivolous things means more money in the hands of the doctors themselves. Still, they wanted to have the party, and the doctor Andy has been covering is coming with her new baby.

"Cate, you have no reason to be nervous," Andy says with an arm around my back.

"Easy for you to say. What if they don't like me?"

Andy stares at me. "I work with them. It's not like they are my family."

And isn't that the crux of the problem?

"And what will your family say when I show up with you at Christmas?"

"It will be fine, Cate."

The doors open and too soon I'm ushered into a glass front office. There are a few people milling about. We don't have any more time to talk about the week to come.

The doctors are friendly as Andy introduces me, but it's the baby who steals the show. The infant is carefully passed around after hands are disinfected with liquid sanitizer. When it's my turn, I feel the tears begin to form in the back of my eyes. I want this. I want a baby and a family. And I want it with Andy. The possibility of this could be derailed depending on how our week goes. I know Andy wants to think that it will be okay. But I've broken Andy's heart once.

"Cate," Andy says. He glances to the woman in front of me waiting to take the small bundle from my arms.

I hand the baby off and I immediately feel like something's missing. The tiny baby who smells like powder makes me want too much in a short few minutes. I sip at the glass of wine Andy hands me and try not to think so hard about a future I want and may not get.

Later as the party wraps up, one of the older doctors with only a small thatch of white hair that clings to the crown of his head, speaks.

"Well Cate, what's the verdict?"

I glanced up confused by the question that's directed at me. "Verdict?"

"We're all hoping Drew will stay with us. And the way he speaks of you, I think his decision largely depends on you."

I turn my head to the side and glare at Drew. He gives me a sheepish smile.

"Actually, I haven't had a chance to talk to Cate about your offer yet."

"Oh," the man says. "Sorry, we are all just so pleased with Drew's accomplishments so far. He will make a great addition to the team. And of course, a second office in DC will expand our client base."

"DC," I say to no one in particular.

That sparks conversation all around me. Drew uses the opportunity to draw me down the hall away from everyone. He pulls me into an office and closes the door.

"Andy, what's going on?"

He takes my hands and my heart begins to race.

"I planned to talk to you about this later tonight. I didn't expect they would put me or you on the spot like this."

My eyes are wide because I don't know what he's about to do.

"Cate, I love you and I always have, you know this."

I nod. I'm so very afraid he'll get on one knee. I'm not sure I'm ready for that.

"Roslyn is coming back part-time to the office. However, they want to bring me on full time. To help justify the cost, they want to open a satellite office in DC. I'll be there most of the time but will have a couple of days in Baltimore a month and will rotate hospital hours in both DC and Baltimore. It means I could move to DC."

"That's great," I say.

His smile dips. "You don't seem happy."

"It's not that. I'm just overwhelmed. It's a lot. But it sounds like a fantastic opportunity."

Even I know the smile on my face is a little weak. I try to crank it up because isn't this what I've wanted?

The delight on his face falls. "You don't want us to move into together."

"I'm not saying that. I just need some time."

He nods. "You're right. I've grown to enjoy the area, but I'll be honest with you. You sweeten the deal. If you don't want this, if you don't want me ..."

He stops, not finishing his thought. I want to tell him everything is great. The words are stuck in my throat for reasons that make me itch to run. I promised him I wouldn't.

He takes my hand and opens the door. He leads me back to the main room as hugs are being doled out and coos are being made over the baby. I feel like I'm having an out of body experience. I can't explain what's come over me and why I'm not happy when moments ago, I was dreaming of babies with Andy.

The drive back to his place is quiet. We get undressed and do our nightly ritual without saying much. I know Andy is hurt and I never meant to be the one to hurt him. It's almost awkward when we climb into bed. Still he pulls me close.

"Cate," he says softly.

"Yes." I feel the panic rising in me, unsure what he will say or ask of me.

"I want this shot at a future with you. You have all the reasons in the world to be scared. And I know you said you wouldn't run. But I won't hold you hostage. If you can't be with me, it will hurt like hell, but I would rather you say it."

I keep my clam trap shut at first. He lets out a long suffering breath of air. I meet his pleading eyes.

"I'm scared." It's a truth he deserves to know.

"What are you scared of?"

"Everything. I'm scared of how people will react when they find out. Mostly, I'm scared my heart can't handle breaking a second time."

"No one else matters. Just you and I. And I swear Cate, I won't break your heart."

"You can't guarantee that."

He doesn't counter because he knows there is truth in my words. Instead, he wraps strong arms around me and holds me tight. He strokes my hair while I let out quiet sobs.

When finally the tears ease and I can speak, I whisper the words, "I love you."

"I love you, too." He breathes the phrase and I find myself searching and listening to the beat of his heart. It's a long time before I can sleep.

Tomorrow is the party at the hospital. His future partners will be there. I need to have some answers for Andy in the morning and I fear what I want. I don't think I'll be able to feel solid about our relationship until it's out in the open with our family and friends. That means I need to tell him about Jenna's party. No doubt Ben will be there.

TWENTY-EIGHT
Present

---◆---

IN HIS ARMS, I WAKE up feeling safe. I lay still, content in his comforting embrace. I want to memorize his smell, his touch, his love, so I'll never forget it. And I know it's the past that continues to haunt me. Yet, he's still here even after my minor freak out over finding out he wants to stay in the area for me.

When he begins to stir, I turn to face him.

"Good Morning."

He presses his lips to mine. "Morning."

I reach to twine my fingers in his hair. "Your hair is getting long."

He gives me an impish grin. "I know. You want to cut it for me?"

I shake my head, knowing I'm dancing around the unspoken issue, so I push forward. "About last night…"

He takes my hand and presses a soft kiss to my fingertips. "I'm sorry. I shouldn't have sprung that on you, especially with everyone there watching."

"It wasn't your fault," I say. He hadn't been the one to bring it up. "And besides, I want you to stay."

A cautious smile blossoms on his face. "Are you sure?"

"I am, but…" I hesitate because this is the hard part. "We have to tell our family and friends."

As much as it scares me, it has to happen.

He nods, and his expression sobers. "Are you going home for Christmas?"

"I'm going down for the week."

His words don't falter, which makes me wonder if he's already thought about this.

"We can tell everyone then. I have to work most of the week. I should make it into Charleston by Christmas Eve."

I remember something I haven't yet brought up. It seems both of us have been holding back just a little.

"Jenna's having a Christmas Eve party."

He nods like he already knew.

"It's a good place to start."

His eyes hold me like an anchor, so I press forward.

"Ben." It's both a statement and question. I know he understands.

"It will be fine."

I shake my head. "Easy for you to say. No one will hate you."

He's quick with a retort.

"Cate, no one will hate you either. I'm surprised Jenna didn't crack and tell Ben about us already."

Frankly, I am too. "He'll be mad we kept this from him."

"Babe." He kisses me softly. "We can't worry about everyone else's feelings. This is about us. And you are it for me and you have been."

He clears his throat, only to cover his mouth with a fist and let out a cough.

My body locks up as if I've been flash-frozen.

Slowly, I force the words out of my mouth. "Are you okay?"

He nods, but coughs again. "It's nothing, a tickle in the back of my throat."

I say nothing. He's not stupid. He knows what's running through my head.

"Cate, babe, it's the season for colds and flu. I see patients every day. They have germs. I'm okay. I swear. I probably shouldn't kiss you, though."

He gives me a teasing grin, but doesn't let me respond. He soothes my worried soul with tender touches and wondrous kisses on my body. I lose myself in feelings that aren't emotions. He makes me forget that life is fragile, that we are fragile.

We spend a lazy morning in bed and he hasn't coughed anymore. I've let the worry go for now. At some point, he gets up and makes us breakfast. I feel so spoiled I show him my appreciation in all the ways that has him gripping my hair and calling out my name.

I don't even know how we make it to the hospital's Christmas party later that evening. Andy holds my hand as we walk into the ballroom of the hotel next to the hospital.

"Convenient," I say to Andy as he ushers me through the front doors.

"They wanted staff to be able to come over and be close if they are called back in case of an emergency."

The dress code isn't black tie. People come in a variety of outfits from very casual to semi-formal. The black dress I'm wearing is somewhere in the middle. As I take in the room, which isn't as fancy as the balls I've been to over the past few months, the décor is nice and more comfortable than some pretentious places I've been. I'm not sure what to expect, but it isn't the warm welcome I get from Becca.

"Hi. Cate, isn't it?"

I smile. Andy is behind me speaking to some of his colleagues and Becca is positively beaming. Before she can say anything else, a man not much taller than her comes over and slips an arm around her waist. Her face lights up and I understand where her glow comes from. I couldn't be happier for her.

A hand gently touches the small of my back and I turn to the side to see Andy standing next to me. A little more than cordially, he says, "Becca, Fredrick."

Becca gives Drew a megawatt smile and Fredrick matches her.

"Drew," he says. "And this must be—" says Fredrick, the ginger, with a possessive arm around Becca.

"Cate," I say holding out my hand.

"Nice to meet you."

He gives me a business handshake while Becca smiles at Drew. "Fredrick tells me I have you to thank for convincing him to ask me out. He says you gave him the push he needed to take the chance."

Drew laughs as if she's exaggerated the story. "He was almost there. I just got him to realize that sometimes it's good to take a risk."

His eyes brush over me and I wonder if he thought I was a risk when I kept running from him.

She steps in and gives Drew a quick friendly hug. I'm surprised when I feel no hint of jealousy. It's clear she's smitten with Fredrick. "Thanks." Then in almost a whisper, she adds, "I think he could be the one."

Her smile borders on shy as she steps back and lets Fredrick put his arm around her. I start to calculate when this all happened, considering her bold statement of Fredrick being her one. Only someone calls out the name Drew from across the room. We turn and see Désirée barreling toward us. She stops short when she sees me.

"Drew?"

I'm not sure why there is a question in her voice. I glance over my shoulder and see that Becca and Fredrick have been roped into another conversation. So I don't feel so bad that we've rudely turned away from them.

"Désirée, I'm surprised to see you here. This is a staff event," Andy says questioningly.

"I'm on the board now." Her tone is brusque and she's busy checking out all the places we touch as Andy has me tucked against his side. "I hear that you might be moving to another hospital."

She glances between us.

"I'm moving to DC to be closer to Cate," Andy says matter-of-factly.

For a second, her eyes narrow before they open with wide-eyed, fake glee. "Congratulations. I hope to get a wedding invitation soon."

She's probing and I'm prepared with an answer, but Andy beats me to it.

"We'll be sure to mail you one."

It's hard to hold back a snicker as her smile flattens out. I know she expected that he'd say something to contradict her. Instead, he's given her exactly what she doesn't want to hear.

"Great, I look forward to it." She spins on her heels and stalks away.

I let the laugh come out that I've been holding back.

"That was brilliant. Too bad we have no invitation to send."

Andy's magnetic blue eyes gaze into mine. "You never know."

My hand stills midair with the wine glass I've been holding. I'm not sure what to say to that.

"Drew," another person calls and we are pulled into another introduction and conversation.

Later, I'm finally able to step away as a long winded doctor draws Drew into a conversation with so many nonsensical five syllable words, my head starts to spin. I've just picked up one of the yummy calamari appetizers when a woman steps into my personal space.

Her blonde hair is carefully styled in an updo, but I recognize her as the one who couldn't keep her lips to herself and off of Drew.

"You may have won this round, but if you manage to marry him, you'll still lose. Half of the doctors here cheat on their spouses with nurses and other staff. I mean, they spend more time with us than they do at home with their spouses."

Everything about her looks angry.

I can't stop the quick retort that barrels out of my mouth. "You realize that if you didn't walk around with a sneer on your face, any one of the single guys here tonight would ask you out. You're an attractive woman whose beauty is hidden behind hate and envy. A genuine smile and happy thoughts would go a long way toward getting a man that wants you. And a bit of advice—no man wants to be chased. Men like to do the chasing."

I think of HockeyHo as I shake my head feeling so sorry for the woman before me. I pivot and plow right into Andy. He must have come up while I was talking.

"Cate." My name is but a whisper from his sly and half parted smile. He leans down and kisses me right in front of the woman and anyone else nearby to see.

I still don't know her name, but I don't care either—especially while Andy is touching me. He puts an arm around me and I turn back to face her. Only she's stalking off before we can share any other words.

"I sure am one lucky woman." I glance up at the man I call mine.

Andy appears mystified. "Why is that?"

"My boyfriend is like a super star."

He gives me a cheeky grin. "I'm lucky too. Do you know how many guys have come up to me tonight and begged me to tell them you were just my sister so they could ask you out?"

I shake my head. "No way."

"Yes, way, my beautiful Cate."

He makes me feel beautiful, but I don't say it. Instead, I teasingly say, "So it's my beauty you want."

"Pot and kettle and all that. You called me a mega model." He winks at me.

"Did not." I playfully slap at his arm. "Super star, Doctor extraordinaire, the man who could have any one he wants."

"And he wants only one woman. The one before me. So why don't you let me take you home so I can get even luckier?"

He kisses me again before we leave the party and when we get back to his place, he makes good on his promise.

Days later when I arrive at my parents' house in Charleston for the holidays, I sit in the kitchen with my mother.

"You can't stay more than a couple of days?" Mom pouts.

"I promised Jenna I would help get her place ready for the party. It's just easier if I stay with her."

I don't want to feel like a kid sleeping at my parents' house. They will want to know my every move, especially with my younger sister and brother at home. I plan to spend every night with Andy when he arrives. Which is why I'm staying with Jenna and not them because they would never allow it.

"You're coming Christmas morning to open presents."

I sigh. "Mom, I'm not five."

"I know. But you'll always be my baby."

She kisses the top of my head and I feel bad.

"I'll be by Christmas day at some point." I take in a deep breath and just say the words I've been thinking about all day. "And I'll be bringing Drew with me."

I don't bother calling him Andy because that's not how they know him and they will think I'm talking about someone else.

Shannon breezes into the kitchen. "So what's this about Drew coming?"

My sister is apparently still boy crazy. I don't remember being that bright eyed every time a hot guy's name was mentioned in a conversation. She was like this a few years ago and nothing's changed. Mom says nothing while she continues to cut out Christmas shapes in the cookie dough when she pauses. I decide to clarify my words. "Drew and I are back together."

Mom doesn't acknowledge my words, only continues what she

was doing being uncharacteristically quiet.

Shannon, on the other hand, goes for sarcasm. "Of course you are. I bet he's giving it to you real good."

"Shannon Forbes," Mom warns. "Stop being sassy. Go upstairs and clean your room."

She heads out and my brother walks in. "What's going on?" he asks when he spots the fury on Mom's face.

"Cate is shacking up with her boyfriend and doesn't want to tell Mom."

Eric shakes his head and does an about-face as I yell, "I am not shacking up with Drew."

Shannon waves a dismissive hand and I'm left alone with Mom whose stewing on Shannon's words or mine. I'm not sure. It could be both.

After agonizing moments, she finally says, "Are you sure that's a good idea that you and Drew get back together?"

I've expected a reaction, just not that one. "Why?"

"Catelyn, you and I both know how hard everything was on you. Are you sure you can handle this?"

"Hard on me? I'm the one that ran. Do you not like him or something?"

She'd never indicated she had a problem with him. I don't understand why she's on my side and not his.

"It's not that. He's a fine young man. I'm just worried about you."

"Don't be. I haven't been this happy since," I wave a hand in the air. "Since then."

I don't tell her that I had the very fears she's mentioned. I don't want her to worry because Andy is great and he's mine. Somehow, it will all work out.

Dad walks in and glances at us. "What's with the long faces?"

I dive in headfirst and blurt, "I'm seeing Drew again."

Dad's reaction is far different from Mom's. He walks over and places a comforting hand on mine. "I'm glad. Now I understand that smile when you walked in the door, not that I'm complaining. Any man that can make my baby happy, is good enough for me."

"Thanks Dad."

Mom doesn't say any more over the next few days. Shannon does her best to annoy me and Eric and I play video games as he tells me about making the basketball team. Dad and I get a tree the next day and as a family we spend the time decorating it. It feels good to be home and I haven't felt that way in a while.

When I arrive at Jenna's the next night, Ben is there.

"Catie Bear," Ben says wrapping me in a hug.

I don't correct him because Ben and I became best friends during all of the bad days that summer.

"Ben, I feel like it's been forever since we've talked."

"It has. And I hear you have news for me."

Damn, Jenna. But I'm surprised she hadn't spilled the beans so far.

"Drew." I clear my throat because I'm more afraid of his reaction over my parents. "Drew and I are back together."

He nods, not at all surprised. "Figures. I guess I'm the last to know."

He gives me a look but it isn't condemning.

"I'm sorry. I didn't want anyone to know until we figured it out. I wasn't sure if it would work. Plus, I wasn't ready for the backlash."

"Backlash?"

"I don't want anyone mad because we're together."

"Why would anyone be mad?"

I stop and close my mouth for a second. "Isn't it obvious? I walked away." I amend that. "No, I ran. You were there. I wasn't even sure he'd forgive me."

"What would he have to forgive? You did what you thought was best at that time. No one blames you, Cate. Least of all me."

I hug him and barely stop myself from crying. "I wasn't sure how you and everyone would feel."

He pats my back while I continue to hold him tight. He's like my big brother as much as he's Jenna's.

"I'm happy for you, Cate. I'm happy for both of you. You deserve it."

As much as I'm grateful he's fine with all of it, I worry about him too.

"What about you?"

He pulls back and I can see the sadness in his eyes. He shrugs and tries to give me a playful smile when he speaks, but I know he feels some truth of his words. "I'm all alone here in Charleston now."

I shake my head feeling like a mama bear that needs to protect her cub.

"That's not true. You've got Jenna. And you can always come up for a visit. We would love to have you."

He nods.

"By the way. I heard you're bringing someone to the party."

He shrugs. "She's a warm body."

"Warm body, that's not a very good description," I say with halfhearted humor.

"What do you want to know? She's pretty and intelligent? Well, she is both of those things, but I'm not expecting any more than that. We all aren't lucky to have what you two have, Cate. I'm not expecting a fairytale ending."

I narrow my eyes at him.

"With an attitude like that, you won't get one either. She could be your happily ever after if you give her a chance."

I see the humor leave him and he's got his dead serious face on.

"She can warm my bed, but nothing will thaw this cold heart."

He points to his chest and I place my hand there.

"Don't bullshit me Ben Rhoades. I know you now. You aren't the cold-hearted bastard I used to think you were." Which is probably the reason my crush on him died shortly after it began back when I was a preteen. He had a reputation of breaking hearts and bad boys were never my thing. "I feel your beating heart and you deserve to be happy."

"I am happy. I'm happy for you and Drew." He steps away like he's in a hurry. "Anyway, I've got to get going. I have to help my parents move furniture or something." He grabs his coat. "It was really good seeing you, Cate."

Then he is gone. I stand there worried about him. He hasn't been himself or so Jenna's told me. When she comes downstairs with her purse, she says, "Where's Benny?"

I'm still trying to think how I can help him as I mutter, "He left, something about helping your parents."

She snickers. "I'm glad you're here. I have an excuse not to go over there. Mom's in her re-decorating mode. And ever since Dad put the brakes on her shopping, she rearranges furniture every month instead." She rolls her eyes. "Let's go find a dress. I need something that will make Brandon jealous."

Two nights later, I watch as Andy and Ben talk in one corner. Jenna and some cute guy chat in another. My parents and Jenna's are sitting on the couch and other various people are having great animated conversations.

For a Christmas Eve, I pronounce all is fine in the world. So far, everyone has taken the news well that I'm with Drew again.

When the front door buzzes, I watch as Ben opens the door. When the McKnights, my in-laws walk in, Andy is immediately by my side. My heart races when their eyes lock on me, I know the conversation to come will be the hardest of any I've had so far.

TWENTY-NINE
Past

———————◆———————

"AND? TELL ME ABOUT YOUR scans, Drew." His expression, the downbeat look on his face, pretty much says it all. But he has to speak, and I know he needs to get it off his chest, even though he doesn't want to tell me.

He shakes his head. "It's come back. I lit up the pictures like a fucking Christmas tree. It's everywhere. I'm stopping all treatment." He holds up his hand to prevent me from talking. "I've been in every one of their conferences, Cate. I know the outcome data on all the protocols and I've failed everything. I want to live what little there is left of my life feeling better than I do right now. I don't have much time, but what I do have, I want those days to be enjoyable. I know this should probably be partly your decision, too, but I'm making it on my own. I have some things I need to take care of, business and personal things, and I wouldn't be able to do a damn thing if I feel like shit all the time. I hope you can understand my point here. I'm sorry I've put you through all this shit."

He offers up a sad smile and I throw myself at him. I don't know how I'll live without him. One thing I *do* know—this world will be shit without Drew McKnight.

"Me? You're worried about me? I want you to at least consider trying, Drew."

"It's no use, Cate. If I thought there was the slightest of chances, I would give it a go. But there isn't. Try to understand."

The words I want to say I can't, because I want to scream and yell. I want to shake him and tell him NO! Don't give up.

"Cate?"

My head jerks up. "What?"

"Look at me. I mean, really look at me. And take your blinders off." He holds his arms out. "This is cancer, killing me. It's what it does; it's called advanced disease progression. I'm at the point of palliative care."

"I-I don't know what that means."

"It means Rosenberg will make me comfortable with whatever he has to use. Pain meds, maybe some low doses of chemo."

"But you just said you were done trying chemo."

"For a cure. This would be for pain management. That's what palliative care is. I'll be comfortable, I promise." The ironic thing is his voice has a soothing quality to it.

"Drew, are you good with this?"

He lets out a short laugh. "I don't really have a choice, do I?"

No, he doesn't. It's not like he ordered this off the menu.

"Jesus, I don't know what to say."

"All I want you to say is that you accept my decision and pray for a miracle."

I look at him and say, "It's not like I have a choice, do I?"

He gives me a sheepish look and shakes his head. "No. I'm sorry."

I blow out a shaky breath. The time has come for me to face facts here. It's not like I haven't had these thoughts before. But when you're presented with them like this, it's like having ice water thrown in your face.

I don't know where the calm comes from, but I'm numb as I ask, "Do your parents know?"

"Not yet. Will you go with me when I tell them?"

"You know I will." I lay my head on his chest. "What about Ben?"

"I hope you don't mind, but he's on his way over."

"No. I don't mind." The truth is I'm kind of glad he's coming.

Ben never knocks, but for some reason, he does tonight. When I open the door, I can see the fear in his gray eyes. His dark brown hair is disheveled and I know why. He keeps running his hands through it, as he's doing now. Then he jerks me into his arms and we stand there, two dazed souls, trying to comfort each other. We hear Drew's voice calling from the other room.

"Stop sniveling out there and get in here you two."

"Leave it to him to say something like that," Ben says against my shoulder. Then he sniffs, wipes his eyes, and gives me a weak smile. Holding out his hand he asks, "Ready?"

We walk in together and Ben asks, "Since when have I ever sniveled?"

"Since you decided to take me on as your best friend and carry this cancer thing around with you." Then Drew blurts out, "I'm not gonna make it, dude. This is my last hurrah."

"I figured that's what you were gonna say. You wouldn't have called my ass over here for anything else. Good news usually gets delivered with a phone call."

"Damn, the dude grew some neurons and they actually started firing." Drew grins. Or tries to anyway.

Ben shakes his head. "Every now and then my common sense flares its head."

Drew looks at me and says, "Cate, can you give us a minute?"

It gives me the break I need so I run up to our bedroom and call Jenna. I'm nearly hyperventilating by the time she answers.

"Hey and I know it's not good. Ben's already hit me up with his suspicions."

"He's quitting everything," I tell her and I explain.

"Oh, Cate." Her voice conveys her heartbreak. Then I hear her sniffing and it starts a round of my own.

"What am I going to do?"

"I don't know, but you'll be doing it in great company. You'll have Ben, me, Letty, Ray, and your parents. Drew has quite the fan club and that means you'll have tons of support."

"As great as that sounds, it won't replace my husband." And I turn into a sobbing mess. Jesus, if I can't even think about it, how the fuck will I function through it?

Jenna reads my mind because she says, between tears, "One hour at a time. Or maybe even one minute at a time. And sometimes, one breath at a time."

"I'd better get back down there and I've gotta pull myself together first."

"Cate, it's okay if he sees you cry."

"Yeah, but I don't want the rest of our days to be filled with nothing but that. I want his last days to be good, you know?"

"I know. I'm here if you need me."

"You always are."

I go into the bathroom and look at the woman in the mirror. Red, puffy eyes with lips to match distort my face, and it has become my normal look lately. I splash cold water on me, hoping to rinse some of the swelling away, only I know that won't do it. What I need is a five-pound bag of ice to do the trick.

When I rejoin the guys, Ben looks as bad as I do, so I head to the liquor cabinet and pour him a tumbler full of Jameson. His hand shakes as he grabs it from me. Then I wedge myself next to Drew and wrap my arm through his.

"Can I get you anything?" I ask.

"I hate to make you get back up again."

"Dammit, Drew, I'd climb fucking Everest for you." I teeter on another round of tears, and he pulls me into him.

"Babe, all I want is one of those IPAs I love."

"I can handle that." I fly off the couch and grab one out of the refrigerator and bring it back to him. I'm back in seconds.

He laughs. "Cate, it's not a race."

But it is. A race against time. The question hangs over me ... how much? A year? Months?

He knows and he says, "Babe, like I told Ben, it's somewhere in the neighborhood of six months, give or take."

My hand clenches Drew's thigh and my eyes connect with Ben's. *Six months. By summer he'll be gone.* I try to calculate in my accountant's brain how many more nights I have with him. Six times thirty equals one eighty. One hundred and eighty days and nights with Drew. And then nothing.

Ben empties his glass, jumps out of his seat, and pours himself another. I jump off the couch and run out the back door. Oddly enough, I don't cry. I stare off into the distance and think about what I'll do with myself minus the love of my life. I hear the door open and assume it's Ben.

"You must be going as crazy as I am, wondering what the fuck your life will be like without the most important person in it."

"Actually, I'm more worried about you than anything."

I turn to see Drew standing there. He walks up to me and wraps me in his warm embrace. I brace myself for his words.

"Cate, listen to what I'm going to say. The reason I'm doing this is because I want my last days to be good ones, you know? I'm going to ask something really huge of you. I want you to take a leave of absence. I know you're just kicking your career off, but I want you with me, every day, every hour, especially now, when I feel like doing things. Because right now I feel pretty good. And now that I'll be off treatment, I'll be even better. I want to go places, do things. Live. For the next five or six months, or however long I have, I want to hang out with Ben and Jenna, party, watch hockey, go to the beach, spend time with my parents and yours. If you're working, we won't be able to do half of these things. You know money isn't an issue. Can you do this for me?"

Without even thinking, I say, "You know I will. There's nowhere else I'd rather be and honestly, I haven't given work a thought. I'll give Joseph a call tomorrow to see what I need to do."

For the first time since Chicago, I see his blue eyes sparkle. "Thank you."

This is my Drew. Thanking me for taking a leave of absence to watch him die. What the fuck do I say to that? He takes care of the awkwardness for me.

"Oh, and Cate, do me a favor. We all know I'm going to die. Let's not tiptoe around any of this. It will get really weird if you do. I'd rather lay this shit out on the table. You know? And not dance around the issue. And by the look on your face, I know I've just shocked you, but it's the truth. No running into the closet with Ben and whispering behind my back anymore, okay?"

"You've accepted all this, haven't you?"

"Yeah, and it's sort of a release. My only concern is you."

I make a huge decision here. Not because I want to, but because I *have* to.

"Stop. Right here and now, I want you to stop being so concerned about me. I'll be fine with whatever happens. My choice is that you'd be here forever and ever, but if the powers that be choose otherwise, I'll deal with it, Drew."

"You promise?"

I make an X over my heart. "Cross my heart and hope to die."

"Never do that."

"Okay, bad choice of words, but you know what I mean."

Then he grabs me and kisses me in a way he hasn't in weeks.

"Hey, have you all forgotten about me?" Ben asks, interrupting us.

"No, I just had to kiss my wife," Drew says.

Then Ben twitches his brows and holds up a pipe. "Anyone wanna smoky smoke?"

"Hell yeah," Drew says.

Boys will be boys, even if one is dying of cancer.

The visit with Drew's parents is as difficult as I'd imagined. How can you prepare yourself to tell your parents you have a terminal illness? Drew is as calm as can be, but I'm the one who has the most trouble. Letty and I cling to each other like static electricity. But they're happy to hear that Joseph agreed to my six-month leave of absence. If it goes longer than that, I will have to give up my position. I don't give a damn. Drew comes first as I explain to his parents.

The next few months are filled with side trips to Asheville, Savannah, and Hilton Head, where Drew and I spend precious time together doing things he loves to do, like fishing, sailing, and sitting and watching the sunset. When we're at home, Ben, his parents, my parents, and Jenna are usually there, not all at one time, but it's a show of love and I'm thankful for every one of them.

Four months have passed and Drew is holding his own. One day he suggests we take a vacation out to the California wine country. I'm shocked because it's a long flight and the time change worries me because it might fatigue him.

"Cate, I'll sleep on the plane and they do have beds in California."

"I don't want you to get run down."

"I won't let myself. I promise."

He seems so strong, and if this is what he wants, who am I to deny him? But I do one thing first. I call Dr. Rosenberg and have a chat with him. He laughs. "Cate, Drew is a physician and also knows his limitations. If he wants to go, then go."

"But ..."

"But nothing. You both know what the eventuality is. Let him get his wish."

"You're right."

If Drew wants the wine country, then he shall have it. And he gets it. We're tipsy more than we're sober, I think. One day Drew says, "I don't think I've tried a wine I haven't liked."

We laugh and sip, and eat, and one day at dinner when the

waiter asks if we'd like to see a wine list, we both shout, "No!" We agree we've had enough for the day.

By the time we get home, Drew's energy begins to lag. He doesn't complain, but I can see it in the longer naps and the earlier bed times. He's using fentanyl patches for pain and sometimes has to use the lollipops laced with it, too. But one thing Drew doesn't do is complain. If he's in pain, he slinks off and uses a lollipop, but I can usually tell by his eyes, or the shade of his skin, which has lost its usually tawny glow and luster. His hair is growing in, but the chemo he takes for pain keeps it at that downy stage, like a newborn's, and I love to rub my hand across it. It's one thing that Drew loves, too, and in fact he asks me to do it a lot. He says it's soothing.

He's down to nothing, as far as weight, and he was right about the sweats. It's what he lives in these days. He mentions it again today.

"Any chance you can buy me more of these? I hate to wear the same things over and over."

"Oh, sure. They're so soft, I'm sure they're comfy."

"Yeah. And I don't have to worry about them falling off this bag of bones. I'm down to nothing, Cate, there's no use in denying it."

He's right. I can't. He's nothing but a shadow of what he was six or seven months ago. I have his clothes pushed to the back of the closet so he isn't confronted by them constantly, but I sneak back and look at them. It's sad when I see how robust and strapping he used to be compared to what he is now.

"I won't. But I'm also not going to tell you anything negative either, Drew. I'll get you whatever you want. You know that."

"Thank you."

Later that week, he sits in his favorite chair, a large recliner, so I hop in with him and snuggle next to him. "How's my guy today? Feel like doing anything? A movie?"

"Nah, I'm good right here."

"Hungry?"

"Not really. Just wanna chill."

"You got it."

Minutes later he's sleeping. It's what he does mostly these days. I slip out of the chair and call Ben. I usually give him an update every couple of hours. And then it turns into a tearfest for the two of us. And poor Ben. He has to work with a career to maintain throughout all of this. I'm not sure how he's keeping this shit from falling out of the briefcase—trying to sell stocks and investments while his best friend is dying. I'm so thankful I'm not working.

"You stopping by after work?"

"Cate, what the fuck do you think? I should just move in with you."

"Hey, there's plenty of room here."

"Yeah, I know. But I have a place of my own."

"Rent it out."

"Um, yeah, but what about after ..." He trails off and we both fall silent. It's a powerful moment. "I didn't mean ..." he starts.

I blurt out, "You could stay with me for while. I may need you."

"You won't."

"I won't what?"

"Want to stay there."

Oh shit. I never thought about it, but he's right. There's nothing that could make me stay here. This is ... was ... our place. This was supposed to be where we had kids.

"I guess not. Need a roommate?"

It's another awkward moment. Then Ben fixes things.

"I'll see you shortly. Need me to bring dinner?"

"Sure. Can you pick up Chinese? His favorite egg rolls and won ton soup?"

"You bet. What about you?"

"I'll eat what he doesn't." His appetite has gone to nothing these days.

Ben says he'll see me in about an hour.

Drew eats half an egg roll and half a cup of soup and I don't eat much more. Ben tries to cheer up the house, but Drew falls asleep on us and it's the two of us staring at each other, wet-eyed. The TV provides white noise as Ben and I stare ahead.

"What do you think life will be like without him?" I ask.

"Empty."

"Kinda like right now?"

"Yeah."

"He always tells me he loves all the pieces of me with all the pieces of him. Why did all the pieces of him have to get sick? Why couldn't one piece of him get sick? A piece that he didn't need?"

Ben scrubs his face. "I dunno, Cate. I wish I had an answer for you. But just for the record. I love all the pieces of him with all the pieces of me, too."

It's only a short fifteen days later when Drew wakes me up in the middle of the night. That's not quite accurate because I'm not really sure when the last time I truly fell asleep—and I'm talking deep sleep—was. I hover in that place somewhere between sleep and awake. Things have declined rapidly in the last couple of days. My head spins when I think about it.

His voice rasps as he calls my name. "Cate?"

I'm out of the bed saying, "What is it?"

"I think it's time. I want to go to the hospital."

The words I've dreaded for weeks punch me in the gut, deflating me. But I refuse to let him see it. "Yeah, okay. Let me get dressed."

"Cate? I think you need to call 911. I'm pretty sure I can't get up to walk." Yesterday was rough. He had a tough time standing at all. He inhales and it's then I hear the faint rattle that lies deep in his chest. Oh, God, how will I ever get through this? As is Drew's usual way, he talks me through it all, telling me everything will be fine. This, my Drew, comforting *me*, on *his* deathbed.

The EMTs arrive and load him into the vehicle, and I follow behind in my car. I call his parents, Ben, my parents, and Jenna on the way. When we arrive at the hospital, I'm at his side, holding his hand and biting my knuckle as they wheel him in. Even though this journey has been long and filled with ups and downs and I've had time to prepare for this day, I'm not ready. At all. Letting go of this man will be next to impossible. I watched that movie where the mountain climber became trapped under a boulder and was forced to amputate his own arm. That's how I feel right now. Losing Drew will be like cutting out my heart. I know—it's cliché, but it's true. Part of me will die with him. There's no other way around it.

Ben and Jenna arrive and we all hug and cry in the hall, and then all go in and hug Drew. Ben practically crawls in his bed. When his parents get here, we step out to give them time alone with their only son. When I think of what they must be going through, my dying heart hurts even worse. And Drew, knowing the man he is, must be trying to be brave for them. But at this point, in these final moments, there is no more he can do or say to boost their spirits. I still have a hard time wrapping my brain around how all this could happen. No doubt they do too. My parents and siblings make an appearance, but my mom is worse off than me. I think she hates to see her daughter suffer. I don't want Shannon and Eric to remember Drew like this, so I send them home after a brief visit.

The day inches by. Ray and Letty take a break by going down to get some food. My parents leave and so does Jenna, promising to return that evening. Ben takes a bathroom break and says he's going to grab some coffee. I ask him to bring me back a cup.

"You need to eat, Cate."

"Not hungry, Ben." He holds his hands up in the air, backing off. He knows not to push the food issue. We have this unspoken rule between us about these kinds of things. "I'll be back in fifteen or twenty."

"No hurry."

It's just the two of us now. I watch Drew as his chest moves up and down. His eyes flutter open and he motions me to his bedside. Then he starts talking and his voice is surprisingly strong. But the things he says plow into me like a fucking tank and I want to curl into him and die right with him. He tells me how he knew from the first moment he set eyes on me I was his and that he's sorry it turned out this way. Gah, like this is all his fault! Then he tells me to go home.

I nod and suck back my tears. "Okay. I'm going to go home and shower, because I'm kind of rank. I love you too, Drew. More than I can say."

"Cate, stop. That's not what I meant. I want you to promise me something, okay? Swear to me right now." His voice is firm, much stronger than it has been in days.

"Okay. What is it?"

"I want you to leave this room now and go home, but I don't want you to come back after you shower. I want you to say your goodbyes to me right here, right now."

"What!? What are you saying?" My heart stutters in my throat.

"I'm saying what you think I'm saying. I love you so much more than having you sit here by my side for the next few days. I don't want that. You swore to me, Cate."

"Drew, I can't." Tears stream unchecked down my cheeks, because I can't let myself think of the inevitable. Drew is my life, my heart, my everything.

"Yes, you can. Now, go. Turn around, walk through that door, and don't ever look back. All my stuff is boxed exactly like I asked you to, and you know what to do with it. My parents and yours will be here, along with Ben. But you, you don't need to be here. I don't want you to be here. I want you to remember me as I was, when I was healthy, during our best times. Now, look at that door and take your first steps into your new life, Cate. And promise me you'll live. Just live, Cate. Do it for me."

"You can't mean this. Drew, I'm not walking away." And instead of walking, I make a move to crawl in his bed.

"Don't, Cate. You're making this harder for me. It's ... have you ever heard of stories where people can't let go? That's what you're doing to me."

My hand flies over my mouth to cover the sob.

"Please. For me. If there's one thing left you can do for me, do this last thing."

I back away from his bed, looking at his murky eyes, no longer the crystal blue of his healthy days gone by, and I turn and run blindly from the room. I don't know where I'm going, I just have to leave his room for a moment to think, to figure out if I can do what he's asked. My eyes are so misted with tears, I'm blind, and as I turn the corner I crash head on into someone. Arms reach out to steady me and prevent me from slamming on my ass as my own arms windmill. I'm sure whoever I just careened into must think they've been attacked by a banshee, because I'm wailing, and look a mess, not to mention I smell like a skunk.

"Hey, are you okay?"

"Hell no," I shake my head. My words come out choked through another sob. "No, I'm not okay," I manage to say. Irrationality burns my gut. Isn't it obvious? "Do I look like I'm okay?" I rub my eyes so I can get the buckets of water out to see.

"Here. Come with me."

I don't have a choice. Whoever this person is takes my arm and walks me somewhere. He opens a door and says, "Sit." A handful of tissues magically appear in my hand. I blow my snot-filled nose and wipe my eyes again, but still I cry.

I feel guilty at my earlier irritation. Someone is trying to be nice and I'm being a bitch.

"I'm sorry. I ... I ... my husband is ... he's dying ... and," I sniff loudly, "he just told me he wants me to leave."

"Your husband?"

I finally look at my savior. His lab coat screams "physician." My eyes are cloudy with tears so I can't really make out if he's young, old, short or tall. I can't seem to stop my heart from tearing into shreds.

"Yeah. You may know him. Drew. Drew McKnight. He's a fellow here." I blow my nose into a clean tissue and add it to the wadded ball of used ones.

"Ah. Yeah. I mean, I sort of know him but never got the chance to work with him. I've heard great things about him. And I'm terribly sorry." He introduces himself, but I don't catch his name. My brain is too much of a mess to take notice. "I'm also an oncology fellow. I'm a year ahead of your Drew."

"Look, sorry I dumped on you."

"Don't be. Can I offer you some advice? The last days … he won't know. He knows it, too. He's trying to protect you. As hard as it is, that's all he's doing. Be with him if you want."

A giant breath gushes out of me. "Thank you. I need to go."

"Mrs. McKnight?"

"Cate," I say dabbing at my eyes.

"What?"

"My name. It's Cate."

"Oh. Cate then. I'm on call and here tonight. If you need anything, tell the nurses to page Dr. Mercer. I'll be here to help if you or Drew need me."

I take his hand. It's comforting. "Thank you."

Swiping the tears off my face, I head back to Drew's room. Ben is here and I motion him into the hall. When I tell him what Drew said, he looks embarrassed.

"You knew, didn't you?"

"Yes, but he swore me not to tell you. I'm sorry Cate."

"Well, I just can't do that. I can't leave and never say goodbye."

"I told him that and I told him it wasn't fair of him to ask that of you. But you know Drew. He's always thinking of everyone else."

"I am going home to shower and then I'm coming back with my stuff to stay for however long. I ran into one of the oncologists who's on call. He told me to stay." I start to cry again. In a weepy voice I say, "He said Drew wouldn't know if I'm here anyway."

Ben's arms grab me and we both tremble as we cry. Then he

asks, "Are you okay to drive?"

"Yeah. I'll be fine. Nothing but a few more tears."

"Text me as soon as you get home."

"I will."

It's a quick turn around trip for me and I'm back at the hospital, but when I walk toward Drew's room, I wonder if I should linger in the hall. I text Ben and he meets me right outside the room.

"He knows you're coming back. I told him it wasn't fair to do that to you."

"What did he say?"

"He told me I sucked in Drew-fashion."

That gets a smile out of us, albeit a small one. Ben and I get bed seats, and by that I mean in his bed. I lie next to him for most of the time, other than when I have to pee or get something to drink. Letty sits next to the bed in the recliner and holds his hand or touches him in some fashion, and Ray only looks on, disbelief etched on his features. I think he held out hope until the bitter end and now that it's here, it's too much for him to face.

At ten, I get up and walk down to the cafeteria and grab a muffin and a coke. After I choke a quarter of the muffin down and sip the coke I'm flicking the crumbs around the table when a shadow crosses over me. I glance up and see that it's the physician that helped me earlier. I'm a bit embarrassed to admit I don't even remember his name.

"How're you holding up?"

"How does anyone ever hold up when the love of their life is dying at the age of twenty-nine?"

"Probably as well as you are."

"Then not too good."

"It's a shit hand of cards he was dealt, Cate."

"Yeah, it's not fair. And all I keep asking myself is why can't the bad people get shit like this? Drew never has a bad thing to say about anyone. He was always the good guy, you know?"

"It's what I've been told. Everyone says he's the golden boy. Smart as hell and the greatest diagnostician. He was like a god around here. When he had the recurrence, everyone was just sick about it. Let me tell you, he had the best care, Cate. His case went all over the world. There wasn't a stone left unturned."

I reach out and touch his hand. "Thank you for telling me this. We haven't been here long enough to meet a lot of the other fellows, so I didn't know. I appreciate that."

He digs in his pocket and pulls out a card. "Listen, if you need anything, just call. I'm out of here in about an hour. But the whole department is on this thing. You should know that. This has been really tough on Rosenberg. Everyone loves Drew."

I look at his card briefly and say, "Thanks. You've been very kind." Then I gather up my crumbly muffin and coke and head back to the room.

Two days later, my Drew, my husband, the only man I've ever loved fades away as he takes his final breath, with me in the bed next to him, Ben holding one hand and Letty holding the other. It's very peaceful—for Drew. For me, my world shatters into tiny pieces as all the pieces of Drew leave this world. All the pieces of me remain behind, broken and … alone.

THIRTY
Past

❖

DREW'S FUNERAL TAKES PLACE ONE week before our first anniversary. Drew being Drew, left Ben explicit instructions on how he wanted things handled. So Ben took care of mostly everything. It was a good thing, too, because I was in a state of perpetual numbness. Ray and Letty handled the venue, choosing the same church Drew and I were married in.

I am told later that people attended from his residency, his hockey team including Sam and Caroline, from his medical school class, and his fellowship program. I see none of them. The church is nothing but a blank slate, all I am is a huge empty space, and the place where my heart used to be is a black hole. I am hollow, vacant. The minister says some lovely things, but I don't really follow. Ben sits on one side and Letty on the other. I squeeze both of their hands, just to make myself feel something, anything.

The minister allows anyone to come up to the pulpit to say something about Drew, if they wish. I see many people step up and speak, but I hear nothing. Not until Ben. He has to untangle his fingers from mine when he walks up to take the microphone. His hands tremble as he digs into the pocket of his suit coat and pulls out his speech. Ben's eulogy is the one I listen to and my heart latches onto it, hanging on every syllable.

He starts when they met, in kindergarten, and progresses

throughout their lives. But his delivery is priceless. It's funny but punctuated with moments of love, not enough to bring everyone to sobs, only enough to get the points. It's his story about Drew learning to ice skate that brings down the house.

"So he says, 'Dude, I'm serious. I'm going to learn this if it kills me.' And you have to picture Drew—six feet three inches in one of those leotard outfits, right? So I say to him, 'You do know you'll be in recitals and stuff, right?' And he says, 'Yeah. Will you come watch?' And he's serious. So he goes at it like you've never seen. He comes home all bruised up and tells me about how he's learning these Salchows and axels and is all geeked out about it. I'm talking Drew McKnight everyone. Figure skating! So he finally gets to the point where he has to perform all these jumps and things and he begs me to come watch. I'm his best friend. What am I going to say? So I head over to the ice rink and I see huge Drew in the midst of all these seven and eight year old girls in pink tutus. It would be like seeing The Rock taking ballet. No kidding. Each time he performs, or one of the little girls does something, they all high five or fist bump each other. And Drew is right in the middle of them. It was freaking hilarious. But I swear to god, that night, the man comes home, puts the figure skates in the closet, trades them out for a pair of blades and picks up hockey like he was born to play. And that was Drew McKnight."

You can hear murmurs throughout the church and Ben's right. Drew never did anything without purpose, or without a goal in mind.

"And one other thing Drew did, was ask me to a Purdue football game and alumni post party. So we went. My sister Jenna and her best friend and roommate, Cate Forbes showed up. Drew took one look at Cate and said to me, 'Dude, who's that girl with your sister?' When I told him, he said, 'I'm going to marry her one day. Introduce us. Now.' It took a few weeks to persuade Cate to agree to a date, but damn if he didn't. And Cate, you made him the happiest guy on Earth."

He gently folds his papers in half and says in a soft voice, "You will be missed, my brother." Ben walks down and takes his seat next to me, grabbing my hand and squeezing it. I know it could not have been easy for him to do it, but Drew would have been proud if he could have been here. Something inside my heart tells me he heard every word.

If the attendees expect me to speak, they will have to be disappointed. Now my body is broken apart by silent sobs. Ben's arm wraps around me as I lean against him for support. The question that won't leave hits me again. How will I live without him?

The church has kindly allowed us to greet the mourners in a large room, so we have food and drinks available. There are so many people, it's impossible for me to keep up. Half of the time, I find myself in the bathroom, splashing water on my face, trying to rinse my tears away. I never bothered with any makeup today and that was the best call ever. I would've looked awful by now, even with the waterproof stuff. At one point after fixing myself up, I glance over at Ben, and his hair looks like a hurricane got a hold of it. He can't keep his hands out of it. I can hear Drew's voice in my head saying, "Babe, go fix that shit up for him. He looks like hell."

So that's what I do. I scoot next to him and grab his arm. "Come here a sec."

"What?"

I do my best to straighten out the wreck of Ben's wavy nest.

"That bad, huh?"

Scrunching up my face, I say, "Yeah. It sort of looked like you just woke up after a week long bender."

His arm moves up to run through his hair and I trap it in my hand. "Stop. That's what's causing this mess."

He holds out his hands. "Okay. Okay. I'll do better. I'm just …"

I swipe at my face and say, "I know. We all are."

"We need a fucking drink, don't we?"

"And we'll have some, as soon as this is over."

We move back to the crowd. When the last person has filed through, we all finally take a breather and sit. Ray and Letty look like they've aged twenty years. I feel like I have, too. Ben's hair is a wreck again and I laugh. It's one of those inappropriate laughs, that you try to hold back, but just can't. Everyone looks at me with questions in their eyes.

Shaking my head, I say, "It's Ben's hair. I can hear Drew saying a bunch of crap about it."

Everyone laughs and the Drew stories start. Ben invites everyone over to clean out his liquor cabinet and we migrate to his house. Ray and Letty and my parents leave after a little while, but

Jenna and I stay the night. We drink ourselves silly and all crash on the floor, with sleeping bags, pillows and cushions from the couches and chairs.

In the morning, I wake up and look around. Ben and Jenna are still passed out. I roll over and see all the empty liquor bottles on the coffee table. It's a surprise I'm not puking everywhere. I sit up and go to the bathroom. On the way back, I pass a shelf that's loaded with pictures of Ben and Drew. It's impossible for me not to stare at them. What a pair they are. Or were. A sudden wave of anxiety barrels into me, and I nearly drop the picture in my hand as I slide to the floor. My chest pounds with pain as I realize I can't ever go home. I can't walk through that door again, knowing Drew won't ever be there to greet me with those stunning blue eyes of his. A wave of nausea rolls over me and I clamp my hand over my mouth. Ben is there, pulling me up.

"What happened?"

"I can't go home. I … ever. I can't ever go back there." My entire body shakes.

"It's okay, Cate. You don't have to."

"No, you don't get it, Ben. I can't walk in there at all."

He grabs my hand and we go into his kitchen where he fixes me a glass of water.

After a few sips, and Ben talks me through this anxiety attack, I calm down.

"Cate, this is a new road for you."

"Ben, it's not about a new road. It's about Drew not ever coming home. I don't want to be in that house. Period."

"Okay. Okay. I get that. Come with me."

He takes my hand again, and this time we go to his office.

"Have a seat," he says, pointing to a chair. "Look, you don't have to go back there. In fact, you should sell. But, I have something for you."

"You do?"

"Yeah. You know our guy. He always planned for everything. I was to give this to you the day after the funeral. Here." Ben hands me an envelope.

I look at him, not knowing what to do.

He nods. "Open it. I'm supposed to stay with you while you read it."

"Okay. Is this going to tear me up into even more pieces?"

"I don't know." There go his hands through his hair again.
The outside of the envelope says, "My Loving Cate."
I open it gingerly.

My Dearest Cate,

If you are reading this, then the inevitable has taken place. We've had many discussions about what would happen after my passing, but knowing you as I do, I knew I had to write this. That's also why I've given this to Ben. (I hope the dude has followed my instructions!)

I hope you don't hate me for trying to send you away from the hospital (although I was fairly certain you would be too hard headed to leave). You had already been through the worst of the worst, and I didn't want you to go through that, too. I wanted you to carry our best memories forward, to remember me in my healthy days, when we were happy and fell in love, and loved with abandon. I never told you this, but if I'd had a crystal ball and could've seen the future, I would've run far, far away from you as fast and as hard as I could have. Not because I didn't love you. I hope you know that. My heart was as tangled up in yours as was possible. I don't think I could've loved anyone as hard as I loved you. I would've run because I never would've put you through this horrible journey. And I can only hear you ranting now. But stop. It's done. It's over. And I didn't know. So we fell in love, married, and the rest, as they say, is history.

But this ending was not part of my plan, as you know. I had such great visions for us. The large house with three kids. Growing old together and spoiling the hell out of our grandkids. I saw us holding hands, sitting on our rockers, watching the sunsets, sipping our wine. Taking luxurious vacations (which may or may not have included side trips to Blackhawks games), and me spoiling the hell out of you. Words will never express to you how sorry I am that I couldn't fulfill those visions.

Now here comes the hard part for you, Cate. You made me a promise and I'm going to hold your feet to the fire on this. You swore to me you would move on afterwards. You would go forward and find someone else and live your life. That's what I'm asking you to do. Oh, I know you can't do this immediately. But don't you dare sit on your ass for years and pine away. And knowing you, that's exactly what you'll do. You're such a hard ass sometimes. But I'm not going to let you get away with this. This time, you're going to hold up your end of the bargain. This is a huge world, Cate. I was not the only person in it for you. Don't tell yourself that and don't be naïve. Open yourself up and let yourself love again. The worst thing that could happen and the last thing I would want are for you to be alone and be lonely. You've been through way too much in your young life already. You promised me, and by God, you'd better not renege on this. So I'm giving you six months. Too short you say? I say bullshit. You're going to pack up your boxes, because mine are already packed, and get the hell out of here. Sell the house. Do you hear me? Move. Get the hell out of there! Give all my clothes to charity. The few items I've tagged will go to Ben or my parents. You already have what you want. Everything else is tagged for the charity I've designated.

There's enough life insurance money and money from my trust fund that you'll inherit for you to be comfortable for however long you want. You'll need to work only if that's what you want to do. Ben will help you with all of this— he's your money guy. This will give you time to figure out where you want to end up living. Go. Explore the world if you want. Seek out a new life for yourself. And find that special someone. Make sure he treats you well. And don't settle. You deserve the best of the best, Cate.

Do me a favor. Always remember the better times and know that I loved all the pieces of you with all the pieces of me.

Forever and then some,
Drew

P.S. Look out for Ben and tell that dude to stop running his hands through his hair. He's going to go bald and end up looking like me, but he won't be as sexy!

Leave it to Drew to try to make me laugh at the end.

"Did you read this?" I ask Ben.

"No. Why?"

I hand it to him. His eyes run with tears until he gets to the last line. Then we both laugh.

"Asshole." Then we cry-laugh and hug.

I look at Ben and ask, "Will you help with all this? I think I'm going to take up Jenna on her offer to move in. Most of my stuff will have to go in storage once the house sells. I want to leave it furnished so it shows better."

"Sure, I'll help, but why don't you make it easy on yourself and hire some moving company."

"Oh, Ben, I don't want to spend the money. I haven't worked in six months and I'm not sure about the finances."

Ben laughs. "Did you not read the letter? You have no idea, do you?"

"About what?"

"Your financial status. And you're a damn accountant."

"Should I be insulted?"

He shakes his head. "No. If it were anyone else other than Drew, I might say yeah. But not with him. Cate, let me just say you can afford it. The moving company."

"And you know this, how?"

"I'm your fucking broker. Like the letter said—I'm the money guy. Drew left you well cushioned. He's a trust fundee. I've handled his investments for years and you're his sole beneficiary."

"It was him I wanted. I never paid attention to his bank account. It was just us and battling fucking cancer." I almost sob.

The money thing never entered the picture for me and it's not something I want to focus on right now. Ben must notice it because he keeps pushing.

"Here. Hold on." Ben pulls up a chair and we both sit at his computer. He logs into his brokerage firm and pulls up Drew's account. "This is your account." Then he scrolls down and shows me the numbers. It's seven hefty figures worth. "This won't include his life insurance, which will add another million."

"What?" I wipe my face again, because I'm still crying off and on throughout this whole conversation.

"You heard me. You know about Drew's mom, right? Her family?"

"Well, yeah."

"That's where his money comes from. Your house? You know it doesn't have a mortgage on it, right?"

"Yeah."

"So, Cate, add another seven hundred grand to your bottom line."

Jesus. How did I not know this?

"You never talked about money with him?" Ben asks.

"No. Never. Looking back, that sounds really dumb of me."

"No. I'm sure if the conversation ever got close to the subject, he would steer it away. And he wasn't frivolous with it either."

It's hard to take in. I knew money wasn't an issue, but I just never dug into it. "Ben, someday when our heads are screwed on straight, we need to find a way to do something with some of this money as a tribute to him."

"Yeah. I think you're right. By the way, I'll be with you at the reading of his will and all."

"Good."

"So, a moving company then?"

Letty calls the following week and says the reading of Drew's Last Will and Testament will take place at their home. The attorney is a close family friend so they decide to do it there. Ben picks me up at Jenna's and we go together. Afterwards, I ask Letty if she's okay with all this. After all, it's sort of her money.

She sighs. "Drew loved you more than his own life, Cate. Of course I'm okay with it. It was his will that you have it all."

Then I tell her about my plans to move and sell.

"I think you're wise. It would bring nothing but more tears and heartache for you, dear, and God knows we've all had enough of that." She dabs her eyes as she talks. I ask myself if it will ever get easier to talk or think about Drew.

Seven Months Later

The house is mostly staged, all pictures of Drew and me are packed and stored. The movers have come and all my belongings are in storage. It's finally listed and I'm living full time with Jenna again, just like old times.

My position with Ernst and Young was given away, but I interviewed with Price Waterhouse and was given an entry-level auditing role with them. I'm starting all over again. I'd be lying if I'd say I wasn't depressed. I think about Drew every day. He's everywhere I look, in everything I do. But I guess that's the grieving process, or at least it's what everyone says.

During my lunch break today, I make a run to the hospital. I'm still dealing with insurance stuff, so I furnish the billing office with just one more piece of information they need. The woman tells me to come back in an hour so I decide to grab a quick lunch in the cafeteria. As I walk down the corridor, I turn the corner and run smack into Dr. Mercer. Once again, his first name escapes me. I give myself a pass because the night I met him I wasn't exactly in the right frame of mind.

"Cate."

"Dr. Mercer." I extend my hand to him.

"I thought we passed all the formalities. Please, call me Drew."

THIRTY-ONE
Present

———◆———

IT'S THE FIRST DAY OF spring and I stand by the window of my apartment and gaze out as the sun makes its first appearance for the day. Today is moving day and nervous excitement wouldn't allow me to sleep. Arms circle me and draw me back into a firm chest.

"Morning, beautiful."

I turn in his arms and press my lips against his. "Morning."

"I didn't expect you to be up so early."

I shrug. "I've rarely seen dawn since I moved to DC."

"It's pretty impressive, but it has nothing on you."

My lips curl and then, I watch in stunned silence as shirtless, looking sexy as hell Andy kneels down on one knee. My heart stops. The sunrise is forgotten as no light shines on me like the man before me.

It's been several months since the awkward conversation between Drew's parents and me. They seem genuinely happy that I've found someone else. Their support and love has meant the world to me. Now that everyone knows, there is nothing to stop me from charging forward into a new life except myself.

Andy's eyes, so much like Drew's, sparkle up at me. My chest ceases to move.

"Sweetheart, breathe."

Every sound is caught in a vacuum as I let out a breath I know I've been holding for a few years.

"Cate, you lit a fire in me long before I knew what that fire meant."

They say when you die, your life flashes in front of your eyes. I have that surreal moment now. Everything begins to slow and the memories since the day I met Andy comes back like a sledgehammer to the chest.

~ About seven months after Drew ~

I rush into the hospital hating that I have to be there. But the insurance company needs some paperwork signed off in order to finalize benefits. It's something I should have done months ago but I couldn't bear it.

The woman in front of me has no sympathy for me. I'm sure she's seen and heard it all. My circumstances aren't dire—at least to anyone besides me.

"You can pick up the form in an hour. That's the best I can do."

I nod and walk to the cafeteria. I haven't had lunch and I don't want to leave and come back. While I'm deciding whether or not to go with a Cobb or Caesar salad, someone says my name.

"Cate."

I turn and it takes a moment for me to recognize the face. I'm not sure why; his eyes are the spitting imagine of Drew's.

"Dr. Mercer." I extend my hand.

There is no way I could forget this man's kindness. I practically sobbed all over him the day Drew asked me to leave his hospital room for good.

"I thought we passed all the formalities. Please call me Drew."

I nod, but it's hard to say that name without breaking out in tears.

"How are things?" he asks.

Grief over takes me and a tear slips through my defenses.

"It's okay, Cate. I shouldn't have asked. Let me buy you lunch."

I glance up at him. "I'm not ready to date," I blurt.

Dr. Mercer looks at me, shocked, and I realize my mistake. With a polite smile, he says, "I'm not sure my girlfriend would appreciate me asking anyone on a date. I just thought I could offer you an ear."

My face must turn beet red.

"I'm sorry. Ever since I took off my rings, I've been getting hit on occasionally."

I hadn't wanted to take off my engagement and wedding rings, but every time I looked at them I couldn't stop crying. After several months, Mom finally suggested that I take them off, not because I want to forget Drew, but so I could remember him without the tears.

"I can't say I blame them. But I totally understand. It's going to be a long time until you can be better."

I'm glad he didn't say be okay. I'm not sure I can ever be okay.

"I don't know if I'll ever be better."

He nods sympathetically. "Have you considered a support group?"

"Been there, done that. And don't get me wrong. They help so many people. But I feel like a fish out of water because most of the people there are so much older than I am. I don't want to take antidepressants, but if I don't turn a corner soon, I think I may start."

"Don't be afraid of them. They aren't habit forming or anything like that. But let me ask you. Have you tried running? Studies really do show it can help with depression."

"I used to run. But haven't in a couple of years."

"Why don't you try? Running can help clear your mind and get the endorphins going to make you feel better in general. I run with a group and you can join us if you'd like."

His words ring true. He is a doctor and I've heard that about running before.

"I feel like there is a cloud that follows me everywhere. I can't even go to my house and move the boxes Drew thoughtfully packed so I wouldn't have to. The house is staged; I just need to get those boxes out if I truly plan to sell the house. That's hard, too. I don't want to sell the house we picked together, yet I can't imagine living there without him."

Out of his pocket, he produces tissues like he did the last time tears flowed down my face.

"Small steps, Cate. Rome wasn't built in a day."

Dr. Mercer takes both salads and steers me to the register. I find myself sitting as I continue to release the words I've been so scared to say knowing everyone must be tired of all my crying.

"I can't ask his parents, they've been through enough. Ben, his best friend, is a wreck just like me. He suggested a moving company because I don't think he wants to go in there any more than I do. I watched my husband slip away in that house and I just can't go there. I don't want to ask my parents because they've practically packed up the house for me."

"I can get the boxes for you."

I glance up and meet those azure blue eyes so much like my dead husband's and the hurt bubbles up like a geyser.

"I can't ask you that."

"Why not? Drew was one of ours. You can't imagine how he's missed around here. I didn't know him well, but I can't imagine anyone else that wouldn't offer to help you in any way."

After some more convincing, Dr. Mercer drives behind me to my old house after I pick up my paperwork. His shift is over and with some directions from me, he enters the place I once called home. It doesn't take him long and he comes out with Drew's stuff.

"There is one marked for you."

I nod and he puts it in my trunk. "I'll take the rest for you to Goodwill."

"Thanks for everything, including lunch," I say.

He smiles warmly. "Don't mention it."

~ Eight months after Drew ~

When the news comes, I'm so overwhelmed, I find myself in the park running down a path. The pads of my feet smacking the ground are the only noise in my head. Dr. Mercer was right. Only it took me one more hardheaded month to take his advice and try running again.

For the first time in a while, I feel alive. I can't believe how much I've missed this. My heart races from exhilaration and not depression. I'm in no way fine, but I feel marginally better.

I run around a corner and glance up to see those striking blue eyes. For a second, my heart skips a beat. Then I realize the blond hair doesn't belong to my Drew but to Dr. Mercer.

"Cate."

"Dr. Mercer."

"You're not going to call me Drew are you?"

I force the words out of my mouth because he's been nothing but kind to me. "Drew."

The name is like a bitter pill on my tongue. My Drew should be with me right now.

"Tried running, eh?" he asks with an eyebrow raised.

"You were right. It clears my head. It's what I need from the news I just got."

"News?"

We continue to jog in place as other joggers pass. And for some reason it's easy to talk to him.

"I got a really good offer on the house. A nice family with a baby on the way wants the house. They love it." I manage to say the words without crying. "They will make it the home it was meant to be."

He nods but doesn't offer any words of encouragement. He tilts his head toward the trail. I nod and take off in the direction I had been heading and he follows. We run for a while until I get back to my starting point.

"You should join our group."

I glance up at him after toweling off my face. I've stopped and start to stretch but he's still moving. Apparently, my thirty minutes is just a warm up for him.

"The one I mentioned a while back."

When I still show no signs of recognition, he says, "There are a group of us that run daily. It doesn't require any socialization. You don't have to talk at all during the runs. Sometimes it's good to run with other people. They help keep you motivated."

I bend forward to shake out my muscles. When I straighten he adds, "There is a morning run at six and an evening run at six. Pick your time, it's not formal or anything. We usually gather near the statue."

"It's sounds fun. I'll think about it."

"Good. And it was good seeing you, Cate."

"You too."

~ A year and a little over two months after Drew ~

Jenna stares at me like I'm lying to her.

"I swear, we're just friends."

Her face softens. "You know it's okay to date other people. Drew didn't expect you to be a hermit."

I glance away. "I'm not ready, Jenna. I'm just not. I'm not sure when I'll ever be."

She doesn't understand when you find the love of your life, who can ever match up to that. And it won't be fair for me to see anyone while comparing them to Drew.

"I've seen pictures of you two. You sporting a huge smile. You ran in the 10k prostate cancer race. You have breakfast with him a few times a week and sometimes dinner. He helped at your yard sale and he moved furniture with Ben."

"It's incidental. We are only friends. He's dating someone. As far as the race, it was a challenge. I did it and can mark it off my bucket list. I doubt I'll run in any more races. And I haven't seen him in a few weeks."

"Why?"

I shrug. "I've been running most mornings. He hasn't. I assume he's running in the evening. It's not like we call each other to coordinate our schedules."

"Un huh."

I groan. "He's with someone. You're reading our friendship wrong."

"You have to admit he's hot."

I shake my head. "I've never looked at him that way."

She stares at me like I grew antlers. "He's gorgeous, Cate. There's no way you don't see it."

I shake my head.

"He reminds me of…"

"Of what?" I ask.

"Never mind. I would date him."

"Good, I'll pass that along if he becomes single."

She dismissively waves my words away. "You do that. Anyway, why don't you date someone, anyone? And make them take you to dinner. You're too skinny."

I roll my eyes at her. "Look, I have to go."

"Running this afternoon hoping to 'run' into a certain someone?" She makes air quotes with her fingers.

Ignoring her, I rush out the door. Only Dr. Mercer is there. I try not to notice him, but Jenna has me assessing him differently when the run is over and we are all stretching out so our muscles won't cramp up.

When he tugs off his shirt and begins to towel off, I have to admit he would be a good catch for someone. Just not me.

"You up for dinner?" he asks.

I smile and nod. Outside of Jenna and Ben, I haven't had many close friends and he's become one. We sit at a popular deli waiting for our salads and sandwiches.

"How have you been? Is everything okay?" It's the first time I've seen him not give me a smile.

"The truth is, my girlfriend broke up with me. She's tired of my hours and how I get called in at odd times."

"Wow, she had to know that going into the relationship."

He purses his lips. "She did. Says she thought she could handle it."

"I'm sorry. Did it happen today?"

He shakes his head. "No, a few weeks ago. I guess it's really hitting me today. I've been so busy with work, I haven't had time to think about it."

We've become so comfortable with each other, I don't think twice when I ask him my next question. "Did you love her?"

He glances up thoughtfully. "I wouldn't say love. But she won't be the only woman who can't put up with my profession. It kind of sucks to think that my job will be a turn off."

"Somehow I think she's in the minority." Jenna's words come back to me. "Anyway, I have a friend," I begin and map out my plan for setting up a blind date.

Two days later, Jenna completely blows me off.

"No way. That's your doctor. I saw how he looked at you at your yard sale. His eyes narrowed anytime a guy came up to ask you the price of something."

"We're just friends," I say for the millionth time.

"I'm still not going out with him," she says adamantly.

"But you said you would date him and I set it all up because of that."

Jenna won't change her mind. Therefore, I find myself walking into the bar and lounge to find him surprised to see me.

"I'm sorry," I say sheepishly.

He seems resigned. "She doesn't want to date a doctor."

"No, it's not that." I don't want to lie to him. "She has this crazy idea about you and me."

His eyes go wide and it stings just a little. I'm not even sure why. I like him as a friend, but I guess knowing he wouldn't be interested in me at all hits the old ego like a wrecking ball.

"Why don't you stay? We can make the best of it. I don't get many nights like these that often."

Feeling guilty I set up this date without talking to Jenna first, I agree. It isn't a hardship. I enjoy spending time with him. We never seem to have trouble coming up with conversation topics.

"Dance with me," he says later.

I meet his eyes. "Are you serious?"

"Yeah, why not? You've been moving in your chair for the past half an hour," he teases.

"Fine, why not?" I accept more just because he said it so much like a dare.

I take his hand and we dance. The fast moving songs have my heart racing like I'm running. For that time, my mind is free and clear, and I see the man before me for the first time. He's good looking if not gorgeous, just like Jenna said. Somehow, I think I've known that. I've only ignored it until now. His girlfriend is a fool. He's a great guy and will make someone a good husband one day.

When the night is over, he walks me to my car.

"I had fun."

"Me too," I say.

After I click the lock on my car, he opens the door so I can get inside. For the craziest of moments, I wonder if he will kiss me. The moment passes and he doesn't. So I drive away and get back to my daily life.

~ A year and four months after Drew ~

"You're finally going out with him tonight?" Jenna asks, genuinely surprised.

"It was last minute. His date canceled. He asked if I could go with him." Then I add, "as friends," before Jenna can get any ideas.

"Friends my ass."

"Jenna, we are just friends."

"But you like him."

It's the first time I hesitate in my response. "I don't think I'm ready. Drew—"

Jenna cuts me off. "This is going to sound harsh, but Drew is gone and he's never coming back. And we are all sorry that's the case. But you promised him you would live. I'm sorry I have to pull that card, but it's been long enough. No one is going to fault you for moving on."

Her words still bounce in my head as I drink my glass of wine. When he turns his back, I down the rest and give the empty glass to the waiter.

When he turns back to me, I feel the need to fill the space. "You know everyone," I say, nervous for the first time.

"My parents know everyone and thus they know me."

"Your family and Jenna's."

Jenna would probably get stopped every few steps. This benefit has all the old families in attendance.

"It's tough sometimes, like tonight when I would rather be talking to you than some stuffed shirt who knows my dad or mom."

I find myself staring at his lips while he talks. I wave a hand at my face suddenly feeling flushed.

"Are you hot? Do you want to want to walk out on the terrace?"

I nod frantically because I can't stop staring and it's stupid.

He takes my hand and leads me outside. The night is cool and we stand by the marble railing staring out into the night. We start to talk at the same time.

"No, you go ahead," I say.

He seems to take a breath. "Cate, I'll be honest with you. I'm glad you're here with me and not someone else."

"Really?"

"I like you, Cate. I think I like you more than you're ready to hear. And I've tried to be patient and not push, but Cate—"

It might be the wine, but I move in and silence him with my lips. I press them to his and savor the moment for a second. His hand snakes behind my back and I start to feel warm all over. It has to be the wine. Three glasses might have been the courage I needed.

When I pull back his eyes are heavy on mine. "Cate—"

I shake my head. "I want this. I want you, if you'll have me." I take his hand. I've known him for almost a year and a half. This isn't rushed, my subconscious tells me. We've taken time to get to know each other. And I need to know. I need to know if I can move on. "Let's see if they have a room."

He stops and holds my hand so I can't move toward the doors.

"Are you sure? I can wait." He scrubs a hand through his hair. "Hell, I have been waiting."

His words puzzle me for a second.

"You had a girlfriend?"

He shakes his head. "I had a girl. She was more than a friend but not by much. And maybe that was my fault because I've been infatuated with you since the first time I saw you. It was the wrong time, so I backed off. Now—"

"Now you're talking too much. Let's just see where this goes."

When I wake up in the morning with him naked in the sheets, I completely freak out. I get dressed while he sleeps and I rush out without saying goodbye.

~ A year and seven months after Drew ~

It takes Jenna talking me down from the ledge before I'm able to talk or see the good doctor again. I'm scared of the feelings he's creating in me. He's been a great friend and being with him beneath the sheets made me want more. Still, I feel like I'm cheating on my dead husband.

He finally coaxes me out to have lunch with him. He's been understanding, letting things take a step back in a slower gear. I'm grateful for that. I still feel somewhat guilty for feeling anything for anyone other than my late husband, Drew McKnight.

Yet, Drew Mercer makes it impossible not to have a good time. He's telling me horror stories about working at the hospital.

"I walked into the patient's room without knocking. Mind you, he's a ninety year old man, and his wife was in there with him." Drew's brow rises. "The two of them were getting it on like they were newlyweds. I have to say, it gives me hope for the future."

"He was in his nineties?" I ask.

He nods. "And she was probably in her late eighties."

He gives a shudder but laughs. We're both cracking up while enjoying an afternoon eating outside at a bistro when I see Ben.

Jenna's brother looks lost and I know he's been having a rough time. My laugh quiet and suddenly guilt consumes me like a ball of fire. How can I be laughing with another man? Drew's best friend is still bereft with grief. I'm Drew's wife. I should be worse off.

"I can't," I say, my mood changing lightning fast.

"What?"

My face feels flushed as I suddenly feel out of breath and I know I appear like a crazed bipolar patient off their meds. "I can't do this. I'm not ready. How can I possibly be happy when he's in the ground?"

"Cate, please." He reaches for me. For the briefest second, I pause. "I think I've fallen in love with you."

His words only catapult me from my seat because I'm starting to fall myself. How can I possibly take that leap with someone else? I belong to Drew. I bolt from the restaurant and from his life. I ignore his calls. I refuse to see him.

Weeks later when my boss offers me the transfer of a lifetime, I know I have to take it. I can move to DC and start fresh in a new city where memories of my Drew won't haunt me.

"You can't move without telling him," Jenna berates me.

She's right. Yet, I can't talk to him either. He doesn't deserve what I did to him. He's been nothing but good to me. So I write him a letter explaining that I'm leaving town. I ask for his forgiveness and for his understanding. I leave with strict instructions to Jenna for her not to tell him where I've gone if he should ask. Only fate put us together again.

Present

I take Andy's hand in mine. "There are a few things I need to show you and do before I can answer you."

When we get to my place, he sits on the couch when I go to my room to get something. I come back to the room and sit next to him before I hand him the letter. It's the letter Ben gave to me from Drew those many, many months ago.

THIRTY-TWO
Present

———◆———

I WALK UP TO ANDY, or Drew, as I should now call him, and hand him the manila envelope I received last week. It was from Ben, which surprised me a little, but the mysterious contents intrigued me even more. Inside were two more envelopes, one addressed to me, and the other said, "The One—Cate—DO NOT OPEN!"

When I read the letter in the one addressed to me, my emotions were all over the place as I was thrown by the handwriting. Of course, I should have known he would've thought of everything. And he did.

Cate,

If you're reading this, then Ben has deemed it was the appropriate time to pass this along, which means you have found THE ONE. Ben's instructions were to send you this when he knew you had either fallen in love again, or were getting married. I hope, for your sake, that you are the happiest woman in the world. It is my most fervent wish that you live life to its fullest with the man of your dreams.

The other envelope is for him. Don't you dare open it. If he chooses to share it with you, that is his business.

Be happy. You deserve nothing less than the best.

Yours, Drew

Tears clouded my vision when I read it.

Now I stand before my other Drew, or Andy, and hand him his letter. His eyes ping back and forth between it and me. "What is this?"

"It's from Drew. Ben sent it."

A V forms between his brows and he turns it over a few times in his hands as he stares at it. He sits on the couch with his forearms resting on his thighs. I can't even imagine what he must be thinking as he holds a letter from his girlfriend's deceased husband.

"This is pretty weird, Cate."

"Yeah, I know. If you don't want to read it …"

"No, I do." He fills his lungs with air and very gently opens the thick paper. Inside, I see the familiar handwriting, but I don't dare peek. I walk to the other side of the room as he reads. He stops for a moment, wipes his face, and continues. When he's finished, there isn't a dry part of his face. Tears freely run and he does nothing to stop them. His arm extends out to me with the letter in his hand.

"You should read this."

I take it from him and exchange it for a handful of tissues. Then I begin.

To THE ONE,

Since you're reading this, Cate has either consented to marry you or has told you she's fallen in love with you. If you haven't yet asked her to marry you, you'd better do so. Love—those words don't come easy for her, nor does she say them frivolously to just anyone. So you are one lucky bastard, let me tell you. And with that being said, I would ask that you treat her like the most precious bird alive. Most people think their loved ones need to be treated like gems. But gems are hard, and don't need special care. Cate does. Don't let her fly away. I'm sure she wanted to run from you. She probably felt guilty about loving you. Tell her I said to forget about that damn guilt. It's a useless emotion that will bring her nothing but more pain. If she's chosen you, you'd better do everything in your power to deserve her, because she's special.

Cate changed my life. She has a way of putting her handprint on things and when she does, they are never the same again. She did that to me. She put the extra beat in my heart, made the blood flow faster through my veins, made my soul burn brighter and my sprit grow deeper. Once she entered my life, I knew there was no going back. I hope she does that to you, too. I once said that getting cancer made me more empathetic. That wasn't true. It was Cate who did that to me.

I wanted her to move on and to find someone else after me, and I'm glad she did. My friend, Ben, has my permission to kick your ass if you're not good to her. And he will. He's that kind of guy. But I'm hoping he doesn't have to because I truly want you to make her the happiest woman on Earth. For everything I put her through, she deserves it.

Now go and do her right. Treat her well and love her with everything you've got. You won't be disappointed.

Drew McKnight

The letter flutters out of my hand because I'm incapable of anything, standing, seeing, talking, or breathing. Andy's scent is all around me, so I know he's there as I break into all the pieces Drew loved.

"Cate, baby, it's going to be okay."

I'm not so sure. Drew has been gone now for almost three years, yet the pain still stabs me in the chest like it happened yesterday. I feel like one of the pieces of me left with all the pieces of him when they departed this world.

"I'm sorry. It just came back. He was always a good guy and here he proves it in death." I sob. "I'm sorry," I say again.

"There's nothing to be sorry for. You wouldn't be the woman I fell in love with if that letter didn't affect you. He loved you and I have big shoes to fill."

I let him hold me as I continue to cry. Somewhere as Andy holds me with no judgment, no jealousy, no anything but all of his love, a piece inside that was missing fits into place.

As the tears slow, I realize I'm blessed for having Drew for the time I did. He showed me what love is, what it was meant to be. He gave me the tools to know when love was right. He gave me all of him as I had given all of myself in return. He wanted me to find love again. And I have. I hadn't been sure until this point that I had a hundred percent to give back to someone else. But I was wrong.

I think back to something Drew said long ago. He said he didn't believe in one soul mate for everyone. And I'm grateful he's right. Not that I wanted him to pass from this earth and from me. But I'm humbled to have found someone else I could love so completely, who loves me the same way.

Immeasurable eyes, the color of calm clear seas, cornflowers blowing in the breeze and the skies on the clearest days, wait patiently as I break over another man. It's then I know for sure that I'm the luckiest woman in the world. Not many people are given a second chance at love. I won't waste mine.

"Yes," I say.

He has no idea that while staring at him, I know I've built myself up again and I'm ready to take the plunge.

"Yes?"

"Yes, I'll marry you if you'll have me."

EPILOGUE

Andrew (Drew) Mercer

———————◆———————

THE DRIVE ISN'T LONG AND neither is the walk. Cate's hands are linked in mine and she's not sure why I brought us here because I haven't told her. There's no noise as we walk across the grass to a place of eternal rest, or so they say. The birds are even respectful as a peaceful calm greets us as we make our way to the stone.

It isn't fancy, because according to all I've learned, it wasn't Drew's style to be. The marble headstone is simple and has just the right number of words.

Andrew Standford McKnight
Cherished Son
and
Loving Husband

I glance down at Cate. Nerves are starting to get the better of me. I squeeze her hand while I run the other over my hair. I try to smile to encourage her as I search for the words I haven't exactly practiced. I turn away from her to give my attention to the headstone.

"I'm not sure how to do this." I pause, still unsure of what I want to say. Diving in, I say what's in my heart. "McKnight, I don't really expect that you are here, but I hope in some way, you hear me. I would like to respond to the letter you wrote. Most importantly, I hope for your blessing of Cate's hand. Just so you know, I asked her father and he approved, but I need your approval as well." I blow out a breath. The guy wrote a letter that could have moved a mountain. "I can't reply to your letter with words on a page, so here I am. You're right that Cate is someone special. And I know that part of who she is today has been shaped by how you loved her. I'm grateful for that role you played in her life. I promise you I will treat her like she is the last of her kind because she is. I plan to only love one woman and she's the one. She's my bird and I promise to keep her heart safe and love her with all of me, the same way you did. She had no idea why we came, by the way. But it was important for me to tell you that she's in the right hands before she walks down the aisle. I don't ever expect her to stop loving you. I'm not that petty or jealous because I know she's capable of loving both of us. You mean the world to her and I plan to do my best to make her as happy as you did. You are sorely missed and this woman, our hospital, this world was a better place with you in it. And without you, there is a part missing. I expect you to watch over our girl when I can't. And may we meet again one day sometime very far in the future."

Still holding Cate's hand, I watch as she lays a bunch of flowers at the foot of the headstone. I didn't ask why she chose the flowers she did. I figured they meant something and according to the web, they did. The white carnations represent remembrance. The purple lilacs mean first love and the gladiolas represent strength of character. They are great choices for everything I know about the man.

I hand Cate some tissues from my pocket. She gives me that shy smile she gave me the first day we met. Then I knew there was something special about her, but she'd been a colleague's wife. Today, she will become mine.

We get to the church on time, but Cate's mother still hustles her away. Something about me not seeing the bride on her wedding day.

I'm sent to the boys' room where I find Mitch, Dave and Ben sitting around talking, looking hung over.

"Where have you been? Jenna's furious you both missed the brunch buffet."

"I had business to take care of," I say offhandedly. Ben was Drew's best friend, but what Cate and I did this morning is between us. If she chooses to share, she will.

Mitch laughs. "That's code word for banging his bride before the wedding."

He's wrong about that. Jenna convinced Cate that us not having sex the month before the wedding would be good for the honeymoon. As much as I've tried to explain to Cate that my balls in fact do appear to be blue, she's been unwilling to give me a second opinion. She tells me she's just as needy as I am.

"No sex, thanks to his sister." I point an accusatory finger at Ben.

He shrugs. "She has all kinds of stats on that shit."

Dave just looks amused and changes the direction of the conversation. "Your sister is really hot. Is she still dating that guy?"

Ben's eyes grow horns and appear as though they are glowing red. "I've heard enough about you two to know neither of you should ever think about my sister."

Mitch laughs. "All's fair in sex and booze at a wedding."

Ben's about to say something, but Dad knocks on the door. "Time."

The guys eye me, but I'm not nervous. I want Cate with every fiber of my being. My only wildest fear is if she'll break her promise and run. And even that fear has diminished over the last several months. I trust her completely.

At the altar, when they begin to play that familiar tune, I stand and stare at the door opening. I wait until Cate appears and when she does all the air is sucked out of my lungs. She's so fucking beautiful I can only blink. Mitch taps my back and I remember to breathe.

Her hair is pulled back in some elaborate way I can't focus on because her face is radiant and I still can't quite believe she's mine. My gaze lowers to the dress I hadn't been allowed to see, let alone hear about. It isn't quite white and has fabric that hangs purposefully off her shoulders, leaving her collarbones exposed. That skin alone is enough to get my dick hard. Like the sex deprived guy I am, I focus on the little amount of cleavage she has on display and lick my lips. I feel like an asshole as I try to hide my hard on as my gorgeous bride walks toward me with tulips that look almost white in her hand. But from what I overheard the bridesmaids say at the rehearsal dinner, they are actually a pale yellow. Knowing what I do about Cate, I'd searched for the meaning and yellow tulips means hopelessly in love. She has no idea that she's talking about me because I'm just that far gone when it comes to her.

When her father hands her off to me, I don't hear the minister. He spoke at the rehearsal, so I know what he plans to say. I stand in awe of my bride feeling like the luckiest bastard on the planet. Then I have a moment to say a prayer for feeling guilty. If not for Drew McKnight passing from this world, I wouldn't have this opportunity. I know what I have to do. When it comes time, I am ready.

I take her hands in mine and stare into the windows of her soul because she needs to know I've never felt this way about anyone else and I never will. She is my first and my last, my only and now is the time to not only tell her, but tell the world.

"Cate McKnight, I knew when I met you I wasn't your first love. That honor belonged to Drew McKnight. And his shoes won't be easy to fill. I'm thankful to him for encouraging you to love again, thus giving me the greatest opportunity of a lifetime to spend it with you." I want to glance at his parents who sit somewhere in the pews to the left of me, but I refuse to take my eyes off my girl. "I knew this when I decided you were the one with whom I wanted to share my life. Your beauty, your heart, and your mind encourage me to be the best person I can be. And I vow that I will do whatever it takes to be, if not your first, your last love. I promise to love you without reservation, encourage you to achieve all of your goals, laugh with you, comfort you in times of distress, always be open and honest with you, cherish and be faithful to you for as long as we both shall live. For this is my promise and my solemn vow."

I see Cate's tears and reluctantly, I let her hand go to produce a tissue from my pocket. This is something I did the first day we met and it seems as important. She smiles at me in a way that tells me she remembers as well, and dabs her eyes with it. Then she takes my hand again and it's her turn.

"Drew Mercer, I didn't think I could love again or even want to. When you came in my life, you came with your patience and understanding. You offered friendship and encouragement in my time of need. Our love wasn't hurried. It came over time in a way that scared me at first, but made me feel secure in the end. Drew McKnight did leave big shoes to fill and not because he wore a size fourteen." That gets a few laughs and even a chuckle from me. "But I know Drew would approve of you knowing you could handle the job. I promise from this day forward I will give you all my love and you will not walk alone. Your love is my anchor, your trust, my strength. I give you shelter for your heart and may my arms be your home. I willingly give you all that I am and all that I will become. My love for you has no beginning or no end. For this is my promise and my solemn vow."

I want to kiss her now. I want to take her in my arms and tell her that her words are my own. But I wait as the minister has us say a few more things before he finally lets me kiss my bride. Her lips are my lifeline and I have to break it off, otherwise I'll have a serious tent in my pants. When she pulls backs, she leans up again. Her lips slide against my cheek and up to my ear.

"There is one more thing I need to tell you, husband."

I wait as everyone gets on their feet ready for us to walk down the aisle joined hand in hand.

"We're having a baby."

And I thought there was no greater joy in marrying the woman I love until I hear those words.

After pictures and the cutting of the cake, I can't wait any longer.

"Where are we going?" Cate asks as I take her hand in mine and drag her along with me.

"The limo." Her eyes grow in size and it only makes me harder. "Fuck Cate, you can't look at me like that. I won't last."

The door is unlocked and the driver is nowhere in sight. I take her down NFL style, full on tackle. My hands gather more and more of her dress with no end in sight.

"How much fabric does this dress have?"

She laughs. "Wait, let me help you."

She's teasing me and she doesn't know the state I'm in. Seeing her and not being able to touch her for the last month has made me lose all finesse. I kiss her hard and her teasing dies away. She fists her hand in my hair, tugging me closer and I know she's as desperate as I am for me to be buried balls deep inside her.

There's no need for a condom, as if I'd worn any since that first time without one—which explains the baby thing. After I dip two fingers inside her and find her wet and ready, I dive in.

I groan out my relief because she's heaven. I languish being inside her skin to skin. When her nails dig in my ass, that's her sign, telling me to move. I oblige and rock myself forward hard and at a steady pace.

"Harder," she begs.

I lift her ass off the seat and angle her differently. I know just how to set her off and give her her first orgasm in seconds. Her pussy milks my dick, almost setting me off. But I'm not ready yet. It feels so damn good to be inside her again, I want it to last. So as a diversion, I think of work for a second and that halts everything. Leaning down, I capture her lips in a searing kiss. She tastes like the sweetest cake and I feel myself building again.

It isn't long before I'm saying, "Fuck Cate, I'm going to come."

My words rocket her second orgasm. Her back arches off the seat and I ride her all the way back down. My climax jars me so hard, I collapse on top of her when I'm done.

"I hope you believe me now that my balls really were a nice shade of blue."

About eight months later, I stare into the eyes of the woman I love so completely, I'm mesmerized every time I look at her. I try not to smile at the frantic look on her face. She's totally out of sorts as they wheel her into labor and delivery.

"Andy, don't let go of my hand." Her plea for my support does something to my chest and I feel almost like beating on it.

"Never," I say gently as she squeezes the ever loving life out of it.

"It's not fair, you're all calm. You don't have to push a turkey out of Louise. I mean how do they know she's ready? She doesn't have a basting button on the side of her head."

"We doctors don't know. We usually leave that up to the baby. That's why our daughter has made her opinion known on the subject."

Cate glares "You know it's a girl, don't you?" She whips out an accusatory finger pointed in my direction. "You said she. You promised it would be a surprise and you wouldn't sneak and find out."

They set the gurney in the room and prepare to shift her over to the specialized bed they use for the delivery. She doesn't let go of my hand. I have to stretch in order not to pull her off it as I make my way around and next to her.

"I didn't find out. You called her 'a her' and I went with it."

Her eyes narrow and I swear the chuckle I'm holding in will burst out of me. Before she can say anything else, her face gathers at the brow, pinching in pain. "Andy, I want pain medication."

It had been Cate's idea to go without meds. I'd supported her decision either way. "Okay, let me see if Dr. Yancey is on the floor."

I'm about to let her go when a man walks in as Cate continues to squeeze my hand like it's an orange and she's trying to make juice. The man holds a chart, but I don't recognize him.

"Dr. Carter," Cate says in surprise.

His face grows a smile at my wife in a way that says he's familiar with her. "Mrs. Mercer, it's good to see you again."

I hold up a finger. "A moment."

He glances up at me and I'm sure he's dealt with plenty of fathers over the years.

"Sure."

When Cate's pain passes, I kiss her knuckles. "I'll be right back. I'm just going to step over here and talk to Dr. Carter." I nod at the nurse and she steps over to reassure Cate while I confer with the good doctor.

Three steps and I stand to one side of the room with the other man. He gets the jump on the conversation to come.

"Dr. Mercer, your wife has nothing but great things to say about you. I'm sorry we haven't met. Apparently, the two times I had the pleasure of seeing your wife, you had emergencies that kept you away."

I take his proffered hand and shake it.

"Nice to meet you Dr. Carter. My wife mentioned you." She had. She hadn't said he was a he. Not that it should matter. I get to the heart of the matter. "Cate wanted to go without an epidural; however, she's changed her mind."

"I'm sure you know it all depends on how far along she is. Can you tell me about her contractions?"

I run down medically how labor began with her water breaking and what we did since that point. We'd opted to stay at home where I walked with her, rubbed her back and generally got her through the pain until this point. Last checked, I clocked the contractions at about five minutes apart and told him so. Although things had progressed on the drive over, she'd been so worried, I found myself talking to her instead of timing the pauses between her pain.

"As long as she's not crowning, I can send the order for an Anesthesiologist to come down."

"Andy, I think I need to push."

Dr. Carter and I turn to see Cate. Her face is strained like she's physically holding herself back. Frozen, we both watch as the nurse checks her.

"Dr. Carter, I think it's time."

He glances at me and I feel like an ass. He's a doctor, not a pervert. I nod giving him permission to do his job as I quickly make my way over to Cate.

"It's too late isn't it?" she asks.

I give her my hand and push tendrils of hair off her forehead. "Let's see what the doc says."

Dr. Carter gives us the news. "Go ahead and push Cate the next time you feel it."

And just like that, my gorgeous wife pushes our son into the world.

Over five years later, I steer my car through the streets of DC to get home. Traffic is ridiculous despite it being before rush hour. I'd hoped to be home by now. I pull into our Great Falls neighborhood in Virginia, just outside of DC. Our home is lit up and a smile forms on my face. When we first bought the place, Cate had been reluctant. I sold her on the safety of the neighborhood and good schools.

When I open the door, the real reasons for the large five bedroom house come running toward me.

"Daddy," shouts my two and half year old daughter. Her blonde curls bounce as she wraps herself around my leg. I pry her off so I can toss her up and catch her, sending her into a fit of giggles. Her pink princess dress circles her before she lands in my arms. "Daddy, Dew called me a baby and said I need a labodomee. What's a labodomee?"

I laugh for several reasons. One because she hasn't yet mastered the word Drew, opting to call him Dew instead. Ethan had proved too much for her as well. Two, a lobotomy. I shake my head wondering where he hears this stuff.

"Ethan," I call out. I had intended to ask my five-year-old about school. Instead, I will have to address his treatment of his sister.

My son with his dark hair so much like his mother's is decked out in scrubs and carrying a doctor's bag. He strolls around the corner as if all's well in the world wearing a plastic stethoscope around his neck.

I bend down so we can talk man to man. "Ethan, let's talk like men."

"Then call me Drew, Daddy, just like Grandma calls you. I wanna be a man, just like you, Daddy."

It's hard to maintain my parental look. "Okay, Drew, did you call your sister a baby?"

His face changes to remorseful as I'm sure he knows he's in trouble. "Emma cries too much and babies cry. So she's a baby."

I can't argue with that logic and good thing my daughter who clings to my chest chimes in.

"He says my castle is just a bed, not a princess castle."

I sigh. "Drew—"

"Dad, she's needs a reality check."

I chuckle unable to stop it. "Where did you hear that?"

"Mom said that to Aunt Shannon."

I shake my head only imagining the conversation that preceded that statement. "You need to be nice to your sister and not tell her she needs a lobotomy."

"But Aunt Shannon told Uncle Eric he's crazy and needs a lobotomee. And Emma's crazy."

"Ethan Andrew Mercer." I glance up to see Cate with her Mom face on. She does a better job at maintaining a stern face than I have in the past few minutes. Only, to me, she looks sexy as hell doing it. "You won't go trick or treating if you're mean to your sister. Now apologize."

Drew's head bows and he manages to eke out a "Sorree Emma."

"Now go eat your snacks on the table before it gets dark."

Food is more important than me as my kids rush off to the kitchen table. I stand so I can kiss my beautiful wife. It lingers and my hand catches the curve of her ass.

She giggles, which turns me on because she doesn't laugh like that often. I have to shift because my scrubs won't hide the evidence of my arousal. And that's a conversation I'm not prepared to have with my kids.

"What was that for?" Her smile is infectious and it spreads on my face.

"You're so damn beautiful, Cate. I swear you get prettier every day."

Her eyes warm her face. "You are full of shit. I look and feel like a beached whale."

I rub her belly with my other hand. "Any day now."

"Any day? My due date was two days ago. And I really don't want to have a Halloween baby. Can you imagine throwing a party every year on Halloween?"

I laugh because she's been talking about this since we first found out she could deliver near this day.

"Then you should get off your feet."

I bend and catch her off guard. I lift her in my arms.

"You're crazy. I weigh a ton." She heartily laughs.

"You two should get a room." I glance up to see my sister-in-law.

"Shannon, can you watch the kids for a few minutes?"

"Sure." She winks at us. "Just as long as you take that somewhere else."

I don't ask twice. I carry my wife up to our bedroom and close the door behind us. I set her down in her favorite chair in front of the fireplace where I remove her shoes and massage the bottom of her feet.

"Really, you brought me up here for that?" She may be joking, but there's heat in her eyes.

"Believe me, I want you. Sex, however, can bring on contractions and you said you wanted to wait another day."

She shrugs. "It's up to you, but you'll be sorry. Six weeks will be a long time to wait."

It isn't like Cate and I have been abstaining. We've had sex every night this week because she was ready to give birth hoping to avoid this day.

"I'll do whatever you want."

"Or maybe, I'll do you."

She urges me to stand and come around to the side of the chair.

I follow her instructions because I know what she's about to do. And I'm right. She gives me the best damn blow job of my life. Practice can certainly improve on perfection. I didn't think it possible, but it is.

Later, after I take the kids trick or treating, we sit on the back deck on a porch swing. Ethan finds a place in his mother's lap as Emma curls herself in mine. Our two kids sleep as my fingers twine with Cate's.

The swing rocks back and forth in a calming rhythm. Cate's eyes are closed and her features smooth out. Her lips are curved as if she's having a pleasant dream. And I think about how lucky I am.

Cate decided not to work after our son was born, which was her decision. Still, my wife can't be idle. She started the Drew McKnight foundation, which serves people with Ewing Sarcoma, both young and old. She's hired full time people now, but she still oversees it and watches the financial end of it like a hawk. She used some of the money Drew left her to start the non-profit and she involved Drew's parents who have become true activists on the subject. We named them honorary grandparents to our kids. It was something I wanted to do and Cate too, so she readily accepted. Their faces light up every time we bring the kids around to visit when we're in Charleston. And they come up to spend time here as well because we have plenty of room. In fact, after the baby is born, we will have rotating grandparents visiting two weeks at a time to help Cate as she nurtures our latest gift to the family.

I don't know how Cate does it all, but she doesn't want to hire a nanny either. She's a superhero to the kids and the best wife ever to me.

"Cate," I call out. I can't help myself.

"Hmm." Her eyes flutter open, clear, and focus on me.

"I love you and our life."

I tell her I love her every day. Yet I feel the need to confess that to her.

"I love you too, and our life."

I lean over and kiss her, careful not to wake our children.

Then I see it. Her face forms a frown. "It's time."

I nod, grateful Shannon has been staying with us. She wanted to be here to help. She doesn't have classes the next few days and offered to come and stay for this very reason. I pick up the kids and carry them to bed. I tuck them in and kiss their foreheads. On the way, I knock on Shannon's door and tell her what's going on.

Then I walk back down and gather my formidable wife in my arms remembering how messed up I'd been when she left me the first time. I'd assumed after that I'd never find love. But fate brought us back together and I knew I had to win her over. Even if we did have to fight to overcome the cruel, we hung on to the beautiful and it was damn worth it.

A FINAL WORD

Life is strange in that you often believe it is a compilation of events that mold you into the person you eventually turn out to be. In my case, however, I believe Drew McKnight (not his real name) impacted me in such a way, everything else paled in comparison. My Drew rearranged my priorities and turned me into the person I am today. The Drew in this novel is as close to the real man as I could make him. He was kind and generous, and never had a bad thing to say about anyone. I wrote it in the pages of this book, and I'll say it again here—only the good die young. *AMH*

A THANK YOU

We'd like to thank you for taking the time out of your busy life to read our novel. Above all we hope you loved it. If you did, we would love it back if you could spare just a few more minutes to leave a review on your favorite e-tailer. If you do, could you be so kind and **not to leave any spoilers about Drew/Andy and the big twist in the story.** Thanks so much!

———————————◆———————————

A MESS OF A MAN

Devastated by the death of his best friend since childhood, **Ben Rhodes** finds himself on a path of self-destruction. The only thing in his life he hasn't managed to wreck is his career. Leaving a trail behind of women he's felt justified in destroying, Ben only thinks clearly when he stares into the clear cubes of ice at the bottom of an empty glass of Lagavulin, until her.

Samantha Calhoun is on her way to meet friends when she makes a brief stop at the market. With her hands on a melon, she glances up to find herself lost in a set of alluring steel grey eyes. The man has to be the Produce God himself, as just staring at him, he's ruined her for anyone else with his tall, dark, and desirous good looks.

When his eyes land on her, his steps falter for the first time. It's like he breathes a different kind of oxygen into his lungs. He knows he has to have her because she will be his game changer—his life altering *one*.

Only she has no idea of the journey she's about to undertake when he asks for her number. He can't help but drag her into his wreckage, ultimately tackling the biggest test of his life. She will be his regardless of the mess of a man that he is.

ABOUT THE AUTHORS

---◆---

A.M. HARGROVE

Reader, Writer, Dark Chocolate Lover, Ice Cream Worshipper, Coffee Drinker, Lover of Grey Goose (and an extra dirty martini), Puppy Lover, and if you're ever around me for more than five minutes, you'll find out I'm a talker. A.M. Hargrove divides her time between the mountains of North Carolina and the upstate of South Carolina where she pursues her dream career of writing. If she could change anything in the world, she would make chocolate and ice cream a part of the USDA food groups. Annie writes romance in several genres, including adult, new adult, and young adult. Her books usually include lots of suspense and thrills and she sometimes ventures into the paranormal, sci-fi and fantasy blend.

TERRI E. LAINE

Terri E. Laine, USA Today bestselling author, left a lucrative career as a CPA to pursue her love for writing. Outside of her roles as a wife and mother of three, she's always been a dreamer and as such became an avid reader at a young age.

Many years later, she got a crazy idea to write a novel and set out to try to publish it. With over a dozen titles published under various pen names, the rest is history. Her journey has been a blessing, and a dream realized. She looks forward to many more memories to come.

Other Co-authored Books by A. M. Hargrove & Terri E. Laine

Cruel & Beautiful Standalone Series:
Cruel and Beautiful
A Mess of a Man
One Wrong Choice

The Wilde Players Dirty Romance Standalone Series:
Sidelined
Fastball
Hooked
Worth Every Risk (Wilde Players spin-off)

Standalone:
A Beautiful Sin

Other Books by Terri E. Laine

King Maker Trilogy:
> Money Man
> Queen of Men
> King Maker

Kingdom Come Duet:
> Kingdom Come
> Kingdom Fall

All The Kings Sons Spin-off Standalones:
> Arrogant Savior
> King Me

Chasing Butterflies standalone series:
> Chasing Butterflies
> Catching Fireflies
> Changing Hearts
> Craving Dragonflies
> Songs for Cricket

Him standalone series
> Because of Him
> Captivated by Him

Blinded by You Duet:
> Honey
> Sugar

Married in Vegas standalone series:

Married in Vegas: In His Arms
Absolutely Mine

Other Standalones:
Ride or Die
Thirty Five and Single

Other Books by A. M. Hargrove

ADULT NOVELS

The Kent Brothers Novels:
ACER
RAIDEN
CRUZE (TBD)

The West Sisters Standalone Novels:
One Indecent Night
One Shameless Night
One Blissful Night

The West Brothers Stand Alone Novels:
From Ashes to Flames
From Ice to Flames
From Smoke to Flames

The Men of Crestview Stand Alone Novels:
A Special Obsession
Chasing Vivi
Craving Midnight

Standalones:
Secret Nights
For The Love of English
For The Love of My Sexy Geek
I'll Be Waiting

Exquisite Betrayal

The Edge Standalone Series:
Edge of Disaster
Shattered Edge
Kissing Fire

The Tragic Duet Standalone Series:
Tragically Flawed, Tragic 1
Tragic Desires, Tragic 2

The Hart Brothers Series:
Freeing Her, Book 1
Freeing Him, Book 2
Kestrel, Book 3
The Fall and Rise of Kade Hart, Book 4
The Hart Brothers Series Boxset
Sabin, A Seven Novel--A Hart Brothers Novel Spin-off

YA/NA Clean Romance
The Guardians of Vesturon Series:
Survival, Book 1
Resurrection, Book 2
Determinant, Book 3
reEmergent, Book 4
Dark Waltz, A Praestani Novel
Death Waltz, A Praestani Novel

Stalk A.M. Hargrove

If you would like to hear more about what's going on in my world, please subscribe to my mailing list at my website.

Please stalk me. I'll love you forever if you do. Seriously.

Website – www.amhargrove.com
Instagram @amhargroveauthor

For more information about books, newsletter signup and links to other social media can be found on website.

Stalk Terri E. Laine

If you would like more information about me, sign up for my newsletter at my website. I love to hear from my readers.

Website – www.terrielaine.com
Instagram @terrielaineauthor

For more information about books, newsletter signup and links to other social media can be found on website.

Made in the USA
Monee, IL
16 September 2021